Bought at Boo
April 13, 1989

D1046627

First Father,
First Daughter

MAUREEN REAGAN

First Father, First Daughter

A MEMOIR

LITTLE, BROWN AND COMPANY
BOSTON   TORONTO   LONDON

FIRST EDITION

Library of Congress Cataloging-in-Publication Data

Reagan, Maureen, 1941–
    First Father, First Daughter: a memoir / Maureen Reagan. — 1st ed.
        p.   cm.
    ISBN 0-316-73631-7
    1. Reagan, Maureen, 1941–   — Family. 2. Reagan, Ronald — Family.
3. Presidents — United States — Children — Biography. 4. Presidents —
United States — Biography. I. Title.
E878.R42A3   1989
973.927′092′4 — dc19
[B]   88-38403
                                                                   CIP

10 9 8 7 6 5 4 3 2 1

MV-PA

Published simultaneously in Canada
by Little, Brown & Company (Canada) Limited

PRINTED IN THE UNITED STATES OF AMERICA

This book is dedicated with great affection
to Ronald Wilson Reagan, who made it all possible,
and to Dennis Cormac Revell, who makes it all fun.

Contents

Acknowledgments

I COULD NEVER HAVE PUT THIS BOOK together without a great deal of help. Organizing nearly fifty years of daughter-father relationship into manageable pieces took time and care. The story is mine; the book is a collaborative effort.

Thank you to Dorothy Hermann for organizing the material.

Special thanks to Daniel Paisner, who took on the herculean task of gathering all the pieces so it comes together with one voice. The fact that it took his time away from his newborn baby, Jake, makes me more grateful.

Thank you to Fredrica Friedman and Little, Brown for believing in this project.

Thank you to the White House photo office, whose photographers have captured all our memorable moments.

Thanks, also, to my friend Gary Bernstein, whose photographic skills make me look like I always dreamed.

Thank you to each and every member of the U.S. Delegation to the U.N. Conference in Nairobi. The success we enjoyed there was also a collaborative effort, and you are my best friends for life.

Thank you to the wonderful people who have labored with me over the past five years at the Republican National Committee. Your long hours and hard work have made all our successes possible.

First Father,
First Daughter

PROLOGUE

The Start of Something

WHEN I DREAMED about this day, it had California written all over it: sun-drenched, brilliant, sapphire-blue skies, swaying palm trees against a gentle, cooling ocean breeze, here and there puffs of cotton-white clouds — the whole bit.

But while some dreams do, in fact, come true, others die hard. On this day the sun smiled someplace else, the sky looked like a campaign-soaked charcoal-gray suit, and the palm trees weren't swaying so much as they were kicking up a fuss. It was a cool and nasty January morning, on which California was doing precious little about leaving its mark.

And yet, surprisingly, it didn't much matter. Oh, sure, it would have been a wonderfully fitting way to frame an already wonderful day, but as I boarded one of two United Airlines charters from Los Angeles International Airport, I noticed our plane was filled with more warmth and sunshine than any of us knew quite what to do with. It was a little like California inside — albeit climate-controlled — and I was glad about that for the warm touch of home it offered. We were about to take off on an extraordinary flight, headed east to our nation's capital for an extraordinary occasion, and I'm willing to bet there wasn't one person on board who cared a hoot about the weather.

You see, in just three days — at high noon on Tuesday, January 20, 1981 — my father, Ronald Wilson Reagan, would become a father to us all, when he was sworn in as the fortieth President of these United States, and that was sunshine enough for any of us.

First Father, First Daughter. . . .

It's hard to describe precisely how and what I was feeling as we taxied toward takeoff, but I'll try. For one thing, I was numb and tired. Positively thrashed. I had been up all night tending to last-minute details in the office to free up my calendar for the long weekend away. Plus, I was still on overload from the fall campaign: I had been in twenty-seven states, bringing home my father's message over what was basically a two-month period. Before that, I had beaten the bushes along with everyone else in the primaries. I'd been in more towns than you'd find on most road maps. I'd eaten so much fast food that I no longer recognized dinner if it didn't come in a microwavable container. I had been pushed out of the way and had my feet stomped on by more Secret Service agents than you could stuff into a Ringling Brothers Volkswagen, and I'd lent new meaning to the term "frequent flyer" — we all had — as I'd stumped and shook hands and campaigned my way from sea to shining sea.

It was wonderful.

But exhilarating as it may be, a life on the road like that can take a lot out of you. Our would-be First Family was so displaced by the all-out campaign that when we'd bump into each other during our many months on the road, we would, literally, bump into each other from fatigue.

"Well, Dad," I used to say when we both happened to be in the same place at the same time, "I guess I'll see you when I see you."

He'd come back with, "Come to a banquet and we'll have dinner together."

OK, so now you know how I was feeling physically, and to a certain degree emotionally, but through my to-the-bone exhaustion, I was also ridiculously and hopelessly excited. I may have been sitting there stuffed into a cramped airline seat, but to me it was as comfortable as cloud nine.

On the plane with me were my soon-to-be-husband, Dennis Revell, my brother Michael, his wife, Colleen, and their three-year-old son, Cameron. We were all still in a campaign mode. You have to understand, after what we'd all just been through, it was very difficult to wind down, to shut off one valve for the sake of another. The euphoria of election night passes quickly, and it is right away replaced by a nagging sense that there is still a mission to accomplish, a message to get across, an election to win. I guess it takes a while for the reality of it all to sink in, and even though we'd had two months at this point to get used to the reality of Ronald Wilson Reagan as our fortieth President, it was still sinking in for many of us as we took off that nasty January morning. Here's another bet I'm willing to take: I'm sure I wasn't the only one on board who kept thinking of the Inaugural as just another campaign trip.

Of course, it was much more than that. Much more. In fact, this trip and the days immediately ahead were so much more that it was almost frightening to contemplate. It can all get pretty intimidating and overwhelming if you stop too long to think about it. I remember I leaned over to Dennis as we were taking off, and I clutched his arm and said, "We did it!" That was all I could think to say, and having settled on that, I wanted to say it again and again: "We did it! We did it! We did it!" I sang out louder and louder with each pass, until Dennis finally leaned over and took my hand in his (probably as much to loose the vise grip I had on his arm as to share an affectionate moment), and answered me back softly, "Yes, we did it."

Well, we did.

I'm almost embarrassed to admit what I did next: I giggled. It wasn't a laugh-out-loud giggle, the kind you move away from at not-so-funny movies in not-so-crowded theaters; it was more like a private smile. I'm sorry, I couldn't help myself. It's not every day you leave home to fly cross-country to witness your father inaugurated as President.

It's not even every four years.

Anyway, the captain turned off the no-smoking signs, and

as people began to wander about the plane I tilted my seat into serious recline and let my mind do my wandering for me. I flashed back on the nine short weeks since the election. Dad, of course, was busy selecting his Cabinet and laying the groundwork for his administration. There was hardly a free minute in his busy days — everyone, it seemed, wanted a piece of his time (and everyone, it seemed, managed to get it) — and we all worried that we'd have to wait four years to get his attention. He and Nancy also had the details of closing up the house in Pacific Palisades to attend to, which were no small matter.

The rest of the family was swept up in the excitement right along with the folks. There had been an emotional Christmas at their house, the last we'd likely spend there. My brother Ron was on hand, with his new wife, Doria, and my sister, Patti. Michael was there with his family. The most talked-about gift was this hand-painted toilet seat with a presidential seal; I don't remember who gave it to Dad, but it was the season favorite. (I'm not sure what's become of it, but it's probably in storage with everything else the folks own.)

I remember Ron being thrown by the idea of not seeing the house again; he had grown up in that house, and understandably, it held a lot of special memories for him, even though I only knew it as a place to visit. (I mean, I'd never actually lived there or anything.) Patti, too, appeared a little upset about this particular aspect of the move. But the emotion of that moment, for me, had as much to do with what was happening outside our family gathering as it did with what was going on within it. We had all worked long and hard to help bring Dad to this crowning moment, and I had worked longer and harder than most. I couldn't wait for the payoff. I wanted desperately to put this scene on fast-forward and flash ahead to the White House; I was anxious to see how Dad's administration would turn out, to see how the many programs and ideals he had talked about during his campaign would take shape, and to see how the lives of all Americans would change over the next four years and how the lives of my family, gathered here about our last Christmas tree in the Pacific Palisades house, would also change in the bargain.

The President-elect made a holiday toast that had surprisingly little to do with his new job or with any momentous leave-taking, and a whole lot to do with his family being together under one roof. He's like that, my father. Having all of his children at smile's length means more to him than I can ever hope to put into words on his behalf. He's always saying how good it makes him feel when we're all together like that — how rich, how warm, how full — and on this particular holiday I'm sure he felt like the richest man alive.

"This is for all of us," he said, lifting his glass. "Not for what we're about to become, but for what we've been, to each other, for so many years."

We drank it all in.

Looking back, Christmas seemed a brief pocket of calm. Private family moments like those, we all knew, would be harder and harder to come by in the years ahead, and we seemed to want to hold on to each moment for longer than we should. In our attempt to savor that special day, to let it resonate, we had tried to shut the world out for one last time before things got beyond our control, but, still, the world was watching.

We were all of us about to trade one merry-go-round for another, and right then, at Christmas, we had relished being between rides.

But Christmas only lasts one day, and by the next morning we were all back at it. Full speed ahead. There had been a lot of grand send-offs for Dad and Nancy during their last weeks in California, one of the grandest that I attended being a luncheon at the Biltmore Hotel in early January, hosted by the Los Angeles Central City Association. The place was absolutely jam-packed with well-wishers and supporters. The catering director, a friend of ours named Bernard Jacoupy, was determined that even though there were one thousand guests, he would serve a deliciously fantastic California meal. And he did! The steaks were all done just right — thick and juicy and cooked to perfection. Even the asparagus was al dente! If you've ever tried to pull off a menu like that over dinner for eight, you'll appreciate the trick when it's turned out for a thousand.

Jesse Unruh, the treasurer of California and Dad's opponent in the 1970 gubernatorial election, had been one of the speakers, bidding a fond farewell to the President-elect. Charlton Heston, the actor, grabbed one of the biggest laughs when he got up and said, "I voted for Ronald Reagan for President before anybody else in this room." (He had voted for him as president of the Screen Actors Guild some thirty years earlier.) And then my father took his turn at the podium, with no notes, and he just spoke about how he and his family and his friends were not at the end of a road but at the beginning, about how much he was going to miss everybody, about how he and Nancy were off to live in "government housing" in the East (this last pulled in a laugh bigger than Chuck's), and most of all about how it was time for America to once again be a shining city on a hill. Well, as most of you already know, I come from a show-business family, and you'll have to indulge me, from time to time, a show-business expression. Here's one: Dad sure knows how to work a room. Here's another: by the time he stepped down, there wasn't a dry eye in the house.

Well, there wasn't a dry eye on this particular United Airlines charter, either. Like me, the weary travelers on this plane took a special pride in having helped Ronald Reagan to victory. We all had our roles to play in his campaign, and now that it was finally over, culminating in this grand inaugural trip, you could hardly see your way past the whoops and hugs and huzzahs throughout the cabin. It was an emotional bunch, this, tireless Republican campaign workers and supporters who believed in my father and in his vision of what this country could be, and should be. I shared his vision as well, wholeheartedly, and even though in my younger years we'd invariably seen different shades of the same color, we'd recently adjusted our tints to at least something resembling the same levels.

First Father, First Daughter. . . .

It was a scenario I had already spent years getting used to. Keep in mind, it was me, a brash young woman of twenty with a flowering passion for politics, who had first told my father, over a rare lunch together in 1961, that I thought he could be President in twenty years. It just took me a while to convince him — and the rest of the country — that I knew what I was talking about.

And so, as we hit cruising speed and brushed past a slight patch of turbulence, I settled well into my seat and into my thoughts with an overwhelming sigh of satisfaction. It often surprises people when I tell them this, but there was no *by-golly-gosh-gee-whiz!* to what I was feeling at this time, not even a hint of mild disbelief. I didn't have to pinch myself. I was prepared for this moment. In fact, I had fully expected it. As the back-slapping and picture-taking died down on board, I started to lose myself in a big hardcover book I'd brought along just for this purpose. I wish I could remember what book it was — for posterity's sake, as well as for the publisher's — but I do recall it was a mystery, and as I became absorbed in its pages I was thinking to myself, We're off to meet our destiny.

But no matter how prepared I was, I wasn't ready for what hit us as we touched down at Baltimore-Washington International Airport. There Dennis and I were met by Van Logan, a San Francisco architect who had always volunteered his time to the Reagan campaigns and who had been my traveling companion for the 1980 fall campaign, and right away we were scooped up in a whirlwind of inaugural activities — receptions, concerts, luncheons, parties — that would take us straight through the next three days. We would barely have time to catch our breath, I realized as Van thrust a schedule into our hands. It made me feel tired just looking at it.

Twenty-one events in three days!

I had been looking forward to spending at least a few minutes with the President-elect and future First Lady before all the excitement began, but our plane had been delayed and it was all we could do to make it back into Washington in time for our first function, a State Department reception honoring Robert Gray and Charles Wick as Inaugural cochairmen, hosted by our future secretary of state, Al Haig. We wouldn't even make it to Blair House, the official presidential guest quarters, where we would be staying, in time to compare notes with the folks or with the rest of the family. We wouldn't even have time to shower and change.

We made our way through District traffic in high style, in a sleek black limousine, with our two Secret Service agents (who since the election had stopped pushing me out of the way and stomping on my feet and instead had signed on as my traveling companions for the next while). I couldn't recognize the landscape passing quickly by my window. Maybe it was because I was tired, or maybe it was because of something else, but the familiar surroundings of the approach to our nation's capital looked suddenly strange to me, almost new. Although I had once attended college in nearby Arlington, Virginia, and had worked for a time in downtown Washington, things seemed as though I was seeing them for the first time.

In a way, I was.

Again it hit me: First Father, First Daughter. . . .

The President. My father. The President's daughter. Me. For an instant I flashed on an image of all the daughters of our past Presidents. Many of them were anonymous, faceless young women who left no lasting mark on history. Many more were too young to have much impact anywhere but the society and life-style pages: Caroline Kennedy and my most recent predecessor, Amy Carter, came quickly to mind. And yet there were others, including the prankish, witty Alice Roosevelt, the talented Margaret Truman, and the accomplished Julie Nixon, who emerged from the shadows and became respected public figures in their own right. Of course, I would be much older in this position than the others were in their times. At forty, I'd already achieved a certain reputation — some would even call it a mild infamy, I'll admit — in my own political career, and in my career as an actress and entertainer. I wondered what kind of marks I would leave, if any, when our time had come and gone.

But I was shaken from my wonderings before too long. There, on the horizon over the Lincoln Memorial, I could see a stunning fireworks display honoring the occasion. It's hard to imagine a more spectacular sight. Again I wanted to grab Dennis's arm and sing out "We did it! We did it! We did it!" but this time I restrained myself.

There's one thing you should know about our Inaugural traditions and festivities. They're a lot like your wedding, or if you've never been married, they're a lot like your second cousin Sarah's wedding. What I mean is you get so caught up in the relentless excitement that if it weren't for pictures and stories and mementos and press accounts, all you'd have to remember it by would be one big happy blur. The events roll on one after another, and the overall effect is like being in a movie run at a too-fast speed.

The night was far from young when we returned to Blair House to refuel. Blair House is actually five separate row houses, and the folks' quarters were set off from the rest of ours. They'd been there for a couple of weeks already when we hit town, and by the time we returned late that night, Dad and Nancy had called it an evening.

Oh, well. . . .

A part of me was hoping that our stay here would be like a mini–family reunion — now that we're grown and scattered about the country, these times are so rare, and I remembered how Dad loves it so when we're all together — and in fact my room was clustered with Ron and Doria's, and with Patti's, and with Michael and Colleen's, in a kind of suite with a common sitting room, but we were all kept so busy that even those close quarters didn't provide much in the way of a family visit. Nancy's parents, Edith (or Deedee, as we called her) and Loyal Davis, were off in another corner of Blair House, along with Nancy's brother, Dr. Richard Davis, and his family, and Dad's older brother, Neill, and his wife, Bess. We'd pass each other in the halls on our way to or from whatever it was we were racing to or from, and we'd find enough time to agree that never in Dad's career as a movie star and politician had we attended anything quite so glamorous or quite so exhausting.

More than that, we didn't find time for.

We did get to see the folks the next morning, but only in passing. We were sitting down to our breakfast just as they were getting up from theirs, and thinking ahead to the wall-to-wall schedule awaiting us, I said, "Excuse me, Dad, but did we win something?"

He didn't miss a beat and answered back, "Yes, and I've decreed that next time the losers get the Inaugural."

We were pushed and pulled in so many directions over the next few days that I'm surprised one of us didn't snap. It seems everyone in Washington wants to give a party during the Inaugural weekend, and the way it works is you divide up the future First Family members and send representatives to as many different events and parties as possible. In our case there weren't all that many of us, and so we were run pretty ragged. The first stop for Dennis and me that next morning, Sunday, was to represent the family at a luncheon honoring our diplomatic corps, hosted by Pepsico Chairman Don Kendall at the Organization of American States building.

In the middle of all the excitement, I saw Dennis chatting happily with Anatoly Dobrynin, the longtime Soviet ambassador; the ambassador, a rotund, jolly fellow whose eyes never stop moving (he takes in everything!), was busy convincing Dennis to part with his "First Dog Inaugural Flight" campaign button as a souvenir. (The button had been printed by some friends of ours in honor of my dachapoo, Barnae, who "got down on all fours" in her own campaign for First Family Pooch.) After considerable cajoling, Dennis gave up the button, figuring our new President was already known for his sense of humor and wouldn't mind if such an artifact entered campaign-collectible circulation.

On the way upstairs to the luncheon, we ran into Vice President–elect George Bush and his lovely wife, Barbara. Now, I've always liked Barbara Bush — she's a fun person with a great sense of humor — and I was a little concerned to see her with her leg all bandaged up.

I asked her what had happened.

"Oh, my dear," she said to me in explanation, "last night I tripped on the stairs and they had to stitch me up. Please tell your father he doesn't have to worry about who the klutz in his administration will be — I'll take the job."

We didn't see the folks until later that night at a concert at the Kennedy Center. They were seated in the box next to ours, and when they came in we kind of waved and then they kind of waved back, and in that small exchange it occurred to me that the next four years could become a series of waves and fleeting visits if we weren't all careful. During an intermission I found my father's ear long enough to relate Barbara Bush's barb, and he all but roared in appreciation. Even though it was just a short moment before his attention was pulled away by some other presidential exchange, it was still a way for him and me to keep close, to touch base, to anchor us as a family during this most hectic time.

The next day, Monday, found us at a Distinguished Ladies reception at the Kennedy Center in honor of Nancy Reagan and Barbara Bush, but not before I was roused (not so) bright and (exceedingly) early for a cycle of appearances on the network morning shows. I made quite a picture in ABC's Washington bureau at seven A.M., dressed in the black velvet suit I was planning to wear to the reception later that morning. That's another thing about Inaugurals that you have to just pick up as you go along: you're always overdressed, which means you're always dressed weirdly. When you're on the frantic pace we were on, with one event leading directly into another, there simply is no time to stop and change clothes between appearances. So the practicality of it is that you get dressed so far ahead of time you end up being overdressed for wherever you might be at any particular moment just so you're not underdressed for the next event. If that sounds complicated and confusing, it's because it is.

And so I was in that same black velvet suit I was planning to wear at noon when what I should have been in was my pajamas. Later that afternoon we would attend a business-attire reception dressed in black tie for the gala to follow that evening at the Capital Center. That was quite a scene. They wanted to get us out there early to beat the traffic, and so the bulk of the family spent nearly two hours in a kind of holding room, waiting for the show to go on. (It turned out we beat the traffic to a pulp, we got there so early.) My grandmother Deedee Davis was with us then, and what you need to know about her by way of introduction is that she could spin the most risqué yarns you ever did hear! She had the longest list of dirty jokes of any human being on this earth, and she chose to fill the two hours' down time in our little holding room by holding forth like some bawdy comedienne. By that time Deedee was in a wheelchair, and she didn't see very well, and she didn't hear very well, but as long as she was on, she was bright as a penny. And that night she was a pure pocketful of shiny Lincolns.

One joke stands out still: Dad's pastor, Don Moomaw, was with us at the time, and Deedee began telling him about some of the work she did with a local school in Phoenix. She segued very smoothly into a story about President Carter visiting the school during the campaign. She made the transition so masterfully that the reverend never realized he was now into one of Deedee's "stories."

"So there was Carter," Deedee said, "and he was on the

lake in this rowboat with three kids, and all of a sudden he fell overboard and hit his head on the boat. The kids jumped in and pulled him to shore.

"The President couldn't thank these boys enough. He told them he might have drowned if they hadn't saved him, and he asked them if there was anything he could do to repay the kindness.

"Well, the first boy sheepishly asked for an appointment to the Naval Academy, which Carter said was doable. The second boy, a bit more bravely, asked for an appointment to West Point, and Carter agreed to that as well.

"Finally Carter turned to the third boy and said, 'And what would you like?'

"The third lad replied, 'Well, Sir, if it's not too much trouble, I'd like to be buried in Arlington National Cemetery.'

" 'Buried at Arlington!' Carter exclaimed. 'Why, you're too young to be thinking about that.'

" 'No Sir,' replied the young man. 'When I go home tonight and tell my Dad I saved your life, he's gonna kill me!' "

The reverend caught the punch line full in the face, and he laughed for about five minutes.

Well, we couldn't have asked for a better opening act, because by the time the show got under way we were as warmed up as we could be. What I remember most of all from the incredible show that followed was Jimmy Stewart, retired Brigadier General in the Air Force Reserves, and Omar Bradley, retired General of the Army, who was in a wheelchair at the time, coming out on stage together to give their friend the President his first salute. Now, I'm an easy target when it comes to stirring emotional moments, and Dad's dear old friends really got me with this one. I think they got Dad, too. (If you'll indulge me again, there wasn't a dry eye in this house, either, at least not in the presidential box.) The comedian Rich Little lightened things up some when he came on and did an impression of Dad that was so outrageously funny he seemed like the President's evil twin; we found out later that Rich was just terrified before he went on because he didn't know how the President and his family would react to his shenanigans. He needn't have worried; like Dad, he knew how to work his room. Even Johnny Carson seemed a little tentative when he came out with his battery of jokes at the President's expense, though I'm sure his uncertainty was just part of the act. He kept looking up at Dad's box after each joke, as if to say, "Is that OK? Is that OK?" and each time he looked up with his sad puppy-dog eyes for some kind of presidential approval, Dad would just lose it all the more. All the news footage and photos from that evening show Dad, and the rest of us, just having a grand old time.

But all of this was mere preamble to what lay ahead. Tuesday was the main event: Inauguration Day. We were up at first light (or at least I was; who could sleep on the morning of something like this?). And what a brilliant day it was! Our home state of California paid us the visit we'd missed just a few days earlier, turning a winter's day into sixty sunny degrees. For a moment I thought about not wearing a coat, it was such a spectacular day, but then I decided that might be seen as just a touch too arrogant for a Californian.

Our first stop was Saint John's Episcopal Church on Lafayette Square, where we listened to sermons by the reverends Billy Graham and Don Moomaw, who had recovered sufficiently from his run-in with Deedee the night before. From there we took our place in the family motorcade, which inched its way slowly to the Capitol. The sidewalks on either side of us were lined thick with overwhelmingly enthusiastic crowds; almost everyone, it seemed, was waving flags or displaying some other tribute to the old Red, White, and Blue. When I look back on that marvelously slow crawl in that motorcade, what I remember most vividly is the faces and hands along our way — everywhere I turned, there was nothing but faces and hands, faces and hands.

What a moment! I had seen accounts of previous presidential inaugurations on television since 1953, but I had never experienced one firsthand. I was convinced that nothing could ever compare with the dignity and majesty of this morning, or with the outpouring of real affection displayed along our way.

The swearing-in was to take place on the west face of the Capitol. Nobody in history had ever been sworn in on the west face, and there's a story that goes along with that. You see, when L'Enfant designed our nation's capital, he thought the District was going to grow toward the east, so that's where he put the door to the Capitol. By tradition, the President is sworn in in front of the building, and then he ends the ceremony by walking in through the front door. Sounds good, right? Well, L'Enfant got it all wrong. Over the years Washington has grown toward the west, and the front doors of the Capitol now look out over a parking lot.

But on this day, thanks to some renovation work on the east face, the ceremony was held overlooking the great lawn of the Capitol, facing west. Spreading before us, as far as the eye could see, was a sea of people. I'm sure there was some lawn, or pavement, beneath the feet of these people, but darned if I could see any of it through the crowd. On the east face only eight thousand people can witness the inauguration, but due to the change of venue, on Tuesday, January 20, 1981, more than thirty-two thousand were able to witness this particular piece of history. Thirty-two thousand people!

I looked down toward the Washington Monument directly before us, rising from the crowd, and I wanted desperately to freeze this moment, to capture its beauty and splendor in such a way that I could call it all up again at any time.

I don't think any of us wanted this day to end.

At 11:40 A.M., against a jubilant fanfare supplied by U.S. Army trumpets, Dad mounted the podium, and at precisely noon he took the oath of office as prescribed by the Constitution: "I, Ronald Reagan, do solemnly swear to protect and defend the Constitution. . . ."

First Father, First Daughter. . . .

I was sitting with the family in back of the speaker's rostrum, doing my best to fight back tears, looking as proud and regal as I could manage in the purple coat and hat I'd had made for this special occasion. I listened as my father, our new President, talked about the need to remedy the severe economic problems and runaway inflation then plaguing our nation. I listened as he told the American people that big government had long been the cause rather than the solution to our problems. And I listened as he promised to build a better, stronger America and to strive to give Americans a better life through less government. These were the central messages of his campaign — the very messages I'd helped him get across during the previous months — and now, as he was taking office, these messages were taking shape as the central themes of his new administration.

"The crisis we are facing today does not require of us the kind of sacrifice that so many thousands were called upon to make," he said, gesturing toward the sloping hills of the Arlington National Cemetery. "It does require, however, our best effort and our willingness to believe in ourselves and to believe in our capacity to perform great deeds, to believe that together, with God's help, we can and will resolve the problems which now confront us. And after all, why shouldn't we believe that? We are Americans!"

As ever, Dad knew how to work his room, even a room (or a lawn) as big as this.

When the ceremony came to a close, I turned to Michael and I noticed he was fighting back the same tears I was. We leaned into each other for an emotional embrace — the tears at this point were winning — and I sang out once again, "We did it! We did it!" Now, anyone who knows me will tell you I'm usually never at a loss for words, but I seemed to be stuck on this "We did it!" line, which was just as well, because nothing else would have so accurately captured what I was feeling at that moment: pride, accomplishment, relief, purpose. "We did it!" That said it all.

From the west face we were ushered into Statuary Hall, a huge, rotundalike room in the Capitol that is just awe-inspiring, where there was to be a luncheon with Congressional leaders and Inaugural participants. On the way in Dad had been given word on the release of our American hostages in Iran — ending over a year of captivity — and he capped the proceedings with a special toast. "With thanks to Almighty God," he said, underneath a beaming expression, "I have been given a tag line. Some thirty minutes ago, the planes bearing our prisoners left Iranian airspace and are now free. We can all drink to this one."

Dad's Inaugural parade was a far cry from the one held to honor Thomas Jefferson, when a group of Navy mechanics had spontaneously escorted the new President from his boardinghouse to the White House. There was nothing spontaneous about this celebration — for logistical and security reasons, the entire affair had to be mapped out and plotted to the nth degree — but the emotions behind it were every bit as joyous. At Ronald Reagan's parade, thousands upon thousands of onlookers lined the route from the Capitol to the White House and cheered the President and the First Lady, and the Vice President and his wife, as they passed in sunroofed limousines. Again the recurring image is of faces and hands, faces and hands, leading the President and the First Lady on their way to their new home.

We joined Dad and Nancy in the White House reviewing box, along with various government officials and close friends, including General Omar Bradley and his wife, Kitty. From where I was sitting, I could see Dad getting all choked up when he spotted the high-school marching band from his hometown of Dixon, Illinois. He's always been a sucker for that kind of nostalgic sentiment.

During a break in the parade proceedings, he made a second announcement to those of us in the viewing stand, which added to the exhilaration of the moment: the hostages had arrived in Germany.

I sat watching him, and I felt safe, secure, the way many daughters do, I think, in the presence of their fathers. Our relationship is no different in that way, except I found myself wondering, on the heels of these hostage bulletins, how soon it would be before the rest of the country would draw the same kind of comfort from him and his reassuring manner that I had drawn for the past forty years. I wondered how I'd feel about sharing that part of him with the rest of the country and, to a degree, with the rest of the world.

First Father, First Daughter. . . .

That evening we all met at the White House, done up in our finest, for our first First Family portrait. Dad and Nancy had been moved in that afternoon, and the "government housing" Dad had joked about already looked like it was agreeing with them, though their living quarters still lacked the personal touches that would fall into place in the coming weeks. I was wearing royal blue sequins and velvet; Nancy looked stunning in a white beaded Galanos; Patti was a vision in red chiffon. The Reagan men were done up in tails. We were every bit the picture of a family who knows this is a once-in-a-lifetime moment: we wanted to look our best.

After a champagne toast — which tasted particularly sweet because it was served to us for the first time by the attentive White House staff — Dad announced he and Nancy must be "to our coach and away." (He talks that way sometimes.) They had a whirlwind tour of ten balls ahead of them, but Dennis and I only had one, and so when we all separated to attend our assigned celebrations, I whisked Dennis off on a short detour. Sure, our attendance at the ball was important, but I had something I had to do first.

I wanted to see the Oval Office.

We'd all slaved over hot political coals for too many years for me to put off seeing "the prize" any longer. I corralled a White House usher and asked for directions, and he escorted us down the stairs and through the colonnade to the West Wing, where Theodore Roosevelt had first moved the presidential office from the White House proper.

We stepped into the room, and I was right away overwhelmed. If these walls could talk, I was thinking; or, better, if I could have listened in. I'd only seen pictures of this fabled room, and here, now, with its rich history spread before me, I thought I'd died and gone to Heaven. This was what we'd worked so hard for, what we'd dreamed about for so many years. This was where Ronald Reagan, my father, would meet with other heads of state, where he would see to the day-to-day management of the greatest nation on this good earth.

The Oval Office!

Now, you have to understand that we hadn't had a chance to put up any personal pictures or other odds and ends to make Dad feel at home in his new office, so in a sense it wasn't yet entirely his. The place, on its unaccustomed day of transition, looked more like a display in a museum than a functioning office. I took advantage of the relatively bare surroundings and stole a brief memory that I will always cherish.

There, for the first and only time during Ronald Reagan's presidency, I sat in my father's chair.

This has got to be the biggest *wow!* in the history of big *wow*s. And always the tourist, I made Dennis take my picture.

I would never take that seat again during Dad's term, but on that night it didn't seem like such a bad thing to do. Yes, it was the President's chair, but in a way it wasn't all his yet. He hadn't used it yet, anyway.

Dennis and I departed the south portico for the Pension Building, where we were expected. The official Inaugural balls, which began in 1809 when James and Dolly Madison kicked off the tradition, are complex, jammed events. Lately, they've been filled by contributors as a way of financing the elaborate (and expensive) Inaugural festivities. For Dad's inauguration ten balls were scheduled, plus local parties in eighty-three cities via closed-circuit television. As is the custom, Dad and Nancy had to visit all ten balls before the night was through, and by the time they got to me, playing host to well over a thousand Reagan supporters, they looked to this First Daughter like they were just about ready to drop.

Outwardly, though, they seemed to be holding up pretty well. Dad was resplendent in his tails, and Nancy looked like a fairy princess the way she had her hair swept back into a chignon ornamented by four pearl-and-diamond clasps.

"You're our eighth stop," Dad whispered into my ear as we hugged and kissed. "We haven't even had a chance to dance."

"Well," I said, indicating the large dance floor at the head of the room, "dance."

And they did.

The band played "Moonlight Serenade," Dad put his arm tenderly around Nancy's waist, and they danced for the very first time as President and First Lady. I can't tell you how many times I'd watched them dance before this special evening, but like everything else in this new light, they seemed different somehow, as if they were moving together for the first time.

We were scheduled to leave the very next day, and as we were getting ready to depart Blair House, I felt torn. I didn't want to leave Dad and Nancy and the rest of my family so soon after something like this, even if I did have my own life waiting for me back home.

I felt torn also because Washington is an addictive town, and politics is an addictive business. I often tell people it's not a habit you can easily kick, but you can go into remission if you work real hard at it. And so, hooked before, I was really worried as we flew into Washington about how I was going to feel leaving the seat of power so quickly and going back to California. Was I going to get hooked all over again, in such a short time? I knew there was no place for me in Washington, the nepotism statutes (and political realities) being what they were, and so I was biting my nails over this one. I was afraid I'd get back on that plane heading west and feel like I was missing something. I thought it'd be like when I was a kid and my parents had a party, and when it was time to go to bed, I'd try to stay up as long as I could because I didn't want anything to happen without me.

But we got on the plane, and all I felt was exhausted. Spent. I wanted nothing more than to return home, to sleep in my own bed. The Inaugural, for all its wonder and pomp and circumstance, was the most draining thing I'd ever experienced in all my life. And if you're looking to break a lifelong addiction to Washington and politics, it's the best aversion therapy they've got going.

Seven and a half years have passed since I took that return trip, and a lot has changed. But some things haven't. It's still an odd sensation to think of my father as the President of the United States. It took me a while to get used to calling him Mr. President, and I only slipped once or twice and called him Governor. And even that moniker sounds, well, off, when attached to your dad. But the biggest change has been in our own relationship, and that's been a change for the better. We've grown closer during his time in office, not because of his position as this country's leader but because after all these years we've finally settled into a nice, loving way of being with each other. The precious times we've shared over the years have grown more frequent, and more precious; the moments of a lifetime together have begun to resonate with the years, to the point where they carry, for both of us, a rich and enriched meaning, moments that began when Ronald Reagan was a tall, handsome young movie actor who had just learned that in nine months his life was going to change.

Oh, how his life was going to change. . . .

I

1941–1962

1

The Hollywood Kid

My MOTHER wanted to name me Ronald, after my father, but things didn't quite work out the way she'd planned. I guess even then I had a mind of my own.

The birth announcement they sent out tells the story:

THIS IS THE ANNOUNCEMENT WE WERE GOING TO SEND:

HEADQUARTERS
FORT REAGAN
1326 LONDONDERRY VIEW
HOLLYWOOD, CALIFORNIA

SUBJECT: EXTENDED ACTIVE DUTY

1. GENERAL RONALD REAGAN, JR., HAVING PASSED FINAL TYPE PHYSICAL EXAMINATION, IS AVAILABLE FOR ACTIVE DUTY.

2. GENERAL REAGAN WILL ASSUME COMMAND OF THE POST EFFECTIVE JANUARY 4, 1941.

FOR THE EXECUTIVES:
A. STORK
AIRCORPS MEDICAL DIV.

BUT IT'S HARDLY APPROPRIATE FOR . . .
Maureen Elizabeth Reagan
IS IT?

Even though I had the temerity to be a girl, I was one of the most publicized and photographed children in all of Hollywood. I've got the overflowing scrapbook to prove it. Both of my parents, Ronald Reagan and Jane Wyman, were featured players at Warner Brothers during the late 1930s (and on into the '40s and '50s), and their courtship and resulting marriage were given the typical star treatment accorded to romancing movie stars of the day, particularly to romancing movie stars under contract to the same studio. They had met on the set of *Brother Rat* — a light comedy about life in a military school — and quickly became an "item" in the society and gossip pages. The movie magazines called them the ideal Hollywood couple, and in a way I suppose they were, at least in the eyes of their studio bosses; for a while, at least, theirs was a match made in press-agent Heaven.

When I came along, the Warner Brothers publicity department issued a veritable album of photos, and a stream of press releases, one of which quoted my father as saying I was "the most wonderful baby in the world." Of course, privately he had confided to his mother, Nelle, that I was "such a homely, red thing," but a line like that had no place in the Hollywood promotional machine of 1941, even though, to judge from some of the publicity stills from just after I was born, his description seemed pretty much on the money.

Oh, do we have pictures from that time! Studio photographers took countless posed shots — roll upon roll upon roll — of our happy little family, which then turned up in fan magazines and newspapers all across the country. We must have sold a lot of tickets to a lot of Warner Brothers movies, or at least somebody must have thought we'd sell a lot of tickets, because flashbulbs, I'm told, played as big a part in lighting my first months on this earth as sunshine. I'll never forget this one particular shot of me in my mother's arms, taken in her hospital room just a day or two after I was born, me looking pretty red and homely and Mother looking perfectly coiffed and made up and propped up in her bed; I must have seen that picture in a hundred different places. There were other shots, too: my parents leaning in over my crib, or playing with me on the lawn, or shopping for baby clothes in exclusive Beverly Hills boutiques.

You get the picture.

My parents had already grown accustomed to this kind of attention. As part of the fabled studio system, which governed the film industry during that period, they spent their time off the set forever under the watchful eye of the publicity cameras and the society reporters. From the stories I've collected over the years, it seems they couldn't even go out to dinner or to the supermarket without attracting considerable attention, and some of my earliest memories — beyond the infant publicity blitz — put me and my parents at the center of at least some kind of attention.

Even their relationship had a chance to flower on center stage, as they traveled with a troup of young performers on a tour sponsored by the legendary Hollywood gossip columnist Louella Parsons. Remember, the entertainment industry was in something of a transition during that time, moving slowly from vaudeville to burlesque and then into a kind of meeting of stage and screen. For a long time in the thirties and forties, and even on into the fifties in some parts of the country, you'd find movie theaters combining live, revue-style entertainment with feature films; a lot of just-starting-out performers during that time, Ronald Reagan and Jane Wyman among them, supplemented their incomes and got some much-needed exposure making personal appearances like these. On this particular tour, Louella Parsons would get up on stage and introduce the performers in "her stable," as she called it, and then the young stars would do a little song and dance or a short sketch, or take some questions from the audience, or whatever.

As a matter of fact, my parents had announced their engagement on stage during one of Louella Parsons's "vaudeville-style" tours — a routine that wasn't exactly in the script — and from that moment on "Aunt Lolly" had taken credit for bringing them together. Like my father, she was another Hollywood transplant by way of Dixon, Illinois, and she was pretty much a fixture in our household during the early years of my childhood. I still have some clippings in which Aunt Lolly figured publicly that my parents should have named me after her, because of the history they all shared. (Nobody ever has told me where the name Maureen came from, but Elizabeth was after my mother's best friend, Betty Kaplan; Aunt Betty, incidentally, a warm, beautiful lady who was very dear to me, was the first professional homemaker I ever knew.)

One of my most enduring memories about Louella Parsons is that she was someone I wasn't supposed to talk to too much, which I know now was because of her position as the industry's leading gossip columnist and her insatiable thirst for a good story. At the time I just knew to keep my mouth shut. That was the story of my growing up — be nice to people, but don't tell them anything, because your parents make good copy — which explains, I think, how I grew up to be so good at letting people think they know a few things when in fact they don't know the first thing.

But I'm getting ahead of myself here. Before we get too far along, and as long as we're talking the language of Hollywood, let me give you a little "back-story": Dad was born in the prairie hamlet of Tampico, Illinois, during a raging snowstorm on February 6, 1911. The story goes that on the night of Dad's birth, neither the local doctor nor a midwife could get to the house on account of the storm, and as the hours passed, my grandfather Jack was afraid he might lose his wife, Nelle, in childbirth. And so he set out in the blinding snow and howling winds to seek help, which he finally found in the form of a kindly midwife willing to brave the elements. The doctor, too, eventually made his way through the storm, and shortly after he arrived, a future President was born, looking decidedly less stately than he would in later years.

"He looks like a fat little Dutchman," Jack remarked to Nelle, giving first voice to a nickname that would stick with my father for years. "And for such a little bit of a Dutchman, he makes a hell of a lot of noise."

Jack, a shoe salesman, was often out of work, and the family moved all over the state of Illinois, eventually settling in Dixon, a pleasant, peaceful little town somewhat larger than Tampico, located about ninety miles south of Chicago. Dad always said Dixon was the kind of place where a kid could lose his dog — a Boston terrier, say, by the name of Bobby Jiggs — and before too long one of the local policemen would turn up in the driveway with the dog in his car. "Everybody knew everybody else," he used to tell me. "Not like today." The way he'd spin the story about Bobby Jiggs, it was like a fairy tale, because we lived in Los Angeles, and even in those days, as much as you thought you knew the town, it was far too big a place to know everybody, certainly far too big a place to get the local police to fetch your dog home.

Later we'd poke holes all the way into Dad's story, when we had two Scottish terriers — Scotch and Soda — who used to love to dig their way under our fence and go off exploring. One time our phone rang very early one Sunday morning, and a very nice man introduced himself and said, "Mr. Reagan, I'm the pastor of Saint Victor's" — a Catholic church about two miles away from our house — "Your dogs have been sitting under the back pew since the seven-o'clock mass, and I think they've had enough religion!"

But let me get back to Bobby Jiggs. Oh, my father loved that dog! He told me once about a clever game he'd invented to help pass the long summer hours. There was this porch at the back of the Dixon house, which was built in an old Victorian style, and behind the house there was a kind of sloping hill. The porch was above ground level, and what Dad would do was he'd tie himself a fishing line around a stick (without the hook, of course) and fly-cast off the back porch, down this hill, and Bobby Jiggs would grab the stick and Dad would reel the dog in.

As an adult, I visited the Dixon house and stood for a long time on the back porch, looking down on the slope of lawn, and what I was thinking about most of all was this particular game my father had cooked up. I had this wonderfully odd scene racing through my head — a boy struggling to bring in a yipping, airborne terrier — and captured in that image was one of the clearest pictures I've ever had of my father as a young boy. Oh, I've seen actual pictures — worn and frayed by the years — but it is this moment, colored by his fanciful retelling, that frames his childhood in the way I can best understand.

"I can't tell you how many hours we spent doing that," Dad explained when I returned from my Dixon visit wanting to know more. "And I can't for the life of me tell you how we got started. It just seemed a whole lot easier than running around all over the place with the dog."

Dad tells wonderful stories. That's one of the things I re-

member most about him from the earliest years of my growing up. He'd get me in the car, where I was a captive audience, and we'd be driving along, and before I knew it I'd be
thoroughly absorbed in whatever it was Dad had to relate. Or
he'd sit me down on his lap and just draw me into his world.
His stories were like magnets, the way they could pull you
along. He had the keen ability to tell stories in such a way
that the listener would feel transported into another time and
place. And, oh! did I love to listen!

There's one about him and a borrowed pair of pants that
I've never seen reported elsewhere, and so I'll tell it for him
here. It seems that during his teenage years, there was a style
going around Dixon (and, I presume, elsewhere) that called
for the young men to wear these ridiculously wide-legged pants.
You'd have to see these things to believe them, and even then
you'd have some trouble. These weren't just bell-bottoms, these
things were huge! But ugly as they may have been, they were
all the rage, and Dad simply had to have a pair. Now, Jack
barely made enough money selling shoes to keep his family
fed and clothed as it was, and he certainly didn't make enough
money for his son to fritter away a good chunk of it on a pair
of height-of-fashion pants. So Dad had to settle for borrowing
a pair from a friend of his, and he put them on right away
and set off on a proud stroll along the streets of downtown
Dixon.

Well, that night Jack came home and said to my father, "You
and I are going shopping tomorrow for a new pair of trou-
sers." And the next day Dad was taken to the store and fitted
for a conservative pair of straight gray pants. Apparently Jack
had also been downtown during Dad's stroll, and he'd been
standing on the corner talking to a friend when the friend
said, "Would you look at that fool over there in those ghastly
pants? What kind of father would let his son out of the house
looking like that?"

There's a footnote to this story: during Dad's second term
as President, on a quiet, family evening at the White House,
I was flipping through a book on past Presidents when I spotted the tale of a former head of state who had the very same
reaction to the very same style of pants worn by his own son.

"Dad," I said, bringing the book over for his inspection, "take a look at this."

He scanned the page for the indicated passage. "Why, that's the same pair of pants Jack got so upset about," he said, and then he reminisced some more about that glorious time and place in his life. It only takes the slightest impulse to take Dad back to the wonders of his youth, and to take whoever's listening along for the ride.

Another favorite story took place on one of Dad's first dates. There was a heavy rainstorm, and what happened was he took the young lady home and stopped in for a cup of coffee, hoping that the storm would pass. But in the half hour or so he was inside, the temperature outside dipped, so what had been rain turned to sheets of ice, and by the time Dad came to the door there was this slope of sheer ice leading down to the street. The young lady said, "Ronnie, you're going to fall." And my father said, "No, I'm not," and with that he sat himself down and slid all the way to his car.

"See," he said, turning back to the house as he stood up, "I didn't fall."

Over the years I've run into a number of women who knew Dad during his high-school years; one woman in particular told me that she and her friends all had crushes on him, and that they would regularly drive by his house, hoping for a chance encounter. But despite their open displays of affection, she said, "Your father never gave us a tumble."

When I spent some time campaigning in Illinois in the 1960s, I would from time to time run into people who said that they had known my father. It seems he was quite the social butterfly; I'd hear tales of Dad courting this girl or that girl, or singing drinking songs in some bar or other, or cavorting until all hours with his pals. And yet whenever I'd relate to him these stories of his "misspent youth," he'd put on this little wry smile that he has and deny everything.

OK, Dad. Noted.

As I said, Jack didn't have a lot of money. Dad has often told me his family lived a hand-to-mouth existence, and his older brother, Neill, would regularly quell his dreams of going to college, saying, "Poor people don't go to college."

But my father was determined to achieve his goal. Still in high school, Dad started working as a lifeguard at Lowell Park, a three-hundred-acre recreation area on the treacherous Rock River, which ran through the center of town. A beautiful forested park, it was named for the poet James Russell Lowell, who had been so taken with its beauty that he had written his "Ode to a Waterfall" in its honor. Dad was paid fifteen dollars a week to keep people from drowning in the turbulent river. He took his work so seriously that as far back as I can remember, our kitchen windowsill sported a clock with the inscription *"To Ronald 'Dutch' Reagan, From 77 Grateful People Whose Lives He Saved While A Lifeguard At Lowell Park, Illinois."*

With the money he earned, Dad put himself through Eureka College, a Disciples of Christ school in Eureka, Illinois, a small town near Peoria. He adored the college — he describes it as a "small-town, ivy-covered campus" — and over the years he's remembered his time there fondly at every chance. There are very few things in this world that Dad will light up at the mere mention of, and Eureka College is right up at the top of that list. There have been many times, he has told me, when he has wished himself back onto that cozy campus, to be once again that ambitious young man about to carve his own path through the world. Between his studies in economics and sociology, life-guarding at Lowell Park, and his job as a busboy in a girls' dormitory, he still managed to play football and swim, two of his all-time favorite activities. He also organized a student strike against a college ban on smoking, drinking, and dancing. (No wonder he was a popular figure on campus.)

Dad graduated from Eureka in 1932, in the depths of the Depression, but he did not pursue the business career for which he had studied. He'd been bitten by the acting bug in a high-school production and had a relapse in several college shows, and he'd decided he wanted to try his luck as an entertainer. He's always gone about things systematically, my father, and he quickly set his sights on the fledgling radio industry, figuring the best (and fastest) ticket into the world of entertainment would be as a sports announcer.

So he hopped into his car and set out for Chicago, where a woman in NBC's personnel department told him to hop back into his car and turn right back around. She said the best way to break into big-time radio was to start in a small market ("the sticks," she called it) — sound career advice that still holds in today's broadcasting industry. Dad followed her counsel, going from one small-town radio station to another throughout the Midwest, knocking on as many doors as station managers could slam in his face.

Finally he arrived at WOC-Radio in Davenport, Iowa. There he was interviewed by the program director, Peter Mac-Arthur, an arthritic old Scotsman who hobbled on two canes. When MacArthur told my father he couldn't give him a job — partly because of his inexperience, but mostly because he'd just hired someone else — Dad's frustration over his sought-for career reached the boiling-over point. "How the hell do you get to be a sports announcer," he yammered, "if you can't even get a job in a radio station?" He stormed out of Mac-Arthur's office in a huff.

But to Dad's surprise, MacArthur hobbled after him as fast as he could. "Hey, wait up," the program director shouted out toward the elevator banks, saving himself, as Dad now recalls, "a couple of steps." "What makes you think you can talk to me like that?"

"I'm sorry, Sir," my father said, "I just wish someone would give me a chance."

"All right," the old Scotsman said. "Here's your chance. Do you think you could tell me about a football game and make me see it?"

"Sure," Dad said. "Tell me when."

MacArthur set Dad up in a studio, with a microphone and an engineer, and Dad launched into a lavish description of a game he had played for Eureka College the previous season. He remembered it like it had happened that afternoon, and he let fly with the most vivid account he could muster, he was so eager to win the job. The way I've heard the story, Mac-Arthur was so impressed by Dad's expressive play-by-play — he said things like "a chill wind is blowing in through the end of the stadium" and "the long blue shadows are settling over the field" — that he offered him a job right then and there.

With his foot in the door, Dad eventually moved from Davenport to WHO-Radio in Des Moines, where he covered football, baseball, prizefights, and track meets. And because of the station's unusually strong signal, reaching several midwestern states, Dad became one of the best-known sports announcers in that part of the country, and he developed quite a following.

He's got stories from this time as well. Like the time when he was broadcasting a Chicago Cubs game and the sports wire supplying him with the play-by-play information went dead. You see, in those days, sports announcers called the game based on the Western Union reports that were fed in to the studio. As a result, the broadcasts were not exactly "live," as they are today; in fact, the extraneous details that made a game come truly alive — whether a shortstop moved to his left or to his right to field a ground ball; whether a batter struck out swinging at a fastball or a curveball — were often left to the announcers' fertile imaginations. They were not at the stadium watching the game along with the fans; they were someplace else, offering a secondhand account. The hard facts of the game were reported accurately, but they were often embellished to the point of creative license.

Anyway, on this day, Augie Galan was at bat when the Western Union ticker inexplicably shut down on Dad. But he's always been quick on his feet, my father, and in desperation he announced that Galan was fouling off pitch after pitch after pitch. Pretty clever, huh? He didn't want to say Galan had gotten a hit, or that he'd grounded out, because the fans would read in the newspapers the next day what had actually happened; he also didn't want to interrupt the drama of the game by reminding listeners that he wasn't actually there watching the action unfold with his own two eyes. Galan must have fouled off a few dozen pitches while Dad prayed for the ticker to spring suddenly back to life. When it did, several minutes later, Dad found out what he'd missed (Galan had popped up the first pitch for an out) and he had Galan do the same on the very next pitch.

His career would take a turn for the unexpected in 1937, while he was covering the Cubs' spring training season on Catalina Island. There a friend introduced Dad to Bill Meiklejohn, a Hollywood agent who pegged my father as the next

Robert Taylor, one of MGM's most promising young leading men. Meiklejohn arranged for a screen test at Warner Brothers, to which Dad happily consented, figuring he had nothing to lose but the few hours he'd put into it. The test went well enough, Dad thought, but when he was finished he was told it would be some time before Jack Warner, the studio head, would be able to see the results of the test. He was told to stick around in Hollywood for the verdict, but my father, true to the values he carries to this day, was not about to give up a sure thing for a long shot. "I'll be on the train tomorrow," he told the folks at Warner. "Me and the Cubs are going home."

And that's what he did. But he did leave Meiklejohn on the case for him on the West Coast (my father may shy away from the long shots, but he covers his bets), and a day after he returned to Des Moines, he received the following telegram from his new agent: "Warner wants you for a seven-year contract. What shall I do?"

Dad returned the wire immediately: "Take it before they change their minds. I'm on the next train."

Well, as you can probably guess, Ronald Reagan arrived in Hollywood before Jack Warner could rethink his offer, and he was put to work right away in a small role for which he was pretty well suited. He played a brash radio announcer in a 1937 movie called *Love Is on the Air*, in which he dashed into a room, his fedora at the back of his head, grabbed a phone, and yelled, "Give me the city desk, I've got a story that will crack this town wide open!"

A star wasn't exactly born with that one bit appearance, but Dad was on his way. Movies like *Accidents Will Happen, Swing Your Lady* (with Humphrey Bogart), *Boy Meets Girl* (with Jimmy Cagney and Pat O'Brien), and *Girls on Probation* (with Susan Hayward) quickly followed, and later in 1938 he would take the role in *Brother Rat* that would change the course of his life and begin the course of mine.

Jane Wyman, his costar in *Brother Rat* and for the next several years off-camera as well, had a somewhat less circuitous route to Hollywood than Dad's. She was born Sarah Jane Fulks, in St. Joseph, Missouri, and moved with her family to California in time to attend Los Angeles High School. During school she worked part-time painting chocolate on donuts — how's

that for a glamorous job? She always had a love of performing, and she managed to win occasional jobs "dancing in the
line" at Paramount.

With that experience she landed a Warner Brothers contract, and she spent several years there before she got her first
starring roles; she would always play the wide-eyed innocent,
and then the worldly-wise best friend, before her big break
into drama in *The Lost Weekend*, with Ray Milland.

The two Warner Brothers players were married on January
27, 1940, at the Wee Kirk O'Heather, a Hollywood wedding
chapel. Mother was a stunning bride in a pale-blue satin gown
and a mink hat with matching muff. Dad, despite a bad case
of the flu, looked sharp in his navy-blue suit. He was running
such a high fever and sneezing so often that he was barely
able to drag himself out of bed in time to make it to the chapel
and to the reception held afterward at — where else? — Louella
Parsons's home. Of course, there was an elaborate account of
the wedding in the papers the next day, and Aunt Lolly got
her hands on a few tidbits that escaped the attention of some
less well connected reporters.

Mother was pregnant with me when she and Dad filmed a
movie called *Tugboat Annie Sails Again*, with Alan Hale and
Marjorie Rambeau, so I suppose we can stretch here and call
this my movie debut. There's a scene in the movie in which
Mother gets knocked into the water, and I cringe every time I
see it, knowing I took the fall with her.

You know, it's funny, but when you grow up in a houseful
of movie stars, you tend to date the pivotal moments in your
life by what movie your parents were working on at the time.
I suppose we all use our own yardsticks against which to measure the passage of time, only in my case the yardsticks are
displayed on the big screen for all the world to see. For instance, I was born on January 4, 1941, about a year after my
parents' marriage, and a few short months before the release
of an otherwise forgettable movie called *You're in the Army Now*,
in which my mother was featured in what still ranks as the
longest screen kiss in movie history, clocked at a full three
minutes and five seconds, against the lips of Regis Toomey.

How's that for a yardstick?

(Incidentally, that record kiss was recently challenged by no less a romantic lead than the comic Pee-wee Herman, in the 1988 movie *Big Top Pee-wee*. But Mother's record, I'm happy to report, still stands; most of Pee-wee's record-settingly long smooch wound up on the cutting-room floor.)

Like most people, I remember very little about my very earliest years. One thing I do remember is that we practically lived at the famous Brown Derby Restaurant, on the corner of Hollywood and Vine — talk about your prime locations! — where I would dine happily on chicken à la King and rub tiny elbows with some of my parents' famous friends. (Chicken à la King was my regular fare; I could actually sit myself down and say, "The usual," and the waiter would know what I was talking about. Later, as an adolescent, I would graduate to a dish called Spaghetti Derby, and then, as an adult, to the famous Cobb Salad.)

"Uncle Bob" Cobb and his wife, Sally, were old family friends, and I used to relish our visits to their restaurant. I had the run of the place, and I would hop around from one table to another, poking my nose around where it didn't belong, just like I was in my own living room. I remember the walls of the restaurant were lined with wonderful celebrity caricatures. (Jimmy Durante's, by the way, had an extra frame for his legendary schnozz.) While the adults talked, I'd spend hours staring up at the pictures, trying to figure out who was who, and what was what.

At that time, the Hollywood Brown Derby was the "in" restaurant among the movie set. It was the place to see and be seen, much like Spago and The Bistro today. Whenever an aspiring actor, director, writer, or agent had lunch there, he'd have himself paged, to help get his name out before the assembled bigwigs and make it appear he had important business to attend to. This became such common practice that if you happened to be one of the well-known bigwigs dining at the restaurant, you began to pray that you wouldn't get a legitimate phone call, because the resulting page would invariably send out the signal that you were down on the level of the up-and-comers. All of this, of course, has become pretty much of a Hollywood cliché over the years, but it had its beginnings at the Brown Derby, and at the time, when I was a little girl standing underneath the cartoon images of the famous people sitting across the room, I put two and two together in such a way that the movie business came gloriously alive for me.

(Eventually the Cobbs opened a Beverly Hills Brown Derby, which was closer to where we lived, and we became frequent dinner customers there. Of course, the new place was never able to duplicate the kind of see-and-be-seen success of the original, but we would go there just the same. The decor at the Beverly Hills restaurant was much more subdued, and the walls this time were covered with photographs of Academy Award winners. What a thrill it was to dine out with Mother and sit underneath her picture, for 1948's *Johnny Belinda*! I used to imagine that every eye in the restaurant was fixed on us.)

I have very specific memories of my father tiptoeing into my room when I was supposed to be asleep. He'd peek over at me to see if I was awake (which I always was), in a way that was almost conspiratorial, and then he'd sit himself down and read me a story. My favorites were the fairy tales of Hans Christian Andersen, though once in a while I'd get a dose of the Brothers Grimm, which I found a little too spooky for my young tastes. Sometimes, too, I'd be treated to my father's stories about his own growing up, which to me were as wonderful as anything penned by any writer. He'd sit with his legs crossed in a chair over by the window, and whether the stories were his or someone else's, I would listen anxiously from my pillow, not wanting to miss a word.

But whatever the story, he'd always cap it off with my favorite bedtime song. I wish I could find the title — Dad says he doesn't know where he first heard it — or a good way to convey in print the beautiful, lilting melody.

We had a little game worked out about that song. "Please, Daddy," I would threaten playfully, "I won't go to sleep until you sing to me."

And then he'd start in, with a soft, deep, and soothing baritone that could lull any daughter to dreamland in ten hot seconds. The lyrics, unadorned and unaccompanied, will have to do:

Stars are the windows of heaven,
   Where angels peek through;
Up in the sky, they keep an eye on kids
   Like me and you;
'Cause stars are the windows of heaven,
   Where angels peek through.

As I grew up, I was always surprised that Dad never played the song-and-dance man in his work, because he loved to give it a go in private. Really, his voice wasn't half bad. We were always singing together, or to each other. We even went so far as to work out old vaudeville routines, one of which became a part of our own little act when company came over.

"Hello, Joe, what do you know?" Dad would begin, borrowing the immortal opening line from one of Charlie Foy's most famous routines.

"I just got back from the vaudeville show," I'd respond.

"Can you sing and dance?"

"Well, I'll take a chance. . . ."

And so on. Our big finale line was, "We're not Warfields, Cohans, or Foys, we're just a pair of entertaining boys." How I loved that routine! (And how Dad loved it, too! He'd call me out for a performance before their company had a chance to take off their coats and sit down!) We would sing and dance and do a little time step as we reminisced about Marilyn Miller and George M. Cohan and all the other vaudeville greats. When Dad talked about the old vaudeville days, I would feel like I was sitting there right next to him in the theater, soaking it all up, and when we put on one of our routines, well, it made me feel a little like Shirley Temple or Margaret O'Brien; playing opposite my father, an actor who was quickly becoming one of the most recognizable movie stars of the day, made me feel all the more connected to the material and all the more at home in the role of performer.

Dad was a born performer, and all the games we used to play together required some type of acting or leap of imagination. He has always had a fondness for the poetry of Robert Service, and when I was a little girl of about three I would beg him to act out "The Shooting of Dan McGrew," one of the

Canadian writer's most famous works, about a saloon in the Yukon, and one of my favorites.

He would really ham it up:

A bunch of the boys were whooping it up in the Malamute saloon;
The kid that handles the music-box was hitting a jag-time tune;
Back of the bar, in a solo game, sat Dangerous Dan McGrew,
And watching his luck was his light-o'-love, the lady that's known
  as Lou.

I would sit mesmerized as he went deeper and deeper into the story of the stranger who stepped in out of the night and could play the piano with every lustful emotion; I must have known the poem by heart — goodness knows, I'd heard it enough times — and by the time Dad was nearing the end, he'd have me in the palm of his hand:

Then I ducked my head, and the lights went out, and two guns blazed
  in the dark,
And a woman screamed, and the lights went up, and two men lay
  stiff and stark.
Pitched on his head, and pumped full of lead, was Dangerous Dan
  McGrew,
While the man from the creeks lay clutched to the breast of the lady
  that's known as Lou.

He stopped short there during one particular retelling, and I'd heard the poem enough times to know it was not quite finished, so I was completely surprised when my father gasped suddenly for air and fell onto the floor. I waited for a minute or two for him to get up, but he just lay there. I was panicked, and I ran over and began beating him on the arm to get him up; he had made the final shootout scene seem so real I thought he had died. I shook him awake, and even when he opened his eyes, it took Dad a good long time to convince his gullible daughter that he was indeed very much alive.

Shortly after I was born my parents built an eight-room house on a curving, steep hill above Sunset Boulevard. The house had a huge stone fireplace and big picture windows, with a magnificent view of Los Angeles and the Pacific Ocean. And leading up to it was the longest driveway I ever did see; if you'd asked me then I would have told you it was a thousand

miles long. Before the house was even finished, Dad had seen
to it that the swimming pool was fully operational. People like
John Payne and Anne Shirley, Bill and Ardis Holden, George
Burns and Gracie Allen, and Johnny Green and Betty Furness
were frequent guests and favored friends, and I would play
with their children, Julie Payne, Babbie Green, and Ronnie
and Sandy Burns.

One of my earliest friends was Lynne Wasserman, daughter
of Dad's agent, Lou Wasserman, and just as Jack had pinned
Dad with the lifelong nickname Dutch, so too did Lynne Wasserman weigh me down with one of my own. The first stum-
bling block to our babyhood friendship was that she couldn't
pronounce "Maureen" and I couldn't say "Lyndie" (which was
the nickname her parents were trying out), so we became
"DeeDee" and "MerMer." Lynne was fortunate enough to
outgrow "DeeDee," but I have been known ever since as
"Merm" or "Mermie." To this day my father seldom calls me
by my given name.

By all accounts I was a precocious child, a characteristic my
father encouraged. He saw all of his children as a challenge,
and he relished the battle of wits we would wage. In that respect Dad was certainly not a traditional father. As early as I
can remember, he treated me as an individual, someone able
to make my own decisions; of course, he would guide me along
masterfully until my decisions were pretty much in line with
his own.

Mother also encouraged me to be independent. One of her
favorite expressions was, "If I get hit by a Mack truck tomorrow, you'll have to take care of yourself." At four I had the
dubious distinction of being the only kid on the block who
knew what a Mack truck was.

I think every kid tries to run away from home at least once,
and I was no different. I tried it twice, as far as we can now
determine. The first time was when I was only three or four
years old. I didn't get very far. I announced to Dad that I was
leaving as he sat by the pool, and he calmly waved goodbye
as I started down the hill and out of sight. I waited for all of
two or three minutes, which seemed like an eternity then, before I returned my little blond head into my father's line of
vision and asked, "Why didn't you come after me?"

"Because," he said, "I knew you'd be back."

The second time I was a little older, and I made more of a good show. One night Mother gave me a stern lecture on the virtues of hanging things up. "If you're going to live in this house, you're going to learn how to hang things up," she said. "If you're going to live in this house, you're going to do as you're told."

"Well," I said, all of five years old, "Maureen is leaving." (I had intended for the line to carry significant dramatic effect, though I'm told it came out sounding more like "Moween is leaving" than anything else, which considerably dulled its impact.) I packed my doll and her clothing into a small suitcase and got my coat.

When I got downstairs, my parents were waiting for me in the front hall. Dad handed me a dollar bill for expenses and said, "Write, Mermie, if you get work."

Out the door I went. What I know of this story is what my mother later told me, and as she remembers it I walked quite deliberately down our long, winding driveway and onto the very quiet street below. As I continued down the street, with my hovering parents hiding behind the backyard fence and monitoring my every move, I began to realize how dark the street was, and gradually my steps slowed. Feeling suddenly frightened, I sat down on my little suitcase in the middle of the street to ponder my next move. I'm sure I made quite a picture! After what must have been a minute's contemplation, I stood up and with visible determination began the short walk back to the driveway. When I finally reached the house, my parents were seated in the living room, where I had left them. I rang the doorbell, announced, "Moween is back," and marched upstairs to unpack.

I got to keep the dollar, though, which I consider to this day a victory of sorts.

With two rising movie stars in our little family, our lives naturally revolved around the movies my parents were making. Both Mother and Dad were highly dedicated to their craft, but there were clear differences in their approaches to work. The line in Hollywood at that time was that actors were the kind of people who took their work home with them, meaning it was difficult to shed whatever role you were working on simply because the cameras were shut down for the day. It all has to do with style; there are some actors who can turn it off at the end of the day, there are some who don't need to, and there are some who simply need to live with the person they're playing for longer than the shooting schedule requires.

Dad, for example, was playing mostly personality parts, so he was able to put a lot more of himself into his roles than he needed to absorb from them; had he followed the path of *Kings Row* (1942), a serious, breakthrough role that was something of a departure for him, then he might have adopted a different approach to what would have been a much different career.

Ask him his favorite role, and without a beat's hesitation he'll tell you it was the part of Drake McHugh in *Kings Row*, one of his best films. In it Dad played a handsome young man-about-town who becomes romantically involved with the daughter of an insane doctor. When McHugh is injured in an accident, the doctor sadistically amputates his legs to pay him back for the perceived immoralities done to his daughter. When Drake awakens from the anesthetic, he realizes that his legs have been amputated and cries out, "Where's the rest of me?"

I was too young to remember Dad's preparation for the part, but he told me later it was the hardest role he ever took on as an actor; he felt that having to portray the utter shock and disbelief of this young man, in five words, was the most exciting challenge of his acting career. He told me that although he had rehearsed the scene again and again at the studio and at home and had consulted psychologists and disabled people, he was still unsure of how to perform the scene as its date on the shooting schedule came closer and closer.

Finally the day of reckoning came. When he arrived on the set, Dad found that the prop man had cut a hole in the mattress at about hip level; he had also put a supporting box underneath the bed, which Dad was supposed to rest his hidden legs on. He climbed onto the mutilated mattress and spent the next hour in a stiff, awkward position, with nothing to do to fill the down time except contemplating his torso and the empty space of sheet where his legs should have been. Gradually the sight began to terrify him. In some weird way he began to feel that something terrible had happened to his body. The director, Sam Wood, asked Dad if he was ready to shoot.

"No rehearsal?" Dad asked, pretending bravado.

By the time Sam Wood called "Action," Dad was so distressed by the distorted sight of his body that he managed to deliver just what was needed on the first take: "Where's the rest of me?" To this day he has difficulty describing exactly what he was feeling when he reached down to where his legs should have been, after all that time. The five-word line came to mean so much to him over the years that he even used it as the title for an autobiography he published in 1965.

But as I said, *Kings Row* was a departure for Dad. Most of his movies were a lot less heavy than this one, and as it turned out, there was a lot of Ronald Reagan in almost every role he played.

Mother was another story. There was very little Jane Wyman in any of her screen performances, and at the same time there was all of Jane Wyman in each and every role. What I mean is that she would immerse herself fully in whatever role it was she was playing. In fact she lived through every role to such an extent that it was hard to recognize her when she came home. My recollections of her during this time are of many different people. Now, this is not necessarily a good thing or a bad thing, it's just the way it was.

You have to remember, her career consisted mainly of serious, weighty roles. She may have started out playing ditzy blondes, but she wiped the smile off her face pretty quick. When she was doing Ma Baxter in *The Yearling*, we hardly saw her smile for six months. No exaggeration. She was this earth-mother-dirt-farmer-starving-to-death-type person every hour of the day. She wasn't acting this way deliberately, it was just the way she approached her work. Sure, it would have been nice if she had taken on a lighter role once in a while — something in a carefree, Holly Golightly mode, perhaps — but Mother's career consisted mostly of one depressingly serious part after another: *Johnny Belinda*, for which she won a best actress Oscar in 1948; *The Glass Menagerie*; Edna Ferber's *So Big*; *The Blue Veil*; *Magnificent Obsession*. In her work she was always the heroine or the victim; she was always struggling to survive. I wonder now if there was a casting director at Warner Brothers who would look over scripts and say, "Aha! Sad, depressing, emotionally gut-wrenching — let's get Wyman!"

Do you remember the movie *The Blue Veil?* That's the one where in the first reel Mother's recently widowed character loses a baby and then becomes a governess; she spends the rest of the movie saying goodbye to one child after another. What a depressing movie! And she had to live with this character every day! No wonder it sometimes was difficult to get a smile out of her. It wasn't until I got to be a teenager and she started doing "Jane Wyman's Fireside Theater," a 1950s television anthology series that allowed her to play a different depressing character each week, that I realized what was happening.

You see, movies in those days took about three to six months to shoot, which meant we had to live with Mother's wide personality swings for months at a time, but television dramas were often cranked out in less than a week. By that time we would sit around and wonder whether Mother would come home from work as a Maryknoll nun or an ax murderess, but we'd learned to accept her sudden about-faces as part of the territory when it came to Mother and acting.

The hours were also tough, for both of them. It seems one of them was almost always working on the weekend, or too tired out from the busy week preceding it. This was fairly common in two-movie-career families in those days. Under the studio system, as a contract player, you moved from one project directly into another.

So all of this meant I spent a whole lot of time with a woman named "Nanny" Banner, a Scotswoman who was small of stature and great of heart, who was hired by my parents to help take care of me. By all accounts, she did a wonderful job. It was Nanny who decided the time had come for me to see my mother on the screen. While I knew what they did for a living, I had never seen any of my parents' movies, and so Nanny packed me up one afternoon in 1945 and carted me down the hill from our house to catch the streetcar to Hollywood, stepping off at a movie theater featuring Mother's current film, which if memory and family legend serve was *The Doughgirls,* with Ann Sheridan, Eve Arden, and Jack Carson.

The movie, set against the backdrop of World War II and concerning the personal problems of a group of young people, was lighthearted and funny enough to be considered appropriate fare for a young child; Nanny had done her homework on that front.

I'd been to movie theaters before; that part of this outing was familiar. But what was decidedly unfamiliar was the sight of my mother interacting with the other characters on the screen. Nanny would remind me from time to time that Mommy was playing make-believe, or some such, but I'm sure the effect on my young mind was addling at best. According to Nanny, I had difficulty following the story line and not talking back to the screen, but I was able to follow what was going on closely enough so that when Jack Carson's character grabbed my mother's character in a tussle of sorts, I ran down the center aisle and shrieked, "You can't do that to my mommy!"

I turned every head in the place, and Nanny and I were shushed back into our seats.

I don't think I was old enough to fit the pieces of the puzzle together in anything resembling the right way, but I'd be surprised if any child of movie-star parents can put it all together on the first pass. A few years later Dad was recovering from a broken leg in Saint John's Hospital (he had broken it during a charity baseball game that pitted the Hollywood Stars team from the Pacific Coast League against a bunch of actual Hollywood stars), and hospital rules didn't allow kids to visit all that often. My grandmother Nelle thought it would help the situation if she took Michael (whom you'll meet more formally in the pages ahead) and me to see Dad's latest film, *The Hasty Heart*, which was Michael's big-screen baptism.

Nelle hadn't counted on the fact that the picture took place in an Army hospital. Michael was old enough to understand about Dad's broken leg, so he was mildly confused by the sight of his father without a cast. What got to him most was that Dad could leave the hospital to appear on the screen but couldn't come home to spend time with us.

Looking back, I think it must have been a strange way for a little girl to grow up, having to comprehend seeing her parents, on screen, adopting new personalities and forming relationships at considerable remove from the realities of her own day-to-day life. I'll never forget the time Alexis Smith, Dad's beautiful costar in *Stallion Road*, visited our house. She and Dad were having some publicity photos taken when I arrived home from school. I walked up to my father and he started to introduce me, but something told me there wasn't supposed to be another woman besides my mother in our house — particularly one so glamorous — posing for pictures like these, interacting so warmly with my father. When she offered her hand, I refused to shake it, and after a mild temper tantrum I was finally sent to my room by my very embarrassed father.

But despite the occasional psychological hurdles in growing up as the daughter of Ronald Reagan and Jane Wyman, movie stars, I developed a fast fascination with Hollywood. I was a quick study. As far back as I can remember, I would question my parents about the movies they were working on, about their costars, their wardrobes, their rehearsals. I would tag along and spend the day on the set whenever I was invited, and sometimes when I wasn't. This was always a special thrill, though I forever lived in dark fear that I would make some dreadful noise that would horribly mess up the film.

From the first, Dad warned me not to yawn on the set — a rule of thumb for any first-time visitor — because a yawn is contagious; it can travel from one person to another, and if it reaches an actor in the middle of a scene, it can ruin the take. Also, my friends would all share horror stories about how they messed up their parents' films — with the noise from their squeaky patent-leather shoes or with the soft slam of a door upon entering a sound stage when the red light was flashing — and I would walk around quieter than any mouse, afraid that I would make or cause some kind of peep that would cost me my ticket into this wonderful place.

Because I was so timid, I sometimes acted in ways that must have seemed a little mysterious to my parents. One time, on the set of one of Dad's westerns, he asked me to join him on horseback for a ride down to the lower lot for his next scene. I wanted to jump right on — he's never known me to refuse a ride on a horse, before or since — but because I was so terrified of doing something wrong, I refused.

I became so enamored of life on a Hollywood set that by the

time I reached kindergarten I told my father there was no need for me to go to school.

"I want to be an actress," I told him.

"Well, Mermie," he said with a straight face, "it isn't every little girl who knows exactly what she wants to be when she grows up."

"That's right," I said, "and I don't have to go to school to be an actress."

(I had it all figured out.)

"But don't you think you should still learn to read and write?" Dad tried. "How will you be able to sign autographs if you don't know how to write?"

OK, so I lost that argument to Dad's too-sound reasoning, but after the first day of school, when I'd learned how to write my own name and mastered the fine art of signature signing, I picked up where I left off.

"Don't you think you should be able to read?" Dad said this time around. "When you're an actress, you'll have scripts to learn and contracts to sign, and I'm pretty sure you'll want to know how to read."

"You can read them to me," I shot back.

"I'd be happy to," Dad said, "but what will happen if I'm not here one day, or if I'm away working on another movie, and you get a new script and can't understand a word of it? How will you be able to figure out what you're supposed to do?"

OK, so I lost that round, too. But I never lost the dream of someday doing what my parents did for a living. The world of movies and movie stars seemed like such a magical place to a small child. When I visited them on the set, I'd pretend I was a grown-up actress on a break between scenes, and I'd stop in at the Warner Brothers commissary to stare open-mouthed at the stars sitting quite normally at their tables. I'd sit myself down and grandly order an iced tea, into which I would systematically stir seven teaspoons of sugar, and then I'd sip very slowly, the very picture of Hollywood royalty, and I remember thinking, Someday this will be what my life is like. . . .

2

A Penny Saved

SOMETHING WAS IN THE AIR as we turned the corner into 1945, though at four years old I'm not sure how much of it I was able to pick up on, even if family legend says I picked up on almost everything. For the better part of the previous year I had been after my parents to get me a baby brother, and for a little girl that age to get an idea like that in her head, she must have sensed that something was going on; she must have overheard a conversation or two.

Anyway, I'd gotten it in my head that a baby brother was something you could just pick up at the store, certainly at a wonderful store like Saks Fifth Avenue, where I'm told I would make regular visits to the toy counter — particularly around Christmastime — to see if they had any in stock. I also asked for a red scooter on the same visits, lest you think I was barking up the wrong tree entirely: I may have been only four years old, but I wasn't born yesterday.

Dad played right along. He'd smile helplessly (and hopelessly) as the people behind the counter fumbled for an appropriate response. He also insisted that if I wanted a baby brother, I would have to save up for him. And I saved diligently, stashing away a penny here and a penny there until my piggybank positively jingled with the effort. You've heard of a

Christmas Savings account, right? Well, Mermie Reagan opened up her own little Baby Brother account; the only interest it accrued was my own — and, I suppose, my parents' — but the account grew as fast as my meager wages would allow. Instinctively I must have known that there was a time frame for getting baby brothers (you had to order one, right? and then you had to wait a good, long while for delivery?), because when my parents told me one unusually warm afternoon in March that I would get the one thing I wanted most in the entire world, my first thoughts were of the red scooter.

When they called me down the stairs later that night, I made sure I had my play clothes on, because I wanted to try out my new prize. A scooter. It wasn't even my birthday, and Christmas wasn't coming for almost a whole year. I couldn't wait to see it.

But there, in my mother's arms, was the baby brother I'd been asking bewildered toy clerks for. Dad says it was a funny sight watching my eyes grow bigger and bigger as I stepped down the stairs, as the reality of what was happening sunk all the way in. I didn't know what to do, whether I should walk over to Mother and see the baby up close, whether I could go touch him or — better! — hold him, whether I should talk to him. What does a four-year-old know about how to act around little babies? I stood there on the third or fourth step from the bottom, just looking.

"Well, Mermie," Dad finally said, probably as much to break the tension as anything else, "where's the piggybank?"

The piggybank! I'd completely forgotten. Dad tells me I ran back up the rest of the stairs almost faster than my short legs could carry me, and was back down in just under a flash, piggybank in tow.

We cracked it open and counted out ninety-seven cents, all pennies, and to my mind Michael Edward Reagan was worth every last one! (Dad — good for him! — kept the money, which I guess evens my tab against the dollar I conveniently forgot to return after "running away.")

Clearly there must have been conversations I'd overheard. I know now that you just don't go out and adopt a baby without some serious thought and discussion; I also know there is considerable paperwork to attend to and a lot of phone calls and other back-and-forthing with attorneys and adoption agencies and whatnot. It takes time. These days such a procedure can take many months, sometimes years, and sometimes even longer. In 1945 the process was much more manageable. Michael has since found out that his was a private adoption, so the back-and-forthing did not take as long as it could have, even if it took just long enough for me to sense what was going on.

The story I got then from my parents, and the one I heard throughout my growing up, was that they had decided to adopt because there were so many children in the world in need of the love and care and happy homelife they could provide. They thought it was important for families who wanted children, and who could provide for them, to take in children who might otherwise grow up in institutions or foster homes.

I'm sure that was part of the story, but it wasn't the whole story.

It has always been my understanding that for some reason, my parents didn't think they could have any more children naturally. I've also sensed that my mother didn't want to go through the pain and suffering of childbirth again, not after what I'd put her through. She can tell you the most adorned story of the day I was born — right down to what she was wearing when she went into labor and how much pain she endured throughout. You can hear every minute of eight and a half hours of agonizing labor, and a minute and a half about me.

That's my mother.

So whether they thought my mother couldn't conceive again, or whether she didn't want to, or whether something else was going on, I don't know. I do know that a couple of years later, in 1947, my mother became pregnant again, and not long after that gave birth to a little girl, four months premature. The baby only lived for one day. I remember very few details about that sad ordeal, other than the fact that my parents had a baby and the baby died. I was too young to even know if they had a chance to name the baby, or if they even had a name picked out. It's something we hardly talked about, then or after. Later, when I was older, Mother pointed out to me the places in *Johnny Belinda* where she looked heavier than usual; she was just coming out of that unhappy pregnancy when she started filming, and she hadn't yet lost all the weight she would lose by the time shooting was completed. Here again we measured the moments of our lives by Hollywood's peculiar yardstick, but that was as far as our discussions ever went about the little girl who was my sister for one day: I learned what it did to my mother professionally, on camera, but not what it did to her emotionally, off camera, or how she was able to handle a devastating disappointment like that and still go on with her life.

That, too, is my mother.

During her pregnancy, my father was filming *That Hagen Girl*, with Shirley Temple. In the movie Shirley Temple played an illegitimate teenager who tries to commit suicide by jumping into a lake, and Dad, playing her older suitor, had to jump into the lake to rescue her. Over and over again. They shot take after take, until the director was grudgingly satisfied. I don't recall where they were filming, or what time of year it was, but the water was freezing. The numerous retakes took their toll on Dad; he woke up feverish the next morning, and within a few days, as he was leaving a premiere, he doubled over with a pain he described as "being stabbed in the chest."

It turned out he had a serious case of viral pneumonia; in fact, it almost claimed him. I vividly remember the night later that week when an ambulance came to take him to Cedars of Lebanon Hospital. I had an enormous teddy bear as a small child — it must have been five feet tall — and I stood behind the door to my room, clutching tight to my furry friend, watching through the crack in the frame as the ambulance attendants took Dad downstairs on a stretcher. I was so scared. I couldn't make sense of what was going on, but I knew enough to know my whole world was hanging in the balance. I'd been cautioned to stay out of the way, and so all I could do was huddle in a corner of my room, crying and clinging to my teddy, petrified, until someone finally found me and told me that Daddy would be in the hospital for a few days, but he'd be all right.

Of course, that was simplifying things somewhat; I found out later that he almost died. In fact, he maintains to this day that there was a certain nurse at the hospital who kept him alive by literally commanding him to breathe; Dad said he obliged her "out of courtesy," which sounds just like him. It was while he was still in the hospital that Mother went into premature labor, and what I remember most about that terrible time in all our lives was that my parents were kept apart from each other by circumstance. It's funny what a child can pick up, and what I picked up was that my parents were not able to be together when they should be together.

But let me get back to Michael. The thing I recall most of all is that he was a very sickly baby. He caught everything that came along, and some other things nobody could trace. Mother used to say he had rickets; I don't know if that was the case, but for the first couple of years, until he was well past two years old, we were kept pretty much apart. "Look but don't touch" — that sort of thing.

By the time Michael was well enough to take on the role of playmate, I was being shipped off to Chadwick, a boarding school, for part of the summer. I was six years old, and the arrangement was for me to stay there for six weeks, interrupted in the middle by one weekend visit home.

Summer school! At six years old! I had wanted to go to camp, and for months I'd been hounding my parents to send me; I was always asking for permission to do things that kids two or three years older would do, and this was just one of a long list. Well, Mother just couldn't say no, but she couldn't say yes, either, and so what she came up with was that I would be going to a summer camp of sorts. I think she convinced Dad that it was just what I wanted, and besides, she figured, the experience would be very good for me. But it wasn't exactly what I had in mind. When I came back home for my midsummer break, I had a case of viral pneumonia to call my very own, and so I spent most of the rest of the summer in bed, which seemed to me a much more pleasant alternative than returning to Chadwick for the next three weeks.

Michael's childhood, particularly his early childhood, was much different from mine. For one thing, our parents reassessed the publicity quotient and decided it was tough enough to raise two kids and tend to their own careers as movie stars without having to deal with the problems and dangers of overexposure. From the day they brought him home, they sought to separate their professional and personal lives to whatever degree was reasonably possible. Missing, then, for Michael, were the flashbulbs that dotted my infancy. Gone, too, were the occasional items in the newspapers and fan magazines. Michael never knew any of that, at least not to the degree that I did, and I have to think a difference like that goes into shaping the kind of person you're going to become.

Publicity about me also slowed down at that time, even though publicity about my parents was still climbing. By this time their stars were shining even more brightly than when I was born. They were getting bigger and better parts, in bigger and better movies. I was too young to miss my place in the limelight, of course, and without the extra attention, growing up in Hollywood was not unlike growing up in Baltimore or Kansas City or any other place. Well, I'll admit, it was a little bit different — Jack and Mary Benny and George and Gracie Burns would probably not have come to Baltimore to use the pool! Kansas City, maybe, but not Baltimore.

But the biggest difference for Michael was that he had an older sibling to teach him the ways of the world, or at least the ways of the Reagan household. He had me to pave the way with Dad, or Mother, and he had me to help him get his hands on what he wanted. I knew which strings to pull and which ones to leave alone, and I could explain the differences for him. He also had me to spill the beans that he was adopted. Now, in my defense, it's not all that unusual for an older sibling to tease a younger one with lines like "Oh, yeah? Well, you're adopted!" In our case, however, the taunt just happened to be true. Michael remembers that he came upstairs to tell me a surprise one day — that I was getting a new dress or something for my birthday — and I didn't want to hear it, so I said to him, "Well, *I* have a surprise for *you*. . . ." That's when I dropped the bombshell.

I don't think he was mature enough to understand what being adopted meant — my parents weren't keeping the news from him so much as they were waiting until he was older and better able to process this piece of information — but I decided it was time for him to know.

When my parents stepped in to clear up the mess I'd made, they bent over backward to make sure Michael understood that being adopted wasn't a bad thing, that it didn't mean they loved him any less, or any differently, than they loved me. He took some convincing, I guess because it was such a hard thing to grasp. From his perspective, one minute he was sitting there, minding his own business, and the next thing he knew, he was adopted. I remember listening in on the discussion, and by the time my parents were through, they'd made such a convincing case for adoption that even I went around saying I was adopted for a while — they made being adopted sound so much better than just being born, as I was.

My mother corroborates Michael's story, and I'm sure it's true, except for the part about my motivation. I doubt very seriously I decided to tell him he was adopted because I didn't want to know I was getting a dress for my birthday. More likely, I must have been jealous about his being the baby in the house, about his being sick all the time and getting all the attention that used to be reserved for me alone.

I think we both measured the attention we received from our parents, mostly because there wasn't all that much of it to go around. They were both as busy as ever; more often than not, they were working six days a week. Like many children of famous people, Michael and I were left to the daily care of people like Nanny Banner. Oh, we were well taken care of, don't misunderstand me, but as an adult I now realize that there's a distinct difference between the care provided by a parent and the care provided by a paid caretaker. We weren't neglected, by any means, and we knew even then that the reason our parents weren't around was because they were busy, not because they were ignoring us. It was simply one of the prices all of us had to pay for their success. I think Michael had more difficulty than I had in coping with this fact of Hollywood life, perhaps because he was younger and, having just found out he was adopted, needed a great deal more reassurance and affection than I did. Or maybe I'd gotten used to their schedule by then, and now it was Michael's turn to get used to it.

Oh, Michael, too, spent his share of time on the set, even though he says now he doesn't remember going all that often. I think it's true that I went more often than he did, mostly because it was somewhat more comfortable for Mother to take a little girl with her into dressing rooms and such than a little boy.

There was one time with Michael that I remember particularly well, when we went to meet Dad on the set of what was to become one of my very favorite movies, *Bedtime for Bonzo.*

For a long time before our visit Michael and I kept hearing these wonderful stories about this playful and bright chimpanzee starring with Dad in his new movie. A chimpanzee? Starring in a movie? It sounds like old hat now, and it is, but at the time the notion that animals could be trained to follow a script was fairly new. We heard story after story, until both of us could think of nothing we'd rather have than an audience with Bonzo.

Well, I'd gotten all dressed up for the occasion. I remember I was wearing a bright red hat with a feather in it, which comes to mind not because I have such a keen eye for detail but because Bonzo had such an eye for bright red hats with feathers in them. We have dozens of pictures of his thin, hairy arm reaching up to grab my hat. (I don't mind telling you, I looked a whole lot better in it than he did!)

I was kind of disappointed in Bonzo. I was expecting this cuddly, lovable little guy, like a neighborhood dog, and what I got instead was almost like a little man. Bonzo was not only humanlike, he was very clearly adultlike; Michael and I could have gone for something a little more childlike. Still, it was fascinating, watching him move about the set and take direction. Neither of us had ever been around a monkey before. God, was he smart!

Some time after the movie was released (I guess I must have been about ten), Bonzo figured again in my young life. Dad and I were alone in the car — which is where we would have all of our most serious talks — headed out to the horse farm he owned in Northridge. "There's something I think you need to know about Bonzo," he said quietly and with what it seems to me now must have been great effort. "There was a terrible fire where he lives, and the flames were too high. They just couldn't rescue him. Everybody did everything they could. I'm sorry, Mermie, but I wanted you to know before you heard about it from the kids at school."

This was the first experience I'd ever had with death, and I can tell now that Dad put considerable thought into just how to handle it. He's always been that way when it comes to his children: any important moment or rite of passage that he has a chance to think through in advance, he'll think all the way through. I think he feels there are certain things in life that are just too important to leave to fate, and telling me about Bonzo's passing was one of those things.

"So we won't be seeing him again?" I asked sheepishly, even though I hadn't seen Bonzo since that one time on the set; I hadn't even thought of him except for when I was watching the movie.

"No, Mermie, I'm afraid not."

At this point Dad remembers that I was crying, though I think my tears had more to do with the weight Dad seemed to be attaching to his words than with what he was actually saying. Bonzo's death was a tough concept for me to get a grip on, but the thing that was bothering me most was the seriousness in Dad's voice. It's funny to me now, even a little sad, that we all saw our way through our parents' busy schedules to find touchstone moments like these, to learn about such a thing as death through the sad tale of a chimp who played alongside Dad in a comedy.

Another special memory on a Hollywood set came when I was about six, when I was called upon to make my visible screen debut (not counting my "in utero" performance in *Tugboat Annie Sails Again*). In those days Warner Brothers was churning out musicals starring people like Jack Carson, Dennis Morgan, and Doris Day, in which the studio's stable of contract players would appear either in cameo parts or as themselves.

One night Dad came home and told me that I had to go to bed early so I could be up in time to go to the studio with him and Mother the next morning. I was going to be in one of their movies! Now, I guess I must have been a pretty jaded six-year-old, because my first thought was not to jump for joy, like most kids would have done, but to sulk because going to bed early would also mean missing my favorite radio show, "The Cisco Kid."

"Dad," I pleaded, "if I go to bed early I won't hear them tell the joke at the end, and I won't hear them say, 'Ah, Cisco,' 'Ah, Pancho,' at the end. That's my favorite part."

"Mermie," Dad said, "you'll only be missing the show this once, and it's not every day a little girl gets to be in a movie. Remember how you've always said you wanted to be an actress?"

"I remember."

"Well, here's your chance."

I didn't have an agent, so I struck my own deal. I agreed to go to bed if Dad promised to wake me up in time to hear the "Ah, Cisco," "Ah, Pancho," part of the program. He consented to my demands, but once I was asleep he switched off the radio, and that was the end of our agreement. I suppose if I'd had an agent I could have gotten Dad to put something in writing.

Anyway, my debut was to be in a delightful musical extravaganza called *It's a Great Feeling.* Dad's cameo scene was with Carson and Morgan in a barber shop; Errol Flynn was also cast in a small role. Mother, too, was cast — as herself — and the script had her being called into the office of a producer (played by Bill Goodwin) and told that she would be directed in the role of "Mademoiselle Fifi" by Jack Carson. She reacted by fainting dead away on the floor.

At that point a blond kid entered the scene (yours truly) with a glass of water in her hand and said, "Here, Mommy, take this."

Piece of cake, right?

Well, not quite. I didn't exactly have the hang of it. In fact, I thought I was just terrible, certainly the weak link in an otherwise fine production. Everybody else gushed about how wonderful I was, but I was sure they were just being polite. Over the years I have had a few opportunities to watch my screen debut on the late late show, and I've come to the conclusion that the late late show is not on quite late late enough. If you happen to come across *It's a Great Feeling* late one night, and you stay awake until that scene, do us all a favor and change the channel for a minute.

This is what life was like in the Hollywood of my growing up.

My father's mother, Nelle, whom I always called Gramsie, filled much of the void left by my parents' careers. A petite, fiery woman with auburn hair and sparkling blue eyes, she was a constant in our young lives, and I don't presume to speak for Michael here, but she was a steadying influence in mine.

When both their sons migrated to California, it wasn't long before Nelle and Jack made the move out west, too. Dad bought a house for them just below Sunset Strip, right at the border of Beverly Hills and Los Angeles. At the time of their move Jack was still doing what he could to make ends meet, with only some success, and Dad eased the move somewhat by putting his father to work as a personal assistant of sorts. My grandfather was too proud to take a handout, and this was Dad's way of seeing that his father had what he needed while he held fast to one of the things he needed most: his pride. Jack had had several heart attacks by this time, the residual effects of a lifelong drinking problem. By the standards of today he was disabled, and finding and securing almost any other kind of job was virtually out of the question.

I'm leading up to a story here. When *Knute Rockne — All American* premiered at Notre Dame in 1940 (that's the movie with the famous line, "Let's win one for the Gipper"), Dad took Jack along as his guest. He had a strange relationship with his father — he loved him dearly, but at the same time he had been embarrassed in his youth, I think, by Jack's public bouts of drinking — and he was looking to make a kind of peace with Jack before it was too late. He knew that his father, being the quintessential Irishman, would get a big charge out of a trip to Notre Dame, and the V.I.P. treatment he'd receive. Now, keep in mind that Dad was worried about Jack's heart and about Jack falling once again off the wagon and doing some horrible damage to himself.

Well, the morning after the big premiere, Jack was nowhere to be found. Dad searched Notre Dame high and low; his father's bed hadn't been slept in. My father got to imagining all kinds of worst-case scenarios. Finally, who should my father see strolling into the hotel but Jack, laughing loudly and singing songs with one of the brothers he'd met the night before! Dad's first thought was that this clergyman had found his father someplace and was simply leading him back to his room to sleep off a rough night; his next thought was that the two of them had spent the night over a bottle — or six or seven. Of course, as it turned out, there was another option that Dad hadn't counted on. The two men had indeed been out all night, but not drinking; they had simply lost track of the hours, talking and singing and laughing and having a grand old time.

Dad told me later that during the banquet the night before, he had looked over to where Jack was sitting and seen the most beatific smile on his face. He said it must have been the closest thing to Heaven Jack had ever known, being there at Notre Dame on an occasion such as this. And in that brief moment, Dad said his emotions ran the gamut from guilt to sadness to love to respect: guilt that he hadn't been more understanding of his father's drinking problems, as a child and a young adult (when he was about eleven, Dad came home from school one cold afternoon and found Jack sleeping on the porch, the snow sticking in clumps to his hair; though Dad was a thin and scrawny boy, he somehow found the physical and emotional strength to drag his father into the house and to bed); sadness that he could now see the end of his father's life more clearly than his father could see the beginning; love for the man who, through hardship, had given his family everything he could and had helped my father to form the values he holds still; and respect for the way his father struggled through his illnesses with as much dignity and grace as he could manage.

I never knew my grandfather, not really. Jack died shortly afterward, when I was five months old, of a heart attack. There's a story that goes with that, too. As I said, Jack and Nelle lived in a house bordering two cities, and in those days there were a lot of jurisdictional disputes between city agencies. One of the areas of conflict, though my grandparents didn't know it at the time, was ambulance routes. Well, when Jack had what would prove to be his fatal heart attack, Nelle called the nearest ambulance, which happened to be a Beverly Hills ambulance. Not only did the ambulance refuse to cross the boundary line to make the pickup, they didn't alert Nelle to their decision. And so she waited and waited for an ambulance that never came, that never intended to come, and she watched her husband die.

My parents were in New York at the time, and my father, in those days, didn't fly, which meant it would have taken them four or five days to traverse the country by train to make it home for Jack's funeral.

"Look," Nelle told him, "I know how you are about planes. If you get on a plane now and anything happens, I will never forgive myself. That will just be it as far as I'm concerned. Take your time and get here when you can."

Jack had been dead for about a week by the time my parents returned home. Nelle held off on the funeral until they got home. They were all sitting in the church where the funeral service was held — I think it was Saint Victor's, down on Holloway Drive, which was Jack's parish — when something wonderfully unusual happened to my father. We've talked about this recently, during a quiet night at the White House, and I was so moved by my father's recollection of how and what he was feeling that I went back to my room and wrote down what he said, in case I ever wanted to call his words to mind again.

I'm glad I did. "It was a grand California day," he told me, "and we hadn't been in California long enough to not gasp at the beauty of a California day. But despite the weather, I was just desolate. I was beyond crying. My soul was just desolate, that's the only word I can use. Desolate. And empty. And then all of a sudden I heard somebody talking to me, and I knew that it was Jack, and he was saying, 'I'm OK, and where I am it's very nice. Please don't be unhappy.' And I turned to your grandmother, who was sitting with me, and I said, 'Jack is OK, and where he is he's very happy.' And it was just like it went away. The desolation wasn't there anymore, the emptiness was all gone, and I've always felt silly telling this to anyone because it sounds kind of weird, but it's true. It's exactly how it happened.

"Only one thing bothered me," he went on, "and it still bothers me. Why me? Of all people, if he was gonna come back and talk to somebody, why me?"

"Dad," I said, "maybe you were the only one who was listening."

But I digress. . . .

Gramsie was something of a clairvoyant, and she was absolutely convinced that one of her sons was going to be President of the United States. The trouble is, I think she thought Dad's older brother, Neill, was targeted for the job, so she only wins so many points for her vision.

She was also a Bible-thumper of the first order. At some point in her life — nobody knows whether it was in childbirth or during an operation — she claimed to have had a near-death experience. Years before scientists would document the phenomenon, she could describe in vivid detail what it had been like: the bright, brilliant light, followed by the feeling of floating on a cloud, and finally, the knowledge that she was close to death. Gramsie would always say her life had been totally altered by the experience, and even if we take her account at the barest of face value — that she nearly died, and lived to tell about it — then I suppose it was.

What is beyond question is that Gramsie came away from the experience thinking that her work here on this earth wasn't finished, and that she had been called back because she was needed to preach the Gospel.

When she and Jack moved to California, Gramsie became very active in the Hollywood Beverly Christian Church. When I was two, I began attending their Sunday school, where I eventually earned a gold cross for perfect attendance. Of course, there was little doubt that I would get to church on time for class, because Gramsie insisted that I stay at her house on Saturday nights.

Gramsie still lived in the house my father had bought for them down the hill from us, a small place on Phyllis Avenue, just below the Sunset Strip. She used to keep an old snapping turtle named Crusty out back, and after church Michael and I would go out and feed him lettuce.

I looked forward to our Saturday nights there all week long. We would always have dinner on stools by the cutting board in her kitchen, with my favorite meal — strange as it now may seem — being Spam. Then we'd get dressed early for bed, turn in, and switch on the radio, and Gramsie would do her part to counterbalance whatever good influences she would see to it that I received the next morning. We'd listen to the family fare early in the evening, after which I'd usually pretend to be asleep. Then, with my eyes closed and my breathing slow and sure, I'd listen to shows like "Gangbusters" and "Inner Sanctum," shows that were on late because they were too scary, or too "adult," for little children to hear. I would hold my breath and hope that Gramsie had fallen asleep, or that she would think I had. And every week, without fail, a hand would reach out of the darkness and shut off the radio just after "Inner Sanctum." To this day I'm convinced that she knew I was listening; little kids aren't as clever as they think.

My grandmother was always deeply concerned about her fellow man, and she selected a number of facilities and organizations in the Los Angeles area to benefit from her good works. She regularly visited Olive View, then a small hospital for patients with tuberculosis, whom she entertained with dramatic readings. Dad once confided to us that Nelle had been a frustrated actress in her youth and had dragged him along to some of her readings so he could tell her whether or not she had the right stuff to make it in Hollywood, even at her advanced age. She also made regular rounds at the veterans' hospital, the children's hospital, and the county jail.

Years later, when Dad was at a banquet, the waiter asked him if he would rather have a juicy sirloin steak instead of the rubbery chicken being served to everyone else. (Don't go getting ideas; this favor was tendered long before my father ever ran for public office, so there were no strings attached.) Dad, thinking the man was a fan and admirer, thanked the waiter profusely and offered to sign an autograph or pose for pictures in exchange for the nice turn.

The waiter waved him off with a shrug. "Nah," he said, "that's all right. I used to have TB, and Ma Reagan always came to see me in the hospital. How is she?"

One time when Michael and I were sick with the flu, Nelle came to visit us. Our sickness didn't stop her from telling us about a family who had just moved to Los Angeles with no money and little more than the clothes on their backs. The details of her tale are now cloudy, but the feelings of charity and good-will-toward-man she inspired in both of us were enough to drag us out of bed and get us to go through our books and toys and clothes to find whatever we could to give them.

Well, I guess you could say we went overboard on this one. Nelle went downstairs overloaded with our gifts, and even she admitted to my father that she might have gone too far. I had given her two dresses with the price tags still attached! Dad evidently explained that she had obviously appealed to our most generous instincts, albeit a bit too forcefully, but that there was no way to explain excess generosity to children. The donations would stand, he said, as long as Gramsie promised to use a somewhat softer sell in the future.

Of course, Nelle never did learn to tone down her appeals. She had the gift of making you believe that you could change the world. I like to think she passed that gift on to me, and it's the nicest legacy she could have left behind.

I realize, too, that I've inherited a lot of my passionate family feelings from my grandmother, who, though she was kind to everyone, never forgave or forgot a harsh word against any of her brood. If a critic gave Dad, or Mother, a bad review, she would grumble about it for weeks. She always took the time to make sure people didn't get the wrong idea about her family. I don't remember what prompted it, but once she sat me down and said, "Mermie, always remember that your father is a man of firm principles." And then she proceeded to tell me a story I'd already heard, about my father resigning from a golf club — Lakeside Country Club — when he learned that Jews were excluded from membership.

(The reason I already knew the story about Dad and Lakeside was that one day George Burns, Jack Benny, and a group of some of Dad's friends — all of whom happened to be Jewish — came by to make him an honorary member of the golf club they were starting, Hillcrest Country Club; Dad had never spoken publicly of his decision to leave Lakeside, but I guess word had gotten around anyway. Hillcrest, incidentally, has thrived, becoming one of the most exclusive country clubs in the Los Angeles area.)

In this one respect, my father was very much like his father, who abhorred discrimination of any kind. When my father was a young man, Jack wouldn't let him see D. W. Griffith's

Birth of a Nation because the film dealt with the Ku Klux Klan's persecution of black people. Another time, Jack went into a hotel during the dark days of the Depression and, after being assigned the last available room in town, was told by the clerk, "You'll find the accommodations to your liking, Sir. We don't permit Jews here." Jack was irate. "I'm a Catholic," he told the clerk, "and if you don't take Jews, then I guess you don't want Catholics, either." With that he stalked out of the hotel, and he spent the freezing winter night in his car. (The sad footnote to this one is that on this night Jack caught such a terrible cold that he eventually contracted a pulmonary infection, which would lead a few months later to the first of his several heart attacks.)

Although Dad inherited his father's intolerance for discrimination as well as his Irish charm, wry humor, and keen ability as a storyteller, I've always said that Nelle, with her kindness, generosity of spirit and energy, and good works, had a greater influence on him. From what I can piece together, Jack and Gramsie were two very different people; it's amazing to me that they got along as well, and as long, as they did. She was as dry as he was wet. Jack, I'm told, was something of a cynic, and believed that energy and hard work, with a little luck for good measure, were the only ingredients for success, while Nelle believed that sweetness and charity could transform the world into a better place.

I was twenty years old when she died, after suffering for many years from osteoporosis and a creeping senility that today would no doubt be diagnosed as Alzheimer's disease. She spent the last several years of her life in a nursing home. She never lived to see her son take his first political steps toward fulfilling her vision, even if it was the wrong son doing the fulfilling.

Like Dad with his father, I had a vision, of sorts, about Nelle. I don't make any claims of clairvoyance, the way my grandmother did, but this strangely soothing encounter had a profound impact on me. I told Dad about it the same night he told me his story about Jack. I was living in Washington at the time, and at about six-thirty in the evening, which would have been the middle of the afternoon in southern California, I was sitting idly in my apartment when I suddenly felt like someone had kicked me in the stomach. Really, it was an incredible feeling, and it led to inexplicable fits of crying and melancholy that lasted through the night.

The next morning I got a telegram from Dad, telling me that Nelle had died the afternoon before, and I put that news together with the strange feelings I had experienced the previous evening. I held that telegram in my hand and felt, for Nelle, a tremendous sense of relief, an unburdening. Now, at last, she was free from her suffering. A voice somewhere in my head told me she'd been alone for so many years; now, it said, she's not alone anymore. I listened to the voice, and I felt fine, at peace.

To this day I can remember the first telephone number I ever learned to dial: CRestview 1-0358.

It was Gramsie's.

3

Separating

Well, as you probably already know, most matches made in press-agents' Heaven don't exactly have legs, to borrow an industry term.

Ronald Reagan and Jane Wyman separated in the summer of 1948. I was seven years old. Michael was three. The news of their impending divorce took me completely by surprise. I think it took everyone in my family by surprise, except of course my parents. I never heard any rumblings leading up to it, and very little was ever discussed with me afterward. One day they were together, the next they weren't; that's the way I saw it. You have to remember, I was just a precocious seven-year-old kid, and though it seems natural to me now that parents would shield children of that age from the details of something like this, at the time all I could think was that it had snuck up on me from out of nowhere.

All I could think was that things would never again be the same.

I was right.

Dad had the unhappy task of breaking the news to me. He took me out to dinner one night — I wish I could remember the name of the restaurant — and it was just the two of us; at three, Michael would have been too young to understand what

was going on. In a lot of ways, at seven, I was also too young
to understand what was going on, but with me they at least
had to try.

On the drive over my father and I had another one of our
important car conversations.

"Mermie," he said, "there's something I have to tell you
that's not going to be easy for you to hear." His voice was
gentle, almost soothing, and it was clear to me even then that
he was choosing his words very carefully. "It's not going to
be easy for me to say, either."

"What?" I said back. "Tell me." I had no idea what was
coming. Remember, this conversation took place only a few
months after Dad's bout of viral pneumonia (and that horrible
night when he was carried off on a stretcher), and Mother's
premature delivery, and so the first thoughts stepping forward from the back of my mind were about my parents and
hospitals. I thought maybe someone was sick.

"Your mother and I won't be living together anymore," he
said. "I think we'll get along much better if we live apart from
each other. It's the best thing." The rest of what he said —
about how he would still be my father, how he would always
be my father; about how he'd still be around for me when I
needed him and how he hoped I'd be around for him when
he needed me; about how we'd still see each other, all the
time, and about what fun we'd have, all the time — I remember now as a blur. He was going through the same motions
that all divorcing fathers go through now, but for him it was
entirely new. It was entirely new for me, too, and I wasn't
really listening. I'd heard the first part — I heard the word
divorce somewhere in there — and I guess I must have thought
I didn't need to hear the rest. For some reason I seem to remember looking out the car window as he was struggling
through his explanation, and gazing into the clear, black night,
thinking I was looking into a dark, empty hole.

I must have tuned back in in time for his closing remarks,
because I can still hear Dad saying, "Just remember, Mermie,
I still love you. I will always love you." His voice was cracking
a little as he spoke.

I was crying, but I was being shy about it. I knew something horrible was happening to me, and I knew people cried

whenever horrible things happened to them. When I asked my father about it years later, he told me I was turned away from him the whole time, looking out the window; if I was doing any crying, I wasn't letting on.

Dad put on a game face and tried his best to lighten up the mood inside the car. He reached out for me and said, "C'mere, Shorty" (he called me that, too, sometimes), and pulled me close in a hug. I wasn't making his job any easier. He may have even tried a joke or a riddle or a tickle to cheer me up, but he got no response.

"Hungry?" he asked.

"Not really."

"Not even for chicken à la King?" he tried, enticing me with my favorite meal.

"I guess."

"You guess?"

"I guess."

When I think about that moment, I am still a little girl, my face pressed close up against the car window, my breath fogging the glass. I am still the same little girl who wanted to scream, who wanted to curl right up and disappear, who wanted to cry out "Why?" or "What about me?" or "What about what I want?" I had so many questions racing through my head that night, even as my father was doing his level best to walk me through a gentle explanation; I have those same questions still.

You see, in my family, certain things happen on the surface, and they get discussed on that surface level, but we never quite get below the surface. Mother is like that most of all, and I suppose I, too, am guilty of something of the same thing, at least to a degree. Dad became that way, I think, out of respect for Mother's privacy, and to some extent he remains guarded about certain things to this very day. That's just the way it's always been in my family, and I know a lot of families like that, so I guess it's not unusual. But oh, how I wished, on that night and on the nights that followed, that someone would go below the surface with me and help me to understand what was about to happen to the only world I had ever known. There were so many things I wanted to know! I wasn't even entirely sure what the word *divorce* meant until my family went through it, and I had no one to ask about it, no one to really talk to about it.

I felt completely, and desperately, alone.

Dad, I've since learned, was devastated by the divorce. I know that now, but I didn't know it then. It just never occurred to him, no matter what their problems were, that he and Mother would get a divorce; it was so foreign to his way of thinking, to the way he was brought up. People just didn't get divorced where he came from, in Dixon, Illinois; even in the Hollywood of 1948, people didn't get divorced all that often. Also, he had just told a friend of his that he and Mother were getting along really well for the first time in a couple of years, and then all of a sudden Mother said, "Out, no, go, enough," or whatever, and he didn't know what hit him.

(Whether that's the way it happened or not, I won't ever know, but that's how the story was passed on to me.)

Plus, he didn't have anybody he could talk to about it. None of his close friends had been through what he was going through; certainly no one in his family was in a position to empathize. Bill Holden, the actor, was one of Dad's closest friends at that time, but Bill and his wife, Ardis, were still several years away from their own divorce. Everywhere Dad looked, he was breaking new ground: no one he knew really well was also separated from his children; no one he knew really well was also trading one life and life-style for a completely new pair. There was nowhere for Dad to turn for any kind of emotional support, and even if there had been, I don't know how much support he would have sought; he's a very private man, my father, and he doesn't put himself on the line with too many people. He keeps these kinds of things to himself.

Mother, too, kept pretty much to herself about the whole divorce. Oh, I'm sure she had some very close friends she could have opened up to, but as she had done before and as she has done since, with the other private moments in her life, she chose not to.

With an adult's perspective, I can now see certain telltale signs that things were going sour for my parents. I think World War II, of all things, did a great deal of the souring. For four years during the war Dad put his career on hold and worked making U.S. Army training films — first as a lieutenant, then as a captain — earning $280 each month, which I'll have to admit wasn't bad money then; it's just that, stacked up against an actor's salary, $280 a month didn't go very far. Mother kept on with her career at full pace, and I have to think that the family dynamic was irrevocably changed as she became more and more the breadwinner. She seemed to start making more than her share of family decisions, financial and otherwise. Of course, what happened in my family was not at all different from what happened in other families where women were forced by circumstance into the workplace, but it seems to me now that the apparent role reversal brought about by the war contributed somehow to the shift in my parents' relationship.

Also, I've often wondered if losing the baby the way they did accelerated some of the problems they were having in their marriage or made it seem to them that their problems were not worth working through. Might they have stayed together had the baby been born healthy, at full term? I don't think so. I mean, if they couldn't stay together for the sake of two children, then they wouldn't have stayed together for the sake of three, right?

But let me get back to reality here. Mainly, Dad was floored by what the divorce would do to his relationship with Michael and me, so clearly if there had been another child in the mix, it would have been all the more difficult. He couldn't stand leaving his kids. That got to him in the same big way it got to us. Oh, we would still see him all the time, sure, but we all knew that the nature of that relationship would be forever changed. Now, if he wanted to slip into our bedrooms for a goodnight kiss or a bedtime story as we were drifting off to sleep, he'd have to call ahead to let Mother know he was coming, and he'd have to time it just right. Now, if we wanted to plop down in his lap in the living room while he was reading the paper or studying a script, we'd have to go over to his house to do it. (We'd probably have to call first, to see if he was there, and we'd have to get Mother to drive us.) Now, if we had a question that only he could answer, we'd have to wait until the weekend, or call him up on the phone, to ask.

Dad took an apartment — in the same building he had lived in before he married Mother — and the only things he took with him were his desk and his books. Oh, he also took a stuffed lamb of mine, which sat on his dresser, reminding him of me. I'm sure he also took something of Michael's, but I don't remember what it was. Mother kept everything else. It must have been sad for him, sitting all alone there in his small apartment, thinking about his two children going through their day-to-day without him.

Despite our regular visits, I missed him terribly. Michael did, too. Actually, if we had tallied up the time we spent with him before the divorce and after, I think things would have pretty much evened out, but the way that time was spent was different. As the months and years wore on, we developed our own routine with Dad, our own new way of being together, but it was slow going at first. He wasn't the "Saturday Dad" you hear about in the aftermath of today's divorces; he didn't bend over backward to amuse us during our times together. We amused ourselves. He'd pick us up and we'd drive out to the ranch with him and he'd do his thing and we'd do ours. There was plenty to do: hike, swim, play with the kittens in the barn.

Just around the time of the divorce, Dad sold his first ranch — an eight-acre spread in Northridge that he'd had as far back as I could remember — and "traded up" for a magnificent three-hundred-acre piece of property in Malibu Canyon. For a long time Dad had been worried that the sprawling city of Los Angeles would just sprawl right out onto the track he had laid out for his horses, and so he started to look around for a new piece of property. I think it was just coincidence that it all happened at the same time as the divorce. Anyway, the Malibu Canyon ranch was the ranch of my growing up. There was a whitewashed redwood fence and a big jumping field for Dad's horses (my father built all the jumps himself). The house itself was kind of dilapidated, but Dad got around to fixing it up so it felt like home, which was a good thing, considering the amount of time his children would spend there with him.

Because we were always being shuttled back and forth from Mother's house to Dad's ranch, we wound up spending a lot of time in the car. Dad did almost all of the shuttling, which was OK with us because he had a way of making a car ride

loads of fun. Whenever I think back to the period just after
the divorce, I picture Michael and me in the backseat of Dad's
turquoise convertible, happily engaged in some game or story
cooked up by our clever Dad.

Most little kids just hate being on a long car ride, but for us
the time would just fly. Dad would tilt his head up and catch
our attention through the rearview mirror, and we'd know
from the glint in his eyes we were in for a good time. We used
to love to sit and listen to him talk about the "past lives" he
had lived. One of my favorite tales was about his past life as
a cold germ, and how he had loved to infect everyone with
coughs and sneezes and runny noses; he would flit from nose
to ears to throat, causing all kinds of discomfort to unsuspect-
ing folks. But one day our father the cold germ found himself
suddenly sleepy and desperate for a nap. Searching for a place
to rest, he discovered a dish of fluffy green stuff. He said it
looked like it would make a nice pillow for his head, and he
settled himself down for a short snooze. In his next life, of
course, he discovered that the dish was filled with penicillin.

Every story he ever told us about his past lives had a moral.
(I guess the moral of the penicillin story was "Don't sleep
around.") Once he told us about being a French poodle who
belonged to a fat old lady who did nothing but eat bonbons
all day. The poodle just hated his fat old mistress; she called
him "my oody-woody snookums." So in revenge he used to
go out in the alley and roll around on a dead fish and then
come back into the house and jump all over her. But — darn! —
his mistress thought his mischievous behavior was cute. One
day the poodle trotted into the alley and was just about to roll
on a stone-cold flounder when he was chased by a police dog.
He dashed out into the street and was run over by a truck. In
his next life, of course, he discovered that his mistress had
given him a fantastic funeral. The moral of that story? "Look
both ways before crossing the street."

Another of Dad's games involved "eavesdropping" on other
people's phone calls. In those days the telephone lines were
still above ground, and Dad claimed an unusual ability to listen in on people's conversations as we were driving past their
telephone poles. "Mermie and Michael," he would say, cran-
ing his neck toward the lines, "today I think I'm picking up a

woman's voice. She's talking to someone, I'm not sure who . . . wait a minute, I think it's her lawyer . . . no, it's a policeman . . . no wait — oh, now I know!"

"Who is it, Dad?" We couldn't wait to hear.

"It's her hairdresser!"

The way he'd build up the excitement and say it, it seemed like listening in on some woman's conversation with her hairdresser was one of the most wonderful things in the world. "What's she saying?" I'd ask.

"Tell us, Dad," Michael would insist.

"It's hard for me to make out. I think she has a bad connection. There's a lot of interference. Oh, here it is, it's coming in clear now. She's saying, 'Renaldo, last week my pageboy was on the limp side,' " he'd say, sending his voice as high as it would go in imitation. " 'And my nails were a disaster. I asked you to do them blood-red and then you got to talking to your mother on the phone and you got all mixed up and did them in this disgusting shade of pink. Just look at them. All week people have been laughing at me.' "

Michael and I would be giggling in the backseat.

"Wait a minute, kids, I'm losing the connection. I can't make anything out, there's this terrible crackling. Wait, I hear a new voice. I recognize this voice. Why it's Carrie, your mother's housekeeper."

"It's Carrie!" we'd trill.

"And guess who she's talking to? The butcher. Oh, you kids are going to have a wonderful dinner tonight."

"What, Dad? What are we having?"

"Well, let's see: you're going to have liver and broccoli."

"Yuck," Michael would say. "Liver and broccoli! Yuck, yuck, yuck."

"Wait," Dad would continue, "I take that back. There was some interference on the line. I didn't hear it right. It seems like you're having hamburgers and French fries and peas and a big, thick chocolate fudge cake."

Whatever his predictions, he was always right about what we were having for dinner. He must have had a system worked out with Carrie. Leave it to Dad to go to the extra trouble to make sure the payoff to his games was on the money.

As we grew older, Dad would teach us college drinking

songs, considerably edited. I was twenty-five years old when I finally learned that a ramblin' wreck from Georgia Tech was a little bit more than a "heck" of an engineer. He'd also teach us things like the Army Air Corps song, which of course they use now for the Air Force: "Off we go into the wild blue yonder. . . ." At the end of the song, after the line "Nothing can stop the Army Air Corps," Dad would add his own special tag: ". . . except the cavalry." Well, when I was twenty-two, I was with a group of Air Force people, and guess what? We were singing what had since become the Air Force song, and I put Dad's tag to use. It's true. I sang ". . . except the cavalry" at the end, and these people looked at me like I had about eighteen heads.

I just shrugged and said innocently, "You mean that's not how it goes?"

Dad also mixed in a little history and geography along the way. He'd teach us tidbits of information on the way out to the ranch, and then on the way back he'd quiz us to see what we remembered. In this way we learned, for example, that Brownsville, Texas, was the southernmost point in the United States, not someplace in Florida, as we had thought, and that Maine was the northernmost state in the country, not Washington, as our Pacific Coast upbringing suggested.

There were also impromptu lessons in ethics. In the fall we would often stop at one of the many apple-cider stands in the San Fernando Valley and pick up a jug or two of cider to take home. Dad liked to stop at a different stand each time, and one day we found ourselves in a small general store. Michael and I asked Dad if we could have some animal crackers to hold us over until we got home, and he happily consented and paid the man behind the counter for a box of them. Well, after about fifteen miles or so, Dad could still hear us munching away at our animal crackers, and he figured the box was lasting longer than it should. As it turned out, Michael and I had thought we were each to get a box, while Dad had intended for us to share only one — the one box he had paid for.

Clearly it was just an example of poor communication, but that didn't change the fact that the owner of the small store had not been paid his ten cents for the second box of animal crackers. And so without a moment's hesitation, Dad turned the car around and went back the fifteen miles to pay the storekeeper the dime we owed him and to apologize for the confusion.

That's my father for you.

To their credit, my parents worked overtime to present a united front at holiday times and on special family occasions. They made an effort to get along for our sake. Christmas, birthdays, and Easter we still celebrated together. That very first Fourth of July, for example, found the four of us at a beach house Mother had rented for the summer. Michael, though, if I'm remembering correctly, was sick with something or other and couldn't join us on the beach for the hot dogs and fireworks we had planned, so Mother bundled him up and took him home, which left me and Dad on the beach with a couple of sorry-looking hot dogs and some fireworks without too much pop in them. It was a pretty pathetic Fourth; we all tried hard, but it wasn't quite there.

The picture of what my new life as a child of divorce was all about was becoming clearer and clearer to me as the summer dragged on. Mother had enrolled me once again at Chadwick, only this time for the full year.

Boarding school. Divorce. Predictable, right? Until that time I'd always thought of boarding school as a kind of punishment, a place where you sent troublemaking kids, kids who didn't quite fit in where they were, and a part of me interpreted the decision to send me away to school as a signal that I had done something unspeakably wrong or that I no longer fit in at home. In a way, I didn't; Mother was busy with her career and Dad was busy with his, and both of them were busy building new lives for themselves apart from each other. It must have occurred to both of them, or to Mother at least, that they'd have one less thing to worry about if I was away at school.

Anyway, for whatever reason, off I went. Once again it fell to Dad to do the dirty work. He drove me up to Chadwick and along the way gave it his best effort all over again. I was one tough customer when it came to being cheered up: "Oh, Mermie, you're so lucky," he said. "You're going to just love it up here."

For an actor he didn't sound all that convincing.

The drive in those days took well over an hour, though with the new roads they've built since, you could probably make the trip today in under twenty minutes. I remember we drove along a beautiful country road lined with pepper trees. When we came to the blue and white Chadwick sign on the side of the road, I knew we didn't have too far to go. Dad turned the car onto a long driveway that went straight up a hill. There were fields on either side — big, open fields, the kind you'd find on a farm — and even though I'd been here two summers before, the surroundings looked entirely unfamiliar.

"Dad," I said, "I think you made a wrong turn." (Wishful thinking on my part.)

"No, Mermie," he said, still with the same cheerful voice he had carried for the whole ride, "we're going the right way."

"But it looks like a farm."

"It is a farm."

"But I thought it was a school."

"Well, it is," Dad went on, trying not to grow impatient with me. "It's a school most of all, but it's also a farm. They grow hay and wheat in those fields, and they also raise pigs and chickens and rabbits. And look over there," he said, pointing to a stable off in the distance. "They've even got horses. I hear there are some wonderful places to ride."

"I guess."

"You guess?" he said, doing his best to put a smile on my face. "I guess you'll like it here very much. I know I would, that's what I guess."

Horses or no, I wasn't sure Dad had guessed right. I liked it at home, and I liked it at home with Mother and Dad and Michael and me. All four of us. As we pulled onto the grounds, I wanted nothing more than to turn right back around and go home to our house overlooking Los Angeles, to my pretty, sunny room, to my cat, Rapscallion, who had slept curled around my neck until it turned out I was allergic to her. And I wanted Dad to come home with me, with us. As much as I liked pigs and chickens and rabbits and horses, I would have gladly agreed to never set foot on another farm if only I could have my life back the way it used to be.

But then I remembered that Mother was in the process of

selling the house and that we had to give Rapscallion away to the people who lived across the street from Dad's ranch in Northridge. And, as the topper to it all, I remembered that my parents had gotten a divorce and that Dad was never coming home, at least not to live.

Dad stopped the car in front of the small house where I was supposed to stay. We went inside and met Miss Wallingford, the dorm mother, and she introduced me around to some of the other girls. They seemed like a nice enough bunch, to tell the truth, but they weren't the same as the friends I had at home, and Miss Wallingford wasn't Mother, and this house was nothing like the house I had grown up in.

I walked back out to the car with Dad to get my things. I remember thinking that if we unpacked the car slowly enough they might give my room to another girl, and we would just have to pack up the car and head home, but nobody was waiting for my space by the time we finished. Dad took my hand in his after we unloaded the last of my stuff, and I held on as tight as I could. I didn't want him to leave; I don't think he wanted to leave, either. I'm sure leaving me there like that must have been one of the hardest things he ever had to do.

He bent down and scooped me up in a big hug. "Mermie," he said, doing his best to hold back his emotions, "you're going to love it here. You'll make new friends here. Really. I promise."

"If I don't like it, will you come get me?" I asked.

"If you don't like it, I'll come get you."

"Promise?"

"Promise. But you have to promise you'll give this place a chance."

"I promise."

"Good," he said. "I'm glad."

He held me close again for a few beats more, and then he got into his car and started the engine. I stood in the driveway with tears streaming down my face, waving, as I watched him drive off. I kept waving and waving long after Dad's car had disappeared from view. I thought maybe he'd come back, at least for another hug.

I think we all have a handful of moments in our lives in which events come together in such a way that we gain a new perspective on things, or in such a way that we are forever changed by them. The events of the previous few months — Dad's illness, the baby, the divorce, and, now, being left here at boarding school — came together in just that way for me, and even though I was only seven years old, I had enough going for me to know that from that point forward I was on my own. Really, I know it sounds silly for a little girl of seven to have had an epiphany like that, but think about the hand I'd been dealt: I had no house to go home to; in a way I had no family to go home to; and I was left behind to get along in a place where I had no friends, no roots, nothing. I felt deserted by my parents — mostly by my mother, because at least Dad had driven me up here, but both of them were guilty in my book. It was just me, Mermie Reagan, out to face the world on my very own. Really and truly on my own, as surely as if everyone in my family had been hit by one of Mother's Mack trucks.

During the next few months at Chadwick I began to realize that I was not as alone as I had thought at first. Dad had been right about the place. The people were nice, the teachers were creative, and there were some wonderful places to go riding. Margaret Lee Chadwick, who founded the school, which was set on a hilltop on the beautiful Palos Verdes peninsula, was a remarkable woman. Next to Nelle, she was my favorite teacher. Not only did Mrs. Chadwick stretch our imaginations to new heights, but she also challenged us to excellence. One year she asked her students to write an operetta about Iceland — yes, Iceland! — a place she chose because she knew most of us had never heard of it. We had to study the people, places, music, traditions, and even the sagas of that fascinating land. To this day I know more about that region than most people know about their own country; if they had Iceland as a Trivial Pursuit category, I would clean up.

I lived in a dorm called the Cottage, which had a sleeping porch where about eight or ten of us slept in bunk beds, another sleeping porch that housed four more, and a playroom or common room. Breakfast was served at about seven, which meant we got up at about six-thirty or so. We always made a funny picture in the morning, the way we'd stand in a sort of assembly line, braiding each other's hair. Miss Wallingford, whom we called Wally, would stand at the back of the line doing one girl's hair, and then that girl would work on the hair of the girl in front of her, and then that girl would have someone in front of her, and so on. The treat, every few weeks, was to be the girl assigned to the front of the line.

Classes were held from about eight to four, and we all had chores to do around the dorm, or around the farm, after school. For a while one of my jobs was to take care of a pretty brown goat named Heidi, who became a special friend. I'd spend hours confiding in her about my special problems.

At night the girls in the dorm would sit around in the common room and Wally would read to us, or we'd play some kind of game or do some other group activity. We didn't get homework until the seventh grade, which left the evenings pretty well free for whatever activity the dorm mother planned.

Swimming was a major sport there, which worked out well for me because Dad had introduced me to swimming almost before I could walk. We'd have to trek about a mile down the hill to the pool for gym class, and then a mile back up the hill, and you wouldn't dare be late for your next class. That was all part of the drill. Margaret Chadwick believed that you educated the mind, the body, and the soul, and she did a pretty good job of working on all three.

Many of the students at Chadwick were children of movie stars, politicians, or other famous people. What a relief it was to be around kids who weren't dumbstruck when you told them what your parents did for a living! Many of them also had parents who were divorced, so they were able to help me deal with some of the distressing changes in my life. One of the girls in my dorm was Mary Helen Douglas, the daughter of Helen Gahagan Douglas and the actor Melvyn Douglas. The entire dorm stayed up late one election night when Mary Helen's mother was running for the U.S. Senate, and I'll never forget how crushed the poor girl was once the results were in; it was the first time I'd ever seen up close the powerful impact a political campaign could have on an entire family, and ever since then I've flashed on an image of Mary Helen every time I've come up on the short side of a hard-fought campaign.

I made some good friends at Chadwick, among them Joan Crawford's adopted daughter, Christina. She seemed like such a happy, together kid that I had no idea she was being abused at home. None of us did. In fact, when we were home, Mother and I would sometimes dine with Christina and her mother, and I remember feeling jealous when I looked across the table at the way they interacted with each other. They seemed to be such good pals, and they were always calling each other by these cute nicknames. They acted like friends, and I longed for some of that in my relationship with Mother. With Mother and me things were always so formal, so proper, but now that I know the truth about Joan, I think I prefer Mother just the way she was.

We'd go home on alternate weekends, the upperclassmen one week and the lowerclassmen the next, which was a nice way to do it because then we each had a chance to have the school all to ourselves. On my weekends home I'd divide my time between Mother's new house and Dad's ranch, and I remember not feeling quite at home at either place. Even at that age I knew I was building a life of my own at Chadwick; I had my own routine and my own way of doing things.

Before I looked up, it was already time for our Christmas vacation, and believe it or not, I wasn't looking forward to being home for such an extended time. I counted the days until I could go back to Chadwick. What a difference a few months can make to a newly independent kid!

Anyway, that was our first Christmas since the divorce, and Dad spent it with us. The two presents I wanted most that year were a baton, so I could practice to be a drum majorette, and a long square-dancing dress, so I could look like "the lady that's known as Lou," in the Robert Service poem. Somehow Dad divined what I was wishing for, and he came through with both of them. Where he managed to find a square-dancing dress in my size, I'll never know. I'm sure I was the only kid in all of Los Angeles twirling a baton on Christmas morning and looking like she had just stepped out of a barn-burning hootenanny.

One of the things I discovered that Christmas was how much I missed Michael. And how much he missed me. At three and a half, he had just been getting to the age where we could enjoy each other when I left for school in the fall, and now, at Christmas, I couldn't get over the change in him. We were missing out on our chance to grow up together, to share secrets together, to invent our own private games and special ways of being with each other. I was probably too young for all of this to have occurred to me at the time, but I think I recognized that I somehow felt cheated with Michael; after all, he had cost me ninety-seven hard-earned cents, and I was hardly even getting to play with him.

That all changed in the fall of 1950, when Michael joined me at Chadwick. He was only five and a half years old, which was awfully young to be away from home, but Mother decided it was the proper time, and she was not going to be talked out of it. I was cast in the role of big sister/surrogate mother, which was a tough part to play; I would look over his shoulder whenever I could, but every time I turned up, he'd kind of look the other way, since it wasn't "cool" for a kid to be seen with his big sister.

Michael's dorm was a Quonset hut that was located pretty close to where I had most of my classes, so I would drop in from time to time to see how he was doing. We'd also run into each other when we were waiting in line to go into the dining hall, but other than that, our busy, regimented schedules conspired to keep us apart. Mostly I'd keep tabs on him through his dorm mother, who kept me up to date on some of the problems he was having adjusting to his new life away from home. He had it pretty rough at first. He missed his parents terribly. He cried himself to sleep most nights.

But the biggest problem, as I've pieced it together since, was that Michael was confused about the sudden turns his life had taken. He was unable to draw the proper distinctions among his room at Chadwick, Mother's new home in Holmby Hills, and Dad's new ranch near Malibu Lake. There were so many new things going on in his young life that it was impossible for a kid of five to keep it all straight.

Because he was having difficulty adjusting, the teachers at Chadwick decided it was important that he establish some sort of continuity in all three places. To this end one of them mentioned something to Dad about Michael's love for my favorite goat, Heidi, and suggested that he buy a goat for him and keep it at the Malibu ranch. Dad thought that was a wonderful idea, and he went out and bought Michael a beautiful brown and white Nubian goat, which Michael, with all the imagination a five-year-old could muster, decided to name Heidi.

Whether or not the goat helped to ease Michael's adjustment to Chadwick, I can't say, but he sure did love that animal. He devoted so much of his affection to her and showered her with so much attention that I began to feel jealous, and one day I started working on Dad for a goat of my own. Eventually he gave in and bought me a black and white goat who happened to be Heidi's sister. I named her Nubbin. Nubbin the Nubian.

This business with the goats is leading somewhere — trust me. Michael's goat, Heidi, figures prominently in one of my all-time favorite family stories. You see, during the summer of 1951, when we had the second Heidi at Dad's ranch, Michael and I decided to take her home to meet Mother. If I had to bet, I'd say this brilliant scheme was all my idea, but I'm willing to give Michael some of the credit for coaxing. Together we herded Heidi into the back of Dad's convertible. Somehow we persuaded her to lie down on the floor, and after cautioning her not to let out so much as a bleat, we covered her with our jackets.

Well, when the time came for us to leave, Dad was surprised to find us ready and waiting in his car for the drive back to Holmby Hills. Usually he'd have to round us up for a good long while before we got our act together.

He eyed us suspiciously. "OK, kids, why are you in the car?" he asked. "Are you sick?"

"No, Dad, we're not sick," I said.

"Michael?"

"No, Dad, I'm not sick." Michael was doing his best to beat back a case of the giggles.

Just then there was a rustling from the backseat, which the two of us pretended not to notice.

"What's that under the backseat?" Dad wanted to know.

"Nothing, Dad," I said.

"Michael?"

"Nothing, Dad."

"It isn't Heidi, by any chance?" (Gee, we never could put one over on you, could we, Dad?)

"No, Dad," I said. "Why would Heidi be hiding under our jackets?" (Good tactic, Mermie; answer a question with a question.)

"Michael?"

Well, by this point Michael was about to burst, and before he could figure out something clever to say, like "No, Dad, why would Heidi be hiding under our jackets?," the giggles had their way with him.

When she heard her name and all the giggling, Heidi started to wiggle her way out from underneath the jackets. Her nose emerged from a corner over by the rear passenger door.

"I thought so," Dad said. "All right, Merm, take her out back and let's get going."

"But Dad . . . ," I started in.

"But Dad . . . ," Michael followed close behind.

" 'But Dad' what?" Dad said.

"We wanted to take her to meet Mother," Michael revealed, blowing our cover.

"You wanted to take a goat to Mother's new house?" Dad said slowly, making sure.

"She adores goats," I insisted, thinking maybe we had a fighting chance.

"Absolutely not," Dad said. "Your mother would never speak to me again." But underneath his flat refusal, I must have sensed a little mischief; or maybe I spotted that playful glint in his eyes. Whatever, I thought if we worked on him for a while he'd give in, which is just what happened.

I'm surprised Dad didn't stay for the show. He dropped us off at Mother's, and I put a rope around Heidi's neck and led her to the back door. Michael went in first to show the goat to Mother's housekeeper, Carrie, but before he could get out a word of introduction, Heidi bolted across the kitchen floor and into the dining room.

What happened next was like something out of a Marx brothers' movie. Michael and I followed in hot pursuit, only to stop dead in our tracks at the sight of the poor goat standing in the middle of Mother's immaculate lanai. There was a look of sheer horror on Mother's face as we all stood, anchored to our spots, and watched Heidi slowly embarrass us on the brand-new white carpet.

We couldn't have written a better script — but wait, it gets even better!

Mother shrieked, and when she turned to us, she looked angrier than I'd ever seen her. In fact, her expression rivaled the look she flashed in *The Yearling* when her character, Ma Baxter, finds out that her son's pet deer has eaten most of the family's crops. Fearing a spanking — or worse! — Michael and I shooed Heidi outside, where the poor creature promptly fell into the swimming pool. Now, I don't know if you've ever seen a goat try to swim, and I'm sure you've never seen a goat try to swim in a Holmby Hills swimming pool, but dear Heidi made quite a spectacle of herself.

Michael dove in after her, and finally, after much tugging and pulling, we managed to heave her onto dry land. When we stepped out of the pool to dry ourselves off, we could hear Mother on the phone to Dad, screaming, "I don't care about how busy you are, Ronnie! I want that goat out of my house! Not tomorrow morning! Now!"

Things went from bad to worse. Dad couldn't make the drive back out until the next morning, and so Heidi wound up staying the night. During the course of the evening she somehow managed to escape from where we had tied her up, and then she set about her own interpretation of that scene from *The Yearling* and ate most of the roses in Mother's garden. (Mother improved on the scowl we thought she had perfected as Ma Baxter when she found out what had happened to her flowers!)

Heidi also bleated through the night under Mother's window, which didn't help matters much. Believe me, it was not a pretty scene by morning.

I've conveniently forgotten what punishments were meted out as a result of our caper, but whatever the bill, it was well worth paying. Of course, Mother was not at all amused, but Michael and I suppressed more laughter during that one escapade than we'd let loose with in the years since our parents were divorced. It was a great way for us to let off some steam, and I like to think that somewhere underneath it all — deep, deep down, perhaps, but somewhere — Mother must have gotten at least a small kick out of it. Or at least maybe she's looked back on the incident over the years and allowed herself the tiniest of smiles.

The next morning Michael and I were still biting our lips over the incident as we sat quietly on the curb, waiting for my father to take Heidi and us back to the ranch. When the familiar turquoise of his convertible swept into view, we got up slowly, expecting that he'd come to a full stop and help us into the car. But he merely slowed down as he reached the curb and flung the door open so the three of us could hop in, and I realize now he must have been afraid to get out of the car and leave himself open to the tongue-lashing that was no doubt waiting for him with Mother.

Knowing Dad, I'm sure the idea of a goat running amok in Mother's elegant Holmby Hills home appealed to his comic instincts. He has a great sense of humor, my father, and a terrifically playful sense of mischief, and he pulled a good one on his two children this time, believe me. I know Michael and I cooked up the whole scheme with Heidi on our own, but whenever I've flashed back on an image of that poor goat, doing her business on Mother's white carpet, I can't shake the thought that somehow, some way, Dad put us up to it.

4

Nancy

WHEN I WAS ABOUT TEN, Dad started dating a small, slender actress with dark hair and wide hazel eyes, named Nancy Davis. Now, as an adult, I realize he'd probably been dating off and on since the divorce, but Michael and I were never included in his other courtships the way we were with Nancy. As far as we all knew at the time, she was the first woman in his life since Mother.

The way they met was kind of interesting. When Nancy was introduced to my father, in 1951, she was filming a movie called *East Side, West Side* for MGM. To further set the scene for you, Dad was smack in the middle of his long tenure as president of the Screen Actors Guild. And as you already know, 1951 was the height of McCarthyism in this country, and of the so-called Red Scare, which would prove disastrous to the careers of many Hollywood professionals, including actors, directors, and screenwriters. Well, the name Nancy Davis had appeared on many of the lists of supposed Communist sympathizers published in some of the industry trade papers, and our particular Nancy Davis was understandably concerned about the effects of such damaging publicity on her budding career.

Mervyn LeRoy, the director of *East Side, West Side*, was an old friend of Dad's, and he set up a meeting for his young star. He told her that if there was anything to be done about her unusual and unfortunate predicament, then Ronald Reagan, as president of the Guild, would be just the man to discover what it was.

Before we get too far from the subject, let me just slip in a few words about Dad's career-long involvement with the Screen Actors Guild. From the earliest, Dad was very active in the union, first as a card-carrying member, then as a board member, and eventually as a five-term president. He always referred to his work on behalf of the union as his civic duty; you see, the Guild was designed to be a union in which those actors who had a lot to lose would always be willing to come and put it all on the line for the actors who couldn't speak so well for themselves, and Dad felt called upon to stick his neck out for his fellow actors. Think about it; in how many trade unions do you sit across the negotiating table from the person directly empowered to hire you for your next job? It's a unique situation, and Dad so appreciated the lobbying done on his behalf when he was just starting out in the business that he judged it only fair to return the favor for the next generation of struggling actors when he was in a position to do so.

His Guild presidency took up a lot of his time. Really, I think it took up far more time than he'd bargained for — when he was married to Mother, I know it took up far more time than *she'd* bargained for — but once he found himself in the middle of things, he simply couldn't leave office until he felt his job was done. In some of my earliest memories he is always racing off to some meeting or other or mitigating some crisis on the telephone until all hours of the night. There was always some piece of Guild business to attend to. At times it seemed the Guild was as much a part of his life as acting, he spent so much time at their offices and working on union business at home.

By the time he completed his fourth term, I guess he'd decided he'd more than returned the debt to the acting community, and he stepped aside to let someone else take over. But in 1959, with the threat of a strike hanging over the union, there was a considerable hue and cry among Guild members to return Dad to office; they were convinced that he was the man to handle the sure-to-be-sticky negotiations that lay ahead. In fact, after Dad was elected to his fifth term, I was sitting in Washington, D.C., and watching Bob Hope emcee the Academy Awards when the comedian quipped, "The only person working in Hollywood today is Ronald Reagan."

Indeed.

I felt a tremendous sense of pride in Dad on the night of those Academy Awards; I was sitting there by myself in Washington, virtually a continent away from the rest of my family, and it stirred something in me to know that my father's colleagues had come to rely on him to such a degree that Bob Hope could lampoon his extra efforts. What a special comfort to realize that other people — many other people — drew the same security and assurance from my father that I had for my entire life. I've felt that unique pride in him many times since, but that night was the first time.

Back to Dad and Nancy. LeRoy arranged for the two of them to meet for dinner one night at LaRue's restaurant, on the Sunset Strip. Over dinner Dad told Nancy that his office had discovered four different Nancy Davises, each of whom was registered with the Guild as an actress, and that the union would stand by her record in the event that a case of mistaken identity arose. That out of the way, the two of them went on to talk about "a thousand other things," as Nancy now recalls, and before too long they were as far away from union business as a Guild member and a Guild president could ever hope to be.

When they finished their dessert, the story goes, they found themselves enjoying each other's company so much that they did not want the evening to end. Dancing was out of the question because Dad was hobbling along with a cane as a result of a broken leg suffered in a months-ago slide into first base at a charity baseball game. (The leg was broken in so many places that he'd been in traction for two months following the accident.) So, given Dad's temporary handicap, they decided to go to Ciro's, a well-known Hollywood nightclub of the day, where they watched Sophie Tucker's opening-night performance. Nancy had never before seen Sophie Tucker, and she was so taken with her performance that the folks decided to stay for the second show.

From that night on they were inseparable.

You could tell the two of them were crazy about each other. They weren't lovey-dovey or anything like that, at least not in front of us kids, but they had a natural, easy way of being with each other that suggested they belonged together. They were a perfect fit. Sometimes it seemed like they'd known each other all their lives. Dad was so relaxed around Nancy — more relaxed than I'd ever seen him. Maybe my parents had known what they were doing when they admitted to themselves they'd be happier if they lived apart; with Nancy, Dad certainly appeared to be.

Almost immediately, Nancy became a fixture in the front seat on our famous car-ride sessions. Wherever we went, the drives were filled with laughter and singing and good times. To this day I can't get into a car without wanting to burst out into song, and I have Nancy to thank for that as much as Dad. Our repertoire expanded somewhat under Nancy's influence. At one point, spread out over three or four trips to the ranch and back, Dad taught us "La Marseillaise," the national anthem of France. Phonetically. I don't know why he taught it to us, but he surely did. When I finally learned to speak the language, it was amazing to me how different the words looked in French than in Dad's phonetic shorthand.

We also expanded our repertoire of armed-forces fight songs. For a while there I'm sure I was the only girl in the history of Chadwick who knew the Cavalry song, and I would trot it out at every chance:

> We'll hit the leather and ride, hit the leather and ride,
>   Hit the leather and ride all the way. . . .
> We'll leave the poor benighted infantry behind us,
>   They'll have to eat cavalry dust to find us. . . .

Nancy and I used to sing "I Hear Singing," from the musical *Call Me Madam*. That became our duet. We'd rehearse that thing to death, until Dad would have to lean against the horn to distract us and shout, "Enough, already!" (I think he just wanted us to pick a number he could join in on.) Michael, too, would groan when we announced that we had to try it one more time to get it right. Still, whenever I hear that song, I think of Nancy. As a matter of fact, we were at an "In Performance at the White House" not too long ago, and somebody did that song, and Nancy and I sought each other out across the room and flashed a singing-partners look that said, "Our song!"

Afterward Nancy came up to me and said, laughing, "Well, it would have been better if they'd asked us."

Michael was always kind of quiet in the backseat with me, but he would usually chime in before too long. I think he preferred the games we played to the songs we sang, and his enthusiasm level would always kick up a notch when we started in on Count the Ford Station Wagons or some such. That was more his speed.

Surprisingly — to me, anyway — I didn't feel the jealousy I'd expected to feel when I'd thought about Dad becoming involved with another woman. From the first moment it occurred to me that Dad would someday remarry, I spent a lot of time thinking about what his new wife, and his new life, would be like. Most of the scenarios I painted were like scenes out of Cinderella, but Dad and Nancy erased any anxieties I might have had early on. As I said, they both went to considerable lengths to make me and Michael feel included in their activities; Nancy would come up to Chadwick with Dad to visit, and she would join us on our visits out at the ranch. I especially liked Nancy because when the four of us were at the ranch, she would happily perform one of my most hated chores — whitewashing the thousands of feet of redwood fence that Dad was building.

Dad has always loved to build things, and for as long as I can remember he's been interested in how things work. He's a born tinkerer. Whenever we were out at the Malibu ranch, he'd spend hours in the hot sun building paddocks for the horses, a riding ring, or whatever, all with a manual posthole digger. As I mentioned earlier, he built all of the jumps in our jumping ring with his own two hands. Goodness, would he get absorbed in the sweat and effort of it all! For years he's devoted so much time and energy to getting things ready for his horses that I've often wondered when he finds the time to ride them.

Back then he always had a project going, and he took great pride in his do-it-yourself ability. (Of course, with Nancy, he now had a willing helper to go along with his two not-so-willing ones.) I remember that one day on our way out to the ranch, we stopped at a lumber yard and ordered some supplies to be delivered later that afternoon. Well, Dad came back to the car grinning one of the biggest grins I'd ever seen on his face, and he told us later it was because the lumber man's parting remark had been, "Tell Mr. Reagan I'll take care of that order for him." Dad was simply delighted that the man thought he worked for Mr. Reagan. It just made his day. Part of Dad's charm — and of his appeal as a politician, I think — has always been that he has never taken himself too seriously and can fit right in in almost any environment.

Nancy and I got along right away. We had a lot in common. Her mother, Edith Luckett, was also an actress; her parents were also divorced. And — the biggest coincidence of all! — we both loved Dad. Although she gave the impression of being strong-willed and determined — a first impression she leaves to this day, I should add — she seemed to me to be a warm, compassionate person, certainly sympathetic to the problems of a young girl dealing with the kinds of things I was having to deal with at the time. I know now how hard she must have been trying, judging from the stories I hear of my friends who are trying to forge new romantic relationships and still find room for children from previous marriages. It's tough; in fact, it's almost impossible. As it often plays out, it's one of the few lose-lose situations I can think of, and yet Nancy and I managed to pull it off. I'm sure I didn't make it as easy for her as I could have, and it wasn't always easy for me, but all things considered, we both did a pretty good job.

Nancy's "back-story" has always fascinated me. Her mother, Edith, or Deedee, as we all came to call her, had acted with many of the most famous performers of her day — George M. Cohan, Alla Nazimova, Walter Huston, Spencer Tracy. Shortly after Nancy's birth, Deedee was deserted by her young husband, Kenneth Robbins, a car salesman, and was forced to return to acting to earn a living. Her career kept her on the road a great deal, and while she was on tour, she sent two-year-old Nancy to live with an aunt and uncle in Bethesda, Maryland. Nancy missed her mother dearly and lived for the occasional visits they shared. When Nancy was six years old,

Deedee married a well-known Chicago neurosurgeon named Loyal Davis, who became so enamored of Nancy that he legally adopted her when she turned fourteen. Nancy has always told me that it was like the happy ending to a fairy tale when her mother met Loyal Davis and brought her out to Chicago. I'm a sucker for happy endings.

Dad and Nancy were laying the groundwork for some happy endings of their own as 1951 wore on. During their courtship we all had a front-row seat to another flowering romance. Dad's favorite riding horse at the time was a beautiful black thoroughbred mare named Tar Baby. Sorry, Nancy, but she was the real love of his life! What a stunning-looking animal — black as coal and with a shine to her coat like polished marble. She had appeared in many of Dad's movies, including *Stallion Road*, *The Last Outpost*, and *Cattle Queen of Montana*, before she was retired to his ranch. Also in Dad's stable at the time was a handsome white stallion named Gypsy Minstrel (Gypsy had no acting credits to speak of, I'm sad to say), and it was inevitable that we should all begin to speculate about what would happen if we bred a black mare to a white stallion.

There was only one way to find out.

The result was a gorgeous dapple filly who would later turn light gray and then white — Gypsy's color strain was dominant. But at the time of her birth, this tiny, brand-new foal was simply the most beautiful thing I'd ever seen, and I loved her with a passion.

One day when Michael and Dad and Nancy and I were all standing out in the paddock watching Tar Baby and her foal, we began to discuss a name.

"Why don't we call her Nancy D?" I suggested, paying both Nancy and the pretty little filly the highest compliment I could think of.

There was a long pause while everyone present gave this some consideration, and for an instant I was worried that maybe Nancy would be insulted by my gesture. Really, I was hoping she would realize the impulse was pure affection on my part.

"Yes," Dad finally said. "Nancy D would be a wonderful name."

And so it was.

Nancy D grew to become one of the most beautiful mares

ever to grace a stable, and she followed Tar Baby as Dad's personal riding horse. She stayed with him for the next sixteen years, until just after Dad was elected governor of California, when she finally went to her reward.

Dad and Nancy dated for nearly two years before they got married. Michael and I were off at Chadwick on the appointed day — March 4, 1952 — which was just as well because the folks wanted only the smallest of ceremonies. They were married at Bill and Ardis Holden's house, and Michael and I waited by the phone in the house next door to my dorm for formal notification that the knot had been tied. I think Michael and I both felt a little weird to be sitting in a strange house waiting for a phone call like that, but Dad felt strongly that we should be a part of things in at least this small way. They didn't have much to say to us when they finally called, just "OK, it's official" or something like that, but it was important to Dad, and I think to Nancy, that they make the call.

After a small reception the newlyweds went to Phoenix, Arizona, where Nancy's parents had relocated after Loyal's retirement as chief of surgery at Passavant Northwestern Memorial Hospital.

I was happy for Dad, I truly was. I liked Nancy. And it didn't even occur to me that my life would change in any way now that Dad had remarried. I suppose I might have felt differently if I had been living with him, or if things had been more like they are in divorced families today, where the kids have a room set up in each parent's house. It wasn't like that then. We didn't divide our time between Mother and Dad that way. Mother had custody, and that was that. And besides, I was off at school more often than not. So things didn't figure to be all that different with Dad now that he was married again, except in the obvious ways: now he'd have a house we could go to instead of a bachelor apartment, and we wouldn't have to go out to restaurants all the time.

Mother, too, decided to get in on all the romance, which made 1952 a pretty momentous (and unsettling) year. She moved pretty quickly, becoming involved with a man named Fred Karger, a well-known musical arranger and bandleader. We never became as close to Fred as we'd become to Nancy; we never had the chance. I'll never forget the way Mother had me and Michael brought home from Chadwick on Halloween weekend to meet Fred and his daughter, Terry, who was about six months younger than I was. The deal was, we kids were supposed to go out trick-or-treating together, and when we got back Mother and Fred were waiting for us in the den, and we walked in and they sat us all down and told us of their plans to be married.

Boom! Instant extended family! Just add water and stir.

I can't tell you how odd it was to meet someone one minute and then to find out he was marrying your mother the next. (Actually we'd met him ever so briefly a few weeks before, but this was the first opportunity we'd had to say more than two words to the man.) With Nancy we had at least had some time to get used to her — two whole years! — before we had to also get used to the idea of her as Dad's wife. And Terry! To meet a kid within six months of your own age and before the night is over to find out she's going to become your sister! Talk about your unsettling pieces of news.

Anyway, Mother and Fred didn't waste any time. They eloped the next day. Terry stayed on at the Holmby Hills house with us while they were away. When they got back, Mother's housekeeper, Carrie, gave us these bags of rice she had prepared and positioned us along this circular staircase we had at the entryway to the house, and when the happy couple came in, we all threw the rice on them and screamed some appropriate salutation. I'm not sure, but I think I might have pelted Fred with clumps of rice a bit harder than tradition called for.

Later that afternoon Michael and I were ushered into the car, and Mother's secretary drove us back to school. At Chadwick we got out of the car, and when it pulled away Michael and I just stood there looking at each other, wondering if what had just happened had really just happened. It all seemed too much of a blur to register.

And let's not forget Patti. Patricia Ann Reagan was born to Dad and Nancy that fall, by Cesarean section. It was, I'm told, a difficult birth. I was away at school, too, when I received that piece of news.

So Dad was starting out all over again with a new family, and Mother was starting out all over again with a new family, and either one of those changes, alone, would have seemed emotionally complicated to an eleven-year-old girl. But I didn't even have time to adjust to one overwhelming change before another one was upon me. I was happy for my parents, sure, but I also felt utterly displaced by the whole business. I mean, where did I fit into all this? What about Michael? Would Dad love Patti more than he loved me? Would Mother care for Terry the same way she cared for me?

There were times during that fall of 1952 when it seemed to me that my life was getting away from me, that what was happening to my family was happening apart from me, separate, and that I was being pushed and pulled in so many different directions, all of them leading me away from home. I think this was where my being at Chadwick came in very handy. It was my anchor during this time of upheaval. Remember, I had already decided that I was on my own. I'd written everybody else off at seven, when it seemed to me everybody else had written *me* off. Now, at eleven, it just became a question of being able to compartmentalize the different turns my life had taken, to keep everything in its place. To tell you the truth, it all sounds so much more complicated when you look at it from the outside than it appeared to me at the time, from the inside. Once I was able to deal with my parents' getting divorced, I was able to separate Mother and Dad in my head; at that point whatever happened in Mother's sphere and whatever happened in Dad's sphere was easy to compartmentalize. I could try to deal with each development separately, and any one development didn't necessarily have anything to do with any other.

Besides, I was delighted to have a baby sister. I really was. I thought it was the most wonderful, neatest thing in the world. Of course, to me Patti seemed more like a pet, or a toy, than a tiny person, since I wasn't living with Dad at the time and was only around for the occasional visit, but still, I would flash her picture to my Chadwick friends at the slightest suggestion.

The only time I ever really felt competitive toward Patti was when I was about fourteen years old. I was visiting Dad and Nancy in their first house in Pacific Palisades. Patti must have been about three. I remember she came running over to Dad and plopped down in his lap, and he threw her up into the air and caught her, and when she was on her way down, he said, "Hey, Shorty, how are you?" Well, I died a thousand deaths, because of course that was the name he used to call me. I was stung by the way she seemed to have stepped into the place in Dad's life that had once belonged to me. I was Dad's Shorty. I was the one who plopped down in his lap and got thrown up into the air.

In my brain I knew Dad wasn't doing anything on purpose, and had I been living there I probably would have been delighted that the name had been passed on to a new generation. But that wasn't the case, and the incident simply added to my feelings of isolation. I felt like I didn't belong there. Did I say anything? No. I thought I could handle it, and besides, what could I say that wouldn't have sounded petty and jealous?

Years later, when I was living on my own in Washington and Michael had moved back in with Dad and Nancy at their second Pacific Palisades home, I came to California for a short visit. I think it was 1960, and Patti was about seven or eight. When Michael moved in, the folks had just gotten around to explaining to Patti that he was her brother, which pleased her quite a bit, so Patti came up to me at one point during my visit and said, "Did you know that Michael is my brother?"

And I said, "Yes, of course I know that. And do you know what that makes you and me?"

"No," Patti said, "what?"

"That makes you and me sisters."

Patti burst into tears — actually it was more like an eruption — and she ran from the room crying, "No, it doesn't! No, it doesn't!"

I felt deflated.

Dad was quite embarrassed when he explained to me later that afternoon, "Well, we just haven't gotten that far yet." And there was a reason they hadn't gotten that far yet: I wasn't there. They hadn't had to go that far. They'd just gotten to Michael, and only after it was decided he would move in with them. It seems Patti was introduced to us siblings (or half-siblings, if you want to get technical) on a need-to-know basis, and until that time there had been no need for her to know any such thing about me.

How could this little girl figure out where I fit into her scheme of things if I was hardly around to make my presence felt? I may have carried her picture around at school, but she didn't know that. After all, she had only seen me two or three times in the previous two years. But still, as I listened to Dad's explanation, while I understood it on one level, I started to feel out of place all over again.

I had another one of my life-changing epiphanies in 1952. In the middle of all the adjustments and new relationships, I stumbled upon something that was to bring great stability to my new life, and new meaning — something I would find absorbing and endlessly challenging in the years ahead. In the summer of 1952 Mother and Michael and I were visiting Leah Ray and Sonny Werblin at their beautiful home on the New Jersey shore. Sonny Werblin, you'll recall, later became famous as the owner of the New York Jets football team, but at the time he was a senior executive of the Music Corporation of America, or MCA.

I can't recall the circumstances that brought us to the Werblins' beach house that summer, but I'm glad things fell into place the way they did. First of all, their house was like something out of a storybook: wide verandas, a swing, acres of green lawn, and fireflies in the early evening. And kids! There were tons of kids my own age living nearby, and almost all of them went away to boarding school during the academic year. What an unexpected treat! At home my California neighbors seemed to think I was some kind of odd duck for being sent away to school, but here, in this environment, a prep-school upbringing was a fact of life.

At last I was on some common ground with kids my own age. And the fact that that common ground just happened to turn up in a lovely waterfront community helped to make that summer all the more special.

But the beach and my new prep-school friends took a backseat to the two truly blessed events of that summer: the Republican and Democratic national conventions. For two weeks I sat mesmerized in front of the television set in Uncle Sonny's study, as for the first time in broadcasting history the conventions were given live, gavel-to-gavel coverage. I was swept away by it all. Never before had I felt like such a part of history. These people on the screen were choosing someone who was going to be the next President of the United States! And I was soaking up every delicious hour of it.

I still have a vivid memory of an anonymous delegate who got up in the middle of all the hoopla and started talking about how he had been a soldier in World War II and what Dwight Eisenhower meant to him. I'll never forget how moved I was by his remarks, and it was precisely that kind of stirring human drama that kept me glued to the set. I was completely enthralled by every little development coming from Uncle Sonny's television set. I wanted desperately to be a part of it all.

The adults all thought I'd lost my mind, Mother in particular.

"Why don't you go outside?" she'd say. "It's such a gorgeous day."

"Not now, Mother," I'd say. "I'm busy."

"Seems to me you can watch television any old time," she'd reason.

Right, but it wasn't any old time that an eleven-year-old kid with only a passing knowledge of the way our government worked had a chance to immerse herself in the inner workings of presidential politics. I watched those conventions as if they were some kind of lifeline to another world, to another way of being, to the person I might become. I was even afraid to go to the bathroom or to go into the kitchen for something to eat. I was so afraid I might miss something or lose the connection I had just established.

I was hooked! (I guess that's why they call us political junkies!)

Watching, I decided that being a delegate to a national convention was an achievable goal in life, particularly when I found out that convention delegates held down other jobs for a living. That's great, I remember thinking; I can be an actress and a delegate at the same time.

After taking in both party lines, I decided I liked the Republicans better. They seemed better organized, for one thing, which proves you can fool anybody, right? But, seriously, they also seemed to talk about the ideas and values I'd picked up throughout my growing up, around the dinner table or out at the ranch with Dad. They talked about things we still talk about as Republicans: about how individuals should have more rights than the government, about how people should keep what they earn, about America's responsibility in the world and how there are other countries that depend on us. I kept hearing about our position as the leader of the "free world," which in 1952 was still a relatively new term.

The Democrats, in contrast, were all over the place with their ideas. They were extremely disorganized (and they still are today). They talked about how Americans needed to look inside themselves, which was a very isolationist view. There was no sense of community in their proceedings or in any of their speeches. They attacked problems with big-picture, bureaucratic solutions, while the Republican approach seemed always to rely on a grassroots involvement at the hands-on level.

And so everything I was seeing and hearing from the Republicans matched what I heard at home, which was why I was so shocked to learn in 1960 that my father was a registered Democrat. I couldn't believe it, and we'll talk more about it later in the book when it comes up chronologically, but let me just say here that the Democratic platforms of 1932 and 1936, when Dad was first becoming politically aware, were not dissimilar to the Republican platforms of the 1950s and 1960s. Read them over if you ever have the chance. The party that my father joined in the 1930s sought less taxation and a paring-down of government to the community level; the party that he remained a member of had moved considerably away from that in the intervening years.

When the conventions ended, I tried to convince everyone I knew — other kids, mostly, of nonvoting age — that Eisenhower was their man. I got myself an "I Like Ike" button, which I wore until we won the election.

By the fall of 1953, with my "campaigning" on behalf of the Eisenhower/Nixon ticket long done, very little had changed in my life. I was looking forward to returning to Chadwick for another year. Dad and Nancy, whom I had begun to call "the folks," had moved into the house in Pacific Palisades; Patti was growing up so quickly it was hard for me to recognize her from one visit to the next (and consequently, hard for *her* to recognize *me*).

But the status quo was upset when Mother announced that Michael and I would be leaving Chadwick to move home with her and Fred and Terry. We were all going to be "one big happy family," as she put it, and there was very little Michael or I (or Dad, even) could say to talk her out of it. I would be attending Emerson Junior High School, a local public school where I didn't know anybody! Here I had worked hard to build a nice place for myself at Chadwick, with nice friends, and — oops! — there was that rug being tugged out from under me again. I felt like I was losing my balance, a little like Alice going down the rabbit hole.

Believe it or not, our "one big happy family" lasted just about a year. Mother and Fred would soon divorce, only to remarry many years later; Terry disappeared from our lives. Emerson Junior High was similarly short-lived for me. By the following fall we were primed for the next enormous and sudden change in our lives. When I returned from my summer vacation in 1954, Mother announced that she, Michael, and I would be converting to Catholicism. Well, Mother had always been a spiritual person, but this took us all completely by surprise. Whether this was her way of dealing with her split with Fred, or whether something else was going on, I'll never know, but it all seemed pretty extreme to me. Catholicism! And as if that weren't enough, she told me I would be attending Immaculate Heart High School in Hollywood that fall. That's just what I needed, a convent! But by then I had begun to realize that it was a waste of time and emotional energy to argue with Mother over something like this. Try as he might, even Dad couldn't talk her out of it. She would get something in her head, and the only way to get it out of there was if something else came along to take its place.

I didn't like Immaculate Heart at all. Most of the students there had been together in one of the several Catholic grammar schools that fed into the high-school system in Los Angeles. Only two or three of my classmates lived on the west side of town, where I lived. It seemed like I spent my whole life on the city buses. It took two transfers and well over an hour to get from home to school. The bus stop at Wilshire Boulevard was about a mile from our house, which made for a nice evening stroll in the winter months.

At the end of my freshman year there — my first year — I began to hear talk at home about my transferring to another Catholic high school. The name Marymount kept coming up. Nobody ever talked to me about anything, but I started to hope what I was hearing would come to pass. Marymount had much nicer uniforms than Immaculate Heart, and the school was near UCLA, which was actually bicycling distance from our house. Good thinking, Mother, I thought, now we're getting it together.

As it turned out, I did transfer to Marymount before the next school year, but the Marymount my mother had in mind was in Tarrytown, New York. More than three thousand miles away from everybody! To say that I had mixed feelings about her decision would have been one of the all-time understatements. It was bad enough to feel I didn't fit in at home, in Dad's life or in Mother's, and now I was being sent off to a place where I might not even fit in with the kids my own age. I wasn't exactly looking forward to it. I'd spent enough time summering in New Jersey and on Cape Cod to know that a lot of kids from the East didn't take California, or Californians, all that seriously. In fact, I'd been asked more than once if California had yet become a state, so I wasn't exactly looking forward to forming new friendships with such a perceived strike against me.

Besides, being so far away from home was a good deal different from being away at Chadwick; there I had been only an hour's drive, or an affordable phone call, from home, but Marymount was a country and a telegram removed from what was left of my family. Chadwick promised weekends at home; Marymount promised weekends alone. I was more than a little apprehensive about the distinction.

To help me "fit in" at Marymount, and to help ease my apprehension, Mother and I went out on a full-fledged shopping spree, during which she bought me an entirely new wardrobe, including a navy-blue suit, a breton hat, high heels, and several pairs of white gloves. I looked like a few pages out of *Vogue* when she got through with me.

But despite my new clothes, I did not fit in at Marymount. Not at all. And as I had feared, I felt more and more removed from my family. Everything seemed like a conspiracy to make me an outsider; any friends I made at school would be three thousand miles away from where I lived during the summer and other school vacations. The friends I still had in California had gone on to new circles of friends in my absence. My two "families" did their best to make me feel at home, but I felt socially disconnected. On top of all this, Michael and I hardly saw each other anymore, and when we did, the differences in our ages combined with the distance in every other aspect of our lives to make communication almost impossible.

I spent so much time alone during my early high-school years that I began to wonder if I would ever fit in anywhere. I began to overeat, which I suppose a psychologist would say was to compensate for my loneliness. But at a boarding school, particularly a place like Marymount, there isn't much to do except study and eat. The food, as it is in most institutional kitchens, was starchy and heavy, and by the time I returned home that first Christmas I had put on thirty-five pounds. The deep California tan I had cultivated all my life and taken to school with me had long since faded to East Coast boarding-school pale. I hated the way I looked and felt.

Back home, thankfully, my family went easy on me about the extra weight. Dad slipped in a few quips about my "boarding-school spread," but he was encouraged to see me start reverting to my former self by the time I headed East for the second semester.

My interest in national politics continued unabated. In 1956 I was devastated to learn that Marymount's annual four-day retreat would begin on election night. I had been looking forward to this night for the previous four years, and now I faced the possibility of missing out on the returns just so I could purify my soul, or whatever the purpose of those Marymount "retreats" was.

So there I was in my room on Tuesday night, lying in bed and trying to contemplate whatever it was I was supposed to contemplate, dying for some news of the election. What kind of place, I wondered, allows something like a presidential election to pass by unnoticed? I waited until I was sure the polls had closed and everyone in the dorm was asleep, and then I snuck a small radio under the covers with me and turned the volume down as low as I could manage. The reception was lousy, and the one station I could get clearly had chosen to wait until later in the evening to announce the first returns. They advised listeners to stay tuned, and I did my level best to follow their advice.

I must have fallen asleep, because the next thing I knew a nun was walking into the darkened room for morning wake-up (yes, they wake you up early in Catholic school!). She flashed me a stern, disapproving look and confiscated the radio. And I still hadn't heard any returns!

About a half hour later, as we stood in line for chapel, one of the sisters admonished us to keep to the rules of the retreat. (I think her words were meant for me and my radio, but we all had to listen to them.) And then, just when I thought I'd never learn who our next President would be, she asked us all to pray for President Eisenhower, who had just been elected to a second term.

From the look on some of the faces around me, it appeared that many of my classmates hadn't even realized that Eisenhower was up for reelection or that the previous day had carried such presidential importance out there in the rest of the world. Can you imagine?

Well, retreat or no retreat, I let out a shrill war-whoop of victory and turned every head in the place.

Gosh, they must have thought I was a strange bird! But I told myself I didn't care. Buoyed by Eisenhower's victory, I made a retreat of my very own and a promise to myself that by the time the next presidential election rolled around, I would be as far away from this place as possible.

5

Graduation

DESPITE MY UNEVENTFUL DEBUT at Warner Brothers at the age of six, and despite living so far away from home for so much of my growing up, I spent my childhood living and breathing show business.

I guess it was in my blood.

You would think that since I'd logged all that time on the Warner Brothers lot, on the sets of dozens of movies, and in the constant presence of so many wonderful stars, the big screen might have been brought down to size for me. But that wasn't the case at all. Movies were the most magical escape I could think of, and Hollywood was the most magical place I'd ever been (I hadn't yet been to Washington), and throughout my teenage years I would hope against hope that I could someday earn my living there.

The front-row seat I'd acquired through Mother and Dad only made me cherish movies all the more. I spent my entire allowance in movie theaters; I'd sit through the same movie six or seven times, memorizing the dialogue. When I went to a picture, I would identify completely with the leading lady. I would will myself into her role; I would become her character. When I read a book, I would imagine the dialogue as it would sound in a play or film, or I would act out the various parts.

I had a good ear for music and a good singing voice, and I knew the lyrics to hundreds of songs.

Even as a teenager, I took my lofty ambitions pretty seriously.

No one in my family encouraged me to become an actress or entertainer. They knew how tough it was, how long and hard I'd have to struggle to make a success of it. "This business has been very good to me," my father told me one night, "so I wouldn't tell anybody not to pursue it. But you have to remember, Mermie, there's a good chance there'll be more bad times than good times."

He may have meant something else, but I decided to take that as encouragement.

From my earliest years at Chadwick, I strutted my stuff on school stages whenever I had the chance. Plays, recitals, revues — whatever I could get my lungs on. I loved to sing best of all. During my time at Marymount I performed in several plays and operettas. The most memorable was my first lead, as Ralph Rakestraw in Gilbert and Sullivan's *H.M.S. Pinafore*. Being tall in an all-girls' school (I was five foot eight by the time I was fourteen!) inevitably guaranteed my playing male roles, which would have been fine were it not for the chronic attacks of stage fright that did me in on more than one occasion. Ralph Rakestraw was a simple, low-born sailor in love with Josephine, the captain's daughter. In a scene with Josephine in the second act, my nerves (and my voice) snapped, and with a shrill cackle I cried out my love's name: "Josephine!" I must have sounded like a cat in a blender, because the audience howled with laughter.

I wanted to fall through the floor.

You see, in those days I was a nervous wreck every time I stepped on stage. As much as I loved to perform, I was still petrified by it. On opening night I was such a sweaty mess that the white gloves I wore as part of my sailor's costume were wringing wet. (Poor Josephine, I thought, when we had to hold hands.)

What made my performance as Ralph Rakestraw most memorable, though, was that my family was in the audience on both nights, a rare and special treat when your stage is so far away from home. They hadn't seen me perform since grade school, and I was terribly anxious for a professional opinion on my progress. Dad and Nancy were in New York for "General Electric Theater" and made the trip up to Tarrytown for the Friday show, and Mother was in town to be a guest on "The Perry Como Show" and came up the following night.

Dad's one comment backstage following that night's show — after he expressed some genuine fatherly enthusiasm — was "Try not to overact," which seems to me now a kind of contradiction in terms when you're referring to Gilbert and Sullivan. I don't think my father would have gone very far as an acting coach, because "Don't overact" has always been his standard piece of acting advice. From that time on, whenever I asked for an opinion on how to approach a part I was preparing for or how to read a line, he'd offer up the same pearls of wisdom; he always looked so natural up there on screen, but I suppose he wasn't much into "method" acting.

None of my family had ever been to Marymount before, and I was proud for the chance to show them off and to show my school off to them. Dad and Nancy had never been to a convent before, and a lot of the students and other visiting parents were doing everything short of gawking at them. Well, on second thought, you'd better strike that: there *was* some out-and-out gawking going on. Before and after the performance the nuns were considerate enough to set aside one of the parlors off the main hall so we could have some privacy, but the other parents kept pushing open the door just so they could sneak a peek at a couple of movie stars. "Whoops," they'd say, barging in on our family moments, "I didn't know this room was being used. But as long as I'm here. . . ."

Keep in mind, over the years at Marymount I kept picking up these little mumbled comments and hushed asides about actors and their ilk; visiting parents would explain me and my sometimes loud behavior to their children with "You have to understand how she was raised" or "Well, that's typical" (whatever that meant). And now these same people who had made it very clear that they didn't think very highly of actors were interrupting our visit because they wanted an autograph or a picture.

Go figure, right?

Anyway, the picture Dad and Nancy got of Marymount was

not of the serene, cerebral convent that they'd been led to expect and that I'd described in my letters. Thanks to their visit — and, to a lesser extent, to Mother's the following day — the place was more like a zoo. For a while there I thought they should have put a sign out by the parlor door saying, *"Please Don't Feed the Reagans."*

Interestingly, as I was taking these first tentative steps toward my own acting career, Dad was moving slowly away from his. He didn't know it at the time, and neither did anyone else, but his years-long association with General Electric — as the narrator and occasional star of television's "General Electric Theater" and as a traveling spokesman for the company — would soon pull him completely away from the big screen and toward the small, and eventually out of the world of entertainment entirely.

Here's the story: Dad began his association with GE in 1954, when "General Electric Theater" became one of the first television programs to be so closely identified with one sponsor. Maybe you remember the show. My father would introduce the weekly dramas and plug the company's futuristic products; he'd also star in several episodes each year. At the end of each show Dad would say, "At General Electric, progress is our most important product." I heard that tag line everywhere I went; the kids in school would come up and say it to me all the time.

Part of Dad's deal with GE called for him to make occasional trips around the country to various company plants, basically to boost employee morale and provide the workers with a much-needed break from their assembly-line routines. He was a kind of roving ambassador for the company. He would make several trips a year, usually just for a week or two at a time, or less, stopping here and there to shake hands and pose for pictures and give informal talks, letting the workers know, in groups of a half dozen or so, how much people liked their products and appreciated their efforts. He'd talk about some inside Hollywood stuff as well. They worked him pretty hard on the road. In one day, he used to boast, he once made fourteen speeches.

Before long Dad's appearances grew to where he'd be addressing twenty or thirty workers at a time, and as his audiences grew larger he began more and more to turn the tables on his audiences to try and get a sense of what was on their minds. Increasingly Hollywood would disappear from the talks, and the conversation would turn to the impositions placed on the workers by the taxation demands of the federal government and to how the workers were seeking ways to reclaim greater control of their own lives and their own paychecks. Dad would listen and follow their lead, and as time wore on his talks became more political, as some of his own ideas about the role of government began to crystallize. He began to use the term "encroaching government" to describe the big bureaucracy that he and most of the GE workers found objectionable. He also began to plan out short speeches before his visits, to help him to organize his thoughts and get his message across.

"These people are coming to hear what I have to say," he'd explain to me whenever I asked him why he was working so hard on his speeches, "and I just want to be sure I say something that's worth listening to."

Eventually he'd turn up at a GE plant and find about two hundred people waiting to hear him, and they would gather round and he'd pull up a soapbox and start in on his speech. Workers would bring their friends and their families. These sessions really became like old-style political rallies, with Dad's head poking its way up above the crowd. And then he'd work his special magic on the room, the way he would do so forcefully for the next thirty or so years. I still run into people all around the country who fondly remember Dad's visits and can recognize the ideas expressed in those speeches in the way he built his administration as President.

"As the years went on, my speeches underwent a kind of evolution," he once wrote, "reflecting not only my changing philosophy, but also the swiftly rising tide of collectivism that threatens to inundate what remains of our free economy. . . . The last decade has seen a quickening of tempo in our government's race toward the controlled society."

So what started out as a simple commercial endorsement, with a commitment to a certain number of public appearances, mushroomed into a platform for Dad to deliver full-scale political speeches. Talk about a change of plans! His speeches were for the most part bipartisan, and he stressed that the problems of "encroaching government" crossed party lines. Dad had always been a powerful speaker, and as president of the Screen Actors Guild he'd learned how to speak his mind; now he was blending those skills to become one of the most popular speakers on the circuit. By the end of the 1950s Ronald Reagan was the second most sought-after public speaker in the country, after President Eisenhower.

General Electric, I'm told, was thrilled with all the attention and with the good feeling Dad would leave behind with the workers after one of his visits. (We used to joke that he generated as much electricity as GE.) But in 1961, after Dad had spent nearly seven years on the road for the company and just after John F. Kennedy took office, GE began receiving complaints from certain offices of the federal government, informing them that the message of the GE spokesperson was not entirely appreciated. I've always admired the fact that despite the complaints, GE didn't see fit to ask Dad to change his tune, and Dad continued on his schedule of speeches uninterrupted.

And then one day in 1962 Dad got a call from a friend informing him of a rumor that some agencies of the federal government had threatened to cancel millions of dollars' worth of GE contracts unless the company fired Ronald Reagan as its spokesperson.

Well, Dad checked out the story with his boss at GE, who admitted that the rumor was true. "But don't worry," he told Dad, "we won't be blackmailed."

"Wait a minute," Dad said back, without stopping to think about it. "There are an awful lot of people whose paychecks depend on those contracts. I appreciate your standing up for me, I really do, but I can't abide that."

Dad offered to quit, to spare GE the embarrassment of having to fire him and to save the thousands of jobs that would be lost with the loss of those contracts. I've always suspected, and I'm sure Dad agrees with me on this one, that Robert Kennedy had a hand in all this. I think the Kennedy administration saw in Dad's remarks a backhanded slur against their way of doing things, and their way of doing things wouldn't sit still for something like that.

But once again I'm getting ahead of myself. In 1958 Dad was working for GE, still a few years away from his full-fledged soapbox days, as I finished out my high-school years. I went on from *Pinafore* to star in a number of other Marymount productions, including *Pirates of Penzance, Patience, A Comedy of Errors,* and a variety of religious epics.

For graduation I competed for the school's coveted gold medal in the music category, in a joint recital with my friend Roseanne Walsh. We worked on our program for a full two years, leading up to one Friday night in the spring of 1958. That night I sang songs in six languages, including the "Habanera" from *Carmen* in French, and "Musetta's Waltz" from *La Bohème* in Italian. For our finale we performed Bizet's "Agnus Dei."

I was so nervous! I didn't get along too well with foreign languages in those days, and so Dad's phonetic training with "La Marseillaise" came in handy. Rosie's parents came up from Long Island to cheer us on, and they had to pull double duty because my family couldn't make it. (If I'm remembering correctly, *H.M.S. Pinafore* was the only Marymount performance of mine they ever saw.)

I learned a little bit about show business that night, despite my anxiety. My singing teacher, Madame Theresa, had put two pitchers of water and some lemon slices backstage. I'd never sung such a lengthy solo recital before, so I didn't quite know what to make of these props. I never do things in moderation, so I drained both pitchers and sucked on all the lemons, thinking this would help my performance. Well, by the time I stepped on stage I had no enamel left on my teeth and a tremendous need to visit the ladies' room. Boy, was I glad when that recital was over! (The show must go on, right?) Years later I stood backstage with the talented Carol Burnett at an arthritis telethon in Los Angeles and watched as she gulped cup after cup of water before going on stage. I approached her to caution that the "facility" was a long walk away and that she might want to go easy on the fluids. She looked at the cup, then at me, and then she drank the water and said, "It gives my act a certain amount of urgency!"

Believe me, I knew what she meant.

My bladder problems notwithstanding, Rosie and I just killed 'em. We were terrific, and when we were through I thought we had a good shot at the school's gold medal, a high honor indeed. On graduation day our assistant class mistress, Mother Immaculée, pulled me aside from the procession with a serious look on her face. Mother Immaculée was a very small woman who came up to about my elbows, and she reached up and grabbed me by the shoulder and pulled me down so she could whisper, "You're getting the medal, but don't you dare scream!"

I guess the nuns had had enough of my boisterous enthusiasm by then.

Sure enough, we were awarded the gold medal, and sure enough, I screamed. I bounded up on stage, forgetting my instructions to "glide" like a lady. I was so happy I didn't care. Mother was there, and she gasped and applauded as loudly as I did, even if she did have a few words to say afterward about my not-so-ladylike gait.

Dad and Nancy, though, couldn't make it to my graduation; they had some pressing business back home to attend to, namely the appearance of Ronald Prescott Reagan. Because of Nancy's previous difficulty in delivering Patti, this Cesarean was scheduled in advance, so I was not surprised that they were not at the graduation. Disappointed, maybe, but not surprised.

With the addition of Ron to my extended (and far-flung) family, I didn't know what to feel. With Patti I had felt some sisterly impulses, which were quashed over the years by the distance between us. With Ron I felt elated for Dad and Nancy, but for myself I didn't feel much of anything. I didn't see that he had all that much to do with me. (Sorry, Ron, this is just a seventeen-year-old kid talking.) You have to remember, when Ron was born, I had friends — kids my own age, or close to it — who were having children of their own, so Ron's appearance served as a very telling reminder that I was straddling the frightening fence that separates childhood from adulthood.

For a graduation present my parents offered me the choice of a new car or a trip to Europe, which presented me with a wonderful dilemma. I opted for the trip, which, thanks to a travel-agent friend of Nancy's, turned out to be a glorious chaperoned tour of nine different countries. But the trip wasn't long enough, or glorious enough, because when I got back I realized that Mother had made arrangements for me to attend college in another convent-type situation.

Marymount College (What is this, a franchise? I remember thinking) in Arlington, Virginia, beckoned as my home for the next four years. (In fact, the Marymounts are all connected; the Tarrytown school is the original, and it is known as the Mother House.)

Now, this didn't sit all that well with me. All my life I had been geared in my mind toward graduating from high school. I had never even thought about college. I wanted to go to drama school in New York — I had one all picked out — but in those days you had to be eighteen years old to make a decision like that. That was a much bigger deal then than it is today, and with a January birthday, I was a half year younger chronologically than I was academically, if you follow my math. That was one of my great frustrations, and so I had to rely once again on Mother's decision. She was dead set against my going to college in California; who knows, maybe she didn't want me so close to home after she'd gotten used to having the entire country as a buffer. And she didn't want me at a more typical, liberal arts–type college or a big university. Drama school, she said, was out of the question.

And so she selected Marymount.

Her thinking, I'm sure, was that I would be simply marking time at Marymount, and that once I turned eighteen we'd discuss some other options; until that time she felt most comfortable with my being in a convent environment. Dad kept trying to impress on her the fact that I was old enough to be a freshman in college, and therefore I should be old enough to select my own college, but he didn't get very far.

Marymount was still in a 1950s mode when I got there, which I guess makes sense because it was still 1958. What I mean is that for an all-girls school, it was not progressive at all in the way it treated women. The curriculum was set up so you could study a liberal-arts program or take a typing program. That was their idea of a business education — training you to be a secretary! So I was really not thrilled with the school, since there was no challenge. Not only was I missing out on the chance to prepare for a career as a performer, at Marymount I felt like the college wasn't preparing me for anything. It seemed like such a waste of time.

Within a few months I'd had enough, and at Christmas vacation that first year I dropped the bombshell on my parents that I was leaving school after my eighteenth birthday.

Dad was not pleased. He was the first person in his family to ever graduate from college, and as I said earlier, he looks back on his days at Eureka as among the happiest of his life. He even sold his nay-saying older brother, Neill, on the benefits of a college education and helped to put him through school after he'd graduated. But disappointed as he was, my father was not about to put his foot down with me. He's always felt that his children were equipped to make their own decisions; he would give us advice, and input, and support, but he's not the type to try to stand in our way if he knew we had thought things through for ourselves.

"If that's what you really want to do, Mermie," he said, "then I'll support you with your mother."

Believe me, I needed all the support I could get with Mother. I think I would have had an easier time if I'd announced that I was pregnant. I told her about my decision, and I got calls from three different priests in a matter of hours, each of them singing the praises of a Catholic education. She really brought out the heavy artillery in an attempt to turn me around. When I got back to school after the Christmas break, she even had the nuns start working me over. Mother was convinced I was throwing my life away, and she was pulling out all the stops to see that I didn't.

But there was nothing she could have said or done to make me change my mind. I left Marymount in April 1959 and crossed the Potomac to our nation's capital. Although I still adored politics and found myself looking for work in Washington, D.C., it didn't occur to me to seek a job in government; somehow politics and government seemed to me to be two different things, which meant I was either wise beyond my years or naive as all get-out. Anyway, I took a job as a typist for a small private company (see? my Marymount education did come in handy!), pulling in a whopping $97.87 per payday, every two weeks. The only thing you can do on that kind of money is just barely survive, and so that's what I did.

I didn't get any money or any other kind of support from home, though Dad did offer up this piece of advice: "If someone is paying you to do a job," he said, "then you ought to do the very best that you can do. They're paying you money because they have great faith in you." Sound counsel, I suppose, but the money they chose to pay me didn't suggest they had all that much faith in me — a smart move on their part because I'm sure I was one of the worst secretaries in the history of Washington.

In my free time I still pursued my dream of being a performer. In school there had always been plenty of opportunity for me to get out on stage, but out here in the real world the opportunities were few. There's an old show-business line that goes, "If you open the refrigerator, I'll do twenty minutes," which certainly applied to me at this time. Any light would have done. I sang with a small band on the outskirts of Washington whenever we could get a booking. I traveled up to New York City to attend an occasional acting seminar. I worked with various community theater groups. There wasn't ever a time when I wasn't doing something to bring me closer to my goal; it's just that things weren't quite moving along as smoothly, or as quickly, as I'd envisioned.

I even entered the 1959 Miss Washington competition — a preliminary round for the Miss America Pageant — simply for the chance it offered to appear on stage before an audience. I wasn't crazy about the bathing-suit competition, either from a moral or a personal standpoint (remember, I had just come off a diet of Marymount's institutional food), but I paraded my body around along with everyone else. In those days there weren't many opportunities for young women to get a break in show business or capture the kind of scholarship money available in a pageant like this, and so a lot of girls put up with the demeaning routine. For me it was worth it for the chance it offered to belt out a song in the talent competition. I'm almost ashamed to admit it, but I had a blast during the pageant, I really did. Many of us girls became fast friends; it was like an intense minisorority. I don't know how I would have felt if I had won — I was eliminated in the semifinals — and had had to do it all over again for Bert Parks and his gang, but at the time it was a great way to keep my feet wet until something else came along.

By 1960 I found myself working at the office of two management consultants, still as a secretary. My bosses — Bob Johnson, an attorney from Kansas, and Dr. Irving Raines, a former professor from the University of Maryland — had been active during the Eisenhower administration, Johnson as chief counsel of the Senate Post Office and Civil Service Committee, and Dr. Raines as director of postal rates under Postmaster General Summerfield. During our down time — and for some reason I remember there being a lot of down time — they would regale me with inside stories of how politics, and government, worked.

A small part of my job was to address envelopes on behalf of Vice President Richard Nixon in his campaign for President; Bob Johnson had been a longtime supporter of his. How terribly excited and privileged I felt to be contributing to such an important effort. I had been a Nixon fan since the 1952 conventions, and I agreed entirely with him on foreign policy and most domestic issues, so there was a smile on my face and a song in my heart as I carried out my menial chore. My work there led to an introduction at the Nixon headquarters in Washington, and before long I began spending my evenings stuffing envelopes there.

I've always felt that one of the best ways to learn politics is to do some kind of mindless volunteer work like stuffing envelopes at campaign headquarters. That's the key, being at headquarters. There is so much talk going on, back and forth all day, that you're bound to soak up something if you pay even the slightest attention. You work late into the night with people at all levels of the campaign. Everything happens all around you; you're right in the middle of it. It's like a graduate course in political science; you may not understand it all, but if you ask questions and do some reading on your own, you'll pick up far more than you need to know to move on to the next step, to get beyond simply stuffing envelopes. And even if it sounds intimidating at first, it doesn't take long before you learn the language of precincts and prioritizing and getting out the vote.

It was during one of those long evenings at Nixon headquarters that a fellow volunteer startled me by saying that he couldn't understand how an intelligent man like Ronald Reagan could be a Democrat.

"What are you talking about?" I said, startled.

"Your father," my coworker continued. "I was just wondering what he sees in those Democrats."

"My father's no Democrat," I insisted.

"Is that so?"

"Yes, that's so."

My father? A Democrat? How could this be? For years we'd gone back and forth over the dinner table, discussing world problems and national affairs, and always we had agreed on every point.

I decided this was worth a phone call. In those days we communicated mostly by letter and occasionally by telegram, the price of long-distance phone calls being what it was, but on this I felt I needed an immediate response. I called him the next morning.

"Dad," I started in, "the talk here is that you're a Democrat. Where do they get such things?"

"I'm afraid it's true, Mermie," he admitted.

"But I thought you were for Nixon."

"That's true, too. I'm supporting Nixon's campaign, but I'm still registered as a Democrat."

"Why in the world did you become a Democrat?" I wanted to know.

With that he chuckled and said, "Listen, Mermie, everyone has to have something to be sorry about."

The truth is, Dad was raised in a Democratic household. His father, Jack, was a fervent Democrat who actively supported Franklin Delano Roosevelt, whom Dad also idolized. When Roosevelt won the Democratic nomination, it was the first presidential election in which Dad could cast a vote, and so he signed on as a Democrat because, as he explained, "I was a child of the Depression, a Democrat by upbringing, and very emotionally committed to FDR."

As I touched on earlier, the Democratic party platform of 1932 was not that far removed from the Republican platform of 1960. A shift had taken place over the years, while Dad's party affiliation had remained intact. In fact, he was seriously considering reregistering as a Republican not long after the 1960 election, something he says he'd been putting off for years, when the Nixon people asked him to head up the Democrats For Nixon effort in the 1962 campaign for governor of California. Dad and Nixon had become friendly during the Eisenhower years, and the Vice President phoned to say he was counting on my father to help bring him additional Democratic support in his home state.

So Dad remained a Democrat, and for the sake of the campaign he was determined to stay a Democrat until after the election. But one night he was before an audience in a large auditorium in Orange County, and after speaking for about twenty minutes, he opened the floor to questions. A woman sitting in the second row raised her hand and said, "Excuse me, Mr. Reagan, but are you still a Democrat?"

"Yes, ma'am, I am," Dad replied.

"Well," she said, "I'm a deputy registrar, and I'd like to change that."

What was a future politician to do? Dad invited the woman up on stage, and she reregistered him right there on the spot. The Nixon campaign got a lot of mileage out of that story. And we Republicans have gotten a lot of mileage out of that story ever since; it's great motivation in recruiting deputy registrars, who are an essential but thankless piece of the political puzzle.

The 1960 presidential race between John F. Kennedy and Richard Nixon was the closest in modern political history, and I was thrilled by my fly-on-the-wall view. Nobody had ever "run" so openly for President as these two young politicians. Before 1960 there had always been a draft, or a movement, or some kind of clear indication of who the likely candidates would be; ideas would win out, not people. But now all of a sudden these two young bucks came along and said, "I want to be President," and forever changed the face of presidential politics in the process. Now how you came to be President became as important as what you did when you got there. What an exciting time!

The race that year was so close (less than one vote per precinct would have turned the election) that it marked the first time televised election-night reporting would affect late voting in our western time zones. President Eisenhower even went on television to remind voters on the West Coast that the returns they were seeing on the networks only represented those from the eastern states and that their votes could still make a difference.

Like I said, you hear things when you work at campaign headquarters. As a volunteer stuffing envelopes for Nixon, I was well aware of the perceived voting irregularities of the 1960 election. We heard reports that in Cook County, Illinois, in Dade County, Florida, and in certain parts of Texas, people had voted two or three times for Kennedy. There were also reports of "dead" people voting and of ballot boxes from known Republican precincts that proved not to have a single Republican ballot in them.

To this day I have never conceded the presidential election of 1960. Dad, though, has always been more politic, even from the first: "They won, and I'm afraid there's nothing we can do about it," he said when I called him for some Wednesday-morning quarterbacking.

"They didn't win it, they took it," I insisted.

Little did we know that in just a few short years, Dad would begin to play an instrumental role in helping the Republicans win it all back.

6

A Desperate Exit

THIS IS A TOUGH CHAPTER for me to write, so I may be slow getting started. But please stay with me here, because the events you'll read about in the next few pages contributed as much to shaping the person I am today as anything else in my growing up. And unfortunately, events just like them continue to play a similarly important role in the lives of too many other young women.

In 1961, at the age of twenty, I married a man who was about ten years older than I was. It turned out to be the single worst mistake I've ever made in my entire life. By the time I finally discovered the strength to leave him, I had been brutally beaten, abused, battered, and kicked about the face and head by this man on more occasions than I care to count. On the nights he didn't beat me, I'd lay awake in bed afraid that he would. For the better (or, I should say, worse) part of a year, I was too scared and paralyzed by his threats to do anything about my situation.

Let me tell you how it started.

My husband was a police officer, and we met while he was directing traffic at an intersection near where I lived. I was working in Washington, still as a secretary, and I would stop and chat with this man and his partner when I got off the bus after work. There were a lot of young people in the neighborhood — men and women — who would also stop for a hello on the way home. It was, I thought, a harmless passing friendship with a couple of fellow working stiffs.

In those days the precinct would rotate traffic-duty shifts every couple of weeks — from eight to four P.M., four to midnight, and midnight to eight A.M. — and so we wouldn't see each other for weeks at a time. When our routines again coincided, we'd pick up right where we'd left off, exchanging pleasantries about the weather, politics, the news of the day, and that sort of thing. It was all very neighborly.

One winter day I stepped off the bus to see the two partners huddled up against the cold. Really, it was freezing outside, so cold you could see your own breath, and these poor men were shivering and all but blue; my fingers turned numb in the time it took me to step from the bus to the intersection. So, out of the warmth of my neighborly heart, I asked the two officers if they'd like to stop by for a cup of coffee when the rush hour subsided. It didn't even occur to me to think twice about opening my home to these two men; first of all, it was 1961, and people were a lot more friendly and trusting in those days. Second, and more important, they were police officers. If you can't trust a police officer, then who can you trust, right? Besides, I had always been raised to respect our men in blue, and a cup of coffee on a cold day like this seemed the least I could do.

They stopped by a few more times after that, and I began to feel an attraction toward this one man in particular. He seemed to return the feeling, and one night he asked me if I'd like to join him for a pizza when his shift ended at midnight. Since I was alone in Washington, and not involved with anyone else at the time, it all seemed innocent enough.

I've since found out that men who resort to violence can be very charming when they want to be, and believe me, he poured it on real thick. It turned out we liked the same kinds of movies, we both enjoyed a pizza and a beer once in a while, and we found more than enough things to talk about. Plus there was that physical attraction I mentioned. All the normal ingredients were in place for a romantic relationship to get started, and that's what happened.

Soon — too soon, as it turned out — I started to think of him as the kind of man who would make a good husband. I really don't know why I got to that point so soon, but I think I was anxious to get married because of the way I'd lived my life up until that time: I was very lonely, and very young, and very far away from home, and perhaps I saw marriage as a way to feel emotionally connected to another person and to give myself some validity as a grown-up. Later I found out that this man was married and was waiting for his divorce to come through while his wife was in a hospital with a nervous breakdown, but at the time he was all too eager to step to the altar.

I guess my parents were a little shocked when I called them to tell them we were getting married. I had hardly had enough time to mention him in my letters home, and now all of a sudden they started hearing talk of a wedding. I could sense the hesitation in their voices — in Dad's, particularly — but they didn't say anything, and so I left it alone. That's the kind of parents they are with their adult children: they let us make our own decisions and live our own lives. They said they were happy for me, but underneath there was an uncertainty in their voices, and they didn't sound too eager to meet the young man I'd chosen to share my life with.

Dad apparently was a little more eager than Mother, and he and Nancy made it to the wedding. (For some reason Mother didn't get around to meeting him until several months later.) We were married in a small ceremony in the living room of a friend's house. I was wearing a white lace dress that had been on sale for ten dollars in a downtown bridal shop; the dress was so cheap because it was soiled, and I remember taking it home and using cornstarch on it to get the spots out. It's funny the way those moments, the tiny details, stay with you over the years.

Two days before our wedding my husband-to-be was hospitalized with a severe ulcer attack. He recovered sufficiently to persuade his physician to let him out of the hospital for the ceremony, but he had to return as soon as the reception was over. I spent our honeymoon night by myself, and it proved to be the most tranquil night of our marriage.

My ordeal began a few days after he came home from the

hospital. Right away he began to show himself as an emotionally unstable man, given to violent fits of temper. The slightest things would send him off the deep end. I wrote off his behavior as leftover tension from his ulcer attack, or anxiety over his new marriage, and hoped that a peaceful home environment would calm him down.

But his fits grew more violent and more frequent until one night his verbal abuse turned physical. The first time he assaulted me was after a surprise snowstorm hit Washington; all the streetcars and buses were halted by the weather, so I had to walk the three miles home from work. Well, when I arrived home, about an hour later than usual, my husband turned on me in a fit of jealous rage. The real reason I was late, he insisted, was because I had stopped off to sleep with another man. He was convinced I was having an affair, and there was nothing I could say to make him think otherwise. The more I tried to tell him how ridiculous his assumption was, the more he seemed to believe what he wanted to believe. His voice kept getting louder and uglier. I didn't know what to do to calm him down, and I remember I was thinking, OK, just try to be rational with him and he'll understand, or something like that, when all of a sudden he started punching me and slapping me across the face.

I didn't even have time to get my guard up, he took me so completely by surprise.

I couldn't believe what was happening to me. I mean that literally. I just sat there receiving his blows, not wanting to believe I'd let myself get into a situation like this. I don't know why, but I found myself powerless to fight back. It's hard to explain, but a part of me felt like I was watching all this happen to me, like I was removed from my body, detached and therefore unable to help myself.

My face, when he finally let up, was swollen and puffed and bruised. I tried to eat something, but it hurt to move my jaw; it even hurt to speak. I lay awake in bed that night, unable to sleep from the pain and confusion, and for some reason I kept wondering what I had done wrong. That's the way I was thinking. Do you remember, when you were younger, how when things went wrong you always thought it was your fault, even if it wasn't? That was me that night in bed. I still had enough residual teenage guilt to think that maybe I'd pro-voked my husband into losing his temper with me. It could have been all my fault, I told myself. Maybe I had worried him terribly by not calling to say I'd be late because of the storm, and this was the only way he knew to react.

That night, and during the sleepless nights that followed, I kept telling myself that my husband's physical attack had been merely an aberration, and for a while that indeed appeared to be the case. I never mentioned it to anybody. I don't know why, I just didn't. And as I said, he was able to pour on the charm when he wanted to. Oh, he could be so slippery and slithery, like a snake, but he had me fooled. He wanted me to believe that it wouldn't happen again, and I wanted to believe that it wouldn't happen again, and so that's what I believed. We settled into a typical newlywed routine, and for a time it seemed that that first attack had been a one-time thing.

But by summertime he was at it again. To him, I came to realize, marriage meant ownership, and he would get lost in this irrational, jealous fury anytime he thought someone was stepping in on his territory. It was like I was his turf, and he would quite literally drum that into me, over and over. One morning I joined him at breakfast wearing a waist-length but-toned jacket and a skirt I planned to wear to work that day. He exploded. "How dare you go out in public half-dressed!" he ranted. Then he picked up a glass of orange juice and threw it at me. The juice splashed me in the face; the glass hit me in the head.

That was the first of several times I was made late for work by my husband's rage. I had to take the time to wash the orange juice from my hair, change clothes, and apply some cover-up in the places where I thought I might turn black and blue by the end of the day. When I got to the office I mum-bled some lame excuse to my boss.

As time wore on someone must have seen how lame my excuses really were, but my coworkers didn't really want to know what was going on and my friends were more than will-ing to believe that I was a klutz who kept banging into doors and falling down stairs. That's how I explained away my fre-quent bruises. Oh, they were all smart enough to realize, on some level, what was happening to me at home — I even wore bandages to cover my black eyes! — it's just that spousal abuse and family violence were such dark subjects in those days that people, even close friends or colleagues, just did not want to get involved, and I was too ashamed to seek help from anybody.

It may seem strange that I didn't even share what I was going through with my parents, but you have to understand the distance between us in those days. I don't mean emotional distance so much as I mean physical distance. When I left California after New Year's Day in 1959, I saw my father twice, and my mother once, until Thanksgiving of 1962. I was building a new life in Washington, and three thousand miles were a lot of miles in the early 1960s. People just didn't pick up and jet from Los Angeles to Washington on a moment's notice; neither did they just pick up the phone and visit over long-distance. It wasn't a question of my "keeping" anything from them; it was simply a question of my not seeking them out and confiding in them, which would have been extremely painful and difficult, given the circumstances. Even today I hear stories of young women whose parents discover their abuse only by accident, even when they all live in the same town, so my behavior was not all that unusual.

The one time I saw my father during my marriage — on a short visit he paid to Washington in 1961 — he seemed to sense that something was terribly wrong for me at home, and he tried to open up a dialogue about it without interfering. "Mermie," he said when I met him for lunch at his hotel, "to thine own self be true. I know that's a corny platitude, but you might find it helpful. Whatever the problem is, you have to do what's right for you. That's all that matters."

That was my opening. I should have told him all about it then and there, but something held me back. I wish, even now, that I knew what it was.

Meanwhile the beatings continued. One night that summer the neighbors called the police when they heard strange noises coming from our apartment. When my husband saw the patrol cars pull up outside, he locked me in the bathroom so the police couldn't see the cuts and bruises on my face, ordered me not to make a sound, and then told his colleagues on the force that he was simply moving around some furniture and that he was sorry for the disturbance. (The officers never asked to see me, by the way, though today such a request is standard procedure for all police departments on calls of possible domestic violence.)

The attacks continued. They would come at any hour, for any reason. Or mostly they'd come for no reason at all. Going home from work was always difficult, because I never knew what I'd find waiting for me. One night I worked late, and my boss gave me a ride home. Another police officer saw me being dropped off and decided to tell my husband, who was working the four-to-midnight shift. Well, he came home roaring drunk at two o'clock in the morning, dragged me out of bed, and started hitting me in the face and yelling about how I was fooling around on him.

I was always afraid. There was a deep, black fear in the pit of my stomach that wouldn't go away. It colored my entire life. I never knew when something would happen to set him off. For all I knew, he could be lurking outside my office or sitting in wait for me at home. Like most people, after every violent incident I'd convince myself that he'd never do it again, that there was something I could do to make him stop. I kept examining myself — what had I done? how could I put an end to it? — but by the time I realized that his promises to seek help were worthless or that our reconciliations were always short-lived, he'd be onto a new line of attack. One night when he seemed to think I was gathering the resolve to finally leave him, he started strangling me, and when I fell on the floor he kicked me in the head. The last thing I remember before I blacked out was his saying, "No man will ever look at you again." By the time I regained consciousness he'd gone out, not to return until the bars closed.

I spent a lot of time at the mirror during that miserable time, examining either the visible damage my husband had done to me or the damage I couldn't so easily see. How could I let this keep happening to me? I would ask myself, over and over, fixing hard on my reflection in the glass, trying to look past the welts and the bruises and the cuts and the puffiness around my eyes and jaw. I didn't have an answer. The best I could do was seek, with some makeup or other carefully applied cover-up, to conceal from the outside world what was being done to me inside.

There were quiet moments, sometimes lasting for several weeks, but even during those periods I was always fearful of his next eruption. There was one time when we were at a bar with some friends and I saw a man I had once worked with coming over to say hello. I tried to wave him off because I knew I would be accused of something when we got home, but the man didn't notice. When he got to our table I pretended I didn't remember him, but instead of taking the hint he kept pressing me to remember. I was panicked. Of course, this man couldn't have been expected to pick up on what was going on, but I was certain there would be a scene right there in the bar if this kept up. Finally I feigned recognition, said a quick hello, and sent the man on his way, closing my eyes against what I was certain would be a blow to the face. But nothing happened. That was one of the rare times when my husband acted like a normal human being, and I didn't trust it. I held my breath for the rest of the week, waiting for the other shoe to drop. That was what my life was like. Even when there was a letup, there was no letup.

And while my husband was convinced I was giving it away all over town, he still wanted his share at home. He would always want sex, and it didn't matter to him that I was incapable of any kind of response or intimacy under such circumstances. By this point I felt nothing for him sexually, the physical attraction being long since gone, and yet he kept after me. If I relented, it was simply to save myself from the abuse I knew would come my way; if I refused, which I did increasingly as our marriage wore on, he would beat me, and then he would force himself on me, so I suppose we can also add rape to the long list of abuses I suffered.

There were nights when I lay in bed and stared into the darkness, wondering how to set the bed on fire so he couldn't escape the flames. Some nights I didn't even care if I was consumed by my imagined flames, so desperate was I for a quick release from what I was going through. One time I picked up his service revolver and held it in my hands and realized, to my relief, that I was incapable of murder; it would have been so simple to just pull the trigger, but I knew that wasn't the answer.

Recently I heard a story of a woman who said that the first time her husband beat her, she took a baseball bat to him while he was sleeping and broke both his legs. I wish I'd thought of that. Murder I was incapable of, but how I would have loved to harness the courage to give him back a dose of what he was dishing out!

I reached a breaking point when he hurled one of our kittens, Pixie, against the wall in our bedroom. Can you imagine? It's interesting to me that I wasn't able to come to my own defense, but I was able to come to the defense of this helpless little animal. "She's just a little kitten!" I shrieked, lashing out at him, but he just stormed out of the house. I picked up the badly frightened kitten — I thought the poor thing had broken her neck — and soothed her as best I could, and as I was stroking her back I began telling myself I would no longer sit idly by and allow this man to run, and ruin, my life in this way. It took an incident like this, an abuse to a living thing other than myself, to shake me out of my despair.

That night when he came home I tried to engage him in a rational, adult conversation. As calmly as possible I suggested that we might want to go to a marriage counselor together, that maybe we could talk to someone about his uncontrollable temper, and that if he didn't seek some kind of help I would have no choice but to divorce him.

I can still see the bright, devilish smile he wore when he said, "You won't ever leave me, Maureen, because if you do, I'll kill you."

It was not a threat I took lightly. He had a gun, and I knew from experience that he had no qualms about threatening civilians with it. There was one horrible incident that flashed quickly to mind: one afternoon we were driving around town in our car, and he became enraged when he thought a cabbie cut him off in traffic. I sat by helplessly as he sped after the poor man, caught up with him, dragged him out of the cab, and put a revolver to his head.

Still, through it all I kept my problems to myself. I don't know why I didn't make one simple phone call to my father for help, I really don't. I just didn't, that's all. Maybe I was afraid he wouldn't believe my story, or maybe I was afraid he'd think I wasn't the independent adult I pretended to be. I don't know. I think mostly I was ashamed, and the longer I kept things to myself, the harder it became to finally break down the walls I'd built and share my nightmare with the people closest to me. The longer I went without saying anything, the more I just sealed myself in. That's the way it is with a lot of victims in cases like these, and I was no different.

At some point I resigned myself to my fate and decided that if my husband was going to kill me, then so be it. I would be better off dead, I thought, than continuing to live with the constant fear and anguish he was putting me through. Really, at least death seemed like an escape, which gives you an idea of what I was going through. And so one day, with his threats hanging over my head, I packed my bags and walked out. Let him come after me, I remember thinking. Let him try and find me. I just couldn't take it anymore.

He did come after me, but only to do an abrupt about-face; he wanted us to see a marriage counselor, he said. What turned him around, I'll never know — probably it was just the snake in him, wanting to reconcile — but in hopes of getting him some professional help at last, I agreed to go with him, and we made an appointment with a counselor recommended by a friend. But all the counselor wanted to know was whether I had ever had an orgasm. I was stunned. They were trying to put the blame for my husband's abusive behavior on me! I was enraged, and our visits to the marriage counselor ended after that one session.

You have to realize that at that time spousal and child abuse were not considered the epidemic problems we know them to be today. Many people saw family violence as a myth, and most cries for help in those days were met with comments like "What did you do to provoke such behavior?" Or in my case, "Did you ever have an orgasm?" Just as some still blame the rape victim for inciting a sexual assault, so we blamed the wife or the child who was subjected to domestic violence. In the early 1960s there were no shelters for battered women; psychiatrists and social workers for the most part looked away from the problem. And most police departments had not yet been schooled in identifying and dealing with such cases.

In the first six months after I separated from my husband, I moved five times. I lived at the YWCA, in a rooming house, in a furnished apartment — wherever I could find a safe bed behind a locked door. But everywhere I went my husband would show up and flash his badge and tell some story to the landlord about how I was a psychotic whom he had under surveillance, or some such. Invariably my landlords would believe his frantic stories. He would paint such a picture of me and my fits of violence that they would soon ask me to leave.

In a last, desperate attempt to get my husband to leave me alone, I confided in one of his superiors at the police department. I knew that he admired this man, a sergeant, and I hoped that if the officer knew about this side of my husband's personality, he would see to it that he got some decent professional help. And, I thought, I would help myself in the bargain. Although the sergeant was sympathetic, there wasn't much he could do. His attempt at intervention did no good; in fact, I think it drove my husband to new heights of rage and frustration over my sought-for independence.

It all came to a head one horrible night when I was working late, and alone, at the office. It was like a scene out of a bad made-for-television movie. I heard a knock on the office door, which was locked. When I realized it was my husband, I refused to let him in. He pushed open the mail slot and told me in a menacing voice how dangerous it was for me to be working alone so late at night. And then he left — or at least I thought he left.

I grabbed the phone and called my lawyer, who advised me to wait until I heard other voices in the hall and then to leave the building in the safety of other people.

As I was listening for the sound of other people leaving their offices, I heard another knock at the door. This time it was the night elevator operator, a sweet old man, and I let him in, thinking he would be my ticket out of there. The man told me how my husband had flashed his badge and informed him that I was a psychotic who was planning to jump out the window; he said he was the police officer assigned to prevent my suicide. The elevator operator, trusting authority, had believed this crazy story and let my husband into the building. I listened to this man, and a wave of fear swept over me as I imagined what my husband might be planning to do: I truly believed he was planning to push me out a window and convince people that I had committed suicide.

I was terrified, and I suddenly didn't feel very safe around this kindly old elevator operator. I locked the door and once again called my lawyer, who explained to the elevator operator that I was definitely not psychotic and then advised me to call the police. While I was on the phone I could hear my husband's voice through the mail slot again, taunting me, threatening me. I thought he would break the door down to come in after me, even in the presence of the elevator operator.

The police arrived in less than five minutes — thank God! — and the captain told me that in the past few weeks his men had twice caught my husband staking out the building where I lived. They had warned him on both occasions to leave me alone, but his after-hours "surveillance" had continued. Why hadn't they warned me? It's amazing to me still, the lack of sensitivity or plain old common sense surrounding the issues of domestic violence during that time. Didn't they realize the kind of danger I was in? Didn't they think the fact that my husband was following me was something I would want to know? Or something I had a right to know?

I don't know what the captain said to my husband that night, but it was to be the last time he would try to threaten my life. Afterward I'd find messages from him slipped under my door from time to time, and I'd see him parked in a car across the street from where I lived, but he never made any attempt to hurt me. He would haunt me, but he would never touch me.

When I returned to the apartment we had shared to clear out my things, I found a picture of me in my ten-dollar dress, taken on our wedding day. When I lived there it hung in a frame on the wall. Now the glass was shattered and the picture was slashed. He had taken a knife to it.

We were divorced early in 1962, putting a legal end to my living hell. But I continue to be haunted by him, believe me. It never ends. Oh, I haven't seen or heard from him in over twenty-five years, and all of my visible bruises have long since healed, but I'm still wounded in other, more distressing ways. For a long time, even after I moved back out to California, I could never leave my apartment or my office without instinctively checking all the doorways and parked cars for a lurking figure. My extreme caution colored my entire life and played havoc with more than a few relationships. I have difficulty trusting people. I still tense up and look over my shoulder every time I hear footsteps approaching me from behind. Of course, for the past eight years I've had the benefit of Secret Service protection, which goes a long way toward easing these particular anxieties, but I'm not eager to find out whether the fears and tension will return when Dad steps down from the presidency and my life returns to normal.

When I told my parents about the divorce, I simply told them the marriage hadn't worked out, but I didn't tell them why. The shame and embarrassment I'd felt from the first had by this time grown into something I could not get past. I had built a wall, and I decided to leave the wall intact. That's how I'd learned to deal with everything, to compartmentalize my feelings and close the door on them. If I didn't talk about them, I thought, then I wouldn't have to think about them.

I mention this unpleasant period of my life in a book such as this with a great deal of hesitancy. For one thing, I still haven't spoken openly to my parents, or to anyone in my family, about the details of what I went through. Most of my friends and family know something went horribly wrong with my marriage, but they only know small pieces of the full story. Also, I recall all too vividly the way the press jumped all over Michael's disclosure that he was molested as a child when his book came out in the spring of 1988, and I'm aware that the same kind of attention will likely be focused on this revelation. But I'm also aware that there are thousands upon thousands of women out there who are in situations painfully similar to what I went through, and they need to hear the story of someone who survived her ordeal.

Yes, I suppose this is news-making stuff, but I think there's a benefit in bringing it out into the open. Domestic violence has moved into the forefront of our national concerns — sometimes it seems you can't turn on the television without seeing Phil or Oprah or Geraldo doing a show about it — and it is only through this heightened awareness that we will be better equipped to deal with this epidemic problem. I am gripped by the tales I hear on these talk shows, and I'm traumatized all over again; I sit and listen and once again I'm a helpless and hopeless twenty-year-old woman.

In their voices I hear an echo of my own.

But nobody needs to suffer in silence. Times have changed, and now, thankfully, there are people and agencies who understand and want to help. Seek them out; talk to them. The first step, though, is to confide in someone you trust; let that person know what you're going through, and let that person help you seek help. Don't make the mistake I did; there's no reason to go through something like this alone. Talk to your doctor or a legal-aid counselor, or look in the phone book for the name of a shelter; you can also call the nearest chapter of any well-known women's organization, and they'll direct you to help.

Family violence is a tragic blight on our national landscape. A 1984 report by the U.S. Attorney General on the subject revealed that family violence is cyclical in nature, with a history of violence in one generation suggesting violence in the next. Children in violent homes can "learn" violent behavior in the same way they learn how to speak or the same way they pick up other family mannerisms; it's a part of their environment, and so it becomes a part of them. The report, while admitting that comprehensive and uniform statistics are virtually impossible to compile, indicated that nearly one third of female homicide victims are killed by their husbands or boyfriends, that almost one fifth of all homicides involve family relationships, and, shockingly, that reported cases of child abuse have doubled in the last five-year period for which verifiable statistics are available.

Family violence knows no racial or economic boundaries. You'll find evidence of it in nearly every community — black and white, rich and poor.

Over the years I have spent quite a bit of time learning as much about this subject as I can and taking a public position in favor of private and government spending on shelters in local communities. Whenever I hear a cry for help on behalf of abused women and children, I add my voice to the chorus. In 1985, when Attorney General Edwin Meese was planning to veto funding by his department for a coalition supporting programs for battered women, I was outspoken in my belief that the funding should proceed. People who know me are very much aware that family violence is an issue that is of extreme importance to me, though until now no one has known how deep and how personal my concern has been.

I was foolish and went through my trauma alone, and because of that my recovery took far longer than if I had sought professional or even personal help. The message here is that you don't have to go through such a frightening experience alone.

I'm not sure we can ever erase family violence entirely, but if we talk about it, honestly and openly, we can go a long way toward that goal. I hope the revelations in this chapter will make a positive contribution to the national dialogue.

II

1962—1981

7

Coming Home

CALIFORNIA, to me, has always been as much a state of mind as a place to live. After the harrowing ordeal of my first marriage, I felt I needed to be in California in order to get my life back together. I thought it would be a good place to heal. Oh, I'd missed the beach, and the people, and the easy pace of the West Coast, and I'd also missed my family. But mostly — and I know this sounds silly, but if you grew up in a place like California, you'll be able to relate — I had hated wearing those ridiculously heavy overcoats you have to wear during winters back East. My friend Lynne Wasserman (remember, she was the one who tagged me with the name Mermie when we were little girls) was living in New York in the early 1960s, and she called me up one fall day and said, "I had to put on my winter coat today, and I decided I'm moving home to California."

I knew exactly what she meant.

My coming home was pretty much of a non-event as far as my family was concerned. There were no welcome-home dinners or tearful reunions or anything like that. I kind of just hit the ground running. Dad and Nancy had their life, and Mother had her life, and I was terribly anxious to start in with a new life of my own.

I set up house with a friend of mine named Bobbie Boyd, who was an officer in the U.S. Marine Corps, stationed in the public-information office in Hollywood. We lived in an apartment about a block from the Columbia movie studios. With her help I began making the rounds of studios and agents, hoping for a chance to work in movies or — more realistically, I thought at the time — in television. I decided early on in my pursuit that I did not want to ride on my parents' coattails, and so I deliberately chose not to call on Dad's and Mother's influential friends for a career assist; I'd done everything else on my own, and there was no reason to make an exception with my career.

I went out on so many auditions I began to think of changing my middle name to Rejection. But I did land tiny parts in two movies that first year: *Hootenanny Hoot* and *Kissin' Cousins*, both at MGM. I didn't have more than a line or two in either movie, but it was a start, and it was enough to remind me how much I loved being on a Hollywood set and how much I longed to be there in a much bigger way.

And just as I was gearing up, Dad was gearing down. He had difficulty finding work for nearly two years following his resignation from "General Electric Theater," though I'd be hard-pressed to say the one thing had all that much to do with the other. Yet he emerged from his association with GE with a new national persona: people had begun to see Ronald Reagan not just as an actor but as a strong, influential speaker, a potential leader able to move people with his words and his ideals. Almost immediately after he switched his party affiliation in the 1962 campaign, there was talk in Republican circles that Dad had the intelligence, credibility, and charisma to bring others into the party.

Before I'd returned from Washington, in fact, I'd read an item in a newspaper that said he had been approached to run for governor of California. I immediately sat down and wrote him a letter expressing my enthusiasm for the idea. "Run," I urged him. "You can win back California."

How I wish that I'd saved the letter he wrote back in response. What a priceless piece of presidential memorabilia it would be! "Mermie," he wrote, "I really appreciate your support, but if we're going to talk about what could be, well, I could be President — ha, ha! — but of course, that's not going to happen, is it?''

Dad simply wasn't ready to change careers. He loved being an actor. That was what he did, and he did it well. He was not ready to be a politician. He liked ideas, and he liked having the forum to project those ideas, but he wasn't interested in politics; he was interested in government. (If you ask me, that's one of the qualities that have made him such an effective politician over the years.)

Eventually he signed on as a spokesperson for Borax and as a host of television's "Death Valley Days," which the company sponsored. At the time when the small screen caught up with Ronald Reagan, there was still a kind of stigma attached to television. There was a sense among those who worked in the motion-picture industry that those who worked in the new medium were on their way "out" of Hollywood. That may or may not have been true, and it may or may not have been true in Dad's case, but "Death Valley Days" (like "General Electric Theater" before it) was good, steady work — no small thing for an actor — and so he jumped at the gig.

Across town from my apartment in Hollywood, I had two families. Mother was remarried to Fred Karger, and the two of them shared a small apartment in Beverly Hills. Dad and Nancy were living at the house in Pacific Palisades; Michael had moved in with them to finish up high school, Ron was in kindergarten, and Patti was eleven years old and full of resentment for twenty-two-year-old women named Mermie who sat next to her father on the sofa.

It was nice to be near my family again, but I still didn't feel like I fit in. Their lives were carried on quite apart from mine, and mine grew more and more apart from theirs. I always felt like I was imposing whenever I visited. They all went out of their way to make sure I felt at home, but I just didn't at Dad's or at Mother's. The biggest problem, though, was that nobody knew quite how to act around me: I was an adult, but to them — particularly to Dad and Nancy, with their household full of kids — I was still one of the children.

Work for me was slow and hardly steady. I filled the space between bit parts with acting classes and workshops and community theater groups and a variety of odd jobs. I also continued to be politically active. I shared my interest in politics with a new person in my life, a quiet, dark-haired young man from Peoria, Illinois, named David Sills. We had met while I was still in Washington, and he was a lieutenant in the Marine Corps. Now that we had both relocated to the West Coast, we struck up a relationship.

The folks, this time around, were pleased with my choice. Dad in particular championed David's small-town Illinois roots and his sharp political mind. Mother, too, found him completely "acceptable," and so, with a pocketful of blessings, David and I were married in February 1964 at the Church of the Good Shepherd in Beverly Hills. There was a reception following at Chasen's, with a cake supplied by Uncle Bob Cobb and the Brown Derby, decorated with giant spun-sugar ribbons and bows. Typical Hollywood, right?

David was stationed at Camp Pendleton, and so we moved south to settle in San Clemente, a small town near the base that would later gain fame as the home of Richard Nixon's western White House. Even though I'd supported myself for years, David had some rather old-fashioned ideas about wives' working; essentially he didn't believe in it, and so I reluctantly set aside my Hollywood ambitions and set about doing a job for which I was thoroughly unqualified: keeping house. Oh, I fought him on this one, believe me, but the fact was that San Clemente was not the center of the show-business world, and the pursuit of an acting career from that home base would have been difficult and impractical. And besides, the odd jobs I'd held over the years — typing, filing, sewing, waiting tables — didn't exactly leave me anxious to get to work each day.

I was a perfectly wretched housewife. If David had been my boss and not my husband, I'm sure he would have fired me. Or at least reassigned me. I quickly realized I had to get out of the house, not because it was a raging mess but because I was bored. Conveniently, 1964 was a watershed year in Republican politics. Senator Barry Goldwater of Arizona was about to become our presidential nominee, and the power in the party was shifting to the back-bench conservatives. Thousands of volunteers surfaced all around the country, and in our part of southern Orange County there was a great deal of political activity, mostly Republican and mostly conservative.

I threw my hat into the ring, in a manner of speaking, and signed on as a full-time volunteer. David had political ambitions of his own, but his military status prohibited him from participating in the election, so he was more than happy for me to join the local party organizations as a way of building up his own identity within the party. And besides, to my husband's old-fashioned way of thinking, volunteer work wasn't real work, and he deemed it an acceptable endeavor for his newlywed bride. The thought of never again performing had been gnawing at me for months, but now that I had something to devote my full attention and energy to, the idea didn't seem so bad.

We had only one car in those days, and the routine we'd worked out was that I would drop David off at the base and then cover the Camp Pendleton stickers on the bumpers of the car with Goldwater stickers, so as not to compromise his position. There seemed to be something very cloak-and-dagger about the procedure. I remember I was always worried that I'd forget which sticker should be in place and that I'd be caught in the wrong place at the wrong time, flashing the wrong message.

One of the high points of the campaign was when Senator Goldwater made an old-style whistle-stop train tour between Los Angeles and San Diego, which brought the candidate right through Orange County. There were more than five thousand people gathered around our tiny train station, a pretty impressive number when you stop to think that the population of San Clemente at the time was only thirteen thousand. Supporters had been gathering for hours before the train was scheduled to pull in, and I was one of the volunteers charged with keeping the folks entertained. I was glad for the chance to work a crowd; I sang and told jokes and stories until I was hoarse from the effort.

While I was trudging door to door identifying the voters in my precinct and recruiting volunteers, Dad had stepped forth as the cochairman of the state's Goldwater for President Committee. For months he had driven the length and breadth of California, stumping in every city and town along the way. Because Dad didn't fly, the campaign would maximize his time by sending him out for several days at a clip, scheduling four or five stops in a day. He covered a lot of ground — in his case, literally — and because of his unusually hectic schedule, we hardly found time to see each other.

Somehow, during his wall-to-wall campaigning, he managed to make what would turn out to be his last movie, *The Killers*, based on an Ernest Hemingway story; it was originally intended for television but was released theatrically because of its graphic violence. In it Dad played the heavy for one of the only times in his career. If I remember correctly, the movie failed miserably at the box office, which I took as a sign that moviegoers (and possibly voters) wanted to see the Ronald Reagan they had come to know and respect — honest, trusting, and caring.

I would keep up with Dad's campaign activities off the set through the newspapers or with an occasional phone call. One night I called him at home to compare notes. Goldwater's primary opponent, Nelson Rockefeller, was waging a tough campaign, and by the spring of 1964 things were too close to call. The upcoming California primary, toward which we were all working, came just after Oregon, and Dad and I agreed that our showing in California would have more than a little to do with our showing in Oregon.

"The feeling is that if we win in Oregon," Dad said, "the Rockefeller people will come to California saying, 'A vote for us is a vote for an open convention.' I don't see any way we can beat an opponent named 'open convention.' "

"Sounds to me like we shouldn't win in Oregon," I reasoned.

Dad laughed when I said this and otherwise ignored my comment, but I was entirely serious. When I related the conversation to David later that evening, he agreed that it would be excellent strategy to make California the battleground, since Goldwater's campaign there was much better organized than Rockefeller's.

Well, whether by accident or design, Rockefeller took Oregon by a narrow margin, which left California open for a Goldwater victory, all but clinching the nomination. "You were right, Mermie," Dad said when he returned from the Republican National Convention in San Francisco, after helping to deliver the party's nomination to Goldwater. "Losing Oregon was one of the smartest things we could do."

(And I thought he wasn't paying any attention to me.)

Later on in the campaign, following the convention, I was with a Republican group in southern Orange County that staged a revue called *Washington Hi-Jinx*, which basically lampooned the current Democratic administration with barbed but light-hearted songs and skits. Proceeds from the show would go to help purchase television time for the Goldwater-Miller ticket. One of the prime television buys we contributed to was a paid political broadcast on October 17 featuring a speech by Ronald Reagan entitled "A Time for Choosing." It was one of the most rousing speeches Dad had ever given, covering the issues of encroaching government, high taxation, and world peace, and it served as a call to action for conservatives throughout the country.

"You and I have a rendevous with destiny," Dad said in his closing remarks. "We will preserve for our children this, the last best hope of man on earth, or we will sentence them to take the last step into a thousand years of darkness. If we fail, at least our children, and our children's children, will say of us we justified our brief moment here. We did all that can be done."

Barry Goldwater lost to Lyndon Johnson in what was then considered the greatest landslide in political history, and I learned one of the hardest lessons I ever had to learn in politics. Not only did I learn how to deal with defeat, but I recognized how deep one has to dig in the face of defeat to keep going.

The worst of it came even before the polls closed. There were about a hundred of us working in our small precinct organization, trying to get out the vote. We had been working for weeks, both for the Goldwater effort and for various local candidates. On election night, at about five-thirty, we stopped for a short dinner break; with only a few hours of voting remaining, our work was largely done. As we ate we learned from the network news that Barry Goldwater had suffered a staggering defeat and that "the Republican party is dead." I'll never forget that line.

The polls hadn't even closed in California, and here the press was predicting the demise of our entire party. I was furious. We sat there in stunned silence, defeated, trying to understand why the news media were in such a hurry to bury us. How unfair! Announcing the outcome so early only served to undercut the hundreds of West Coast candidates whose races were still being decided. We all thought it was the ultimate intrusion on our democratic process.

The only thing to do, we agreed, was to get up from our dinner and go back out to the precincts to insure that our local candidates would not suffer defeat and to prove that our party was still very much alive.

But there was a silver lining to the 1964 campaign: my father's career as a politician was launched. His speech had stirred something in the American people and among the powers of the Republican party. His growing list of admirers included some of the party's most influential finance people, including Holmes Tuttle, the automobile king; Walter Knott, of Knott's Berry Farm; Earle Jorgensen, the steel magnate; and Henry Salvatori, the oil tycoon.

Not long after the disappointing 1964 election, David and I went to have dinner with Dad and Nancy at their hilltop home in Pacific Palisades. When we arrived, a copy of the *Los Angeles Herald Examiner* was spread out on the coffee table, folded to a headline declaring Senator Thomas Kuchel — a moderate who had opposed Goldwater in the campaign — as a possible Republican candidate for governor of California in 1966. Dad was on the phone, and from his tone I could tell he was having a very serious conversation.

"What was that all about?" I asked when he hung up.

He indicated the newspaper on the coffee table and asked, "Have you seen this?"

"I've seen it," I said, and then, with my finger pointed right at him, I added, "but what we need is a good candidate for governor."

He shook his head and muttered a playful groan. "Not you, too!" he said. "Mermie, they're closing in all over."

By then Dad was receiving hundreds of letters each week urging him to run. David and I spent many an evening helping Dad and Nancy answer as many letters as we could get through, so I know the tally is no exaggeration. Some of the letters contained petitions with the names and addresses of people who said they would vote for my father if given the chance; others were from people who said they had been so moved by his televised speech that they would immediately join the Republican party if Dad became a candidate. Clearly they were responding to Dad's central message — will the government control the people, or will the people control the government? — as well as to his forcefulness and eloquence as a speaker.

Meanwhile, Holmes Tuttle and Walter Knott had put together an exploratory committee called the Friends of Reagan, and they hired the political consulting firm of Spencer/Roberts to manage the effort. Stu Spencer and Bill Roberts had managed Rockefeller's unsuccessful California primary campaign against Goldwater in 1964, and some of the Reagan supporters from the Goldwater camp were not entirely convinced that they were the right men to do the job, but Dad went along with the committee's decision. It was a decision that would come back to hurt me in a big way.

One of the big problems facing Dad and his "finance people" was his hesitancy about flying. He had witnessed a crash as a young man and had made a vow to himself never to tempt fate by stepping onto an airplane. He took trains whenever he traveled long distances. Well, train travel might be good enough for an actor's schedule, and it might even suit his campaigning efforts on behalf of other candidates, but if Ronald Reagan was to be taken seriously as a candidate himself, in a state the size of California, he'd have to do something about his fear of flying. There were just too many places he had to be, and not enough hours in the day for him to get there by land.

One day, at last, Dad walked into a finance meeting in Los Angeles with the line "Sorry I'm late, gentlemen, but my plane was delayed." He played it like a real actor, with the straightest face imaginable. That was his way of saying he was now flying and was ready to commit himself to this campaign, and he did it in high style.

Everybody got out their checkbooks. Dad's campaign was on its way.

The last half of 1965 found David and me relocated to Anaheim, where he was an associate in a law firm. I was still active as a full-time political volunteer, having been elected the third vice president of the Southern Orange County Communities Republican Women's Club Federated. (The name was larger than the club!) Bill Roberts came over to our new apartment one night to discuss with David and me what was happening with the exploratory committee. Our visit started happily enough when he told us that the polls were very encouraging and that Dad was very excited at the response to a possible candidacy.

But then the conversation took a turn toward the unnerving. Spencer/Roberts, he said, believed that the divorce issue had been the cause of Rockefeller's defeat in 1964, and they were determined not to make the same mistake twice. The consultants were very nervous about Dad's previous marriage, and the very clear message I was getting was that Michael and I were not to be involved in any way in the campaign. In fact, Stu Spencer later suggested to my husband that I dig a hole and pull the dirt in over me until after the election.

Once again I was made to feel like I was in the way, only this time there was a team of paid consultants encouraging those feelings.

I did not agree with their assessment of the Rockefeller divorce issue. I didn't then, and I don't now. Nelson Rockefeller lost the California primary not because he had been divorced and remarried, but because Barry Goldwater was better organized and managed to create a grassroots movement unlike any California had seen for quite some time. He lost because he was not articulating the issues that the new Republican party wanted to hear. The new Republican party, led by people like Barry Goldwater and Ronald Reagan, wanted candidates who would trim the size of government, lessen the voter's tax burden, and further position the United States as the leader of the free world. The new Republican party didn't care about previous marriages or extended families.

I was crushed by Bill Roberts's visit. How dare he see me as a liability to Dad's campaign? Of course I understood the reasoning from his perspective, even if I disagreed with it, but I couldn't shake the feeling of being kicked in the stomach. It was bad enough that I'd grown up feeling removed from my family, but on top of that I was all of a sudden being told by this so-called expert that for the good of the campaign I should pretend that I didn't even exist.

I called Dad to sound him out about the whole thing, and his reaction was predictable. "If you pay someone to manage a campaign," he said, "then you've got to give them the authority to do it as they see fit."

So Michael and I were "rubbed out" by the Spencer/Roberts plan. I wanted to see Ronald Reagan as the next governor of California as much as anybody, and if that meant my not being involved in the campaign, then I wouldn't be involved in the campaign.

But they didn't say I couldn't remain politically active. This was a period of realignment for Republican organizations throughout California, particularly in the California Federation of Republican Women (CFRW). By the end of 1965 there would be a change of leadership that would pit me for the first time against the embryonic "Reagan Group."

A few words, first, about the Federation of Republican Women. Ever since it was begun, as a volunteer organization in 1938, the Federation has been a potent political force on both the national and state levels. In the middle 1960s there were almost half a million members of the national group, the NFRW, nearly a hundred thousand of them in California. Member clubs often pay for headquarters for area candidates and provide volunteers at county party offices; most important, they have been a major source of human power, which is essential for the telephoning, leafleting, and mailing efforts needed in every campaign. According to its mandate, the Federation cannot endorse any primary candidate, which has given the leadership an important role in healing the wounds left over the years by intraparty competition.

At the time the CFRW was the largest political volunteer organization in the country, and it was up for grabs. Women like Ann Bowler, who was on the Republican National Committee, Angela Lombardi and Ann Pike, the incumbent vice presidents of the CFRW, and Louise Hutton, a board member of the Republican State Central Committee, banded together with other women leaders to gain control at the state level on behalf of the so-called back-benchers, those who had been waiting in the wings and who now sought a new direction for the party.

They were up against the entrenched hierarchy of the "Nixon Team," which included Gladys O'Donnell, who was hoping to become the national president of the organization in 1967, Patricia Hitt, a longtime Nixon operative, and Dorothy Goodnight, the incumbent president of the CFRW.

I aligned myself on the side of the opposition, which I saw as representing the interests of a new Republican party; Spencer/Roberts, though, was supporting the incumbent side, which led to a problem. The consultants called my father to insist that he put a stop to my politicking in this area, since they were afraid that the hierarchy of the CFRW would not support him if I openly opposed their candidacies. I was little more than an innocent bystander at this point in my political career, and I certainly was not in any position to stop the defection of the CFRW rank and file, but Spencer/Roberts obviously thought otherwise.

I received a call asking me to break off all ties with the opposing faction of the CFRW. I couldn't believe it. Being asked to step into the shadows during Dad's campaign was bad enough, but now I was being asked to suspend my own political activities.

"This is lousy," I argued with my father over the phone. "I'm not doing anything to hurt your campaign."

"I know, Mermie," he said, "but the guys say this is really a serious problem."

"There is dissatisfaction within the Federation," I reasoned, "and it will continue with or without me. I happen to think it should continue with me."

Remember, my parents have always had a hands-off philosophy when it comes to the activities of their adult children, and I certainly didn't expect my father to break with that philosophy over something like this. It would have been completely out of character for him. "All right," he finally said, proving to me for the first of many times that he only puts so much weight on the opinions of paid political consultants. "But please try to stay out of the line of fire."

Dad won the Republican nomination despite my refusal to

That Reagan smile! — 1941. *(Courtesy Maureen Reagan)*

It's nice to have two dates for a birthday party, but it's sad when you can only remember one of their names. The gentleman on my left is Michael Morris, son of actor Wayne. *(Floyd McCarty/Warner Bros.)*

A snapshot of Gramsie and Mermie outside the Hollywood Beverly Christian Church. *(Courtesy Maureen Reagan)*

At five years old, I was interested in serious reading material . . .

. . . while Dad tended toward the "fluff."

Warner Brothers wanted to
sell Mother's *Night and Day*
and Dad's *Stallion Road,* and
I teamed up with one-and-a-
half-year-old Michael for the
sales pitch. *(Floyd McCarty/
Warner Bros.)*

Dad gave me this photo a few years ago, saying, "Do you remember this old singing duo?"

On a break from Marymount in September 1956, I enjoyed dinner with Dad at the Persian Room of New York's Plaza Hotel.

Graduation portrait, Marymount Secondary School, Tarrytown, New York, June 1958. (*Courtesy Maureen Reagan*)

As a San Francisco nightclub singer in 1963. All of us nightclub singers had beehive hairdos in those days, which is the only reason I haven't burned this picture. (*Courtesy Maureen Reagan*)

The future governor and first lady of California were the guests of honor at a dinner for the Southern Orange County Community Republican Women's Club, Federated. I wonder if they know we only charged five dollars a ticket? *(Courtesy Maureen Reagan)*

I introduced the candidate for governor to a convention of Republican women in 1966. "If he hasn't lost his temper with me," I told the audience, "then he won't lose it with anyone."

This is the only shot I have from my USO tour in Vietnam in 1969. We were aboard a swiftboat between the fishing village of An Thoi and an adviser camp in Ha Tien, on the Cambodian border.

When I was Honorary Chair of the Department of the Air Force Savings Bond Drive in 1971, Admiral Thomas H. Moorer, then Chairman of the Joint Chiefs of Staff, took me on a personal tour of the Pentagon. Here we are at the Hall of Heroes, acknowledging our Medal of Honor winners.
(Courtesy Maureen Reagan)

While traveling through Eastern Europe in 1970, I was reminded of the basic kindness all people have in common. When I took a side trip to Hungary's Danube bend, a very sweet local lady (who spoke no English) sat me down and helped me mend the hem of my skirt.
(Courtesy Maureen Reagan)

It was hands on (and shoes off) in the governor's Sacramento office in 1974. (*Courtesy Maureen Reagan*)

Judy Langford Carter (daughter-in-law of President Carter) and I worked very hard to build the bipartisanship of the women's movement in the 1970s. (*Courtesy Maureen Reagan*)

Producers and casting directors were looking for "cute" and "perky" in the early 1970s. Sometimes this 8 x 10 glossy did the trick.

With Ron and Nancy on nomination night in Kansas City, 1976. *(Courtesy Maureen Reagan)*

Opening-night party for *Guys and Dolls* in San Diego in 1972 found Mother and Van Cliburn busing tables. Looking on is designer Nolan Miller. *(Sam Stone Photographer)*

Lighting up the airwaves for KABC-Radio in the mid-seventies. *(© Roger Sandler)*

back down, and he agreed to speak at a convention of the San Diego Federation. I was asked to introduce him, an honor I was all too happy to accept, only partly because I knew it would tick off the folks at Spencer/Roberts. When I arrived in San Diego I was handed my father's biography, which his campaign wanted me to use as his introduction. But I had already written an introduction of my own, which I was determined to use, and in glancing over the prepared remarks I almost didn't see the following line: "Ronald Reagan and his wife Nancy have two children, Patti and Ronnie."

Two children?

For me to read aloud those words, as his daughter, would have been the ultimate humiliation. I wanted to run away and hide, but I also wanted to stick it to the folks running Dad's campaign and stand up for what I felt was right. Keep in mind, my first priority was to see Dad win the gubernatorial race, and I knew that nothing I was going to say would hurt him. At this gathering I was as much among friends as he was. And so I discarded the remarks prepared by Spencer/Roberts and read from my own notes. I talked about my father's integrity — I told the story about me and Michael and the extra box of animal crackers — and I talked about his vision, and I talked about his tolerance. "After all," I said, "if he hasn't lost his temper with me, then he won't lose it with anyone." I did not deliver the empty rhetoric prepared for me by Ronald Reagan's campaign, but I spoke from the heart about our candidate. And just in case anybody in the audience had forgotten, I reminded all present that the candidate just happened to be my father.

While I was suffering humiliating attacks from within the campaign, Dad was being attacked from without. "This time I'm running against an actor," the Democratic incumbent, Governor Edmund G. Brown, told the press. "I can't act, and he can't govern, believe me." There was even a television program, paid for by the Brown campaign, that showed the governor telling some black schoolchildren that he was running against an actor, explaining, "And you know it was an actor who shot Lincoln, don't you?"

This business can get pretty ugly sometimes. All the nasty stuff, I'm embarrassed to say, was not limited to the Democrats. After all, it was one of our overzealous supporters who printed (and got great mileage out of) a bumper sticker with the slogan "If it's Brown, flush it."

It was during this campaign that Dad's opponents first put forth the idea that as an actor, he was used to learning somebody else's lines; they suggested he was simply repeating the words of professional speechwriters. It was an allegation that would follow him throughout his political career. But in fact Dad had always written every speech himself, and in response to this charge he cut his prepared presentations to half their usual length to allow more time for question-and-answer sessions with the audience.

There can be no denying that Ronald Reagan's skill as an actor, his ease in front of the camera, and his powerful delivery have been tremendous political assets throughout his career. He knew how to read from a TelePrompTer without losing his place, and he knew how to establish rapport with an audience. He also held high the old Hollywood maxim, "When your face is up there on the screen in a close-up, you can't lie to the camera. If you don't believe what you're saying to the audience, then they won't believe what you're saying, either."

(Incidentally, Dad made his last break with Hollywood toward the end of 1965, when he stepped down from his hosting duties at "Death Valley Days" just prior to the campaign, in deference to his busy schedule and in compliance with the FCC equal-time regulations. His friends John Wayne and Robert Taylor helped out by taking turns fulfilling Dad's obligation with the sponsor.)

Since there wasn't much place for me in my father's campaign, I looked elsewhere to keep my political chops wet. Walt Smith, one of the partners in David's law firm, was seeking the Republican nomination in the state's Thirty-fourth Congressional District, and he asked me to organize his campaign. What a thrill! In those days campaigns were usually run by men, but here I was, right in the thick of it, charged with the responsibility of putting together headquarters, enlisting volunteers, lining up district chairpeople, and scheduling public appearances. Walt Smith knew going in that he had only a slim chance of securing the party's nomination, but he thought he'd give it a go just the same. He was concerned about the middle class being taxed to extinction, and he felt that someone had to take a stand for the hardworking families who create America's wealth and buy America's products. As president of the Fullerton school board, he had seen the local mismanagement of public funds firsthand, and he wanted government to be more businesslike.

I agreed with everything Walt Smith said — including, unfortunately, the part about his slim chances. We finished second in the primaries, but coming close doesn't count for much in politics. (A footnote: Walt Smith went on to serve with great distinction as a superior court judge, appointed by Ronald Reagan.)

After that failed campaign I concentrated on our CFRW membership drive, and in that effort I discovered a broad base of young mothers who would have loved to become politically active but because of their commitments at home could not attend our meetings during the day. If we met at night, they told me, then they could arrange for their husbands to babysit. Here I had tapped into an entirely new source of volunteer womanpower, and I wanted to find a way to put it to use. And so we formed a new evening meeting club, which we called the Walter Knott Republican Women's Club, named for one of Dad's chief supporters, whose Knott's Berry Farm in nearby Buena Park, California, was fast becoming one of the country's leading amusement parks and a favorite destination for children. I became the organization's first president.

The Walter Knott Republican Women's Club was active in a variety of programs in the fall of 1966; among other things, we organized neighborhood coffees, where our local candidates could meet voters they might otherwise miss. We also volunteered as a club to cover the fourteen precincts of the small town of Stanton, California, on election day, going door to door to bring in the Republican vote for the benefit of all our candidates, including Ronald Reagan.

On election night, tired out from one of the busiest days in my young political career, I watched our governor-elect make his acceptance speech from Los Angeles on the small television set in our club offices. I lifted a glass of champagne and made a private toast: "Congratulations, Dad. You may not have wanted my support, and you may not have needed it, but you had it, and I hope it helped.

"Tell that to Stu Spencer and Bill Roberts."

8

Governor Reagan

Ronald Reagan was elected governor of California by a margin of nearly a million votes.

After Goldwater's resounding defeat in 1964 and the resulting death knell sounded by the media on behalf of the Republican party, 1966 had loomed as a pivotal election year. Had we not won the governorship of California, as well as some other key elections across the country, the Republican party as we knew it might have died then and there. Political analysts looked on the margin of one million votes in California not only as a clear signal that the Republicans were very much alive but as the dawning of a new era for an invigorated party.

The outgoing Brown administration was not exactly graceful in defeat. They worked around the clock to fill every judicial vacancy before the governor-elect took office. They used the time between administrations to fund pet projects out of the budget for the current fiscal year. They did everything they could to make the transition as disorderly as possible for Ronald Reagan. They made even the most routine communications with the incoming administration difficult.

Now, clearly it isn't all that unusual for a lame-duck administration to make a last-ditch attempt to leave its mark on an office, but it appeared in this case that the lame-duck administration was intent on running its office into the ground. Toward the end of 1966 my father expressed serious concern that what he rightly saw as Brown's irresponsible behavior would continue up until his own inauguration. He was anxious to take office as soon as possible so he could exercise some damage control over the Brown administration, and so he asked Bill Roberts, who had stayed on as part of the Reagan team, to research the state constitution to see what his options were. Bill discovered that the oath of office could be administered anytime after 12:01 A.M. on January 2.

"OK," Dad said. "I'll be there."

The official inauguration — the one with all the hype and hoopla — would take place as scheduled, at a decent hour on January 5, 1967 (a year and a day after my father had formally announced his candidacy), but a private swearing-in ceremony was indeed held just after midnight on January 2.

Dad has never been the sort of man to pussyfoot around about these things.

I visited with Dad and Nancy at the Governor's Mansion in Sacramento on New Year's Day, his last day in the private sector. The mansion was nowhere near the grand, impressive structure I had always imagined. It was a gloomy, rotting Victorian building. If you had to list it with a real-estate broker, you'd have to advertise it under the heading "Handyman's Special." Really, after the euphoria of the election, the place was the most depressing thing I'd ever seen.

"Not exactly homey, is it?" Dad said with a wry smile as I joined him in one of the bare rooms.

"It could use some work," I said.

"The previous tenants should be ashamed," he said, and we both laughed.

Eight-year-old Ron, though, was in love with the place. It had a staircase, and that was all he cared about. He had never lived in a house with a staircase before, and he spent the entire afternoon before the inauguration running up the stairs and sliding down the banister. I had a hankering to join him, but I had a tough enough time getting the folks to treat me as an adult as it was.

Lyn Nofziger, the governor's new press secretary, arrived with the typed copy of Dad's personally crafted inauguration speech, which was to be delivered on the steps of the state capitol later that week. Nofziger playfully weighed the manuscript in his hand and said, "The media want thirty minutes, Governor, and this doesn't feel like thirty minutes."

But Dad hadn't lost his touch for theatrics. "I had counted on applause," he said with a wink.

Right now, though, the most pressing matter was arranging for our family, and Lieutenant Governor Bob Finch's family, to arrive at the rotunda of the state capitol in the middle of the night. The private swearing-in was a logistical nightmare, but we all managed to make it. Or I should say most of us managed to make it: Michael, unfortunately, was snowed in at Lake Tahoe on a ski trip with Mother and couldn't make it down the mountain. Spencer/Roberts may have had their wish on that count, but I wouldn't have missed this night for anything. At midnight David and I stood in the center hall of the state capitol building, under the darkened capitol dome, with Patti, Ron, and Loyal and Deedee Davis; we were all serenaded from above by a choir from the University of Southern California, and I remember being impressed that my father, the governor, could command a university choir even at this hour.

Joining Dad and Nancy on the platform were Bob Finch and his wife, Carol; Chief Justice of the California Supreme Court Marshall McComb; and Dad's dear friend, Senator George Murphy. Murphy, you'll recall, was a well-known Hollywood leading man who preceded Dad as the president of the Screen Actors Guild before retiring from the movie business and embarking on his own political career. The governor, after thanking everyone for making the extra effort to be there, tried to break the tension and quipped to his friend, "Well, Murph, here we are back on the late show." (The press accounts from the next day show Senator Murphy with what looks to be a scowl, presumably due to the lateness of the hour, but he was laughing along with the rest of us at that particular moment.)

Afterward we all went down the steps to the office of the governor for champagne. At that hour of the night the whole thing seemed unreal, almost like a dream. Even though we'd all worked long and hard to help see Dad to this day, I'm sure I wasn't the only one present with the feeling that this moment had kind of snuck up on us. The lateness of the hour added to that feeling. Remember, less than two years earlier Dad had still been hosting "Death Valley Days" on television, and now, suddenly, he was being sworn in as the governor of California. Now, suddenly, he was a major player on the national political scene.

It was a turn of events worth celebrating.

Dad, too, was in a joyous mood. He'd been relatively reserved throughout the campaign, and in public since the election he had shown only his serious, gubernatorial side. But when we got to his new office to make a toast, he let himself relax. He watched along with the rest of us as Ron planted himself in the chair behind his father's desk and began playing with the only piece of office equipment left behind by the Brown administration: a paper clip. Dad leaned over to his young son and said, "OK, Governor, let's go to work."

It was a special, private gathering with family and friends, made richer by the fact that the world was sleeping. It was as though tonight, this moment, was ours, and ours alone; tomorrow we would have to share it with everybody else. I remember looking over at Dad — keep in mind, this was about two or three o'clock in the morning — and he looked absolutely radiant. Not tired but radiant. He was surrounded by people who loved him, in a setting where he would embark on an exciting new chapter in his life.

The "dress rehearsal" came a few days after the real thing. Dad was right about his speech. He may have milked the applause for all it was worth, and he may have stopped a few beats longer than his dramatic pauses called for, but he pulled in his inaugural address at exactly thirty minutes. I know. I timed it.

He spoke about freedom: "Perhaps you and I have lived with this miracle too long to be properly appreciative. Freedom is a fragile thing and is never more than one generation away from extinction. It is not ours by inheritance; it must be fought for and defended constantly by each generation, for it comes only once to a people. Those who have known freedom and then lost it have never known it again."

He spoke about welfare: "We are a humane and generous people and we accept without reservation our obligation to help the aged, disabled and those unfortunates who, through no fault of their own, must depend on their fellow man. But we are not going to perpetuate poverty by substituting a permanent dole for a paycheck. There is no humanity or charity in destroying self-reliance, dignity and self-respect . . . the very substance of moral fiber."

And he spoke about the war in Vietnam: "If, in glancing aloft, some of you were puzzled by the small size of our state flag, there is an explanation. That flag was carried into battle in Vietnam by young men of California. Many will not be coming home. One did — Sergeant Robert Howell, grievously wounded. He brought that flag back. I thought we would be proud to have it fly over the capitol today. It might even serve to put our problems in better perspective. It might remind us of the need to give our sons and daughters a cause to believe in and banners to follow.

"If this is a dream," he concluded, "it is a good dream, worthy of our generation and worth passing on to the next. Let this day mark the beginning."

But before Dad could truly get started on his new duties, he first had to get his house in order. Literally. When I first saw Dad and Nancy in the dilapidated mansion, I knew they wouldn't be comfortable there. Not only was the old Victorian house dark and gloomy and in significant disrepair, it was also a firetrap. There was not a single fire escape in the entire place, only rope ladders that could be thrown out the windows in an emergency — which would have been OK, I suppose, if all the windows hadn't been warped shut over the years.

One afternoon, in fact, Ron and Nancy were alone in the mansion when the fire alarm went off. They ran outside. It was just a false alarm, but the incident so unnerved Nancy that she told Dad she couldn't live in a house that was unsafe. Dad, mindful of the political consequences of such a decision, agreed, and they rented a lovely English-style country house in the Sacramento suburbs, complete with a swimming pool and a beautiful garden.

(Over time the Pacific Palisades house became their weekend retreat during Dad's years as governor; just before his inauguration the folks had sold the ranch in Malibu Canyon to Twentieth Century Fox, which owned the adjacent property and was contemplating building a new studio.)

As expected, the folks' decision to vacate the Governor's Mansion was widely reported in the press and created quite a stir. Dad's advisers had warned him that the move might hurt him politically, and in the days surrounding the decision it seemed that it would in fact do some damage. Soon, though, when the public learned of the hazardous, run-down condition of the place, the uproar died down. A few years later, when the mansion was turned into a museum, the folks were fully vindicated; the upstairs bedrooms were closed to the public on orders from the local fire marshal.

With the move settled, Dad then had to get the state's financial house in order. The Brown administration had left things in a pretty sorry state. Under Brown the Democratic-controlled state legislature had put the state on a new, accrual-based bookkeeping system, which had allowed them to finance their growing budget deficit by borrowing against future revenues. In the short term that worked out fine for the Brown administration, but it was lousy for the state of California. Brown undoubtedly knew there would have to be a tax increase to guarantee the state's constitutionally mandated balanced budget, but he apparently hoped to get through the election before having to reveal the terrible condition of the state's finances.

But when Brown didn't make it through the election, the deficit became Dad's problem. The state was facing a major cash-flow disaster. What no one in the Reagan administration realized was that under the new accrual system, the state had already borrowed a good portion of the next fiscal year's income. Even a tax increase would not have solved the shortfall. California had never had a state withholding tax — in fact Dad had campaigned vigorously against it — but now he would have no choice but to go against one of his major campaign pledges.

In government there are no easy answers, as Dad was learning.

As Dad was adjusting to his new position, I was becoming more deeply involved in the activities of the Federation of Republican Women, locally and nationally. An organizational dogfight was in full yip on the national level, which made our local jockeying of the previous year seem like the stuff of pups. I was to serve as a delegate at the Federation's national convention in Washington, D.C., during which we would elect a new slate of officers.

Let me fill you in on what was going on. The first vice president of the NFRW was Phyllis Schlafly, an Illinois woman whose highly regarded political tome *A Choice Not an Echo* was an influential force behind Barry Goldwater's 1964 presidential bid. She was widely seen as the front-runner for the presidency of the organization, but she was passed over by the Federation's national nominating committee in favor of my old nemesis from California, Gladys O'Donnell.

Now, I have never liked Phyllis Schlafly personally; she has always struck me as a personally motivated opportunist. But politics is not about friendship; it's about supporting a candidate for partisan considerations, not for personal affection. No matter what my personal feelings for her, Phyllis Schlafly was the right person for the job, in my mind and in the minds of a large number of NFRW members; Gladys O'Donnell was not. And so we began a grassroots effort to elect Schlafly to the NFRW presidency from the floor of the convention in May 1967.

I agreed to campaign throughout the Midwest and the Deep South on Schlafly's behalf. I traveled through Illinois, Wisconsin, Minnesota, Ohio, Indiana, Alabama, and Mississippi, meeting with men and women who were working tirelessly to rebuild their party organization and many of whom are still in leadership positions to this day. It was my job to explain to them why the new California leadership would overwhelmingly support Schlafly's candidacy over O'Donnell's, and in the process win them over to our way of thinking.

As the convention approached the opponents were running neck and neck in our informal polls. The outcome of this election would have a considerable impact on the face of Republican party politics in the years ahead, and the campaign was being watched closely by party leaders.

It was even being watched by the governor of California. He called me up one day to see if he could talk me out of going to the convention.

"How can I not go to the convention?" I said. "I'm a delegate."

"Well," he said, "what are you going to do if you lose?"

"We don't intend to lose."

"Nobody intends to lose, but my information is that you're going to be disappointed."

"And just where do you get your information?" I wanted to know.

"It's not important," he replied. "What's important is that you don't destroy the National Federation. What's important is that if things don't go your way, you don't walk away and refuse to participate."

"Why in the world would we want to do that to our own organization?" I said. "If we lose, we'll come back and win next time."

"I hope so," he said, finishing up. "But that's not the way I hear it."

Why can't we ever be on the same side? I wondered as I put down the phone. And where is he getting his information?

As it turned out, the governor's information was pretty much on the money. Gladys O'Donnell won the close election, pushed over the top largely by late-arriving busloads of delegates from New York, New Jersey, Pennsylvania, and other eastern states, whom we had not had a chance to address. The Schlafly campaign cried foul and convened an impromptu meeting of all of its supporters in the basement of the Sheraton Hotel. At the meeting it was revealed that Nelson Rockefeller had financed the late-arrival delegates as retaliation against Phyllis for her role in the 1964 Goldwater campaign against him. And as Dad had predicted, there was much discussion about our leaving the NFRW and establishing a new organization. There was even talk about our leaving the Republican party entirely and supporting George Wallace, who was expected to launch a third-party movement that year.

And the capper to it all came with the announcement that Phyllis Schlafly and her supporters had filed papers in the state of Illinois to form a new organization called the Eagle Forum. She had essentially broken from the NFRW even before the election results were in.

I stepped to the front of the room and asked Phyllis for permission to speak. Thinking I supported her effort, she stepped aside and handed me the microphone. I introduced myself and told those assembled that I was very concerned about the tone of the meeting. I told them that we were all politically active, and as we all knew, nobody wins in politics all the time. We did not need a new organization, I said. We needed to go home and continue to rebuild our party. I went on for several minutes and stepped down to only a smattering of applause. Schlafly and her people were not happy. I wasn't happy, either; I had hoped to be more persuasive.

But I must have said something right (or for all I know, it may have had nothing at all to do with me), because after considerable back-and-forthing, those gathered in that hotel basement finally decided not to leave the NFRW to form a new organization.

Phyllis Schlafly has never spoken to me since, which has been no great loss. Actually, to my mind it's *me* who's never spoken to *her* since. It remains a great disappointment to me that someone whom so many of us trusted with leadership responsibility turned on that trust in a quest for personal power.

For many years the National Federation of Republican Women would live with the myth, born out of that convention, that Nelson Rockefeller had masterminded Schlafly's defeat because he thought she was planning to support Ronald Reagan for President in 1968. But the truth of it is, I think, that the Nixon team saw to it that their own Gladys O'Donnell was elected because they wanted to ensure the support and control of the organization during the presidential race ahead. And the final irony is that Phyllis Schlafly would go on to seek election as a delegate to the 1968 Republican National Convention in Miami, publicly committed to Richard Nixon.

The day I returned to California, I got another phone call from the governor. "I hope you're not upset with me still," he said.

"No, you were right," I said. "I just wish I had your sources. But it all worked out."

"That's what I hear. I also hear you did a lot to stop the walkout."

"I don't know that I did a lot. I tried to, though."

"Well, for what it's worth, thank you."

"You don't have to thank me, Dad," I said. "I didn't do it for you. I did it for me. I did it for the party."

"You did it because it was right," he said, "and for that, I thank you."

"All right," I said, lightening up for the first time in the conversation. "In that case, you're welcome."

While all of this was going on, things were beginning to sour at home between me and David. Well, maybe *sour* is too harsh a word for it, but things were certainly not what they were when we first got married. We had grown apart over the previous months, particularly since he had made the transition into civilian life; he had always had his political ambitions, which he had sought to advance through my political activities, but now that he was no longer in the military, he still hoped to move along on my efforts.

We still shared all of the same interests as when we first got together, save one: we no longer found each other interesting. We had built and managed and scheduled our lives to such an extent that we seemed to share an almost businesslike existence. California has a term for what had happened to our marriage — "irreconcilable differences" — which is what we invoked when we divorced in July 1967.

Dad was shaken by my decision to get a divorce, in much the same way he had been shaken by his own. He thought we could save the marriage. He liked David. And he liked his children to work through their problems to find the best possible solution.

"Mermie," he said to me over dinner one night at his home in Pacific Palisades, "a marriage is a precious thing. It has to be nurtured and cared for. It's not always easy, but it's worth working at. Won't you at least consider going to David and trying to work things out?"

"Dad, you were the one who told me a long time ago that I have to do what's best for me."

"I remember."

"And this is what's best for me," I said, wanting to end the conversation and move on to something else. It was hard for me to explain it all to him; to my mind the end had been coming for quite some time, it was just that he hadn't been aware of it. It was not a decision we had come to lightly.

"All right," he sighed. "But promise me you'll at least go home and think about what I've said."

"I promise," I said, but I knew there was nothing David or I could do to save our marriage; it was best for both of us to just get on with the rest of our lives.

Over the next few months I stayed away from the folks. I even avoided the telephone. It was easier for me to stay away from members of my family than to have to defend my decision every time we got together.

After my divorce I spent a lot of time thinking. Here I was, only twenty-six years old, on the losing end of two failed marriages. I wondered how much of it had been my fault. Obviously the only mistakes I had made with my first husband were getting involved with him in the first place and waiting as long as I did to get myself out of there, but with David I began to recognize certain failings in myself that had contributed to our breakup. I recognized that I could never expect to be someone's partner in life unless we were on equal footing. David and I were not on equal footing, and that was as much my fault as it was his. I had to establish an identity for myself before I could merge that identity with someone else's. I hadn't done that before I met and married David, and I hadn't done that since.

I needed to get my act together.

My first postdivorce crisis was the need to find a job. Suddenly the idea of earning my own living seemed no longer "old-fashioned," as David had thought, but essential. There's nothing old-fashioned about food and clothing and shelter. My first thought, obviously, was toward show business, but I didn't want to go back to Hollywood so soon after my divorce. I don't know — for some reason the idea struck me as scandalous.

So I took stock of what I had learned over the past years and realized that I had developed some marketable skills despite myself. I could organize events, plan budgets, write promotional material and press releases, and speak with some confidence and professionalism before large audiences. Oh, and don't let me forget, I could still type.

The first nibble came from San Diego. Pacific Southwest Airlines was looking for an assistant public relations director. As anyone who's ever worked in public relations knows, the job was mostly clerical work, but it did require a knowledge of event management, promotional writing, and press work. And it paid five hundred dollars per month, which in those days was just barely enough to keep me fed and clothed and sheltered.

I flew down to San Diego for an interview, and I was excited about my chances. And San Diego is such a clean, beautiful city that I hoped it would mark a whole new beginning for me.

A few days later I got a call from PSA informing me that my qualifications were excellent but management was afraid that my relationship to the governor made me too partisan. Too partisan? To work as an assistant public relations director for an airline? I'd never heard of such a thing. Of course, PSA had just conferred Passenger of the Year status on Lady Bird Johnson and Hubert Humphrey, which suggested to me that if they were worried about appearing too partisan, they could use a Republican in their midst.

Coincidentally, on the same day that piece of bad news came my way, another caller was to teach me a very valuable political lesson on the importance of keeping track of friends and favors. As soon as I hung up with PSA I heard from an automobile dealer in Sacramento named Paul Puzak. We'd met in 1966, when David and I had agreed to help a local candidate he was supporting for election, and he was just calling to check in and say hello. What he got was my frustration over my conversation with PSA.

"Let me make a couple of phone calls," Paul said after hearing me out. "I think this can be fixed."

"Please," I begged, "not with the governor's office. That will just make things worse."

"Don't worry, Maureen. I wouldn't do that to you. I've been around Sacramento long enough to know a few other people I can call."

As an automobile dealer, Paul was always being asked for favors by Republicans and Democrats alike, so there were lots of people in town in his debt. What he was hoping to find out was whether a Democrat's acquiescence to my getting this job would get PSA over this partisanship nonsense.

He called me back a few hours later and invited me to Sacramento for dinner the next evening.

We met at a place called Frank Fat's, a wonderful Chinese restaurant that doubles as the political watering hole in the state capital. People were table-hopping all around us. I had never been in the middle of such action — as a new member of the Republican State Central Committee, I barely knew the players in our party — and I was soaking up every minute of it.

I still wasn't sure what we were doing that night at Fat's, besides having dinner, when a man named Jack Crose joined us at our table. When we were introduced he asked me about the PSA job, and I explained that the airline had been concerned about appearing partisan by hiring me, even though there was nothing at all political about the job.

As we talked, there was a commotion over by the doorway as Speaker of the State Assembly Jesse Unruh entered the restaurant. Unruh was the ultimate politico, a powerful Democrat who wielded tremendous clout. The stories about how he kept legislators in line were so outrageous and so farfetched that I can only assume he helped to propagate his own legend. He was a big man physically and carried the nickname Big Daddy. And he could throw his weight around — he would regularly raise and distribute more political donations than anyone else in the state of California. One of his favorite expressions was his own phrase "Money is the mother's milk of politics."

Oh, did he work that room. He stopped at nearly every table, clapping his hands on the shoulders of several legislators at the bar and waving across the restaurant to the tables he couldn't quite get to. It seemed like he knew everybody in the entire place. So you can imagine my surprise when "Big Daddy" walked over to our table and sat down. Was this the man whom Paul had found on my behalf to call in a political favor? I certainly hoped not.

Finally, after making some small talk with Paul and Jack

Crose, Jesse Unruh turned to me and said, "I understand, Miss Reagan, that you're looking for a job that pays five hundred dollars a month."

I nodded my head, anxious to see where this all was going.

"I can get you a job that pays that much a week," he said, and then he turned to the others at the table as if they were sharing a private joke. They all laughed.

I was sure he could find me a more lucrative job, but that wasn't what I was there for. "Thank you, Sir," I said, "but I really prefer the job at PSA."

He looked at me for another long moment and then said, "Jack, take care of it." He turned to me and added, "Nice to meet you, Miss Reagan." And then he smiled and worked his way out of the restaurant.

Later that evening, when we were alone, I told Paul I was concerned about owing a favor to Speaker Unruh.

"It's got nothing to do with you," Paul assured me. "He owes me a favor, and I've just called it in."

I got a call from PSA the very next day and started there the following Monday.

Following that incident, I became very friendly with Jesse Unruh over the years. When he passed away recently I was reminded of something he once said to me in recounting our first meeting. It strikes me now as a more fitting epitaph to his memory than his famous line about the mother's milk of politics. "You know," he said, "political favors are really the currency in which we deal. It must be legitimate and in good conscience, but the more you do to help people, the more they will do for you in return."

It was a valuable lesson, and I got myself a good job in the bargain.

9

Miami, 1968

I HAD A GRAND OLD TIME working at Pacific Southwest Airlines. Really, after so many years as a Washington secretary, it was the first nine-to-five job I'd ever held that allowed me to show some initiative and creativity and put me on an equal footing with many of my colleagues.

Basically it was my job to enhance the public's image and recognition of the airline. One of my big public-relations efforts involved a jumping frog named 727, after PSA's fleet of Boeing aircraft. I convinced my bosses to sponsor the San Diego Jaycees' Calaveras-style frog jumping contest at Del Mar Raceway, just north of the city. We donated the use of one of our helicopters and the services of one of our flight attendants to the event in exchange for the right to enter what we hoped would be the winning frog — 727. I made the case that we would receive wide television and print coverage in the San Diego market and, because of the Calaveras connection, in our central state market.

Well, even the best-laid plans fall apart sometimes. Our fearless frog, warts and all, wound up performing more like a toad than a prince. There was a lot of local news footage showing our helicopter, but there was also film of our 727, sitting still as a lily pad on the pavement and giving jumping frogs the world over a bad name.

A subsequent investigation (there are always investigations when you work for an airline, right?) revealed that the PSA flight attendant who had been assigned to baby-sit 727 during the helicopter flight had allowed her charge to jump from his open jar at about thirty-five hundred feet. He stayed inside the cabin but slammed into the ceiling of the helicopter, and while he seemed to be relatively unharmed in the accident, he flatly refused to ever jump again. I can't say I blame him.

All of this made interesting reading in our *Flightlines* newsletter, but I'm not sure it sold all that many plane tickets.

Oh, well.

Another effort, this one just a tad more successful, allowed me to roll out the red carpet for the governor of California. Dad phoned me one day to let me know he was booked on one of our flights to Los Angeles. My internal publicity machine began to whir, and as soon as I got off the phone I contacted our flight department to let them know about our V.I.P. passenger. You see, it was standard operating procedure to welcome celebrity passengers aboard with a cockpit announcement on the loudspeaker. The only trouble was, the reservations department rarely caught celebrity names in advance, so often as not we would miss out on the chance to promote ourselves as a "star" carrier. Of course, I realize now that our occasional celebrities were not as thrilled as we were at having their presence announced on our loudspeakers, but that never occurred to me at the time.

So that day the governor of California got the full treatment whether he liked it or not, though as a politician, and as the father of the assistant public relations director who had put the flight crew up to all of this in the first place, I'm sure he wasn't surprised.

Besides, Dad was attracting enough attention on his own as we headed into 1968. There was a great deal of talk among party leaders about whether Ronald Reagan would challenge Richard Nixon and Nelson Rockefeller for the Republican presidential nomination. Dad's supporters and advisers — who represented the core of the party leadership in California — were pushing for a "favorite son" candidacy from his home state, which would allow him to test the political waters before committing to a full-scale campaign.

Their reasoning made sound political sense. Republican unity in California was so fragile after 1964 that the "Reagan people" feared a primary battle because of the internal damage it might do to the party; they felt that if Dad filed as a favorite-son candidate, the California delegation could remain out of the Nixon-Rockefeller fray. Also, there was the hope that Dad's candidacy would garner some grassroots support across the country, with which he might emerge as a viable national candidate.

Keep in mind, my father had not only supported Richard Nixon in 1960 and 1962, he had openly campaigned for him; but after Nixon lost the election in 1962, there was the feeling among many that he had retired from politics. He moved to New York, and in the intervening years the Nixon people had made little effort to align with the Reagan camp. He seemed to disappear from the political scene, at least in California. But Nixon had been strategically lining up support by campaigning tirelessly for Congressional candidates across the country in 1964 and 1966, collecting valuable political IOU's that, I'd learned from my friend Jesse Unruh, would translate into delegate support in time for the 1968 Republican National Convention in Miami.

According to party leaders, there was a tremendous amount of support for a Ronald Reagan candidacy in the Midwest and in the South, but as Dad wavered over his decision, some of that support eroded among Democrats and Independents and was transferred to the third-party movement of Alabama Governor George Wallace. The Republican support, however, remained constant, as the rebuilding of our party focused not only on the 1968 election but on the decade ahead.

This was all pretty heady stuff. As an active political volunteer, I found it very easy to get caught up in all the excitement of presidential politics. I would have been pumped up about 1968 with or without my father's involvement. This was what political junkies like me lived for every four years, right? And the way the race was shaping up this time around, it seemed 1968 was going to be the most exciting presidential campaign of my young political lifetime. I found myself looking at the field of hopefuls as "Reagan and Nixon and Rocke-feller" and not, as many would have thought, "Dad and those two other guys." If I had stopped for too long to think that this favorite son who was becoming the fastest-rising star on the national political scene was my father — the man who used to read me the poetry of Robert Service and the fables of Hans Christian Andersen — then I would have gotten myself in trouble.

I tried as best I could to remain objective about the whole thing.

On some nights, though, I would indulge myself, and I'd lie awake imagining what it would be like to see Dad in the White House. Even though we clashed every once in a while, I agreed with almost everything he said and stood for; our differences, when they arose, were generally about methods and party practices and not about issues or policy. My ideals for the most part had been handed down by him, given shape over the dinner tables of my growing up. I couldn't imagine a more forceful, imaginative, and sympathetic leader to take us into the next decade.

The fact that Ronald Reagan happened also to be my father was mere icing on the cake.

It's funny, but the idea of Dad as President is not something I ever talked about with the rest of my family. Even to this day, I don't think we ever sat down, any of us, and said, "Hey, gee, Dad's going to be President! What do you think about that?" To me, at the time, the notion was a glorious new reality and a rich and wonderful possibility, but to every-one else it seemed like the most natural thing in the world. As for Patti and Ron, I guess they had grown up with a polit-ical father the same way I had grown up with a Hollywood father, and so this sudden turn of events must have fit some-how into their thinking about Dad and about what he did for a living. It made a kind of sense to them that it could never make to Michael and me. Michael, meanwhile, had distanced himself as a young adult from Dad's political career to such a degree that I wondered if he thought at all about Dad's pres-idential possibilities; the way he'd dealt with his "dismissal" by Spencer/Roberts was to lose interest in politics in general and in Dad as a politician in particular. As for Nancy, well, she had always been my father's loudest cheerleader, had always felt very strongly that he could achieve anything he set his sights on, and so she was probably not at all surprised to see him emerge as a politician of national timber.

I had known that Ronald Reagan would make a viable presidential candidate since 1961, when his stumping for General Electric was at its peak, and I had told him so at the time, but now that my vision was seeing its way to realistic possibility, I had to stop myself every once in a while to catch my breath.

The domestic issues of the campaign that year focused on an inflation spiral created by the so-called guns-and-butter spending of the Johnson administration and by the mammoth programs proposed by Johnson's "Great Society." Although the costs of these new social programs, which included welfare, food stamps, housing, and health care, seemed in and of themselves reasonable, the down-the-line projections would create whopping federal budget deficits by the early 1980s. The idea of helping people in need is beyond debate and crosses party lines, but most of the proposed expenditures were slated to increase the federal bureaucracy. As Republicans we felt these programs were creating a new middle class of "poverty-program managers," whose goal it would be to perpetuate their own programs (and hence their own jobs) rather than service the communities and solve the problems for which those programs were intended.

Richard Nixon and Ronald Reagan were not all that far apart on these issues, except that it was Ronald Reagan who was better equipped to explain to the American people, in language they could understand, the ways and means by which they could bring government spending in these areas down to size.

Nixon also made his experience in international relations one of the foundations of his campaign. Dad was in no position to dispute Nixon's track record in this area — when Nixon was Vice President, his "kitchen debate" with Soviet leader Nikita Khrushchev had captured worldwide attention — but he was able to sufficiently articulate his own views on the threat of an expansionist Soviet Union.

I didn't see Nelson Rockefeller as an electable candidate at that time, which I know now sounds like hindsight. But whatever it was, I knew that if Dad committed himself fully to seeking the nomination, the battle at the convention would be waged between Ronald Reagan and Richard Nixon. Nelson Rockefeller could hope for no better than the role of spoiler.

This was the climate in which I decided to make one of the most important and difficult decisions of my life. After three years as a full-time political volunteer and several months in a satisfying but nonpolitical job, I felt I was missing something in my life. I wanted something more, but I didn't know what it was I wanted more of. I couldn't explain it then, and I'm not having any better luck with it now, but the upshot of it all was that I found myself needing to get out of California.

You have to remember, Dad's possible run for the presidency made my political activity difficult. The Reagan people did not want me out stumping on Dad's behalf, and the NFRW people, ostensibly committed to the party rather than to individual candidates, were concerned that my efforts would smack of favoritism. There was very little I could do in Dad's California backyard, politically speaking, without feeling that I was ruffling at least one batch of feathers.

And so I packed up my 1965 Chevy Super Sport convertible — which I'd christened Baby — and headed out for America's heartland. My thinking was that the best way for me to spend my time in the months leading up to the convention in Miami was to help increase voter turnout for the party. In California we had helped to pioneer the use of phone banks, door-to-door voter identification, fund-raising solicitation by mail, and many other campaign strategies that we now take for granted. At that time, though, to Republicans throughout the country these strategies were fresh and new and different, and I thought that by helping to implement them in other, more rural areas and enhancing our grassroots capabilities as a party, I could assist the eventual Republican presidential nominee, whoever he was.

The prospect seemed to offer at least some of the answers I was looking for.

Baby took me first to our Midwest and border states, where a two-hundred-dollar honorarium for a local fund-raising speech would keep me going from one town to the next. Along the way I'd meet with as many local organizers as my growing volunteer network could locate, and I'd share with them some of the methods we'd developed in California. I'd also talk generally about the upcoming convention, stressing the importance of a unified party, no matter what the outcome.

One of my favorite stops was the town of Marion, Illinois, not far from Dad's hometown of Dixon. I was the first speaker to pass through Marion, other than their local congressman, in as long as anyone could remember. I think they charged twenty-five dollars a head for a fund-raising dinner at which I was the guest speaker. I talked about the need for a Republican President who would work to unleash the potential of the middle class. I talked about some of the things going on in California, including the governor's pledge that any future surplus resulting from a needed tax increase would be returned to the people. I also talked to them about some of our most recent campaign methods, including the use of computerized voter lists, "door hanger" literature, and phone trees (this last method, incidentally, in which volunteers pledged to make as many as a hundred phone calls a day from their own homes, led to the huge phone banks employed today by every major campaign).

I was such a hit there that in 1976, when Dad made his own campaign swing through town, he called me up to say, "Mermie, I don't know what you said to those people, but you're still very big in Marion, Illinois."

"Marion?" I said back. "Gosh, that was more than eight years ago. They told me I was the first speaker they had had in years."

"I know," Dad replied, "and now there are two of us, because no one else has been there."

Marion was one of many stops I made as our vast political landscape spread out before me. I would think nothing of cranking up Baby to drive seven or eight hours to the next stop. I was a real vagabond. I stayed with friends when I could and found cheap motels when necessary. By the time the first few months of 1968 played themselves out, I had added Iowa, Nebraska, Indiana, Ohio, and Missouri to my itinerary. I'd spread the word anywhere I could find a willing ear.

As the convention neared, the grassroots desire for Ronald Reagan did not diminish, even as the long delegate selection

process brought Richard Nixon closer and closer to the nomination. Remember, in those days we did not have the open
primary system that is in place today, and so it was often the
case that the smoke-filled rooms of the party leadership hardly
reflected the feelings of the rank and file. I collected some horror stories in my travels from local organizations and individuals who had offered support to the Reagan campaign only to
be told there was nothing for them to do. Worse, in Nebraska
the would-be Reagan supporters were advised to contact a field
organizer who turned out to be organizing Missouri for Nixon.
Can you imagine?

I passed these tales on to Dad in California, but he would
explain that the Friends of Reagan organization was primarily
interested in managing the California delegation for his possible favorite-son candidacy. Remember, too, that Dad still
hadn't announced his intentions, and while he was distressed
by the confusion among his supporters in Middle America, he
did not seem overly concerned.

While I had him on the line, I would press him about his
plans. "So," I'd say, "are you going to run?"

"Well, Mermie," he'd begin, "you know my feelings about
this. I've always said that the presidency seeks the man, and
it is unseemly to impose yourself on the nominating process.
The delegates will decide."

"Not even a clue?" I'd try.

"Not even a clue."

Oh, he knew what his plans were, it's just that he wasn't
letting on — not to me, anyway. I think he was uneasy about
revealing anything to me while I was out there on the road
like that. Given my day-to-day, he must have been unsure
about my ability to keep a confidence. It wasn't that he didn't
trust me, so much as that he wasn't sure I trusted myself.
Years later, when I asked him about it, he said his biggest
concern was that some kind of subtle endorsement for his
campaign might seep into my speeches. I can understand that.

Whatever the case, I was as much in the dark about Ronald
Reagan's plans for the 1968 Republican National Convention
as anyone else. As spring turned into summer I began to wonder whether it might be too late for Dad to enter the race. If
he entered now, after all the deliberation and hesitation, and

he wasn't successful, what would that do to his political future? And if he didn't enter the race, would the centrist candidate, Nixon, be pulled further to the left by his opponent, Rockefeller? Was 1968 the right time for the new governor of California to be seeking the presidency? Or was it too soon after his assuming an elected office for the first time? I had so many questions racing through my head that I could only imagine how many more were working their uncertainty on my father.

As I wound up my grassroots campaign with Baby, I had some decisions of my own to make. I still hadn't decided whether or not to attend the convention. As you can imagine, I'd dreamed about attending the Republican National Convention since 1952, but this particular convention didn't seem like an ideal introduction. I had been trying very hard to stay out from under the foot of the Reagan group, and I didn't want Dad's supporters to suddenly think I was turning up without a compelling reason. But then again, I had enough money for a round-trip plane ticket, I had a place to stay in Miami, and I had a ticket to all the sessions.

If my last name had been Smith or Jones, I would have been there in a flash, but I waffled until the Saturday before the convention was due to begin, when I got a phone call from my dear friend Louise Hutton, one of the leaders of the CFRW, who was attending the convention as a Reagan delegate. All summer long we had analyzed the Reagan operation and the way his people would leak stories one day confirming Dad's candidacy and then the next day leak stories denying it, and now she was calling from her Miami hotel to help me make up my mind.

"You must get down here," she said. "You wouldn't believe what the Reagan people are doing to your father. They should either announce his candidacy or select a candidate, but we all feel he's losing ground by being so ambivalent."

"But what can I do by being there?" I asked.

"Well, for one thing you can be here to support your father," she said. "I personally believe he's too late with this thing, and if they announce now, he'll lose. Now, where do you want to be if he loses?"

"You're right," I said. "I'll be on the next plane."

As it turned out, Dad ended his up-in-the-air status while I was literally up in the air. I flew all night to Miami and arrived the next morning in time to learn that Ronald Reagan had indeed declared his candidacy for President. And he had managed to attract some key people to help spearhead the effort, even though at this late date the Nixon team had coopted much of the party organization.

There was tremendous excitement throughout the city. I remember its being oppressively hot, so hot that I would cherish every blast of air-conditioning that came my way. I remember also feeling out of sorts. Now that I had come to Miami, there wasn't very much for me to do. I still wanted to keep a low profile with the Reagan camp — Dad didn't even know I was in town! — and I still wanted to stay on the sidelines until our party selected its candidate.

On the Tuesday night of the convention I was taken for a strange cab ride by Jack Lindsay, who had organized the delegation under the auspices of the Friends of Reagan. He approached me in the convention hall and whispered conspiratorially, "Come with me."

"Where are we going?" I wanted to know.

"Don't ask questions," he said, and he led me out into the hot night and a waiting cab. He gave the driver an address somewhere in the Keys, just outside Miami.

"Where are we going?" I asked again.

"I'm taking you to see your father."

Dad? How did he know I was here? He had good sources, as I'd learned from the Phyllis Schlafly incident, but I was a little startled to have been "collected" in this way.

The governor was staying in the house of a friend in Key West. The place was surrounded by the Secret Service agents who had become a part of Dad's world when he announced his candidacy. It seemed, I don't know, unusual to be taken to see your father under such circumstances; in an odd way it was like a scene out of an old movie, and I was the young lady corralled in the middle of the night to go to the outskirts of town to meet the mob boss, or some such.

It all seemed very clandestine.

"You've got five minutes," Jack told me as I rang the doorbell.

Five minutes? Secret Service men? Strange meetings in the middle of the night? Was this what our lives would be like if Dad became President? The whole incident was a little unsettling.

Lyn Nofziger opened the door and informed me that my father was in the bathroom.

"Does that count as part of my five minutes?" I asked.

(In case you're wondering, Lyn Nofziger does not always appreciate sarcasm.)

As it turned out, Dad's next engagement had been delayed, and we wound up spending about twenty minutes together. We talked about some family business for a while — the standard stuff when father and daughter haven't seen each other for quite some time — and then we got down to the nitty-gritty. "Dad," I said, taking his hand, "do you really want to do this?"

He didn't answer right away. He looked down at our hands, long and hard, and then he said, "Mermie, I wouldn't be doing this if I didn't really want to."

I don't know what it was, but there was something missing in my father's voice. Gone was the gusto with which he had sought the governorship only two and a half years earlier. Gone was the happy gleam in his eye and his bright smile. He seemed very tentative about this major step in all our lives. In retrospect I think it's possible that he sensed something wrong about his decision, that his keen political instincts were flashing him a big red Stop sign.

When our twenty minutes were up we walked together to the door. I tried to lighten the mood. "Dad," I said, "whatever happens, just keep two things in mind. If you don't make it, we'll go horseback riding at home, and if you do make it" — I pointed across the room to the nearest, and cutest, Secret Service agent — "you'll have to let me take him home for my roommate."

We all laughed, even the cute Secret Service agent, and for a brief moment I was in the room with the Ronald Reagan I knew and loved, the Ronald Reagan who would someday capture the heart and mind of the American people and win the presidency.

But that day was not to come anytime soon.

10

Back to the Boards

THE SHORT CANDIDACY of Ronald Reagan in 1968 was built on the wishful thinking that the delegates would split their votes among the three candidates on the first ballot, resulting in an open convention.

Of course, things played out quite differently.

After Richard Nixon won the nomination on the first ballot, there was a good deal of speculation that Ronald Reagan would be asked to consider the vice presidency. In fact, the Nixon people were very anxious to bring my father onto the ticket; there was even talk that they'd trot out their big gun — the ailing Dwight Eisenhower — in an effort to persuade Dad to accept the number-two spot.

"I was holding my breath after the nomination," Dad told me later, "because I knew what a difficult position that would put me in. Boy, was I relieved when they came out and nominated Agnew."

Ronald Reagan was all too happy to return his full attention to the governorship of California, and California was happy to have him back. His run at the White House had indeed been premature, but he would be heard from again. Actually he made himself heard right away, campaigning for Nixon in the few months left before the election. We all did our bit for the Republican cause. I know it often strikes people outside politics as funny, the way we can support a candidate and then oppose him and then support him again. It sometimes seems we go back and forth more times than a duck in a shooting gallery. But there's a reason for that: we do it for the good of the party. I would support just about anybody if he or she had the stamp of the party leadership and if I thought the candidacy would be good for the party and for the country.

In the case of Richard Nixon, all of us had supported him before and all of us had campaigned for him before, and so it was comfortable for us to do so again. By "all of us" I mean the politically active among our friends and family, as well as the people who had put together Dad's unsuccessful effort. I don't know if I would have been able to contribute much to the Rockefeller campaign had he won the nomination, but I would have supported him just the same. I would have voted for him, too.

That's the way it is with us party loyalists.

After the Miami convention I found myself back in California, looking for work and looking to start over for the who-knows-how-manieth time. At twenty-seven now, I still hadn't pointed myself down any identifiable career path: I'd dabbled in show business and politics and public relations (and typing), and I hadn't gotten very far along in any one area. I'd juggled so many different careers that I didn't know what ball to pick up next.

Through some friends I'd heard about an opening on a local talk television program, and that seemed to me as good a place as any to start looking for work. Los Angeles's KHJ-TV was owned by RKO General and featured a four-hour interview–news–talk show called "Tempo." The show was looking for a new cohost, and I arranged for a guest appearance on the show, which would also serve as my audition.

The producers must have seen something they liked, because I was signed on right away. The show aired live Monday through Friday for four hours. There were four hosts: Bob Dornan, who went on to become a congressman from California; Roy Elwell, who later moved on to his own show in San Francisco; Maria Cole, a well-known philanthropist and community activist and the widow of the singer Nat King Cole; and myself. Two of the hooks of the show were the way we pitted two liberals against two conservatives and the way each of us invariably angered at least one member of the listening audience every day.

On my first day the producer threw me what he thought was an easy assignment. I was scheduled to interview two monosyllabic wives of local football players. If memory serves, their celebrity was based on the performance of their husbands on the football field, and we were to fill five minutes with witty patter and inside gossip on the home lives of our heroes.

The interview went something like this:

"Do you attend the football games at home?" I asked, thinking this would be a thought-provoking opening question.

"Yes."

"Do you attend the football games on the road?"

"No."

This wasn't working. I tried another tack: "What do you do to cheer your husband up after a loss? Do you cook him his favorite meal?"

"I don't cook."

Oh. Excuse me, ladies, but why are you here on my talk show if you have nothing to say? This is not a dentist's office; I'm not supposed to be pulling teeth here. As a die-hard football fan, I would have much preferred to interview their husbands. By the end of two minutes we were scrambling — to borrow a term from their husbands' line of work — to fill the time. The producers went to a commercial early to help me save face.

For some reason station management decided to stick with me, even after that inauspicious debut. I settled into a nice routine on the show, and I began to get better as I went along. The combination of news and talk and commentary and audience call-ins was just the right mix for me, and the more I relaxed on the air, the more I was able to pull from my guests and from our callers.

The four hours would just fly! The way we'd work it was we'd meet with the production people early in the morning and go over the schedule for the day. If we needed research on a particular topic, we would pool our efforts and come up with it ourselves. The job required staying on top of as many different subjects as we could get our hands on, because we never knew what might strike a listener as worthy of discussion. It was a real skunkworks operation, and I couldn't imagine a more satisfying way to earn a living.

One time we had Frank Mankiewicz on the show. Mankiewicz, you'll recall, had been Robert Kennedy's campaign manager leading up to the 1968 election; keep in mind, RFK had been assassinated in June of that year, and we were now in the middle of the fall presidential campaign. The thinking was that we'd invite Mankiewicz on to discuss the upcoming face-off between Richard Nixon and Hubert Humphrey from his unique vantage point. We allotted a full fifteen minutes for the interview, which was a sizable chunk of time in our format. The producers had submitted our questions to Mankiewicz in advance, but as the broadcast approached management made it known that we were also to include questions about RFK.

Now, I'm all for explosive live television, but to my mind it seemed entirely too close to such a harrowing turn of events to start pressing Frank Mankiewicz on Robert Kennedy's assassination. It was very important to me to come up with a provocative question about the Kennedy campaign, one that would satisfy management without being ghoulish and invasive, and so would satisfy me. Also, I knew enough to know that whatever I asked, Kennedy supporters would view my comments as partisan.

What I settled on was, "In light of all the information he had accumulated during his years as attorney general, and the tragic murder of his brother, did Robert Kennedy ever express to you any concerns for his own personal safety?"

Harmless enough, right? But as a listener I'd be interested to know the answer.

Mankiewicz answered that he and RFK had never discussed anything of the kind, and it was his opinion that the senator had never worried about his safety, only about what he wanted to accomplish.

Also harmless, right?

Not so fast. The phone lines lit up with people calling in to complain about my indelicacy and my nerve. They sounded like a long-distance lynch mob. "Mr. Mankiewicz," one caller began, "don't you just hate it when people of Maureen Reagan's ilk demean the memory of a great man like Robert Kennedy?" But Frank Mankiewicz — God bless him — stuck up for me and said on the air that he didn't consider my question to be at all out of line.

My job was safe for another day.

But nothing Frank Mankiewicz or anybody else could have said would have saved the day for too much longer. I had only been at KHJ for a few weeks when management made sweeping programming changes that left me out on the street.

Oh, well.

But I was back in my performing mode, and I took the lineup change at KHJ as a signal to hang out my shingle and return full time to the world of entertainment.

I'd forgotten how much I missed it all! It was slow going at first, and I would go out on every audition for which I was even remotely qualified. Television shows, game shows — you name it. As is true for most struggling performers, a lot of my work came in commercials. I hawked everything from Chevrolet cars to Duncan Hines cake mixes, and a whole lot of stuff in between. I'd go out on auditions nearly every day of the week. We used to figure that for every job we got, we'd go out on about a hundred auditions.

Actually I use the term "auditions" very loosely here. They were more like cattle calls. The producers would choose a few hundred people after poring over a casting book with the pictures of every working actor and actress in Hollywood. The thing was thicker than the Los Angeles telephone book! The producers would then group together all the performers of the same "type" — housewife, girlfriend, ingenue, whatever — and bring in the ones they liked for a large-scale reading. I found myself competing with the same people over and over again. I'd regularly go up for parts against people like Mary Frann, who went on to star in the CBS situation comedy "Newhart," and Mariette Hartley, who made those marvelous Polaroid commercials with James Garner and later hosted CBS's "Morning Program." Over time we developed a professional friendship during the long audition hours. I remember we were all up for a bug-spray commercial, with some horribly silly copy, and Mary Frann turned to me and said, "Oh, this one is definitely yours, I can feel it," and I said, "Oh, no, this is the real you!" It was like we both didn't want the part because it was so silly and insulting, but we both needed the work.

Mary Frann landed that one, as I recall.

My family could not have been more supportive. Really, they would watch any commercial or bit part and offer up the most enthusiastic rave reviews. From time to time Dad would caution me yet again not to overact, but he'd be as excited as anyone else whenever I turned up on television. I remember once being told that I looked "realistic" in a spot I did for Crisco Oil; I took it as a compliment.

It was during this time that I first began to feel the burden of my father's legacy. I had always thought that the Reagan name would at best get me into a few doors that might otherwise have been closed to me; at worst, I figured, it would have no impact at all on my career. What I hadn't counted on, though, was a negative impact. Almost as soon as I started trying to hustle up work in a big way, I began to realize that Ronald Reagan's actress daughter was not going to have an easy time of it. One well-known casting director told me he would not consider me for a part because he disagreed with my father's handling of the state withholding tax. A director once told me, "Gee, kid, I like your work, but it's against my religion to do anything that might build up the name of Reagan." An influential producer, table-hopping in a Los Angeles restaurant, stopped by to say, "Oh, yeah, I saw some film on you. You're good, but I hate your old man's politics."

I didn't take any of this lying down, believe me, but nothing I could say did anything more than allow me to vent some frustration. It's tough for any child to follow in a parent's footsteps, but in my case I had three strikes against me: Ronald Reagan's acting career, Jane Wyman's acting career, and now, for the first time in my short stint in show business, Ronald Reagan's political career. I figured a fourth strike every once in a while — being loud, opinionated, and not afraid to put a closed-minded director/casting director/producer in his or her place — couldn't do me any more damage.

But despite all the frustrated auditions and casting calls, I still had enough free time to keep busy in local politics. I was serving on the Republican State Central Committee and on the board of directors of the CFRW, and I had joined the Young Republicans. In early 1969 I was active in a special congressional election in my home district, the Twenty-seventh. The special election came about when Dad's lieutenant governor, Bob Finch, resigned to follow Richard Nixon to Washington. Our congressman, Ed Reinecke, was selected to succeed him in Sacramento, which created a new vacancy in the Twenty-seventh District. It was like a ripple effect. I threw my support and my energies in the direction of one of our primary candidates for the office, Jack Lindsay, the former legislative secretary of Dad's who had taken me to that clandestine meeting in Key West just a few months earlier.

Lyn Nofziger was managing Jack's campaign. Now, Lyn and I were not high on each other's lists of favorite people at the time. As a member of the Spencer/Roberts consulting team in the 1960s, he was one of the folks who decided there was no room for me in my father's campaign or — judging from the press materials they prepared — in his life, either. Because of his efforts to keep me quiet and mine to make as much noise as possible, we were at cross-purposes. At times it seemed like we were at each other's throat.

Every time I think of Lyn Nofziger, I think of the following story. Since he was Lindsay's campaign manager, we worked together very closely leading up to that special primary election, and we began to see past our differences and to form a friendship that has lasted to this very day. Well, Lyn had designed what he used to call "the ultimate campaign weapon," which he unveiled to the rest of the campaign staff one day at a computer firm in Westwood. He had come up with a way to mail a personalized campaign letter, by first class, so it would arrive in every district household on the Monday before the special primary election. Of course, today most households receive letters like these all the time, but early in 1969 it represented real innovation.

Our chief opponent in the primary was Barry M. Goldwater, Jr., a young stockbroker and son of the Arizona senator, who until now had not been all that active on our local political scene. Local party organizations were pretty evenly split over this campaign, and all signs pointed to a dogfight down to the very last day. The Lindsay group, under Nofziger, was hopeful that our unique computerized mailing would put us over the top at the eleventh hour. The fly in the ointment, though, came when former President Dwight Eisenhower died the week before our primary, after a long illness. I walked into our headquarters the day the news about Ike hit, and I sensed that the heavy despair in the room had to do with something more than his passing. I was right: President Nixon had declared the following Monday, the day before our election, a day of national mourning.

The post office would be closed!

Before I go too much further here, I want to clear one thing up. I don't mean to sound callous and insensitive to the very real national tragedy of the loss of one of our greatest Presidents. My heart went out to Ike's family, it truly did, and to the people who had served with him. But Ike, as a politician, would have appreciated the fact that we had an election to win here, and since the primary had not been rescheduled, we had to work through our grief and sympathy and finish what we'd set out to do.

OK. Now, where was I? Oh, yes: all of our beautiful, computer-generated, personalized letters talking about voting in "tomorrow's primary" would not be delivered as planned. We could, of course, get some of the letters out early, so they would arrive on Saturday, but that would diminish the impact, and the mail house's schedule made it impossible to drop the entire mailing early. We sat around a small conference table discussing what parts of the district to mail early to and how to reach the other voters, who would not receive a letter in time for the election.

The Twenty-seventh District in those days covered twenty-four thousand square miles, and in parts of it the largest population groups were jackrabbits, so we decided to mail to the outlying areas and arrange some kind of literature drop to the houses in the center of the district. Then, using a map of the district, we marked off the precincts with the largest numbers of registered Republicans and set off on our way. There was no time to identify Republican households, so we concentrated on precincts that were at least 45 percent Republican as fertile fields for our voter harvest.

In addition to the letters, we gathered every piece of literature we had used in the campaign (we had to make this extra effort worthwhile, right?) and bundled it all together in one neat package for each household; we even ordered an overnight run of twenty-five thousand extra brochures.

We grabbed every volunteer we could find to take materials out to these designated areas, and when Lyn and I looked up from our last-ditch frenzy, we found a nearly empty headquarters. It was getting late, and there was nothing left for us to do but pile into my trusty convertible — you remember Baby, don't you? — with thousands of brochures and tabloids and letters and rubber bands.

I'll never forget that night. Lyn was sitting on top of the convertible's backseat (the top was down, by the way), slipping rubber bands around our packets of literature to make them throwable. He'd package quite a stack, and I was up front, trying to drive and look at the map at the same time, and every once in a while I'd announce a good target territory. Lyn would throw to one side of the street, and the one other volunteer we had with us, who was sitting in the front seat with me, would throw to the other side of the street. We'd try to go slow enough to hit every house but fast enough to make time. It really was quite a scene. And all through the night, Lyn would regale us with stories of his boyhood paper route. "I wish I'd had a car back then," he'd say, letting fly with a grunt. "This is certainly easier."

As the night wore on he began to open up about his days at Spencer/Roberts: "They think they're such hotshot campaign consultants," he said, "but I bet you Stu Spencer has never done this." His occasional grumblings were good-natured, as in "Doesn't anybody know that I'm running this campaign?" or "Where's Jack Lindsay when we need him?" or "What am I doing out here throwing newspapers at doors at this hour?"

By the time we finished five hours later, the sun was thinking about rising and I had the wonderful distinction of having taken Lyn Nofziger out to the precincts the only time he ever went.

(Unfortunately our beyond-the-call-of-duty efforts were not enough for Jack Lindsay to best the name recognition of Barry

M. Goldwater, Jr., in the primary, but that's the way it sometimes goes in politics.)

Now, I look at Lyn Nofziger's recent troubles and can't help
but think back to that night nearly twenty years ago. I've never
wavered in my support of the man who straddled the backseat of my convertible tossing campaign literature with the enthusiasm of a small boy. His troubles, for those of you who
need reminding, began after Lyn left the White House, where
he had been serving as President Reagan's political director,
to set up his own consulting firm. He had a partner who was
supposed to deal with the business and legal aspects of their
enterprise, and Lyn was to head the political planning efforts.
As I understand it, a special prosecutor spent nearly two years,
with unlimited resources, investigating every letter, memo, and
phone call coming from Lyn's office, in an effort to find some
wrongdoing under a law that says that members of the executive branch of government cannot lobby former colleagues
for a period of one year from the time they leave their job.
This law, by the way, does not apply to the members of Congress, who enacted it; a congressman can leave office tomorrow and begin lobbying other congressmen as soon as he cleans
out his desk.

The prosecutor was able to prove to the court's satisfaction
that Lyn had contacted someone in the White House within
that first year. But I don't believe Lyn knowingly broke any
law, and even if he contacted a former colleague, it most certainly was not to persuade him on any political issue. Lyn
Nofziger, despite our early clashes, is one of the most honest
and "stand-up" men I have ever met in all of politics. And
how can we condone a law that applies to one branch of government and not others? It doesn't seem fair. I don't agree
with the conclusions of his recent trial, and I sincerely hope
the appeals process will vindicate him. I will continue to contribute to his defense fund until my bank account runs bone
dry or until justice is served.

But let me get back to 1969. The Tet offensive by the North
Vietnamese army in January 1968 had changed America's understanding of our involvement in the Vietnam war. The story
that most Americans were hearing was that our forces were in

retreat. So instead of applauding U.S. troops for successfully beating back a full-scale invasion from the North, folks back home began to pull away from our commitment to the security of South Vietnam. There was a noticeable shift in the way the folks back home began to think about the war.

I decided — quite abruptly, I'll admit — that I wanted to be there, to find out what was really happening in Vietnam and to do whatever I could to contribute to the effort. I signed on with a USO tour through Vietnam and Thailand. There was more to the USO than Bob Hope; he would head one of the two or three largest shows, but there were dozens of smaller shows touring the country. These were either "handshake" tours, with one or two celebrities or sports figures (Joe Di-Maggio, for instance, was in country on just such a tour during my time there), or small entertainment tours made up of no more than five musicians or performers.

I was to travel with two musicians, another singer, and a stand-up comedian. It was decided that we would leave in early November for a thirty-five-day tour and that we would make an average of two stops a day in Vietnam and then in Thailand. When all the plans were in place, I called Sacramento with the news.

"I'm proud of you, Mermie," the governor said, "and it'll give you a chance to sing some of those armed forces songs we used to sing." Surprisingly, there was no fear or uncertainty in his voice as we spoke; my father firmly believed in our involvement in Vietnam at that time, and he also believed that it was incumbent on all of us as Americans to do our part. If he was concerned for my safety, he wasn't letting on.

"I'll send you a postcard," I said.

You should have seen me in my olive-drab fatigues, wearing steel-reinforced jungle boots (in case of booby traps) that weighed a ton. We weren't going to see any of the infamous poisoned "pungi sticks," but it made the danger seem very real to be outfitted in the same uniform as the troops in the field. Besides the stunning outfit, there were the weekly malaria pills to contend with, huge orange tablets guaranteed to clean out of your system absolutely everything you'd ever ingested. The only way to take the medication without hideous side effects was to break the pill into thirds and swallow one piece with each meal on the dreaded "malaria-pill day."

We arrived first in Saigon and began systematically working our way through the countryside, through the II, III, and IV Corps areas. What a beautiful country it was! Where the landscape remained unspoiled by battle, everything was very green, very lush. I Corps ("eye-corps") was the best-known region because that was the sight of the Tet offensive battle of Hue, but it was located at the northernmost point of the country, and we were there during northern monsoon season, so our travel was restricted from that area. II Corps was the central highlands and the coast, where we had two major bases at Cam Ranh Bay and Nha Trang. It was also the sight of the provincial capital of Da Lat, which was located five thousand feet up in the mountains; when you flew into Da Lat you actually had to increase your altitude to land. III Corps was the plains area around Saigon and out to the Cambodian border; the Ho Chi Minh Trail came down inside Cambodia and then came back into Vietnam through the III Corps area. IV Corps was the lush rice bowl of the Mekong Delta.

We would get up very early in the morning and drive out to the air base, where we'd get on a helicopter and head to a fire-support base in the III Corps area. A fire-support base would appear out of nowhere, it seemed to us. These bases protected the local hamlets, and our forces would work with the South Vietnamese to deter the North Vietnamese from coming south to steal the rice harvest.

Inside the bases (or FSB's, as they were called) there were usually two artillery emplacements, bunkers, and a couple of latrines. (On our visits, out of courtesy, there would often be a hand-lettered cardboard sign marked *"Women"* swinging from one of the doors.) They had people in the field, people out in the bush, people traveling back and forth, and people in the garrison, so there was constant activity. People were coming in and out of the area all the time, and the men were always mindful of the enemy in their midst. I remember one of the men telling me that when they wanted to determine if the Vietcong or North Vietnamese were in the vicinity, our soldiers would visit the local villages and take pictures of the children; if the children didn't accept the pictures, then they knew there were VC in the area.

We would go to two, sometimes three bases in a day, stopping long enough to do a show in each and to talk to some of the men. One time we were flying up-country, and as we were flying we saw a Cessna dropping smoke flares. That was the signal from our spotter planes that there was some activity up ahead, so our helicopter went wide of the area. The sergeant on board became very concerned about what we "civilians" were able to pick up. We told him not to worry, that we knew what a spotter plane was, and then we explained to him what we thought was going on. It didn't take us all that long to pick up on things.

Well, when we finally got to the fire-support base we had headed out for, there was heavy artillery sounding off as we were doing our show. The other singer, Joann Smith, hit a few notes she had not counted on when a round fired just as she was hitting her stride. She told me later it was like being goosed! But she kept singing. Whenever I think of our tour, and our efforts there, I think of that moment.

But there are other moments burned into my memory, too. One early morning we were taken to a small airfield near Saigon, where a gray Marine Corps aircraft was waiting for us with folded wings. Our escort officer, Captain Ed Romano, had mentioned something about "the fleet," but he was very vague about our destination. Since we had no other information, we assumed we were going north to the base at Cam Ranh Bay.

It was early, and we were tired, and we all fell asleep during the flight. When I looked at the time I was amazed at how many hours we'd been airborne. When I looked out the window I was even more amazed that there was nothing but water below us. I looked up and saw over each seat a typed set of "ditching instructions," and as we began our descent I read over those instructions very carefully, believe me. Just then a postage stamp appeared on the water below. We were all looking out the window at this point, and we were all very confused.

We made a lazy circle in approaching the object, which turned out to be an aircraft carrier. The U.S.S. *Coral Sea* would be our base of operations for the next three days, during which time we would also visit the U.S.S. *Long Beach*, the U.S.S. *Biddle*, and the U.S.S. *Truxton*. This fleet was on the northern patrol at the time, almost directly off the North Vietnamese port of Haiphong, but we didn't learn that until later.

The Navy treated us like long-lost relatives. We toured the facilities of the ships, watched flight operations, and ate like kings. On November 10, we even joined the Marine Corps garrison on board to celebrate the anniversary of the U.S. Marine Corps.

Our stay on the U.S.S. *Coral Sea* was indeed a high point of our tour, but always we'd be dragged from high to low by the grim realities of war. There was the tall Hawaiian sergeant who advised us at a reconnaissance battalion on the Saigon River that "Women shouldn't come here"; when I asked him why, he pointed to the barbed wire next to us and said, "This concertina wire is the only thing between us and the VC." Then there was the day we were sitting and waiting to board a plane to go up to II Corps, and Captain Ed Romano kept engaging me in conversation until I realized he was distracting me from something. I looked out the window of our waiting van to discover the reason for our delay in boarding: the cargo being off-loaded from our plane was body bags.

When we performed, the men would sit around in a circle on the ground, drinking Kool Aid, and we would just put up our equipment and set to work. Afterward we would stay and mingle with them for as long as our schedule, and theirs, allowed. I met men who were on their second and third tours, voluntarily, because they felt they were accomplishing something for the Vietnamese and for world peace. They were always delighted to have somebody from home to talk to, and we were constantly made aware that the people we were singing and dancing and talking with could be taken from this world in a flash. That was, after all, one of the reasons we were there.

The Vietnamese were warm, wonderful people, and I began to feel a real affinity for them in the short time I was there. I tend to have a flair for languages, but the only Vietnamese I learned during the whole trip was "Xir ba toi mu'un nuk dah," which means, loosely, "Please, ma'am, I want some ice." In

country you didn't get ice unless you asked for it, and you
never asked for it unless the military was in charge of the
facility.

At night we'd return to the Meyercord Hotel in Saigon, where
the USO had taken over two floors. There were five or six
groups in country the same time we were there. Joe Di-
Maggio, as I said, was staying at the hotel at that time, as was
Tom Tully, a wonderful character actor from the old Warner
Brothers days. We would all gather and drink beer at night
and compare notes on where we'd been that day; among us
we had seen "everything." We'd been "everywhere."

By the time I returned home — or to "the world," as the
soldiers called it — I felt like a different person. I don't see
how anyone could go through a tour like that and not be
changed by it in some fundamental way. I was bursting to talk
about it with people, to share what I'd seen, and to help others understand about our involvement there, but I was shocked
at the way people would turn away and lose interest every
time the subject came up.

It was almost like they were embarrassed to be in the presence of someone with genuine emotions about a place and a
war and a people they had only media-fed emotions about.

It was Christmas when I caught up with my father to talk
about my trip, and I tried to sound him out about this. "I
don't understand it, Dad," I said over a hectic family dinner.
"There's this tremendous lack of interest in what is happening
there. Those men are doing a hell of a job, and it's as though
no one cares."

"I know," he said, "and it kills me."

We didn't get much further than that because Patti was with
us at the time, on vacation from her Arizona prep school, where
she had become very outspoken about our involvement in the
war. She was not about to sit quietly by and listen to her family sing the praises of the men fighting a war she did not believe in; her sentiments echoed many I had encountered since
I'd been home, but in the interests of family harmony we moved
on to another topic.

Later, though, Dad came up to me alone to put a close to
our conversation: "I'm not sure what's happening in this country," he said, "but I don't think I like it."

I didn't like it, either, only I didn't quite know what to do about it. One thing I could do, though, was talk about it, and I tried to get a dialogue going about the war wherever possible. A month later I was invited to address a Republican business group in San Diego on the subject of my visit to Vietnam. By this point President Nixon had outlined his "Vietnamization policy," which stated that our goal in South Vietnam should be to prepare the people there for self-defense. The United States, he said, could keep an invader at bay, as we had done in Korea, but it was the people of the country who had to create their own deterrent military force. I thought his policy made a lot of sense.

I told the audience of local business leaders what I had seen and why I thought the President was right. "If we seek simply a U.S. military victory," I reasoned, "the enemy will merely hide underground until we claim our victory and go home. Then they will reappear and take over as they've always intended."

That remark would resurface and cause one of the most public flare-ups I've ever had with my father. The headline in the next morning's edition of the *San Diego Union* announced: "Reagan's Daughter Says No Need for a Military Victory in Vietnam."

I was steaming. It wasn't the first time a newspaper had distorted my words for its own benefit, and it wasn't to be the last, but I thought in this case the *Union* was way out of line. I immediately sat down to draft a letter to the editor of the paper. San Diego is a military town, and many of my friends there were military or retired military personnel. The last thing I wanted was for them to think I was undercutting our own people in uniform.

But as it turned out, there were other ramifications I needed to worry about first. The national press jumped on the story, and some enterprising reporter asked Governor Reagan what he made of the whole business.

"USO entertainers shouldn't be making foreign policy," he commented.

I couldn't believe he would say such a thing! He knew that headline went against everything we had ever discussed, and agreed upon, about the war, and his flip remarks reduced me in such a public way that I thought no one would ever take me seriously again on any issue. We didn't talk to each other for weeks after that.

I think what happened was that we each forgot the same missing piece of the puzzle: Patti. He had forgotten what my real feelings were on the subject of saving Vietnam because he had another daughter who was becoming quite vocal against U.S. policy there. You know how parents can be sometimes; we kids start to all look alike to them. And I had forgotten about Patti's persistent two cents' worth about the war, and her opposing views.

Instead of addressing the rift head-on, Dad and I brooded on our own. We let the whole thing become bigger than it ever had a right to be.

The letter I wrote to the *San Diego Union* won me a retraction, which I took as a sign that I should mend my fences with the governor, so I slipped the clipping into a birthday card and mailed it off to Dad.

When he called to thank me for the card, there was an uneasy tension in his voice. Things were strained still, but we were both trying to put it all behind us.

"Thank you, Mermie, for the card," he said.

"Did you notice something inside?" I asked.

"Yes," he said. "It's hard to get retractions."

"Not when they're wrong, it isn't."

"Oh, but that's when it's hardest of all," he said, and I imagined, from the tone of his voice, that he was smiling on the other end of the line.

I smiled, too.

The crisis between us was passing, but it would be several years before we could all get past the crisis of the Vietnam war.

The Vietnam Memorial was dedicated in November 1982, on Veterans Day, and there's a story that goes along with that that makes a fitting close to this chapter. I could not make it into town for the dedication, but I did get to see the memorial before Thanksgiving of that year. Remember, there had been a lot of controversy about the Vietnam Memorial, which was a plain black marble wall built into a small hill. Secretary of the Interior James Watt — the numbnut who thought the Beach

Boys were a bad influence on our young people! — led the criticism as people came to look upon the memorial as being a black gash in the earth and an eyesore of an insult to the men who had served their country.

I was overwhelmed by my visit to the wall, and I was immediately transported back to my days in country. I was overcome with emotion as I sat and reflected on the names of the men who lost their lives in that war. I was so moved by the experience, but I wasn't able to articulate what I was feeling until Thanksgiving, when I was visiting with the folks out at their ranch.

My father still hadn't seen the memorial, and I tried to describe to him the way it had made me feel. "It makes you one with antiquity," I said. "You can see yourself in the granite. It's so highly polished it's almost like a mirror, and the effect of it is that you're not looking at something distant, you're a part of it."

He seemed interested, and so I kept on. I told him how it reminded me of the way the Trojan women of ancient times would stand along the road and ask soldiers returning from battle about the fate of their fathers or sons or husbands; here, with the memorial, you could walk along a kind of road and receive the same messages, with the same kind of power.

The President seemed moved by my words, but still he was unsure about making his first visit to share in the experience firsthand. "You have to realize, Mermie," he said, "that when I go to see it, there will be such a lot of noise about my going. There's so much controversy about the wall that I'm bound to offend someone."

"Just go, Dad," I implored. "You have to. It's not about controversy. It's about bringing us all together as a nation over something that has divided us for too long. You must see it."

Sure enough, when he returned to Washington after the holiday, Dad made an unscheduled, unannounced visit to the memorial. There was no fanfare, no press, no aides — just my father, the President, and as few Secret Service people as he could get away with. He walked along the wall, by himself, and had the same experience so many of us have had. As far as I know, his visit was never reported by the media, and he has never spoken about it publicly.

He did speak to me about it, though, the next time we were together. I came east for the White House "President's weekend" in early 1983, and he took me aside to share his thoughts about his visit.

"You were right, Mermie," he said, "it's a beautiful memorial. I don't know why anybody wanted to cause it any trouble."

"I'm glad you got to see it," I said.

"I'm glad you told me about it."

He was so moved by his visit that he didn't want to leave the subject alone. Somehow we went on to talk about that scene in *Gone with the Wind* when everyone comes to the town square and waits for the lists of the dead and wounded, and everyone shares in everyone else's grief. And we talked about what we've done technologically to ourselves over the past century, about how we've begun to encapsulate our grief among small groups of people. Think about it: until the memorial, there was no central place for people to come and grieve over something like this. The telegram would come to you, or a representative from the military would come to you, and you'd go through it all alone. There would be no sense of community, no sense of shared loss.

The Vietnam Memorial, the President agreed, helps us to recapture that lost sense of community, and to heal some of the wounds left by one of the most trying times in our recent history. It makes us all a part of that war.

11

Team '70

FOUR YEARS CAN SEEM like four months in the world of politics, and before any of us knew where the time had gone, it was time for Dad to consider a second go-round as the governor of California.

Surprising no one, he announced that he was very much interested in finishing the job he'd set out to do.

During his time in office the Republicans had won control of the state legislature, so the governor had enjoyed a couple of years with only the most minor of political skirmishes. By all accounts he'd run a smooth, efficient administration, and he was justly proud of California's current state of affairs. Law-enforcement legislation that had been bottled up for years by the Democrats was quickly passed through the new Republican legislature. By reelection time in 1970, 5 percent of the state budget represented funds rebated to local government to ease the property-tax burden on the state's homeowners; the annual budget battle had become a pro forma acknowledgment of the state's need to operate within existing revenues.

And — the best part — his popularity in the polls suggested that the Democrats would have a tough time moving him out of Sacramento.

Dad's opponent in the 1970 election was a man who was by

now an old friend of mine — State Assembly Speaker Jesse Unruh. Unruh was indeed a formidable opponent, one whose main goal was to win back control of the state legislature. I'm sure even he would have admitted that his chances at the governorship were slim, but nevertheless he relinquished his assembly seat in the hopes that his campaign would bring attention to the Democrats in the legislative races. On that score he had a very good chance indeed.

Unruh kicked off his campaign with a splash by picketing the home of Henry Salvatori, one of Dad's earliest financial supporters. He held a press conference there and called Salvatori to task as being representative of "greedy capitalism." I've never been sure why he targeted Salvatori, because the man's philanthropy was widespread and well known, but Jesse Unruh was determined to be as flamboyant, outrageous, and outlandish as possible in order to deflect as much attention as possible from the Reagan campaign.

I remember wondering how Jesse Unruh — the man who had coined the slogan "money is the mother's milk of politics" — justified to himself such an attack on capitalism. The governor must have been wondering the same thing, because it prompted him to remark, "How come all of their finance people are philanthropists, and ours are fat cats?"

Spencer/Roberts reared its ugly head again. They were back in the picture, managing Dad's campaign as well as an umbrella campaign for the other constitutional candidates. They kind of lumped them all together — Ed Reinecke for lieutenant governor, Ivy Baker Priest for state treasurer, Evelle Younger for attorney general, Los Angeles businessman James Flournoy for secretary of state, and George Murphy for United States senator — under the big-picture heading "Team '70." (Flournoy, incidentally, was the only non–office holder of "Team '70.")

And even with all of these candidates to worry about, Stu Spencer and Bill Roberts still found time to worry about me. Once again they tried, successfully, to shut me out of Dad's campaign. Their message this time, in addition to the continued attempt to play down the issue of my parents' divorce, was that I didn't know anything about politics and was an embarrassment to my father.

I had given up feeling frustrated by the Spencer/Roberts attitude toward me over the years. I had long ago traded frustration in for anger. They were not high on my list of favorite people, nor was I up there on their list of pals. If you can believe it, I actually had friends working in the Reagan campaign who truly believed they would have been fired had our friendship become known to Spencer or Roberts. That's how bad things had gotten between us, and now they were telling me I didn't know my ass from my elbow! (Pardon my French, but that was their expression.)

Boy, it was tough trying to keep my mouth shut on that one, believe me.

I may have kept quiet, but I also kept active. I signed on as a volunteer to help run James Flournoy's campaign. Because of his nonincumbent status, it was difficult for Flournoy to raise the money needed to run a statewide campaign against his opponent, Edmund G. ("Jerry") Brown, Jr., the son of the former governor. I also suspected that contributions were coming in slower than expected because James Flournoy was black.

Jerry Brown, a member of the Los Angeles Community College Board, had a well-staffed and well-financed campaign, which painted rather dismal prospects for our candidate. We sent out letters to every conceivable volunteer organization, and we made repeated pleas to the Los Angeles County Party, and through their generosity we were able to keep open the headquarters and pay a skeletal staff through the November election.

Meanwhile, millions of dollars had been raised for "Team '70," with the understanding that some of those monies would be distributed among the secondary campaigns. I fully expected we'd receive at least some of the cash, if not our full fair share, so I designed an affordable radio campaign for our candidate; we knew we'd never see enough money for a television campaign, but a good, statewide radio buy was a realistic possibility. We lined up as many of Jerry Brown's Community College Board adversaries as we could find to help us call attention to our opponent's flaws, and a couple of celebrity voices to sing the praises of our James Flournoy. The entire saturation buy we were proposing would cost only sixty thousand dollars statewide, with minimal production costs.

We made a pitch to Spencer/Roberts to free up the monies we needed for the radio effort, but nobody at "Team '70" would listen to our plan. Of course, I separated myself from the campaign at this point and had my colleague Emil Franzi, who would later be elected president of California Young Republicans, make the presentation. I knew that if Stu Spencer or Bill Roberts had to deal directly with me on this, they'd dismiss the proposal without a first thought, let alone a second.

Even without me, though, the "Team '70" media people would not commit any money.

But we weren't licked yet. We all figured we had one more tree to bark up before we gave in. I had gotten my hands on a copy of Dad's schedule, and we formulated a little surprise for the governor. With what was left of our petty cash we bought a round-trip plane ticket to Sacramento. As you'll see, there was no need for me to bring any luggage.

Even though I was going to argue our case before a friendly audience, I sat on that Western Airlines flight from Los Angeles rehearsing my pitch. I wanted to sound as convincing as possible. For one thing, I reminded myself, it was good political business to have a Republican in the secretary of state's office, to interact with corporations and to oversee elections; that much was obvious. For another, Jerry Brown was following in his father's footsteps on a fast path to Sacramento, and his extremely liberal views promised that he would somehow manage to outmismanage his namesake. Too, the "Team '70" mandate was to benefit all of the constitutional candidates, not only the ones judged by Spencer/Roberts to be worthy of their attention; the proposed sixty-thousand-dollar radio expenditure was minimal and would go a long way toward closing the gap in an already close election.

But most important, I thought, was that James Flournoy was the Republican nominee, and the complete support of his party was due his candidacy.

OK, I told myself as we touched down in Sacramento. I'm ready.

When we pulled into the gate, I deplaned for long enough to turn in my ticket for the return flight and reboard the aircraft. Talk about getting nowhere! There was a passenger scheduled to take the return flight from Sacramento to Los Angeles who I needed to talk to. I had arranged to be on Dad's flight home so I'd have his fullest attention.

"Couldn't you have just come to the house?" he asked, genuinely surprised to see me as I traded seats with his aide Tom Reed.

"I could have," I said, "but this is business, and I didn't want us to be interrupted."

He laughed. Good. I took it as a sign that he was happy for the interruption.

I launched into my attack. Dad agreed with nearly everything I said, as I knew he would. After I saw he was on our side in this thing, we spent most of the flight discussing Jerry Brown and how pleasant it would be to derail his political career before it even had a chance to get started. Dad, I knew, was still smarting from the state of the state left behind by his predecessor.

After a while he called Tom Reed over. "Tom," he said, "we're talking about 'the mother's milk of politics' here. What can you tell me about the 'Team '70' campaign?"

Tom had been listening in, so he knew what we'd been talking about. "Well, Governor," he said, " 'Team '70' is spending money on all the campaigns, but they aren't giving money to any of the individual candidates."

"Wait a minute," I said pointedly. "We have not been apprised of any spending on behalf of our campaign."

It looked to me like Tom Reed was squirming as he assured the governor that the Flournoy campaign would be fully involved in the "Team '70" effort, and that he would personally review our radio proposal. His apparent interest and enthusiasm were enough to satisfy his boss, but in the look he gave me I found no encouragement that "Team '70" was going to keep its commitment to James Flournoy.

By the time we touched down, I'd logged several hundred round-trip miles in just under a few hours, and I didn't know if I'd gained anything for my troubles but a nice visit with my father. Dad seemed to share our concerns, sure, but I knew enough to realize that his support alone would not bring us the needed sixty thousand dollars.

Three days later, in the dim light of an empty saloon at

three o'clock in the afternoon, I was told by a "Team '70" representative that there would be no money for a Flournoy radio campaign. The news itself was hard enough to hear, but the way they chose to deliver it was doubly insulting. I felt like an outcast daughter (which I suppose I was), the way the "Reagan Group" operative ushered me into a corner where we wouldn't be seen. I didn't say anything then because I didn't want to "embarrass" my father, as Spencer/Roberts had so sensitively put it, but I can say something now. What were they afraid would happen if a Spencer/Roberts consultant was seen in public with me? Was I that much of a liability to Dad's campaign? To the "Team '70" campaign?

The "Team '70" representative handed me an unsigned, handwritten list of campaign elements that were supposedly benefiting the Flournoy campaign. He had hoped we'd be satisfied with some "Team '70" billboards and our candidate's name on an election-day doorhanger! That was it. They wouldn't even tell us where our billboards were to be placed or allow us any input on placement.

It was a slap in the face to James Flournoy's candidacy. And indirectly, it was a slap in the face to me.

I called the governor. "Dad," I said, "I'm sorry to bother you about this" — I really was — "but I'm getting nowhere with these campaign people. Isn't there anything we can do?"

"Now, Mermie," he began, "I've had our group check into this, and there really doesn't seem to be any way to win that campaign. There have already been some sizable expenditures made. Sometimes we all have to cut our losses."

"I don't know what you mean by 'sizable expenditures,' " I said. "We haven't seen any, but we're within five percent of Jerry Brown with no money and no media. We can still win this thing."

"I'm sorry, Mermie, but I really have to go along with Stu and Bill. I really believe they're on top of this."

Oh, they were on top of it, all right. They were so much on top of it they couldn't even see what they were sitting on. When it was all over, Dad had been elected to a second term but George Murphy was no longer a United States senator, the Republicans had lost control of the state legislature, and

Jerry Brown had become secretary of state by a margin of 3,234,788 (50.4 percent) to 2,926,613 (45.6 percent).

Jesse Unruh's gamble had paid off, even if he'd failed to unseat my father; the Democrats took back control of the California legislature. (Ronald Reagan and Jesse Unruh, incidentally, went on from this election to become good friends; Unruh was one of the speakers at the Center City luncheon for the President-elect in 1981, and Dad was a frequent telephone visitor during his one-time opponent's losing bout with cancer a few years later.)

Now, I don't mean to suggest here that my sixty-thousand-dollar radio proposal would have saved the Flournoy campaign, because I don't know that it would have. But I am reasonably certain that with a minimal expenditure and some careful attention, Jim Flournoy would have defeated Jerry Brown in 1970. I don't know enough about the other legislative races to comment on those campaigns (I can only imagine that some careful attention might have turned those results around, too), but the "Team '70" power structure didn't believe Flournoy could win as a nonincumbent; they didn't believe he could win because he wanted to run his own campaign; and they didn't believe he could win because he was black. I firmly believe there was prejudice to the decision making that went into all of this — prejudice against James Flournoy because of his race and prejudice against me because of other things.

Spencer/Roberts botched it. In a big way. They managed to snatch defeat out of the jaws of victory. And they said *I* was the one who didn't know anything about politics.

12

What's in a Name?

THE EXCITEMENT of Dad's victory was almost lost in the disappointments of the 1970 California elections. Almost, but not quite.

The inauguration this time around lacked the unique middle-of-the-night atmosphere and the first-time thrill of 1967. In fact, I couldn't even make it to Sacramento on January 4, 1971, because I was stuck in Los Angeles, working. I watched the swearing-in on television and grimaced as Dad tried to explain away the shift in control of the legislature in his address: "By mandate of the people, the power to govern will be shared," he said. "To conclude pessimistically, as some have, that little progress can come from such a situation is to deny the value of the two-party system which has served us so well."

I understood the need for Dad's call to bipartisanship in the session ahead, but I couldn't listen to his speech without thinking that we had given away our legislative control.

But I wasn't there, and I tried to distance myself from my unhappy experience in the 1970 elections emotionally as well as physically. And besides, I was happy to be working. Things were actually going quite well for me in my career. Work was coming fairly steadily around this time — sitcoms, commercials, movies of the week, talk shows, community theater, everything short of my first big break.

My list of credits during the time of Dad's second term as governor is wide and varied. I won't bore you with the whole thing, but I will give you a flavor of what I was up to. I appeared on television shows like "The Partridge Family" and "Marcus Welby, M.D." I had a part in a movie that still turns up on late-night TV, called "Death Takes a Holiday." I appeared on talk and variety shows with people like Donald O'Connor, Art Linkletter, and Merv Griffin.

I even had a lead role in a television-movie pilot for NBC called "The Specialists," with Robert Urich. Jack Webb, of "Dragnet" fame, was the producer, and if things went well in our first outing there was a chance we'd turn it into a series. Imagine, Mermie Reagan with a series all her own! It would have been the big break I was looking for.

I played the part of a doctor with the Los Angeles County Health Department, and Robert Urich was an Epidemic Intelligence Service officer trained by the Centers for Disease Control in Atlanta. Jack Webb was very interested in making the whole thing appear realistic, and so we spent a lot of time at the county health department, learning all about "morbidity reports" and communicable diseases. Since the script called for us to talk about things like "leptospirosis," it was important for us to at least look like we knew what we were saying.

Well, one day a group of us were lunching at a restaurant across the street from the health department building, and I was exclaiming about the latest morbidity report, which contained the names of some diseases I was by now beginning to recognize. As I was talking, the waitress came up to our table and said, "Oh, stop, you doctors are all alike. You're going to ruin your appetites with all this talk about diseases!"

I wanted to kiss her! It was the nicest compliment I've ever received as an actress — hey, Dad! I wasn't overacting on this one! — but since I now knew all about communicable diseases, I decided against the kiss and left a big tip instead.

But I'm getting ahead of myself here. . . .

Around this time I was in a curious place in both my life and my career. Physically it found me — of all places — in Las Vegas's Caesar's Palace hotel. Worse, I was working the lounge. That's right: Mermie Reagan — struggling actress, budding political activist, and First Daughter of the state of California — was smack in the middle of a show-business cliché.

I was a Vegas lounge act.

Now, to be fair, our producers had mounted an entertaining little show called "The Name's the Same," which drew on a wellspring of offspring of Hollywood greats to build a light musical-comedy-variety revue. My partners in song and dance included Meredith MacRae (fresh from the television series "Petticoat Junction"), Gary Lewis (remember Gary Lewis and the Playboys?), Deana Martin, Randy Carmichael, and Patty Grayson, among others, and we all hoofed up a storm in quest of a legitimate buck. The producers had the names Martin and Lewis in lights on the marquee out front (how's that for a gimmick?), but I'll be the first to admit we were all coattailing as much as we were headlining.

There's no business like show business, I'm afraid, except of course when show business happens also to be the family business.

I was between engagements when this particular opportunity knocked, and I told myself that work was work. If I was going to seriously pursue a career as an actress, I was not in a position to turn down a paycheck. Besides, the promise of appearing in Vegas, even in a revue that traded openly on Dad's name, seemed like an important step in my career.

To me, at the time, it was a good gig.

Looking back, I don't think I gave myself enough credit, and I don't think I stopped long enough to hear the unspoken message in the producers' offer and in the audience's enthusiastic response to the show: in harsh terms, "The Name's the Same" told us all that we had accomplished nothing in life beyond being born. Of course that wasn't true, but — and I don't presume to speak here for the others in the show — my first big break was taking longer to materialize than I would have liked. Oh, I was getting parts, but as I said earlier, I had three strikes against me going into every audition, and one was that I was forever trying to cast aside my father's shadow. Even after I found work, I would never know whether I'd gotten the role because of myself or because of Dad or because of some unnatural combination of the two. And underneath it all was this gnawing uncertainty that maybe the career path I had chosen for myself was not exactly headed in the right direction.

Dad, meanwhile, was moving steadily along on *his* new career path. He and Nancy and Ron by now had had four years to get used to their new routine (Patti was away at school, and Michael was living on his own by this time), and they were quite comfortably settled; they were still living in the rented house in the Sacramento suburbs during the week and in their own Pacific Palisades home on the weekends. More often than not their evenings were filled with some banquet or function, which I suppose took its toll on Ron, who was left on his own, and was exhausting to the folks, who prefer a quiet evening at home.

During the summers they had taken to renting a beach house at Trancas, just north of Malibu, for a one-month vacation. That was where we'd do most of our visiting as a family. I'd try to get out there one or two days each week, depending on my work schedule. On the days that all of us were there at the same time, we'd be out body-surfing and Dad would look around and marvel, "My goodness, all four of my pupils, all here at the same time!"

He really was delighted to have the whole family together. I'll admit, it was a nice respite from the busy lives we'd all built for ourselves. We'd all gather in midmorning on the beach, where we had a couple of umbrellas set out for the summer. We'd sunbathe or sit in the shade and talk or read, and then we'd retire to a nice lunch on the patio. The afternoon was spent back on the beach, usually in the water. And then we'd change for a leisurely family dinner and some lively discussion. It was actually quite lovely, a real family vacation.

We would take long walks together on the beach and stop and chat with some of their celebrity neighbors. I remember one conversation Dad and I had with the actor Steve McQueen about rising real-estate prices. The home McQueen and his actress-wife Ali McGraw were renting was on the market for $350,000, which he considered to be entirely out of line. Today, of course, even the most unassuming Malibu beach properties fetch in the millions of dollars; with $350,000 and a little luck you might get yourself a beach chair and a lemonade stand.

During the governorship years, whenever my father was in Sacramento, the demands on his time were so great that I worked out a system with his secretary, Helene Von Damm. I would call and ask her when Dad might have a few minutes to talk, and we'd figure out a time that wouldn't interfere with his hectic schedule. The way it worked out, from Dad's point of view, was that I'd always manage to call just when he had a free moment. He must have thought I was telepathic! When I told him years later that Helene and I had scheduled my "impromptu" calls, he couldn't believe that his own daughter had had to make appointments to talk to him. To someone on the outside that must seem kind of strange, but that's what life can be like when your father is the governor of a state the size of California. There were so many demands on his time that I had to — subtly, at least — demand some time of my own.

I got my call in early, shortly after my Vegas stint, to deliver news of my latest role.

"Greater love hath no daughter than to play the homely role of Agnes Gooch so her father can see her perform," I exclaimed into the phone one busy afternoon in June 1972. Dad hadn't been able to make it to my last show — *Guys and Dolls* in San Diego — and I wanted to give him as much notice as possible that I'd be appearing at the Music Circus in Sacramento with Joanne Worley, in *Mame*.

Gooch is one of the best parts I've come across in American musical theater, certainly one of the best parts I've ever been lucky enough to play. The poor, unfortunate governess-turned-secretary, with her homely appearance and lively spirit, is a comedienne's dream and just what I needed to chase away whatever doldrums were left from Las Vegas. I still laugh out loud when I think of Gooch making a triumphant (and pregnant!) return, singing to Auntie Mame, "I traveled to hell in my new veneer, and look what I got as a souvenir. . . ."

When I auditioned for the role, the producers told me I was too attractive to make a believable Gooch. (Talk about softening the pain of rejection!) But I didn't let that stop me. I went home, pulled my hair straight back in a bun, and wiped off all traces of makeup, save for some heavy, sagging eyebrows. I borrowed a pair of Mother's glasses to complete the look, and then I grabbed an old Polaroid and snapped some pictures. Whatever I'd done to myself, I'd done right (or wrong, depending), because I looked like some serious coyote bait. I raced down to the producers' office with the pictures, and one look convinced them they had a definite hag on their hands. Gooch was mine.

Dad was thrilled, and we were both initially excited when it looked like his schedule would be clear of banquets and functions for opening night. But then, on second look, his calendar told him he was to be in Europe, representing President Nixon — at, among other things, a Fourth of July celebration in Denmark — during the exact two weeks I was to be across the street from the old Governor's Mansion, learning from Auntie Mame that "Life's a banquet, and most poor suckers are starving to death."

Oh, well. . . .

I think Dad always regretted times like these, at least a little bit, the way the tug and pull of his public life kept him from enjoying firsthand the successes of his children. Oh, he enjoyed them with us in spirit, and he was always there for us emotionally, but it's never quite the same as being there in person. There was a genuine disappointment in his voice when he told me to break a leg, but to break it without him and Nancy in the audience. On the other end of the phone, I was doing all I could to hide my own disappointment because I knew deep down that what he was doing was terribly important, at least far more important than coming to see me dressing down as Agnes Gooch.

Mother couldn't make it, either, though she was usually in the front row of my cheering section. She had been in San Diego to help me celebrate some wonderful notices in *Guys and Dolls*. Indulge me for a moment and listen to this *Variety* review: "Maureen Reagan is excellent, delivering her lines and songs on the right note of worldly innocence. Moreover, she has a comedic presence and wide-eyed sparkle." I put that wide-eyed sparkle to work during that spring of 1972 — with John Saxon, Eileen Brennan, and Art Metrano — among the wonderful Runyonesque characters headed for salvation in a floating crap game.

There's a cherished story that goes with my appearance in *Guys and Dolls.* On opening night Mother ran into the pianist Van Cliburn in our hotel (he was returning from a concert) and convinced him to join our party. Toward the end of the evening Mother, who as I've mentioned is an obsessive neat freak, began clearing away the glasses and ashtrays from our table; Van, resplendent in white tie and tails, leapt to his feet and said, "Oh, no, Jane! Let me. I'm dressed for the job!"

Another cherished memory with a show-business connection happened on a rainy night in Texas in 1972, when I was riding in the cast car to a performance of Neil Simon's *Last of the Red Hot Lovers.* The car, which was being driven by Wally Engelhart, an affable comedic actor who played the lead in our show, screeched to a halt, and I looked up from my pre-show musings to see a tiny, wet, bedraggled black dog staring hopelessly into our headlights. Judy Cassmore, a tall red-headed actress (the perfect Elaine Novatio), was with us in the car, and deciding without much biological evidence that this beguiling mixture of poodle and dachshund was male, she named him Barney after the lead character in the play. We quickly discovered that Barney was, in fact, female, and we changed the spelling of her name to Barnea, as in Chelsea. We searched the area for weeks to find Barnea's rightful owner before finally giving up. I felt awful that somebody out there might be wondering about this almond-eyed dreamboat of a pooch, but not too awful; I don't think Barnea minded too much herself, because on that rainy night Barnea found herself a new owner, and she signed on as my faithful canine companion for the next eleven years.

Mother joined us on the road for a performance of *Lovers* (she was a regular groupie when it came to my acting career), and she immediately pooh-poohed the idea of my adopting a dog. She's always been right about most things, and she was right about this — I was on the road as often as not, and that was no kind of life to bestow upon a dog — but then she took one look at Barnea, with her wagging tail and adoring eyes, and she, too, fell in love. She even met us at the airport on our return to Los Angeles. Mother hadn't picked me up at the airport in ten years, and yet there she was in the vintage Rolls Royce she facetiously called The Truck, looking like her appearance there was the most natural thing in the world. Could it possibly have been Barnea she had come to meet?

Possibly. Make that probably. Waiting for us at my apartment was a sign on the door reading, "Welcome Home Barnae," with the last two letters inverted. Mother never could spell, but we didn't want to hurt her feelings, so we changed the poor dog's name yet again. Barnae looked past the error, in the direction of a heaping batch of welcome-home cookies baked in her honor. Mother went overboard for that dog. We all did, and I've got a performance in a Neil Simon play, on a rainy night in an out-of-the-way place, to thank for her coming into my life. She was an otherworldly gift, and we bumped into each other at just the right time for both of us.

It strikes me now that I did a lot of plays on the road during this time. Just before we closed a tour of *Any Wednesday* in Austin, Texas, I was asked by President Nixon's reelection people to participate in a local political event for the fall campaign. (Dad, of course, was not seeking the office with an incumbent President up for reelection.) It wasn't the first time I'd juggled two things at once, and so I did my bit of light comedy at night and squeezed in a little campaign work on the side.

The Nixon people informed me that they were sending "a gentleman from Washington" to help me kick off the voter registration drive in Austin and surrounding parts. The state of Texas is one of several that does not register its voters by party, which means that each party has to canvass door to door to identify which voters will vote for their candidates. That was to be my mission here along with the mysterious Washington gentleman, and I walked up to our designated rally site on this Saturday morning in late September 1972 not knowing who, or what, to expect.

"How do you do?" I heard from over my shoulder, and then I turned to find the extended hand of a kind-looking, bespectacled man. "I'm Secretary of the Treasury George Shultz. I hear we'll be working together" — and then he leaned over as if to whisper, and added — "but what exactly are we supposed to do?"

I was instantly charmed. "Oh, Mr. Secretary," I said, taking his hand. "We'll just ring some doorbells and talk to some people we've never met before and probably have a whole lot of fun."

He didn't seem all that convinced — neither was I, for that matter — but by the time we were through I had proved myself right. We had a grand old time, and he seemed to thoroughly enjoy talking to the people and getting a real good sense of what was in their hearts and on their minds. When we parted that afternoon he gave me a big hug and said, "Well, Maureen, you were right. That was a whole lot of fun."

Secretary Shultz did more than just give me a hug. He also wrote a letter to his good friend Governor Reagan, proclaiming, "I have just met your secret weapon!" And he has remembered our outing over the years. I can't tell you how many times I've been present at some function or other and overheard Secretary of State Shultz explain the workings of the American political system to a visiting dignitary by telling them of his day at my side in grassroots campaigning. And he always finishes up his little show-and-tell by saying, "And it was fun!" I still get a kick out of the fact that I was a part of that experience for him, and that that experience has been passed on to so many over the years.

I also still get a big kick out of being called Dad's "secret weapon," and by the early 1970s I was beginning to set my sights on some important new terrain. All around me the country was waking up to a new way of thinking about men and women and to the new way men and women were thinking about each other. The women's liberation movement was in full swing, and suddenly the traditional male and female roles were thrown into question. Women were demanding equality in every aspect of their lives, including the right to choose a career and a life-style.

Although I did not officially become a part of the movement until 1973 — I'll get to that a little bit later — I suppose I had been a closet feminist all my life. I'm sure there were a great many women out there like myself, women who believed in the cause but did not have an organization or a movement to belong to or a national voice to help them articulate their beliefs and their values. The women's movement did that and

so much more for so many women, but there was a time there
when I was more than a little reluctant to add my voice to the
chorus. You have to remember that the 1960s, politically
speaking, were a time of extreme polarization. If you were a
conservative or a liberal, you didn't dare socialize with someone of an opposing philosophy. That's the way it was back
then. A lot of us formed our attachments and our allegiances
along party lines. We let politics choose our friends for us,
and we let it determine the issues we believed in, the issues
we fought for. It was in this climate that feminism was nurtured, largely by the same liberal Democrats who were so
openly opposed to our involvement with the Vietnam war. To
conservative Republicans like myself and my father, that association made the women's liberation movement suspect at
best.

But the gap between liberals and conservatives narrowed on
this one issue; equal rights for women cut across party lines.
Both sides were bemoaning the fact that a divorced or widowed woman lost her credit rating the moment she was no
longer attached to a man. Both sides watched in horror as the
state of California imposed probate taxes on the entire estate
of a deceased man, even though our community-property laws
meant that one half of the estate belonged legally and right-
fully to the spouse. Both sides were even more outraged to
learn that in the case of a woman's death, only half the estate
was taxed. No matter what your political views, it became increasingly and abundantly clear that we were living in a society where women did not share power equally with men.

In an otherwise enlightened age, we were still pretty much
in the dark on this one.

My transformation from actress to women's liberation activist was quickened one afternoon in 1973 when the microphones of talk radio were once again opened to me. I got a
call from my agent with the news: "KABC-Radio" — a local
radio station in Los Angeles — "wants you to host a talk show,"
he enthused over the phone.

I had just returned from the *Any Wednesday* tour, and I was
not in any kind of mood for prank calls. Since I'd just done
the play, the first thing that entered my mind was my being
out there on my own, filling up dead airtime without even the

small benefits of a script or a rehearsal. But this was no prank call. It may have come completely out of left field, but my agent was serious. "Come on, kid," he coaxed, "you've done this before. You've given speeches before, you've answered questions in front of an audience before. What have all those years in politics prepared you for if not for this kind of show?"

He was right. I was prepared. And so I steeled myself against my nerves and took the job. Before long I was filling the KABC airwaves with four hours of quick-on-my-feet commentary every Saturday afternoon. We covered a variety of subjects from what a young girl should wear for graduation to gun control. My producer, a veteran of local talk radio named Louise Brooks, would comb the community for themes that would ease the strain of booking interviews on Saturdays, when most prospective guests preferred a day at the beach to an afternoon on the hot seat alongside yours truly.

Soon I began filling in during other time slots for vacationing hosts, and that led to a six-day-a-week show of my own, from six to eight in the evening. I would get up in the morning at about five, in time to pick up the network news feed and acquaint myself with the news of the day. I would then set to work lining up interviews to be taped during the day or to be conducted live; since we were on the West Coast, it was necessary for us to get an early start because many of our telephone interviews were conducted with guests in New York or Chicago or Washington. It was quite a hectic schedule, but I was in love with the job and the medium, so I didn't mind.

All along Louise and I had a back-and-forth argument going between ourselves about women's rights issues. As a liberal Democrat she had very definite views on women's equality, and she kept teasing me that if I would just examine the subjects that made me so angry I would find a feminist soul lurking beneath my conservative exterior. Our debate was a good-natured one, unlike others raging among those with opposing viewpoints, and something told me Louise might be right, at least about this particular issue.

Eventually we found a hook for a show on the women's rights issue, which I was not yet supporting: the Republican-dominated Arizona state legislature had failed that spring to ratify the Equal Rights Amendment and instead had passed a comprehensive piece of legislation repealing over a hundred discriminatory laws. We planned to devote our entire four-hour show that week to exploring the legislative future of women.

Louise had arranged an in-studio guest for one hour, and I had arranged a telephone interview with the governor of California (yes, I had an inside track), in which we would discuss probate reform. It was due simply to chance and fate, in concert, that Louise's guest — Dr. Judith Steihm, a professor of political science at USC who taught the provocative course "Sex, Power and Politics" — was scheduled to appear on the show before Dad. We spent the better part of the professor's hour discussing Arizona's legislative reforms, the ERA, and the need for women to be more assertive in business and politics. Despite our opposing political philosophies, Dr. Steihm and I saw eye to eye on most points.

As we were running out of time, my guest turned the tables on me. "Maureen," she said, "listen to yourself. I hear the same thing from so many women. You sit there and agree with me on every aspect of women's equality and still refuse to join the movement of women working for their liberation. You can't have it both ways. We're going to work together and win, or we're going to sit back, do nothing, and lose."

She was absolutely right. How could we be in such agreement on the issues that so affected our well-being as women and as a society, and still allow political polarization to divide us because we disagreed about basic economic philosophy? I turned to Dr. Steihm and said, "Judith, as of this moment, I am a women's liberationist."

We all have certain watershed moments in our lives, turning points where our thoughts or ideals or goals crystallize into something resembling reality. For me this was one of those moments.

It may have been an accident that my transformation to card-carrying member of the women's liberation movement occurred on a live talk-radio show, but it was no mishap. I felt a tremendous unburdening as I said these words, partly because I was acknowledging for the first time that working toward equality for women was something I very much wanted to do, in spite of the fact that it was going to distance me from my father.

Years before, someone had told me I would come of age on the day I identified for myself a personal revolution. Finally I'd found that personal revolution, and at thirty-two I was set to cast some shadows of my own.

But just as my on-air admission lifted one burden, I now felt the weight of another: I had publicly committed myself to the cause, and I now had to help to accomplish the very same goals that a great number of women had been working a great number of years to achieve.

Louise Brooks witnessed my transformation from across the studio. I could see her in the booth, grinning as she held up a note telling me my next interview was on the line. Dad! I'd almost forgotten about him! Before all this happened I had settled on the subject of probate reform for our interview, since I knew he was as incensed as I was at such a flagrant miscarriage of justice.

But now suddenly I had some more pressing matters at hand. "Good afternoon, Governor," I said as all of Los Angeles eavesdropped on our conversation. "You will be happy or unhappy to learn I am now a women's liberationist."

Dad, never at a loss for words, let out a hearty laugh at the other end of the line and said, "I think I liked you better when you were a militant moderate." That got a good laugh out of me.

Before long we had launched into a comprehensive analysis of tax fairness for women, and we both expressed hope that this legislation for probate reform would be passed and signed within the year.

Louise Brooks and I devoted several more shows to women's issues, including one featuring a new phenomenon — rape crisis centers. Only ten cities at that time had any kind of hotline to assist rape victims, and we thought that by reporting this fact to our southern California listening audience, we might create a popular movement for more government and community support in this much-needed area. Rape, as we pointed out, is not a sexual crime. It is a violent act. It is the ultimate violation of a woman as a human being, and to my mind it ranks right up there with child abuse as one of society's most heinous crimes.

People started to take notice of my staunch support of women's rights. The National Women's Political Caucus (a bipartisan feminist organization) and ERA America (a ratification campaign group) called upon me over the next few months to visit other states in support of the Equal Rights Amendment. At meetings in St. Louis, Chicago, New York, and Miami and throughout California, I would come across Republican friends who, like me, believed that these were issues that demanded our attention.

When the ERA was ratified in California in 1972, Governor Reagan endorsed its passage. But over the years his position softened somewhat, and now, looking back, I have to think he was given some bad advice on how to endear himself to some of his more conservative friends and supporters. There's no other way I can reconcile Dad's about-face on this all-important issue.

A few years after my on-air epiphany, I scheduled one of my phone calls, through Helene Von Damm, to talk to Dad about his position. "How can you change your mind on such an important issue?" I wanted to know as soon as he picked up the phone.

"Now, Mermie," he started in. ("Now, Mermie" at the beginning of a call usually meant I had said or done something Dad disagreed with; to this day Dad can't hear the words "I disagree" without keeping me on the phone while he convinces me of his point of view, and even if I said, "Dad, let's agree to disagree about this," he'd continue to prove his point.) "What we really have here is another way for government to interfere in people's lives. I don't know about you, but I don't want to live in a country where women are drafted into combat."

Dad was dishing out the standard arguments. Opponents of the Equal Rights Amendment would regularly paint a picture of battalions of bayonet-wielding women charging the enemy across an open field; whenever we'd mention that the draft had ended and no one, male or female, could be conscripted into military service, they'd turn and try some other tack, only to return to this argument again and again. Hearing this old argument — it was old even then — just made me more determined to prove my point; hearing it from my father just made me frustrated. I knew how tough it would be to win him over; I also knew how important winning him over would be, both for the equality effort and for our personal relationship.

"Dad, just look at the facts," I pleaded, reminding him that Congress already had the right to draft women, even if women did not have full equality under the laws of this land. "Next you'll tell me that the ERA will result in us all using the same toilets," I said. "That's another great argument for why we must depend only on the individual laws at each level of government, with no constitutional guarantee."

"You have the same guarantees as anyone else under the Fourteenth Amendment," he said.

"Yes," I agreed. "We cannot be discriminated against because of race, creed, or prior condition of servitude. But that amendment does not include gender discrimination, because Congress deliberately left it out." I told him I thought the Congressional thinking at the time must have been, "Look, we take good care of our women! They don't need this protection in writing." I told him I thought there was no other way to explain the exclusion.

"Now, Mermie," he said. ("Now, Mermie" at the end of a call usually meant the same thing as it did at the beginning.) "It seems like you've done your homework, but I'm afraid I must disagree with you."

Dad, I thought to myself, borrowing one of his favored and often-parodied expressions, there you go again!

This was one argument I wouldn't back down on. As much as I have always hated disagreeing with my father, I concluded our conversation that day knowing I would never give in on this issue. I also came away knowing that Dad and I would never see each and every issue in exactly the same way; we can agree in principle about some very basic things, but it's all right to break from each other once in a while.

We are, after all, two different people.

From there I would go on to espouse the values and virtues of the ERA wherever I could find an audience — in speeches, at banquets, on talk shows. Anywhere a debate was brewing, I'd take up our side; if there was no debate, I'd try to get one going. I traveled the country reminding women — and men — of the basic principles of the ERA: if a law restricts women's rights, that law will no longer be valid; if it protects women, that protection will be extended to men. I reminded them that the ERA concerned legal attitudes, not personal relationships.

The concept of equal rights for women was not new to that particular time and place in our history. In fact, there is a famous letter that was sent more than two hundred years ago by Abigail Adams to her husband, John, who was off in Philadelphia helping to draft our Declaration of Independence. "In the new code of laws which I suppose it will be necessary for you to make," she wrote on May 7, 1776, "I desire that you would remember the ladies and be more generous and favorable to them than your ancestors. Remember that all men would be tyrants if they could. If particular attention is not paid to the ladies, we are determined to foment a rebellion and will not hold ourselves bound by any laws in which we have no voice or representation."

Her husband replied, "Be assured we know better than to repeal our masculine systems."

But that did not end women's fight for equality. Nineteenth-century women such as the writer Margaret Fuller; Elizabeth Blackwell, the first American woman to graduate from medical school; Victoria Woodhull, the first woman candidate for President; and the mothers of women's suffrage, Elizabeth Cady Stanton and Susan B. Anthony, were only a few of the thousands of women who worked unceasingly throughout our history for women's right to vote and for equal opportunity.

The right to vote was won, under the Nineteenth Amendment, in 1920, but full equality under the law was still not forthcoming. By 1982, ten years after Congressional passage of the ERA, only thirty-five states had ratified the amendment; we still needed three more states to join their ranks before the amendment could become law. But time ran out on the ratification effort, which remains as important today as when it was first introduced to Congress more than sixty-five years ago.

We may have lost the war on this one, but I succeeded in

winning a personal victory. Acting, which had always been as much a private joy to me as it was a public frustration, began to move further and further down on my career résumé as more and more I filled my time with rallying around causes I firmly believed in. Through a chance encounter on a radio talk show and through some very public rolling-up-of-sleeves with my father, I had stumbled upon a new world, and a new way for me to make my way in that world. For the time being, at least, I was headed in the right direction.

And as for the ERA — well, I'm still not entirely convinced that fight is over.

13

Kansas City, 1976

THERE IS A TENDENCY among us political
animals to think in blocks of four years. Time can move along
in chunks, from one election to the next, and the space between campaigns often passes so quickly it seems like a blur.
After Richard Nixon's landslide election to a second term as
President in 1972, the Reagan people (myself forcefully included) all set our sights on the 1976 election year for a second
run at the office. But in the wake of the Watergate scandal
and Nixon's fall from grace, most Republicans remember the
intervening four years as a time they'd like to forget.

So for political animals of the Republican persuasion, those
were four years that couldn't pass quickly enough.

Dad's second term as governor was carried out pretty much
without incident. Now, I read over that line and even to me
it sounds a little like Ronald Reagan didn't accomplish anything during that time, but that's not the case at all. Rather,
with the loss of the legislature to Democratic control, he succeeded in bridging the partisan gap to the degree that he was
able to govern and to manage state affairs with surprising ef-
fectiveness. The even course he'd set out on during his first
term remained straight and true during his second. And all
along his stock as a politician of national influence continued

to rise. To many he was seen as our last great hope for unify-
ing a party demoralized by the Watergate break-in and its
aftermath.

He put a cap on his two-term governorship when he appeared on a local television show called "A.M. Los Angeles,"
on KABC-TV, where I was serving as one of the show's first
hosts. There's a story that goes with that. (There's always a
story, right?) What happened was that the network was due
to carry the inauguration of Governor Jerry Brown at ten o'clock
that morning, which was precisely when we went off the air.
We were having one of our production meetings, and somebody wanted to know if my father would be attending the
ceremonies; I told them that I hardly thought so, and then I
suggested that we have him on our show just beforehand.

Everyone was delighted with the idea, and so was the governor when I invited him. In fact, he later used his scheduled
appearance as an excuse when he was eventually asked to
participate in the inaugural. "I can't," he said. "I promised
my daughter I'd be on her television show."

Anyway, we'd booked Dad for two seven-minute segments
at the tail end of our show. We needed him on the set, live,
at 9:45 in the morning, which meant he ought to be in the
studio by about nine o'clock. Keep in mind, he left office that
very day, and he hadn't sat behind the wheel of a car in eight
years, since there had always been a driver to take him wherever he needed to go. Now that he was on his own, I wanted
to be sure he knew exactly how to get to the studio.

"Oh, I know where that is," he said when I sat him down
to give him directions.

"I'm sure you do, Dad," I said, "but there are different traffic
patterns since you used to drive. You'll be coming in in the
height of rush hour. I just want to make sure you leave enough
time."

Well, he assured me he'd be there with time to spare, and
we began promoting the segments. Really, it was a big coup
getting the governor like that, leading right into the inauguration. Management was thrilled. I was genuinely looking forward to his visit, as was my cohost, Dave Michaels, who now
works at Cable News Network. We'd each come up with a

long list of questions, some tough, some not so tough, all of them interesting.

By 9:15, though, Dad was nowhere to be found. Time was running out. We called Nancy, who informed us that he'd left home with a friend of his over an hour earlier. (Great, I remember thinking, at least one of them can navigate.) Fifteen minutes passed, and there was still no sign of him. We had nothing else in the can to fill the last two segments; without Ronald Reagan, Dave Michaels and I would be left on the set twiddling our thumbs.

In the world of live television this is what's known as a crisis.

Finally, at just after 9:30, one of our writers, Bill Harris (who is now a well-known movie critic and has always been a big fan of Ronald Reagan the actor and Ronald Reagan the politician), grabbed my briefcase and said, "Will your father recognize your briefcase?"

I had no idea what he was up to, but I told him sure, I guessed so. "It's just a briefcase," I said. "We've never talked about it."

Bill was gone in a flash, briefcase in hand, and darted out to the corner of Prospect and Talmadge, just outside the studio. He was scanning furiously up and down the street, looking for a car that he thought might have lost its way. When a likely candidate rolled into view, he stepped out into the street and began waving my briefcase frantically in the air until the car came to a halt. (He must have looked like a lunatic!)

He guessed right on the car, because Dad stepped out of the one he'd flagged down. "It's Maureen's briefcase," Bill Harris shouted. "Come with me!"

(I'm still not sure why Bill thought he needed the briefcase to get his point across, but the fact that he did makes it a better story.)

And with that he grabbed the governor and whisked him through the emergency entrance to the studio with just one minute and fifteen seconds to spare. Dave Michaels and I were in a cold sweat by this point; we were so frazzled, we didn't know what to say.

Dad sat down on the set, cool as a cucumber. We were all

completely unnerved by the whole thing — all was not quiet on the set, believe me — and he was just as calm as could be.

While I was collecting myself, my father leaned in as though he had something to confide to me. "I don't know what you were all so worried about," he said as the director was counting down the last few seconds to air. "I told you I'd be here in time." And then he flashed me his trademark smile.

I've got some other wonderful memories from my stint at KABC. Dan Rather, of all people, came through town on a tour to promote a book he had written about the Nixon administration. (Almost all of our guests, incidentally, were authors, movie stars, or politicians, with books or movies or causes to promote.) I couldn't get over how nervous he was, a man who'd spent all that time in front of the camera. I'm sure George Bush would have loved to have a chance to keep the CBS anchorman on the edge of his seat like I did. But seriously, I'm sure it had nothing to do with my skills as an interviewer and everything to do with the fact that Dan Rather was not used to having the tables turned on him like that. He was used to being the interviewer, not the interviewee, and he was clearly unsettled by the change in his role. You could even see his hands shaking. Other than his nervousness, the only thing I remember about the interview was a great story he told about starting out as a print journalist in Houston and then switching to broadcast because his editor told him his future looked pretty dim unless he could learn how to spell.

I had a chance to interview some fascinating people. Angela Davis, the underground activist, turned up one day with her own book to sell, but she chose as her pitch a vilification of the Reagan administration in Sacramento and the Nixon administration in Washington; I don't think her publisher was entirely thrilled with her salesmanship, but it did make for some interesting television.

Gore Vidal came on with the sequel to his book *Myra Breckenridge*, this one called *Myron*, in which he referred to various parts of the male anatomy by the names of various Justices of the Supreme Court. (I wonder what he would have come up with for Sandra Day O'Connor, had the notion occurred to him a few years later.) It was really quite a book, and if you've ever seen Gore Vidal interviewed you'll know that he is a character. I opened things up with an innocuous line like "First we had Myra, and now we have Myron," and then he just looked at me and tacked on ". . . she said tremulously." That was how the whole interview went, he was just carrying on so. I'll have to admit, he was pretty funny. Finally I just put down my notes and sat back and laughed. I couldn't help it. Besides, it was pointless to do anything but let this man run with it the way he wanted to run with it. When it came time to close the segment, I said, "I'm so glad you were here to take over the show for me." And he said, "Wait, wait, we haven't talked politics." And I said, "You're right about that." And then we went to commercial.

We had a lot of fun on the set. One time we brought my dog, Barnae, out for a spoof commercial hawking a product called Doggie Dent, a toothpaste for pooches. We had a whole script worked out for her and everything. It was a riot!

Dad was watching the show that day, and that evening he gave me a call with his two cents' worth. "I certainly hope you're gonna sell that as a commercial," he said.

"Why?" I wanted to know.

"You didn't see it?"

"No," I said. "We were all too busy laughing."

"Well, Barnae was busy licking away at the toothbrush," my father explained. "It was the perfect testimonial."

"Wanna be her agent?" I asked.

"I'll keep it in mind," he said.

After KABC I worked briefly at its rival station KNBC, hosting a series called "Women In," as in "Women in Banking," "Women in Sports," "Women in Politics." . . . You get the idea. We looked for occupations and specialties where women were very new to the field. For example, we found that in the entire city of Los Angeles at that time, there was only one woman who was the head chef at a major restaurant. I remember pointing out that the women of the 1970s were supposed to still be in the kitchen — at home — but they were obviously not supposed to get paid for it.

From KNBC I went to KNXT-TV, the local CBS affiliate, where I worked on a show called "It Takes All Kinds." It was a Saturday public affairs and human interest show dealing with local issues. One week, for example, we covered the refurbishing of the fabled *"Hollywood"* sign. Did you know that more than fifty years ago, the sign was put up as part of a housing promotion? It's true. At first it read *"Hollywoodland,"* but somehow the tail end of the sign disappeared over the years, and what's left of it has been sitting in the hills above Hollywood, California, ever since, making an inadvertent landmark of itself.

Things were going well for me professionally, even if I had shifted my focus somewhat over the years. I was still going out on auditions for dramatic roles, but I was beginning to fall into casting-director limbo — that awkward period of time when you're too old to be believable in the young adult roles and too young to be believable in the mature adult roles. Parts were few and far between, so I seized on this opportunity for steady work in television news and public affairs programming. Besides, where else could an opinionated daughter of a former governor get a chance to speak her mind before a guaranteed audience in the nation's second-largest television market?

But enough about me. . . .

When Dad left Sacramento in 1975, the wheels were all in place for another run at the presidency. As soon as he left office, he began doing daily five-minute radio commentaries that were syndicated to more than two hundred stations nationwide, which kept him very much in the public ear. It also kept him very busy; it's not easy to research and explore a different topic for discussion every day of the week, but it was the kind of work my father truly loved. He said it reminded him of his early radio days; as a matter of fact, the first two stations in the country to sign on for syndication rights were the two Iowa stations where he had landed his first broadcasting jobs as a young man.

The presidential effort was still exploratory at this point, but if a campaign was to be mounted, it would be a full-scale campaign and not a favorite-son candidacy, as in 1968.

I know this sounds like hindsight now, but I didn't think the time was right for him in 1976. I didn't think the time was right for the Republican party so soon after Watergate. The mood of the country felt oddly like we were all waiting for another shoe to drop. Voter outrage at the excesses and abuses of the Nixon administration was measurable, and it would certainly carry over into this next presidential election. Americans needed time to forgive before they could be asked to forget the Nixon administration. I was troubled, too, by the recent outbursts of political violence, notably the attempts made on the life of President Gerald Ford.

And yet by the summer of 1975 Dad and his advisers were leaning nearly all the way toward a White House run. Dissatisfaction with the incumbent candidacy of Gerald Ford led many party leaders to encourage my father to seek the nomination. Ford was Nixon's President, the thinking went, and the party needed to distance itself as much as possible from the previous administration.

As late as Halloween night 1975, I was still trying to convince Dad to lean in the other direction; he had called a family meeting of sorts to discuss the pros and cons of his decision. Now, keep in mind, Dad had developed a near-constant dialogue with the American people — through his radio broadcasts and through a consuming schedule of public appearances — and wherever he turned, he was being urged to run. Dad felt very strongly that if he didn't declare himself a candidate this time around, he'd be seen as some kind of hypocrite. After all, he'd been calling for a change in our systems for a good many years, and the time had come when he either had to put himself on the line or start changing his message.

So we were all called out to the house to kick it around. We've never been the kind of family for family meetings — in fact, this was the first (and as it turned out, the last) — but Dad wanted us all to have a chance to lay everything out on the table before he went ahead with whatever it was he was going ahead with.

Right away I was transported back to the car conversations of my growing up. There was nothing spontaneous about our little dialogue. Dad had a speech all prepared, and it was clear to me as we all sat down that he had thought about this meeting for a good long while before we all got there.

I gave it my last, best shot. My basic message was for him to wait, to remove himself from the mad scramble to bring new leadership to the Republican party. In four years, I argued, he could bring a fresh vision, fresh hope; the way would be paved for him. Michael, meanwhile, couldn't have been more enthusiastic about the idea; he had become more and more politically active over the past several years and had at last taken an interest in Dad's new career. I was glad for that, even if I didn't share his enthusiasm. Michael's soon-to-be wife, Colleen (they were married the next month), was delighted at the prospect of having a President for a father-in-law. Ron, at seventeen, was more concerned with his costume for a Halloween party that evening than with what his father might do for the next few months. Patti was even less interested and chose not to show up.

Nancy, as ever, was utterly supportive of Dad's wishes and, to a lesser degree, the family's wishes. She recognized the burden all First Ladies and all would-be First Ladies must shoulder, and she said she felt up to it. In fact, she said that she was excited at the possibilities and that she had a great many ideas about changing what until then had been an unassuming role. Remember, in 1968 she was hardly a factor in Dad's campaign, because Dad's campaign was hardly a campaign. This time around, though, she would figure quite significantly in all aspects of the effort, and as a result she would contribute a great deal to Dad's decision making.

We sat around the living room of the Pacific Palisades house, which at that time was decorated with red floral-print furniture, and I stared out at our spectacular nighttime view of Los Angeles and tried to imagine what we would be like as a First Family. But nothing came easily to mind, which I took as a signal that something was wrong. It was like those old games where you're supposed to spot what's wrong with a certain picture. Well, what was wrong with this picture was the timing. It was too soon.

As we were winding down our discussion, Michael kicked in with, "What is your running gonna do to Merm's situation in the business?"

"I don't think it will have any effect at all," Dad replied.

"Yeah," I said, "I'll be a forty-three-year-old character actress by the time you leave office."

"Well," Dad said back, smiling, "how old do you think I'll be?"

"It doesn't matter how old you'll be," I answered. "You're already a leading man."

But despite my caution, Dad made his decision, and he formally announced his candidacy on November 20, 1975, in Washington, D.C., as part of a five-state announcement and campaign swing. Many of my fears were nearly realized right off the bat, when Dad's campaign stopped in Florida to announce at a rally there. A crazed man emerged from the crowd, brandishing a toy pistol aimed at my father. It was only a toy pistol, but the early radio reports of the incident failed to make mention of that, and I was panicked when I got only the first version of the story. I called the local radio station and stayed on the line as new wire copy was being fed into their machines, until I finally heard the whole story and was able to breathe again.

Still, an incident like that so early in Dad's campaign threw me into an anxious depression. I should have been all rah-rah on his behalf — in campaign mode — but I was pulling something back, and this incident pulled me back even further. Why would somebody want to pull a gun — even a toy gun — on my father? And worse, what was to prevent somebody else from turning on him with a real weapon? But then I reminded myself of the question I had posed to Frank Mankiewicz several years earlier, about Robert Kennedy's concern for his own safety. Dad, like every great leader, has always been concerned first for his vision, for what he wanted to accomplish; when he's toiling for America's greater good, I'm sure he doesn't give a thought to his personal safety.

You become hardened to the loss of privacy, to the risk of exposure, after so many years in public life, but in the fall of 1975 I was still somewhat soft in this area. This will take some getting used to, I remember thinking. There are a lot of sick people out there, and presidential candidates and their families are easy targets.

Dad, though, put the Florida "shooting" behind him and set about the business at hand. One of the chief campaign issues was the country's role in international relations, and on that front Dad had staked out two territories that struck a resounding chord with Republican audiences: the Panama Canal and détente with the Soviet Union.

He opposed a treaty that would relinquish control of the canal to the Panamanian government, an act of American good will and good faith that he felt undermined our national defense strategies at a dangerous moment in world history.

On the issue of détente, my father said the Soviets were winning the war of words, painting a picture of the United States as a declining power. That, the candidate said, would quickly change under a Reagan administration.

Of course there were other issues fueling the debate during the primary season, but the signals sent on these fronts served to position Ronald Reagan as a champion of American interests in Central America and of American influence, power, and prestige at home and abroad.

Stu Spencer at last was out of the picture. He had signed on with Ford's campaign. That's politics, right? So with my new friend Lyn Nofziger in charge of the Reagan effort in California, Michael and I were finally allowed to emerge from hiding. It was like being let out of school on the last day. I made speeches on Dad's behalf, and Michael found that he was very good at meeting voters one-on-one, making them feel how essential their support was to the campaign. Remember, this marked the first time Michael was "inside" a campaign — any campaign — and it wasn't long before he was bitten by the same political bug that had gotten its teeth into the rest of us.

In 1976 there weren't as many contested primaries as we've seen in more recent elections, and so the smoke-filled back rooms still held the key to delegate support. (Dad actually delivered over a hundred thousand popular votes more than Ford in contested primaries that year.) In fact, Ford won the kickoff New Hampshire primary by only the slimmest of margins — 49 percent to 48 percent — and yet the press portrayed the incumbent (but appointed) President as an overwhelming favorite for the party's nomination. I wouldn't call a 1 percent margin of victory anything but underwhelming, and neither did Ronald Reagan, who turned a deaf ear to cries that he bow out of the race and save the party from a long primary battle.

As the primary season ground on, the nomination became too close to call. We were hopeful that California, with one of the last primaries, would put us over the top. I even filmed a television commercial for the California primary. Sitting on the floor with a family scrapbook, I talked about the Ronald Reagan I knew, and why he should be President.

But California was not enough. The real battle for the 1976 nomination took place after all the primaries had been held. With the count so close, every day brought telephone calls with news of one or two delegates switching camps. Throughout the summer, as the convention neared, the candidates wooed delegates at every chance. Jerry and Betty Ford invited several uncommitted delegates to a state dinner for the Queen of England. Dad and Nancy responded by inviting several other uncommitteds (and several of the same uncommitteds, I'm sure) to lunch at their ranch.

(Dad and Nancy, by the way, had sold their place in Malibu Canyon when Dad signed on as governor; in 1974, as he was leaving office, they bought a four-hundred-acre ranch thirty miles north of Santa Barbara, overlooking the Santa Ynez Mountains. They've held on to it ever since, and one visit there will tell you why: it's absolutely gorgeous! Really, you can stand on their property and everywhere your eye can see is theirs. They've got a great view of the ocean on one side and a majestic view of the Santa Ynez Mountains on the other. The house itself is a tiny adobe structure with only a wood-burning stove for heat, but the setting is simply spectacular!)

One of the most frustrating campaign techniques deployed by Stu Spencer and his gang was to try to convince uncommitted delegates that a vote for Gerald Ford would get them Ronald Reagan as Vice President. Dad, for one thing, had no desire for the number-two spot, and the Ford people also had no intention of asking him to join their campaign as the President's running mate. It was nothing but dirty pool.

"Only the lead horse gets a change of view," Dad would say when asked about his willingness to consider the vice presidency.

Just before the Republican National Convention in Kansas City, Bob Abernethy of NBC News came out to the ranch to interview our candidate. Michael, Colleen, and I sat on the lawn and watched as Dad laid out the major issues of his campaign. During the interview Dad's new husky — a beautiful

animal named Taaka that he had inherited from a neighbor —
strolled into the picture and listened in along with the rest of
us. But when Bob Abernethy started to ask one of those "Is it
true you're a warmonger?" questions, Taaka stepped in on
Dad's behalf. She took the same offense as the rest of us at
the question, but she was able to do something about it. She
wandered into the shot, jumped up so her front paws were
resting on Dad's shoulders, and began licking his face. Taaka
seemed to be telling the NBC News cameras that nobody
understood her candidate the way she did.

I knew exactly how she felt. I had heard enough of this talk
of Dad's being Ford's Vice President. In fact, a small group of
us, including U.S. Senate hopeful Tom Malatesta, a longtime
Reagan booster, had been giving serious consideration to this
problem. We thought it would be wonderful strategy for Dad
to challenge Ford to a debate at the convention.

Over lunch that day at the ranch, before Taaka's playful defense, I had outlined our plan. "It will solve two problems," I
told my father. "First, it will silence all the talk about a deal
already having been made for you to be Vice President. And
second, there's the benefit of the debate itself. If we can get
support for the idea, the uncommitted delegates will see firsthand who handles himself better in that kind of situation."

"You don't think he'd really debate, do you?" Dad said after
carefully weighing the idea.

"Hell, no," I said. "He wouldn't be that crazy."

"After all," Dad joked, "Stu Spencer didn't work with me
all those years without learning something."

"Right," I laughed. "But whether he agrees to it or not is
not important. What's important is that you throw down the
gauntlet in such a way that you put an end to these vice-
presidency rumors."

Dad and Nancy both liked the idea. In fact, later that afternoon my father mentioned the possibility of a debate to NBC's
Abernethy. The reporter asked if this didn't mean the governor felt he was behind.

"No," Dad said. "To our thinking the race is dead even,
and our object is to move ahead."

As it turned out, Dad's campaign people adopted a strategy
of their own, which was intended to accomplish pretty much

the same thing. It was decided that Dad would choose Senator Richard Schweiker of Pennsylvania as his running mate in advance of the convention. That done, the campaign staff also proposed a rules change at the convention to institutionalize such early selection by all candidates. Their goal was the same as ours: to stop the erosion of support caused by the vice-presidency rumors.

I still believe the debate strategy was sound: it allowed for a popular groundswell of support with virtually no possibility of a backlash. I don't mean to take credit for the idea — I was more its messenger and loudest supporter — but it would have forestalled the feathers Dad's campaign ruffled with the Schweiker selection, because as the Kansas City convention loomed closer and closer on the calendar, it became more and more apparent that the Reagan group would not achieve their goal by the route they'd chosen.

The proposed rules change on vice-presidential selection was defeated at the convention. Oh, it created quite a flap, believe me.

The stage was set for a real shoot-out in Kansas City, and that's about what it felt like when we arrived at the convention hall. There are certain advantages to being the incumbent at a contested national convention. The Ford entourage had arranged for a sky box as well as a second box at the edge of the arena, right above the delegates. The Reagan group was allotted only the one sky box, which was perched high above the convention floor with no similar access to the arena, where members of the California delegation were seated. Even the California delegates and their alternates were separated by a bloc of Colorado alternates.

Stu Spencer, I'm sure, had a hand in all of this. It was actually very shrewd strategy. The Ford family would be mingling with the delegates and would appear, on television screens across the country, to be really involved in the whole nomination process; the Reagan family, though, would be relegated to the rafters and would appear to be either not participating or, worse, disinterested. We made some last-minute changes to our seating arrangements. State Senator Bob Beverly and I managed to convince some of the Colorado alternates to switch places with the Reagan party for the Wednesday night nomination festivities. These displaced alternates would get our sky box — which, for all its failings as a strategic location, really afforded a terrific view of the proceedings — and we would get to present a united front on the edge of the arena, directly behind and above the California delegation.

At a too-close-to-call convention such as the one held in Kansas City in 1976, appearances count for a great deal, as you'll soon see. For instance, the California and Texas delegations were situated on opposite sides of the arena; our Texas people were completely surrounded by the Ford delegations and directly under the arena box occupied by Betty Ford. This struck me then, and it still strikes me now, as an obvious ploy by the Ford people to isolate my father's loyal Texas delegation.

As a means of communicating encouragement across the convention floor, our California delegates would yell *"Viva!"* and the Texas delegates would shout back *"Olé!"* The other Reagan delegations in between would join in the chorus. It really was quite a scene — and a lot of fun — and it had the added effect of bringing the isolated Reagan loyalists from Texas into our celebration.

There was another benefit to the back-and-forth shouting. During the Wednesday night nomination proceedings, as Michael was about to escort Nancy down the stairs to our seats, I noticed that Betty Ford hadn't yet been seated. Obviously she was waiting for Nancy to come in, so she could then step on Nancy's entrance with her own. I didn't like it, and I thought there had to be some monkey wrench we could throw Betty's way. (This is the way you start to think when you're in the middle of a heated campaign.) Suddenly I had an idea. I began clapping and waving at the California delegation, which started up a few rousing *Viva*'s, which in turn launched our Texas delegates into a few boisterous *Olé*'s. Thinking this signaled Nancy's arrival, Betty Ford made her entrance. We quieted the crowd as best we could and allowed the Ford delegates to cheer Betty's arrival. She seemed thrilled, thinking she had cut short the welcome intended for Nancy.

As the Ford noise died down and Betty settled back, thinking she had one-upped us on this one, Nancy made her grand entrance on Michael's arm.

By this point, though, we knew it all would be too little, too late. After the Tuesday night defeat of the vice-presidency proposal, things were looking pretty grim. I remember comparing notes with Ron on where we were losing votes, since our winning was virtually a mathematical impossibility. Dad was counted out when West Virginia's delegation cast its votes for Ford, by a narrow margin. After the final count Ford had collected 1,187 delegate votes, while my father had received 1,070.

That afternoon I managed to steal a few minutes with Dad before we went to the hall for what we all knew would be defeat. "What really makes me sad, Mermie," he said, "is I really think I could make a difference, and now I won't have the chance."

I didn't know what to say, so I just touched him gently on the shoulder.

Later, after the balloting, he came up to me for a hug and said, "Your grandmother always said everything happens for a reason, and we will discover this reason. I promise." He was surprisingly strong and optimistic in the face of such a devastating loss.

He made a courageous showing, too, the following morning, when he met with his supporters in the ballroom of the Alameda Plaza Hotel. I don't think I have ever been more proud of him than I was on that day.

He paraphrased part of his favorite English ballad, John Dryden's "Johnnie Armstrong's Last Goodnight": "Lay me down and bleed a while," he said. "Though I am wounded, I am not slain; I shall rise and fight again."

When Dad and Nancy stepped into their sky box to hear Gerald Ford's acceptance speech on Thursday night, the delegates went crazy. They yelled and rang cowbells and blew horns and in a thousand ways showed their affection for the man who had finished second. I'll never forget the way Dad stood up on his seat so he could wave to everyone over the glass partition. The rousing welcome went on for over ten minutes, which seems like ten hours when you're in the middle of it. To tell the truth, I think Dad was a little embarrassed by the tremendous outpouring of affection, but I'm sure there was a part of him that was just loving it.

Frank Reynolds, the late ABC News anchorman, had been covering the Reagan campaign since New Hampshire, and he was standing behind us with a microphone, keeping up a running commentary for the news cameras positioned across the convention hall. As newspeople go, Frank Reynolds was always fair and a good friend to us Reagans, and even he seemed genuinely moved by the overwhelmingly warm welcome. Finally he leaned into the box and said, "Governor, how does this make you feel?"

"Well," Dad said, "I'm extremely grateful, there's just a great deal of affection, and I'm extremely grateful." He was, understandably, at a loss for words.

Frank Reynolds pulled back and said, "Not exactly journalistic derring-do, but it's his time, and let's let him have it."

Indeed.

After President Ford and his vice-presidential selection, Senator Bob Dole, had finished their acceptance speeches, the President invited Dad and Nancy to the podium. They declined the invitation at first; as my father told me later, he didn't want to do anything to take the spotlight away from the nominee. He knew it was Ford's night, and he was content to be a spectator.

On the second pass, though, Dad accepted this offer of party unity. He was asked to say a few words, and he spoke with no prepared text about America's future and about how this country is the greatest hope of all mankind. He asked what America would be like a hundred years from that day, and whether history would show that freedom prevailed over totalitarian adversaries. Maybe it's because I'm his daughter, but it seemed to me that during the few minutes he spoke, the Kansas City convention hall was quieter than it had been the entire week.

"They will know," he told that quiet hall, "whether we met our challenge. . . . We must go forth from here united, determined that what a great general said a few years ago is true: 'There is no substitute for victory, Mr. President.' "

I sat behind Dad and Nancy on the plane home to Los Angeles. Dad didn't look sad or defeated so much as he looked tired. Worn. But he wasn't letting on, and I knew that despite his strong front, he was bitterly disappointed by his loss. I tried to get inside his head, to feel what he was feeling, because I knew he would never break down and open up to me about something like this. As the plane taxied for takeoff, I thought back to the day we arrived in Kansas City, to the huge welcome he received on the lawn of the Alameda Plaza Hotel. There were a zillion balloons and a tremendous sense of hope and excitement. Now, though, all the balloons were deflated or gone, along with that hope and that excitement.

There were a lot of tears on that plane. The flight attendants who had traveled with the campaign charter for months were all crying. Even some members of the press who had covered the campaign from the very beginning were choked up on this return trip.

But Dad was holding up pretty well, at least outwardly. Inside, though, I'm sure he was hurting. He dropped his share of clues, too, that all was not as well with him as he would have it seem. As we landed in Los Angeles, for example, I noticed that I had one more picture to take to finish up my roll of film, so I yelled after the folks to stop and wave as they were getting into their car to go home. Dad grew suddenly impatient. "Hurry up," he said, almost gruffly, his voice thick with fatigue and tension and disappointment. And then, after I took the picture, he added, "I'm sorry, Mermie, I didn't mean to be short. I'm just tired."

"That's OK, Dad," I said. "We're all tired."

And then we hugged. I was a sobbing mess, but he was still a pillar of strength and dignity and grace. How he managed to hold on to the better part of his emotions, I'll never know, and whether or not he ever let go of them at home with Nancy, I'll never know, either.

As for me, I had shed my first tears for what we'd lost on Wednesday night, and I wouldn't run out of them for the rest of the week.

Lay us down and let us bleed a while, I thought, echoing Dad's Dryden poem. We shall rise and fight again.

14

Third Time's a Charm

THE OTHER SHOE DROPPED.

The Ford-Dole ticket lost out to a peanut farmer from Plains, Georgia, and the Republican party faithful set their clocks on snooze for the next few years.

I left a wake-up call for 1978. By then my acting career had petered out to the point where I was spending more time looking for work than actually working, and so I began to cast about for a new outlet for my energies. (And for a new way to earn a living!) I joined a fledgling operation called Sell Overseas America, which promoted United States exports to foreign markets. It is an enterprise I remain deeply committed to to this very day.

At the time, though, our trade deficit was becoming a serious drain on the economy and needed to be addressed by our business leaders as well as our political leaders; we hoped to contribute to the discussion of the problem and to encourage more American manufacturers to explore foreign markets. To fuel the debate (and to spread the good word), we published a magazine called *Showcase USA*, which I edited. I eventually became so immersed in the magazine and in a variety of trade issues that when the occasional acting job trickled in on its own, I invariably turned it down.

Eventually the trickle turned into a slow drip and then nothing at all. Had there been any one moment where I told myself I would never perform again, it would have been sad, but it was a gradual process for me. I looked up one day and it suddenly dawned on me that I hadn't acted or even gone out on an audition for a period of several months. I missed it, sure, but only when I stopped to think about it; most of the time I was too busy to notice.

By 1978 it had also become clear that Dad would be back for another try at the presidency. Actually his intentions had never been in doubt, at least not in my mind, but it was a few years before his supporters regrouped and started things up again.

There were many in the Reagan camp who felt that John Sears, who ran the 1976 campaign, was not the right man to take the helm for the 1980 effort. I counted myself among them. I urged my father to consider hiring someone else, and in fact he agreed that his interests would be better served by a different person. Dad assured me that under no circumstances would John Sears be involved in his 1980 campaign, but by the time he put his campaign staff together in the summer of 1979, John Sears was right there in the thick of it. To this day I have no idea what changed my father's mind, or who did the changing, but it was an almost fatal mistake, as we'll see.

Sharing power with Sears in these early days of the 1980 campaign were Lyn Nofziger, Mike Deaver, and Ed Meese. There would be a struggle among these four for control of the Reagan effort later. But for now John Sears was calling most of the shots related to campaign strategy.

We all traveled to New York in November 1979 for Dad's formal announcement at the Hilton Hotel. Even Patti was on hand for this one, and the candidate's children all sat together at a center table as we listened to our father outline the issues for his coming campaign. He seemed more confident than he had in 1976; I think the spontaneous show of affection at the close of the Kansas City convention had told him that his time would come, and there was a certain manner about him on this momentous day in New York that suggested that his time was now. He talked about America as a creative giant that could still lead the world in technology and production. He talked about America as a land of untapped natural and hu-

man resources, and he urged us all to turn loose the genius
of free enterprise and the generosity of our communities to
solve our domestic problems.

It was a rousing beginning.

The role of the candidate's family was to be greatly expanded this time around. Finally! I thought. For the first time
I would play a key role in a presidential campaign, and my
first candidate just happened to be my father. What a special
thrill! But I'm getting ahead of myself here. There was still
some resistance to my involvement that needed to be gotten
past.

Michael, who was becoming more and more taken with "the
family business," made a trip with Colleen to central Iowa
months before the caucuses there, and on his return he expressed concern to my father about the lack of organization
he'd found in the counties he visited. This was one of our first
signals that Sears had not laid the groundwork necessary to
take us through the primaries. Michael told Dad that with my
political experience, I could better assess the organization of
the upcoming precinct caucuses than he could, and that I should
go to Iowa. According to Michael, Dad called his campaign
office and told them to make the necessary arrangements.

Great, I thought, I'm on my way. But the campaign people
never called. (I didn't expect they would, to tell you the truth,
but I did wait by the phone just in case.) Before long Michael
and Colleen were back in Iowa, and I was still in Los Angeles,
anxious to be let out of the starting gate. As Michael later reported back to me, Charles Black, one of Sears's deputies, had
ordered Dad's scheduling people not to send me to Iowa. He
was concerned that all I would talk about was the ERA, and
that it would hurt Dad's campaign. When Michael passed this
information on to Dad, the campaign team was again instructed by the candidate to make arrangements for my departure, but again no call was forthcoming.

I had become numb to the insensitivity and shortsighted-
ness of Dad's campaign people over the years. The Spencer/
Roberts attitude — "If we don't talk to her or admit she exists,
maybe she'll go away" — was allowed to persist for so long
in Dad's early campaigns that it became difficult to break away
from that. And even though Spencer and Roberts were long

gone, those who followed just assumed that that was the way things were done.

Dad got around it all for me. I was working at the office one afternoon in late January 1980, just a week or so before the Iowa caucuses, when I got a call.

"Hi," Dad's familiar voice said over the phone. "How are you?"

"I'm fine," I said. "How are you?"

"Good. Want to go to Iowa?" He always gets directly to the point, my father.

It turned out Nancy had a bad case of the flu and would have to miss out on a scheduled campaign swing. Dad was taking the opportunity to circumvent his reluctant campaign team and get me out there in the field on his behalf; he thought that if he saw to the arrangements personally, nothing would get lost in translation.

At last I would hit the road for an official Reagan for President campaign swing!

"When?" I asked.

"Well, tomorrow would be nice."

Now, Iowa is not exactly the hub of the commercial airline universe. It takes a while to get there from here (wherever "here" happens to be), with at least one connecting flight. The only snag was that the next issue of our magazine, which we published six times a year, was going to bed that week; I had to consult with my partners before I could comfortably leave the issue in their hands.

That arranged, I booked a flight for the next night. I had figured, correctly, that Nancy had allowed for a day of travel, and so I could leave a day later than she would have and still arrive in Iowa in time for our first event.

That first event was almost my undoing. On my arrival I was a little bit dismayed to find that there were no briefing materials detailing my father's stand on every conceivable issue. Such a packet is standard campaign stuff and is almost always made available to others stumping on behalf of the candidate. I was suspicious that John Sears had set out a kind of "booby trap" for me to fall into; or worse, I worried that Dad's campaign people were not as well organized as we'd hoped, which would be a political kiss of death in this busy primary season. In my case, I wasn't too concerned about knowing Dad's position on most matters — I was well versed with his record in California, and I'd picked up a great deal about his stand on national and international issues — but I was mindful of being tripped up on something I might have missed.

Well, that's just what happened. At one event a man who identified himself as a union organizer asked me my father's position on Right-to-Work. I told him that as a former union president, Ronald Reagan believed that Right-to-Work was a weapon union membership could use to keep union leadership in line, since it gave them the right to vote for an open shop. He was, however, opposed to a general anti-union, Right-to-Work position. That was an easy one, I thought; I was for Right-to-Work, and we had wrestled with this issue over many a dinner, and I was now simply echoing a line of reasoning I'd heard my father use on me on several occasions.

But as I spoke, I could see one of my father's aides in the back of the room, shaking his head. After the question-and-answer portion of my speech the aide came up to me, wanting to know where in the world I had gotten that answer. I told him that this was what I understood to be my father's position on Right-to-Work.

"But our briefing papers say he's *for* Right-to-Work," the aide protested.

"Well, nobody provided me with any briefing papers," I said. "The family dinner table says he's against it. How was I to know his position had changed?"

I'm sure John Sears was seething when news of the event trickled back to him, but I never heard another word about it, not even from my father.

I spent the next three days driving through seventeen counties in the eastern part of the state — I was the first Reagan campaign person those counties had seen. Can you imagine! The caucuses were less than a week away, and the grassroots enthusiasm my father enjoyed was not being properly channeled throughout Iowa. George Bush's campaign was much better organized in key population centers in the state, and as a direct result of that, they walked all over us in the caucuses.

So much for rousing beginnings.

Let me just give you a rundown and some impressions of the Republican field before we go any further.

I first met George Bush in 1968, when, as a member of Congress, he came to California to campaign for Richard Nixon. He was a guest on "Tempo." I remember thinking at the time, He'll be President one day; then, realizing he could well be competing with Ronald Reagan in the future, I modified my prediction to, He'll at least be Vice President one day. I was sorry to see Bush and my father competing in the 1980 race because I would have supported Bush had Ronald Reagan not been running.

John Connally, who was injured in the Kennedy assassination, had served as the Democratic governor of Texas. He was later secretary of the Treasury under Richard Nixon and became a Republican when he saw his old party moving further and further to the left. He had trouble, however, translating his Democratic political experience into Republican votes, and he spent a great deal of money with no success. The two parties have totally different infrastructures: we Republicans have much more active grass roots than the opposition, which is difficult for Democratic "refugees" to understand. John Connally never caught on to the differences, and so he failed to match his past success as a Democrat with future success as a Republican.

Phil Crane and I had been friends since 1967, when we sat on the floor in a rec room in Illinois during Phyllis Schlafly's campaign for president of the National Federation of Republican Women. He is one of our great conservative intellectuals. As a professor at Bradley University, he wrote a book called *The Democrats' Dilemma*, one of the most fascinating and intellectual treatises I have ever read on liberalism. I have always been saddened at my not being able to bring him round to a more enlightened view on women's role in the world.

Howard Baker was a Republican leader in the United States Senate. Remember, he had supported President Ford in 1976, which did not exactly endear him to the Reaganites, but nevertheless we had all had a long and respectful relationship with the man. And he has a wonderful sense of humor! He loves to tell the story of his grandmother, who reached her hundredth birthday during the 1980 campaign; she was a well-known local politician, having spent many years as the elected county sheriff in her Tennessee hometown. During the campaign she asked her grandson if he could win the presidential race. He assured her that he could. After looking at him pointedly for a minute, she said, "Well, all right, if you really think you can win, I'll support your campaign." I love that story!

Senator Robert Dole had been chairman of the Republican party, and Gerald Ford's running mate in 1976. Because of that he felt an obligation to the party to run in 1980 and to define the issues from his perspective. In my opinion he took a bad rap in 1976 — as if his acerbic humor was responsible for the election defeat, and not the bad aftertaste of Watergate. I have always found his humor on target and self-deprecating.

John Anderson was a member of Congress from northwest Illinois. Many of my conservative friends tolerated him as their representative but always felt he was too liberal and not a party person. (The fact that he wouldn't join the team after the primaries confirmed their worst fears.)

New Hampshire now loomed as all-important, but the Reagan campaign was faltering there as well. Our grassroots effort was almost nonexistent, since paid politicos like John Sears tended to look past the importance of volunteers and local enthusiasm in a national campaign. You have to understand, a Reagan campaign was always a great opportunity to involve new people in politics, but when a campaign team refuses to put those people to work, it can turn into a negative for the candidate, as happened in Iowa in 1980 and throughout the 1976 campaign. That was John Sears's chief failing.

Dad, though, gave himself a tremendous shot in the arm at just the right moment, in a now-famous Saturday-night debate. It would turn his campaign around.

It came about because Jon Breen, the editor and publisher of the *Nashua Telegraph* in Nashua, New Hampshire, decided to sponsor a televised debate between Ronald Reagan and George Bush, the two front-runners. The candidates accepted the invitation, but before long the Federal Elections Commission intervened and declared that the paper's sponsorship would amount to a corporate campaign contribution on behalf of the two participants and was therefore illegal. The debate would have to be canceled. Dad offered to remedy the situation by splitting the cost with the Bush campaign, and when his opponent refused to ante up his share, Ronald Reagan offered to pay for the debate himself. I don't know what made him do it, but it turned out to be a brilliant decision.

When the debate became a Reagan-sponsored event, the other five candidates approached Dad about being included. They pointed out that since his campaign was footing the bill, he would be blamed for their nonparticipation. Jon Breen and George Bush objected to the other candidates' being involved, but Ronald Reagan is a man who lives by the rules of fair play. The other candidates were invited. Breen and Bush opposed the open debate and charged my father with breaking the ground rules.

What ground rules? Breen was not allowed to sponsor his planned debate, and Bush had refused to sponsor his share of a Reagan-Bush debate. Where did either of them get off seeking to establish ground rules under such circumstances? Dad can be a tiger when his sense of injustice is aroused. We've all seen the look by now. His blue eyes, usually soft and benign and pleasant, flash with indignation and fury; his voice, normally soothing and persuasive, can kick up a few notches in volume and force.

Oh, he was a tiger that night!

As the debate was due to start, Ronald Reagan mounted the stage with the other five candidates right behind him. (Bush had already taken his seat on the platform.) The large crowd was delighted at this turn of events and boisterously showed its enthusiasm for the new format. Jon Breen, as moderator, insisted that the debate could only be between Reagan and Bush. When Dad tried to explain why it was unfair to all of the candidates and to all of the voters to exclude the rest of the field from the debate, he heard Breen bark to a stagehand, "Turn Governor Reagan's microphone off!"

That was it as far as Dad was concerned; he'd reached his boiling point.

"Mr. Breen," my father shot back with some heat, "I paid for this microphone."

The exchange was quoted in every major newspaper the following morning, including Breen's own *Nashua Telegraph*; it also made the morning and evening news on all three networks. The line "I paid for this microphone" got such tremendous play that it became part of the fabric of the 1980 campaign. People still remember it. By all accounts the debate was a ringing success for Ronald Reagan and a resounding failure for George Bush.

Momentum was finally swinging to our side, and it had nothing to do with the sputtering campaign efforts being (mis)handled by John Sears and Co.

The following week Dad won the New Hampshire primary with 51 percent of the vote, a stunning majority in a seven-candidate field, and I am firmly convinced that it was that debate at Nashua High School that put him over the top.

On the afternoon of the primary I got word that John Sears was on his way out as campaign manager. Thank goodness! I thought, What took them so long? But then I wondered if it might be too late to undo the damage he'd already done. Keep in mind, the news arrived before the results of the New Hampshire vote were known, so even though Dad was well ahead in the exit polls, he still hadn't formally scored the triumphant victory he would achieve later that day.

So John Sears was out. Gone also was Lyn Nofziger — for the most part, anyway — who had been squeezed from power by Sears and Mike Deaver before the campaign even had a chance to get going. Deaver, too, had disappeared by the summer of 1979, after differences between him and Sears caused an irreconcilable rift in the campaign. Ed Meese was still on board, but I had virtually no dealings with the man; I hadn't known him in Sacramento, I very rarely had any conversations with him during the campaign, and I have only spoken to him to exchange pleasantries in all our years in Washington.

The fly in the ointment in the Sears ouster, though, was that Mike Deaver would be returning.

Since there's no avoiding it, let me deal with my relationship with Mike Deaver right here, as long as it's come up. It's no secret that there was no love lost between Mike Deaver and myself. Through the years we'd locked horns on a number of occasions. We were about the same age, the two of us, and yet he'd always treated me like I was some twelve-year-old kid who had to be kept at bay. And he did it quite successfully for a great many years.

Oh, he was a piece of work. The first time I met him, in 1969, he was on the governor's staff in Sacramento. He has since admitted that he came to my father's administration not because he believed in Ronald Reagan's conservative movement (he didn't believe there was any such thing) but because Reagan was a political train that happened to be leaving the station, and Mike Deaver wanted to be on board.

Our first battle came in his first year on Dad's staff, over the campaign for the position of secretary of the State Central Committee. Louise Hutton, my old friend from the CFRW, was seeking the office, as were Tirso del Junco, who would later become chairman of our party, and Paul Haerle, from the governor's staff. Those of us in the precincts were not particularly pleased at the prospect of having a gubernatorial staffer as an officer in the State Central Committee. Most of the women in the party, myself included, were supporting Louise Hutton.

I went to the governor and asked whether he was supporting Haerle. If so, I told him, Louise Hutton would not pursue the office; if, however, the governor intended to remain neutral, then we were going to go ahead.

"I have to remain neutral," he said. "I could work equally well with any of the people running."

"That's what I thought you'd say," I said.

By the Sunday of the state convention, however, Mike Deaver had begun circulating a letter supposedly signed by the governor, supporting Paul Haerle. What a mess Deaver had created! His maneuvering around the governor's neutrality pitted me directly against the governor on the floor of that convention. It was embarrassing to me, and it was embarrassing to my father, and it was embarrassing to the party.

Another run-in worth noting here occurred in 1974, as the governor was leaving office. Dad called to solicit my support for Rosemary Ferraro, who was running for vice chairman of the state party. "Of course," he said, "I'm going to have to be neutral in this race, but I wanted to be sure you knew about her."

I met Rosemary Ferraro, and I liked her, and I joined her

campaign. End of story? No way. As I telephoned legislators to line up support, I found myself at odds with none other than Mike Deaver, who was making the very same calls, in the governor's name, on behalf of one of our opponents, Bruce Nestande, another gubernatorial employee. I couldn't believe it!

I assured the befuddled legislators that the governor was remaining neutral on this matter, but given the way Deaver had fouled us up on the Haerle-Hutton campaign, my credibility was pretty much shot.

This time I picked up the telephone and complained.

"Dad," I said, "Mike Deaver is making telephone calls that bring into doubt your neutrality in the party election."

"Now, Mermie," the governor said, "Mike and Bruce Nestande are good friends, and I'm sure he is not using my name but simply drumming up support for his friend."

"I'm sure Mike Deaver is doing exactly what I just told you he's doing," I insisted. "Why do you consistently take his side on these things?"

"I'm not taking anybody's side," my father said.

"Well, whatever you do, if he doesn't stop, I'm going to tell people you urged me to support Rosemary Ferraro."

I figured a little hardball wouldn't hurt our chances, and I figured right. Mike Deaver's telephone campaign ended one fast phone call after I got off the phone with the governor.

So after introductions like these, Deaver and I were just short of being at each other's throats throughout most of Dad's political career. I must here admit to being a "soft-shelled crab," though, because it had saddened me to see Deaver depart the campaign the previous summer after his run-in with Sears. I was ecumenical enough to want all Reagan loyalists to be aboard for our big victory, and at that point I still saw him as a Reagan loyalist. So now with Sears gone, the way was paved for Deaver's return, but Mike's ouster had not humbled him, and before the election was won, he would prove to me once again what a rat he could be.

But I didn't allow myself to dwell on Mike Deaver's reappearance. Something happened to distract me. In May of 1980 I volunteered to help in the reelection campaign of Betty Elias, an Orange County judge and an old friend. To help raise money I agreed to be the guest of honor at a reception hosted by the then mayor of Anaheim, John Seymour. As Betty Elias and I waited for the guests to arrive, she began telling me about this wonderful young man who had done so much to get new handicap laws through the legislature. (Betty, incidentally, suffered from rheumatoid arthritis and was very active in supporting legislative reforms benefiting handicapped individuals.) She really gave this guy quite a buildup — she made him sound like God's gift to California, which he may very well have been — but before she'd had a chance to finish singing his praises, the object of her enthusiasm walked up to us to say hello.

"Why, hi, Dennis," I said.

Betty Elias couldn't imagine how we already knew each other. "Is there anybody in the state of California you don't know?" she asked me.

In 1973 Dennis Revell was the Young Republicans' Kern County chairman, and I was their national committeewoman. I was a struggling actress, and he was a political-science student at California State University in Bakersfield. We chatted for a bit at one of our meetings in Santa Barbara and then we went our separate ways. We kept tabs on each other over the years, but we only met that one time.

Now, seven years later, we turned up at the same fundraiser and changed each other's life. Two weeks later, on Memorial Day weekend, we decided to celebrate my first weekend off from the campaign by taking in a movie; we went to see La Cage aux Folles, which was great fun, and as we stepped out of the theater we found ourselves talking up our own blue streaks. We were so relaxed with each other, so natural, that it seemed as though we'd been together for years.

Right away our relationship became a job of creative scheduling. It's been that way ever since. When we remet in 1980 Dennis was just graduating from law school and was handling about 120 cases as part of the California State Bar Certified Law Student program, through which law students are encouraged to "clerk" on cases under the supervision of attorneys. He was putting in fourteen-hour days, and between the campaign and my work on the magazine, I was all over the place with my schedule. We literally had to sit down

at the beginning of every week and schedule blocks of time to
see each other.

Now, I'll admit, I must have been a formidable date in those
days. It's hard enough being brought home to meet your date's
father without her father also being a candidate for President
of the United States. I can't imagine how intimidating that
must have been for Dennis, even though he didn't seem all
that bothered by it. Remember, he had been active in California politics for quite some time — he'd worked as a campaign
consultant to national and local candidates — so he already
knew many of the players on the Reagan team.

But even love couldn't keep me away from the campaign. I
fell into a kind of routine. Throughout the spring of 1980 I
would go to work like a normal person on Mondays through
Thursdays, and then I would leave home for precincts un-
known and travel nonstop through the weekend; I'd usually
arrive home late Sunday night, though occasionally I would
go directly to the office on Monday morning. Dennis and I
would find time for each other whenever the campaign and
our busy schedules allowed. The weeks became a blur of state
conventions, campaign rallies, speeches, hotel rooms, fast food,
and airplanes. Sometimes I'd find myself lying in my hotel
room at night, and I'd have to consult my schedule (or dial
the hotel operator) to remind myself where I was.

Our campaign was run pretty much on a shoestring. That's
no exaggeration. John Sears had budgeted us up against a wall,
spending nearly 90 percent of our monies on Iowa and New
Hampshire and leaving us to apportion the remaining funds
among thirty additional primaries. Most people in the campaign thought Sears had been hoping for a one-two punch in
the first contests, and when that didn't materialize, we faced
a serious financial crisis. Things got so bad that we often needed
to pass a hat at each stop to cover local expenses and gasoline.

Lyn Nofziger and I have disagreed for years about the Sears
strategy. He believes Sears was primed for an early knockout
in Iowa and New Hampshire — which didn't happen, leaving
us short of cash. I don't think John was that inexperienced.

I, on the other hand, have felt for some time that Sears was
torn between his obligation to the Reagan campaign and what
was perhaps a heartfelt commitment to Gerald Ford. If that

was true, and if we had run out of money during the spring primaries without there being any clear winner, then Ford could have entered the race to "save the party." Lyn doesn't think John was that clever.

But even with our dwindling campaign chest, Dad was out there lighting a fire in our early primary states. By the time the California primary rolled around on our campaign calendars, all of Dad's opponents had dropped out of the race. (John Anderson, who for a while had looked to be a formidable opponent, had broken with the party and was contemplating a run as an Independent candidate.) The home-state delegates, who had figured so prominently in our campaign strategy, would now not even come into play — at least not just yet. Even on a shoestring budget, our message won out. There was enormous relief in the Reagan camp now that the nomination struggle was over. But there were to be other struggles ahead.

At the Republican National Convention in Detroit, the decision to remove the Equal Rights Amendment from the Republican party platform caused a tremendous rift within the party. It was to be the major platform battle of the convention. Republican National Committee Cochairman Mary Dent Crisp resigned over the issue and signed on to run Anderson's Independent candidacy in the fall.

In an effort to heal the wounds of the platform fight, Dad invited twenty prominent Republican women — including Massachusetts Congresswoman Margaret Heckler; the former chair of the Republican National Committee, Mary Louise Smith; and the First Lady of Michigan, Helen Milliken — to a meeting to discuss his views on the ERA and other women's issues. He also invited me, even though at first I was reluctant to participate; I was worried that my attendance would be awkward for my father, since I was in complete agreement with the other participants. I didn't see his side on this one at all.

But Dad insisted that he would feel more awkward if I wasn't there, so I accepted his invitation on the second pass. When I arrived to find all the guests wearing ERA buttons turned upside down, I knew this was going to be a potentially explosive session. I was glad I was there. Dad handled himself well —

I'll give him credit for that — and after listening to everyone's comments on the issues, he stressed that though he did not agree with us regarding the ERA, he did recognize the need to change discriminating laws and was committed to legislative reform at the local, state, and federal level. He also indicated — for the first time publicly — his desire to appoint a woman to the United States Supreme Court.

As he said that I flashed back to our last Thanksgiving dinner back at the ranch, just weeks after Dad had announced his candidacy. It can get pretty crowded in that small house around holiday time, but we manage just fine. The way we usually work it is that we set out a buffet spread on Dad's bumper-pool table, and there's room for about eight or ten of us scrunched around the dinner table. There's no dining room or anything, just a table in the middle of the room. Nothing fancy. There's usually a fire going, because that's all they've got for heat. (That's why you've all seen so many pictures of Ronald Reagan chopping firewood at the ranch!)

You have to understand, it's just a tiny adobe house. When they bought it there were only two rooms; it was really little more than a bunkhouse. The folks closed in the patio and pretty much doubled the size of the house, but quarters were still cramped.

But let me get back to this Thanksgiving dinner. Dad, as always, carved the turkey, and as we dug in for a feast of feasts, the subject naturally turned to politics and to Governor Brown's appointment of Rose Bird as chief justice of the California Supreme Court. Offhandedly my father said, "I was going to appoint a woman to the California Supreme Court, but I never got the chance. There was no vacancy."

"Would you appoint a woman to the United States Supreme Court?" I asked, not letting an opening like that pass by.

"I already said I was going to, Mermie."

"I know you were *going* to, but what I'm asking is, will you in the future if you get the chance?"

"Yes, I will," he said. "I think it's time for such an appointment."

"Great," I said, thinking that this would be a sure signal to women that they had the candidate's ear. "Do you mind if I tell people what you've said?"

"Do I mind?" my father said, setting up the table for a nice laugh at my expense. "When have I ever been able to stop you?"

From there to here was a very short distance indeed. But Ronald Reagan still had to sweat a bit before the women in this Detroit meeting room would allow themselves to be won over by his campaign.

"Governor," Margaret Heckler said, "there are many qualified women in this room who should serve in your administration, should you be elected. Will our disagreement on the ERA and other women's issues disqualify those of us who might want to serve?"

"Absolutely not," my father said without a moment's hesitation. "I would be delighted to have any of you as part of my administration."

By meeting's end all of the women in that room were convinced of Ronald Reagan's sincerity and his commitment to women's issues, despite their huge disagreement over the ERA. They decided to support his candidacy, and a number of them would go on to serve in his administration.

There were more fireworks on the Wednesday night of the convention; the fight over the ERA I had anticipated, but this next piece of news took me completely by surprise. There was a rumor making its way among the delegates that former President Gerald Ford would consider the number-two spot on the ticket if he were promised equal power and responsibility. The phrase "co-President" kept cropping up in the early media reports to describe the role Ford was allegedly seeking.

This was quite a story, if it was true. I hoped it wasn't. I had been away from the hotel and the convention hall since late afternoon and had then sat in the box with the family during the actual nomination, so I'd missed the beginnings of the rumor. Imagine how stunned I was when I walked onto the convention floor (I was literally floored) after my father's name was placed in nomination and I was met by Senator Strom Thurmond and a CBS News camera crew, wanting to know what I thought about this "exciting prospect."

Exciting prospect? I didn't think it was all that exciting. It seemed like somebody's idea of a cruel joke! We hadn't worked this long and this hard to share the presidency with Gerald Ford! What was going on here? I wondered. I wanted a chance to check it all out. So I escaped the prying eye of CBS News to try to learn what was happening. Dad and Nancy were back at the hotel with the rest of the family, watching the balloting on television, but as a member of the California delegation, my place was in the convention hall. That was where I'd have to find out what was going on.

I knew there was a phone at the California delegation, so I worked my way back there. They had heard the same rumors I had, but they hadn't been able to get any confirmation from the campaign. I tried to put a call through to the folks' hotel room to clear things up.

I didn't get very far on the telephone, though, because in the middle of all this I was to get the kick of my political career. Bob Nesen, an old and dear friend, was the chairman of the California delegation; an automobile dealer from Ventura County, Nesen was a longtime politico and a longtime Reagan supporter. As you all know, it is the role of the chairman of the delegation to announce the roll-call vote. You've all seen this in convention after convention on television, where the state party leader rattles off a string of state-grown claims to fame ("home of the waffle iron," "home of Larry Bird," "home of the famous Idaho potato," or whatever). Well, it may look kind of silly sometimes, but it's a high honor, believe me. And there was a good chance it would be the only time in Bob Nesen's political career that he'd get the opportunity.

But Bob Nesen did a wonderful thing that Wednesday night. He turned to me and said, "How would you like to announce the vote?"

I knew how excited he was about his role, so at first I wasn't sure I had heard him right. "What are you talking about, Bob?" I said.

He tried again: "Wouldn't you like to stand here and tell the world how many votes California is casting for the next President of the United States?"

"Would I?" My eyes must have gotten as big as saucers, because Bob started to laugh.

"Do you think you can remember how many votes it is?" he asked playfully.

"I think I can handle it."

What a beautiful, gracious gesture! And what a proud, memorable moment!

Meanwhile, we still couldn't get any information on the presumably big doings going on back at the hotel. The roll call of the states was nearly half finished (California, alphabetically speaking, comes up early in the tally), and I was frantic for information. My sources were all dried up or kept too busy by convention business. I couldn't get any phone calls through to the hotel from the delegation phone, so Van Logan — my traveling companion for much of the campaign — and I decided to use the phone in the sky box, which was high up in the arena, near the press corridor. We thought we could at least tap into the latest from the rumor mill. But all we got, still, was speculation and double-talk.

What was going on?

Van and I thought the same thing at the same moment. We looked at each other and gasped, "He's coming here!" There was no particular activity — we just both sensed what was coming. Ronald Reagan was breaking with tradition and was on his way to the convention hall! We raced around the corridor high atop the arena, into a freight elevator, and finally down a flight of stairs. We were out of breath when we arrived at the security entrance just a few beats ahead of the folks. Nancy came through the door and took the arm of their good friend Senator Paul Laxalt of Nevada, the man who'd had the honor of putting Ronald Reagan's name into nomination for President, and Dad put his arm around my shoulders as we walked quietly into the arena.

As we walked along he said to me in a whisper, "Don't react. It's going to be George Bush. It's going to be fine. We're going to make it."

George Bush? How did that happen? How can I not react? And what about all of this Gerald Ford speculation? There were so many questions I wanted to slip in, but before I could ask a single one, he and Nancy were walking out onto the podium.

The crowd went crazy. Most of the delegates hadn't heard the Ford rumors, or if they had, they didn't quite know what to make of them, but Dad's surprise appearance really whipped them into a kind of adoring frenzy. He had come to announce his choice for the vice presidency, and they were honored that he had chosen to make his announcement here, in front of all the delegates who had made his nomination possible, and not in some back room in front of a small group of people or in some press conference.

On the way back to the hotel I managed to get from Dad that there had been some negotiations with Ford but things hadn't worked out. More than that he wouldn't say. I was still in the dark on this thing.

When I got back to my hotel room, I found a note on my door from Michael reading, "See me. IMMEDIATELY. ANY HOUR." I don't remember what time it was, but I'll go out on a limb here and say we were well into the wee hours. The only sound I heard on the way to Michael's room was the shuffling of my feet against the plush of the rug.

I knocked on his door.

"Oh, Merm," he said. "Where have you been?" He practically pulled me from the hall into his room. "I can't wait to tell you what happened."

"What?" I said, as anxious to hear what he had to say as he apparently was to say it.

"We were all sitting there," he started in, "and Dad was in the other room with the guys" — that was our shorthand for Dad's campaign team and advisers — "and all of a sudden they come out and tell me Dad wants me in on this private meeting."

"Was this the Ford negotiation?" I interrupted.

Michael nodded.

"You mean it was real? They were really considering such a move?" I couldn't believe it.

"It was real," he said. "That's what I'm trying to tell you."

"And you were there?"

"Yeah, it was incredible. It went on for hours. I was in on the whole thing. They kept going back and forth with the Ford people, and every time Dad would agree to something, it would be on CBS within minutes. I don't know where they were getting their information, but it had to be from someone in the Ford camp."

"Stick to the story, Michael," I urged. "How did it finally break down?"

Michael was bursting with more excitement than he knew what to do with; he couldn't get the story out fast enough. If I hadn't pushed him along with questions every once in a while, we'd probably still be sitting in that hotel room.

He explained the co-presidency talk: "It had something to do with Cabinet appointments," he said. "I get the impression the Ford people wanted to make State, Treasury, and Defense department appointments. Dad got really mad when he heard this, and he said, 'No, dammit, I'm going to be President of the United States. Please tell Mr. Ford he has three minutes to decide if he's interested.'

"Then," Michael continued, "Dad just stared at his watch, and we all kept looking at ours and at Dad looking at his, and then when three minutes were up, on the dot, he said, 'Will somebody please place a call to George Bush.' He didn't even hesitate."

"And that was it?" I said, wanting to hear more.

"That was it."

"How did they wind up at the convention hall?"

"Dad said he was concerned about all these leaks, and he didn't want the story getting out that George Bush was his second choice, which wasn't really the case. And so he decided to announce it tonight. Dad asked someone to find Lyn Nofziger" — who by that time was back on the team and handling press for the campaign — "to determine where all the press people were. Lyn said they were all on their way to the convention hall, so Dad said, 'That's where we're going,' and off they went."

"So that was Lyn's idea?" I asked.

"That's what he said."

"Very smooth," I figured, recognizing that Lyn Nofziger would turn the Bush announcement into an event; he had the best political instincts of anyone in the business and knew full well that the place to make an announcement like that was at the convention hall, whether the press people were on their way over there or not. "I'll bet the ranch Lyn had to scramble to round up those newsies and get them to the hall before the folks," I said.

I looked at Michael and couldn't fully digest the incredible turn of events of the past several hours. And my baby brother, who until recently had expressed very little interest in anything resembling politics, was able to give me a fly-on-the-wall account of the whole thing! Good for him. Great for him. Oh, how I wished I could have been in that room with them, but I was glad that at least one of us had been there.

We hugged each other. The two outcasts had come in from the cold — Michael had actually been there! we reminded ourselves — and it felt good.

Over the years I've gotten precious little out of anyone else who was in that room that night. I've pressed my father on it more times than he cares to remember, but all the President has ever said to me about the Ford negotiations was, "Well, Mermie, when a former President sends word he will consider being Vice President for the good of the party, there is no way to dismiss such an offer. It must be discussed."

"But did they really want to make Cabinet appointments?" I wanted to know.

"It's unimportant what anybody wanted," he said, trying to shut me up and move on to something else. "Let's just say it didn't happen."

Lyn Nofziger, too, is as tight-lipped as anybody. "C'mon, Lyn," I'd coax at every chance. "Tell the truth. Were the press people really on their way to the convention hall when Dad called you?"

"They were there, weren't they?" he'd respond.

From what I've been able to piece together — mostly from Michael's account and from the press accounts that got out before Dad was able to fix the leak — adding Ford to the ticket would have been a dumb idea. It was a dumb idea at the start, and it was a dumb idea at the end. I'm surprised Dad even considered it for as long as he did. Apparently Ford must have also realized that his offer didn't make much sense, because as the night wore on he kept upping the ante and upping the ante, to the point where he knew he'd set it up so he wouldn't be asked. In my opinion the only people who were in favor of this Reagan-Ford ticket were people like John Tower, Bill Brock, Strom Thurmond, and Henry Kissinger — people who felt they were going to be somehow left out of the Reagan administration (which of course didn't happen).

On the Thursday of the convention, the Republican nominee made his acceptance speech. He kept his word to the Republican women right at the top: "I am very proud of our party tonight," he said. "This convention has shown to all America a party united, with positive programs for solving the nation's problems, a party to build a new consensus with all those across the land who share a community of values embodied in these words: family, work, neighborhood, peace and freedom.

"Now, I know that we have had a quarrel or two, but only as to the method of attaining a goal. There was no argument here about the goal. As President, I will establish a liaison with the fifty governors to encourage them to eliminate, wherever it exists, discrimination against women. I will monitor federal laws to ensure their implementation and to add statutes if they are needed."

At this point in Dad's speech Michael leaned over to me as we sat on the podium and teased, "Now that, my dear sister, is clout."

Yes, I suppose it was.

After the convention the first order of business was a campaign stop for the Republican presidential nominee and his family in the home state of the vice-presidential nominee and his family. Since George Bush was born in Massachusetts, lived in Houston, Texas, but hailed from Connecticut and maintained a home in Maine, there was some confusion about where exactly his home state was.

I was smart-ass enough to ask where we were going.

Dad was not amused. "We're going to Texas," he said evenly.

(As we've since seen, George Bush's grab bag of hometowns — pick a town, any town — brought him some criticism from his opponents in the 1988 campaign but also produced an inordinate amount of "hometown" good will.)

On the day following the convention we all flew to Houston, Texas, to have lunch with George and Barbara Bush and their son Jeb. All of us, that is, except Ron and Patti — Ron was on tour with the Joffrey II ballet company, and Patti was

busy with whatever it was she was busy with. Before lunch —
a delicious hot shrimp dish — Barbara said grace. She began
the blessing just as Michael and Colleen's son, Cameron, came
racing through the dining room pulling a jingling toy belong-
ing to one of the Bush grandchildren. Nancy seemed embarrassed by the interruption, but Barbara paused in the middle
of her blessing and said, "Don't worry, this happens all the
time."

Cameron's interruption broke the ice a little bit. Until then
everyone had been a little tentative in this new company. After
all, we had all campaigned quite bitterly against each other in
the previous few months, and it seemed a bit strained to suddenly put all of that aside to present a unified front. Cameron
reminded us all that we were just two families sitting down
to a friendly meal; George Bush had grandchildren, and Ronald
Reagan had a grandchild, and we allowed ourselves a moment to enjoy that personal common ground before returning
our attention to the coming campaign.

Oh, the campaign! We had hardly had time to savor the
sweetness of Dad's nomination, and now it seemed that our
work was just beginning. The next several weeks promised to
be the busiest of our political lives.

Despite our all-over-the-map life-styles, Dennis and I were
still finding time here and there to see each other, and things
were turning into a real love affair between us. I had been
telling myself for the past fifteen years that I would never marry
again, but it started to occur to both of us that that was where
we were heading. He was twelve years younger than I was,
which worked out perfectly. At Dad's suggestion, I followed
Jack Benny's lead and stopped having birthdays at thirty-
nine, so it would only be a few years before Dennis would
catch up.

And besides, the third time's a charm, right?

The folks were quite anxious to meet him — for a while it
must have seemed I could talk about nothing but Dennis and
the campaign! — but we never quite seemed to pull it off. Finally, on a sweltering Labor Day in Liberty Park, New Jersey,
we kicked off Dad's fall campaign. Dennis had made the trip
east to be on hand. We all rode back to the airport together

following the speech, and Dad and Dennis have been swapping jokes ever since.

OK, I remember thinking. They like him. Great. That's one less thing I have to worry about.

As he had in the primary season, Dad set himself apart in this campaign with a particularly strong debate performance. The League of Women Voters invited the three candidates — Reagan, Anderson, and Carter — to a debate in Baltimore on September 21. Carter declined the invitation, referring to his opponents as "two Republicans." Dad handled himself well against Anderson, an intelligent and quick-witted opponent who was nevertheless no match for Dad's good-natured, commonsense approach to questions; encouraged by Dad's success, the Reagan campaign pushed harder for a debate with Carter. By this time Anderson's support had dwindled in the polls, and he no longer had the 15 percent showing of support needed to participate in the debate, according to the ground rules established by the League of Women Voters. With only one Republican to have to contend with, Carter finally consented, and a date was agreed upon in late October, in Cleveland.

Carter and Reagan had traded barbs throughout the campaign, but this was to be their first opportunity to trade them face-to-face. In my not-too-biased opinion both candidates got off to a slow start, but Dad soon relaxed and hit his stride; Carter, though, remained tense and glowering throughout. At one point in the debate President Carter began talking up the benefits of national health insurance and accused my father of opposing such a program.

"Governor Reagan, as a matter of fact, began his political career campaigning around this nation against Medicare," Carter pointed out.

Dad just looked over at his opponent with a playful glint in his eye and said, "There you go again!" He flashed Carter a look that suggested that the President was a child he'd just caught in a fib.

"There you go again!" became a tag line for Dad's fall campaign in much the same way "I paid for this microphone!" had stood out in the New Hampshire debate. Nine years later, long after people can recall the issues of that debate, they still remember Dad's masterful handling of his opponent.

On the day before the debate I had yet another run-in with Mike Deaver. I put a call in to the residence in Virginia where Dad and Nancy were staying and asked to speak to my father. I wanted to wish him good luck the next night. Mike Deaver picked up the phone and explained that the governor was busy preparing for the debate and couldn't be disturbed; he suggested I call back at seven-thirty that evening, when the folks would have some time to themselves after dinner.

At seven-thirty on the dot I called back, only to be told again that the governor wasn't taking any calls. I was furious. Dave Fisher, from Dad's staff, was on the other end of the phone, and he wouldn't tell me why I couldn't speak to my father or when I might be able to. Van Logan and I had rearranged our schedule to accommodate this "reservation," and now I couldn't even get Deaver on the phone to tell me why my father was unavailable to me.

This was not unusual behavior for Mike Deaver. Annoying, but not unusual. Over the years he had cast himself as a kind of surrogate son to my father, and he was forever creating barricades within our family.

Van sensed my frustration, and he grabbed the phone and very firmly inquired, "Where do you guys get off interfering with a family phone call?"

I didn't hear Fisher's end of the conversation, but I did watch Van nod his head incredulously at whatever he was hearing. "Uh-huh, uh-huh, uh-huh," he would say, and then finally, "You guys are incredible. She only wants to wish him good luck for the debate tomorrow night."

Fisher told Van what he wouldn't tell me: Deaver had given orders that there were to be no calls under any circumstances; he'd even been so specific as to say that if I were to call (and he knew I would!), I was to be told the governor was unavailable.

I couldn't believe it, but then when I thought about it I wasn't surprised.

I was on the road for two months with Van Logan, living out of a briefcase and a carry-on bag and a pocketbook. I had no idea whether we were coming or going, but wherever we were, we would get Dad's message out and canvass support. As we raced for airplanes in city after city I often thought we were in somebody's idea of a bad movie: we were in a kind of vaudeville act, on some ridiculous fifty-city tour, and the days of the calendar would just keep peeling off across the screen. (I guess you can take the kid out of Hollywood, but you can't take Hollywood out of the kid, right?)

In the final week of the 1980 campaign we visited more than twenty-five cities in just six days. That's not a typo — twenty-five cities in six days! Our schedule looked something like this:

Tuesday, October 28	Philadelphia
Wednesday, October 29	Seven-city tour of Pennsylvania Fly to Boca Raton, Florida
Thursday, October 30	Boca Raton, Florida University of Miami Fly to Columbus, Ohio
Friday, October 31	Bus tour of southern Ohio (four cities) Visit circus in Cleveland
Saturday, November 1	Fly to upstate New York (four cities) Event, New York City Fly to Denver
Sunday, November 2	Various events with Senate candidate Mary Estill Buchanan Attend Broncos football game Fly to San Francisco
Monday, November 3	Final campaign swing Chico, California Eureka, California Seattle, Washington Fresno, California Santa Barbara, California
Tuesday, November 4	ELECTION DAY

At about five-thirty on Election Day afternoon, Dad was showering in his Pacific Palisades home when he heard the telephone ring. He stepped out to answer it, dripping wet and with a towel around his waist. Jimmy Carter was on the other end of the line, conceding the election.

Ever since I heard that story I've always answered the phone whenever I'm in the shower. You never know who might be calling.

III

1981—1988

15

Light and Dark

IT TOOK SOME TIME following the hectic Inaugural for the folks to settle into a kind of routine in the White House. There seemed always to be a sense of "Has it started yet?" or "Is this what it's going to be like?" They were waiting, I think, for the presidency to suddenly hit them. We all were. But I suppose that like in any other job that brings with it a tremendous change in life-style, you have to kind of ease into things.

The press, though, was making the adjustment as difficult as possible. They were everywhere, and they had something to say about everything! The folks had expected this on one level, but there was no way they could have anticipated what would happen until they were right in the middle of it. The newsies made much of Nancy's redecorating schemes, for instance, and her fashion sense; we also heard a great deal about Dad's penchant for jelly beans and football and horses. His movies, which could not be shown on television during the campaign because of the equal-time rulings, were suddenly hot properties and began turning up all over the late late show. *Bedtime for Bonzo* once again became a campus cult favorite.

You couldn't turn on the news or open a newspaper without picking up some trivial snippet about the Reagans.

I continued my work encouraging U.S. exports, and the new notoriety at least gave me a chance to get some news attention paid to what was a growing economic crisis — namely, the burgeoning trade deficit.

All of this was quite secondary to the business at hand. What we'd worked for, since Dad's first run at the office in 1968, was the chance to bring Ronald Reagan's ideal of good government to the people, and now that we'd achieved that goal, nothing else seemed to matter.

Nothing else except, of course, Dennis.

We had decided to get married, though to this day there is considerable debate over who came up with the idea in the first place. Neither one of us can remember who did the proposing, which I think speaks more of the whirlwind we were living in at the time than it does of anything else. What we are sure about, though, is that what passed for our proposal happened over dinner at a local Italian restaurant; I had linguini with clam sauce and Dennis had some kind of veal dish and we both had an awful lot of wine. He insists to this day that the linguini with clam sauce was the culprit.

We set the date for Friday, April 24, 1981, choosing the date with the President's scheduling people so that Dad and Nancy could attend on their way to a meeting with Mexican President José Lopez Portillo. I felt good about our plans and was anxious to settle into this next, "adult" phase of my life.

As we were making honeymoon plans of our own, the traditional "honeymoon" period for the Reagan administration was in full swing. Dad was still riding high on the wave of patriotism resulting from the eventual homecoming of the American hostages in Iran, and the country seemed to take to his conservative outlook. Maybe this is just his daughter talking here, but it seemed to me in these first few months that Americans were instilled with a feeling of hope and opportunity they hadn't enjoyed in years. There was a return to a sense of family and community. It was still far too early for any of Dad's new programs or policies to have taken effect, but there had been plenty of time for a new attitude to take hold and shake this country into its next decade.

It seemed there would be many bright days in the years ahead.

But the family, and the American people, were soon shaken from our plenty by a young man named John W. Hinckley, Jr. On March 30, 1981, just sixty-nine days after Ronald Reagan took the oath of office as the fortieth President of the United States, Hinckley tried to assassinate him in front of a downtown Washington hotel.

This was no toy gun, as in 1976. This was the real thing!

I was in my office when Dennis called and told me to turn on the television. There was no other way he could have told me. If he had just blurted it out over the telephone, with one detail following another, I would have fallen into some kind of shock; I needed to absorb all of it at once — the words, the pictures, the analysis, the aftermath — and television allowed me to do that. In an instant I was able to process what had happened and know that my father would be all right. That was all I needed to know: what had happened and what was going to happen. I'd have bunches of time later to let it all sink in, but when you hear a piece of news like that, you yearn to get the bottom line as quickly as possible.

It's the not knowing that kills you.

The bottom line according to the first reports was that the President was unharmed in the shooting. Dennis was still on the phone, waiting for my initial reactions, and when I told him I was fine, he said he was leaving Orange County that very minute and would be in my office in about an hour.

I didn't try to talk him out of it. I needed him there with me. He must have sensed something in my voice that even I didn't know was there.

I left the television set on until Dennis arrived. They kept playing that awful scene — over and over and over — with all the frenzy of activity, the pell-mell confusion, and then the President being bunched up and shoved into a waiting limousine. It was running on almost every channel. Some stations were running it in slow motion (presumably not for the benefit of the President's family). For some reason I remember stopping long enough to wonder how it had happened that there was a working camera on the scene. It's funny, the way you let yourself think of things like that at times like these.

From the first, it didn't even seem like the President had been shot, and in fact my father would later say he hadn't recognized that he'd been shot for several seconds after he was whisked away in the car. It was hard to tell from the herky-jerky camera work what was going on — all the noise, all the commotion, and then, in the wake of it all, the papers and briefcases and bodies strewn about the street. The Secret Service men and the local police doing what they could. It had happened so quickly — the entire scene had played out in just ten seconds or so — and yet I watched it all happen so many times that it seemed like it had gone on forever.

The entire frightening episode is burned, from repetition, into my memory.

About a half hour after Dennis called, I got my first official word of the shooting, and it differed somewhat from the news I was getting in the media accounts. Steve Harrison, the local Secret Service supervisor, called to say that the President had indeed been shot, but the word from Washington was that he was OK.

Is that it? I wanted to cry out. Is that all there is? Or is there more you're not telling me?

But that was it, for now anyway. My father, the President, had been shot. By a troubled young man who couldn't distinguish fantasy from reality. A part of me wanted to believe that if I hadn't answered Dennis's call, and if I hadn't turned on the television, none of this would have happened. I wanted to have the last half hour back. This was the fear we'd all lived with ever since Dad entered public life, but it was a fear we'd learned to place somewhere in the back of our minds. It was something we didn't want to think about, except on some intellectual, philosophical level. This was the kind of prospect you could deal with in theory but not in reality. No matter how long you think about it, nothing can prepare you for when it actually happens. It storms you, it overwhelms your every sense and sensibility, and it leaves you drained and powerless and frightened.

My first and most abiding emotion that day was rage. To this day, when I think back to that horrible incident I am filled with anger and rage and frustration. Now, still, I've got this bottled-up fury inside me as I write this. I thought that maybe with time I might be able to feel some compassion for the young man who pulled the trigger, some pity, even, but nothing has happened over the years to replace rage with a more rational emotion. I honestly don't know what I would do if I found myself in the same room, alone, with John W. Hinckley, Jr.; I only know that it's not something I'd like to find out.

By the time Dennis arrived my office was teeming with local press. I have no idea how they found out where I worked. They were all over the place; we couldn't even get to the bathrooms at the end of the hall. Building management was accommodating enough to find a vacant office on the ground floor where we could ask the press to wait, since none of them seemed inclined to leave the premises without some sort of statement from me. I would have to say something, I knew, but I had no idea what to say. We had no news other than what we'd picked up off the television and that one call from the Secret Service, and we couldn't reach anyone in Washington for an update, but I needed to say something. We had since learned that White House Press Secretary James Brady was also a victim of the shooting — in fact, an earlier televised account had reported that Jim had been killed in the incident — and that a police officer had been wounded as well.

The reporters, despite their hunger for a story, couldn't have been nicer or more sympathetic. Many of them worked the local political beats in California and were old friends. I'd even worked with some of them during my stints in local broadcasting. They seemed almost apologetic about having to put me through these strange motions with them, but that was their job. I understood that. And my job, I told myself (with a helpful reminder from Dennis), was to put on my game face and deal with the press the way my father dealt with the press.

I went out to face their questions.

"No," I said, "we haven't made a decision about going to Washington. We'll know in a little while."

Also: "Everything will be fine. I understand the President is making jokes with his doctors, which we're taking as a very good sign."

And finally someone just asked me a question that didn't allow me to do my tap dance: "My reaction is fury and rage and frustration and anger. I can't believe that in this country this kind of garbage still goes on. Nothing like this is going to happen to this President. Nothing like this is going to happen to my father." I was so furious I could hardly speak, and I excused myself from the reporters. I had to bite down hard to stop while what I was saying was still fit for broadcast.

The next few hours seemed to run into each other. I remember Patti wanted to fly to Washington almost immediately. Michael was so emotional that he couldn't decide what to do. (Ron was already on the East Coast and no doubt already by my father's side.) And me? Well, I couldn't shut off my political valves, and I was very concerned that people might misinterpret our actions and think there was more of a crisis than the White House was letting on. Leave it to me to think of appearances at a time like that.

Anyway, it was decided that we would all leave that night to see for ourselves that everything was OK in Washington, and then we would return to California the next day. Later that evening Dennis and I joined Michael, Colleen, Patti, and a small platoon of Secret Service agents and boarded a California Air National Guard cargo plane for the ultimate red-eye flight to Washington. It was an uncomfortable flight, both emotionally and physically. We were all lost in our own thoughts — on military-issue canvas seats — and I'm sure I wasn't the only one who was desperately hoping for sleep and the chance to escape the day's nightmare for at least a few short winks.

But sleep would not come, and I found myself thinking back to the previous Friday, when I had dined with the folks at the White House while I was on a business trip to D.C. Paul and Carol Laxalt were with us, and I remembered, just as dessert was being served, the President leaning over to his good friend and saying, "I want you to know that the good Lord was watching over me when I chose George Bush as my running mate. He is the perfect partner in this administration." His words now seemed all too prophetic.

Prophetic too had been the encounter the following evening at the annual Gridiron Club dinner, where the press parodies the administration. It's one of the hottest tickets in town, and I had been invited by the columnist Robert Novak. (I had been reading about the Gridiron dinners since 1960, and having the chance to attend one was really quite a thrill.)

At the dinner Jim Brady had come over to say hello.

"Maureen," he said, "we're really looking forward to coming out for your wedding."

"Thanks," I answered. "I'm glad you can be there. And Jim, I'm counting on you to help me keep it from becoming a three-ring circus."

"Sure," he said. "No problem."

That was the last thing he said to me, and now he'd been seriously, almost fatally wounded by a bullet intended for my father.

By the time we reached the White House the sun was getting around to rising. We were all tired and worn out from the trip and from the still-hard-to-believe news of the day before. Most of all, though, we were anxious to see the President, and within a few hours we were sitting alongside Nancy and Ron and his wife, Doria, in the waiting room at George Washington University Hospital.

There was a lot of hugging and kissing (and crying) upon our arrival, but after the hugs and kisses (and tears) no one knew what to do. We'd never been in this kind of situation before. Nancy tried to lighten things up a little and said, "Do you know what your father said to his doctors before they operated?"

"What?" I asked.

" 'I hope you're all Republicans.' "

That got a warm, tentative laugh out of us. We had read in the papers that Dad was joking with his doctors, but it was good to hear it from Nancy. As it turned out, one of the doctors had a sense of history, and humor, and replied, "Today, Mr. President, we are all Republicans."

While Dad was asleep, Michael, Colleen, Dennis, and I went over to the Washington Hospital Center to visit Thomas Delahanty, the D.C. police officer who had been wounded in the neck in the shooting.

I was moved by the officer's loyalty and heroism, and I told him so.

"Please tell the President that I did the best job I could," he said to us in a soft voice.

We assured him that we would. Later it was determined that the bullet that was still lodged in Officer Delahanty's neck was something called a Devastator bullet, meaning it contained a small explosive charge that could have killed him instantly. Devastator bullets are obviously designed to kill people, though the manufacturers insist they are for rabbit hunting. After the bullet is discharged, it explodes on making contact, so the fragments go all through wherever the bullet hits. Fortunately for this young police officer, the bullet was removed before it could cause any further damage. Unfortunately for our friend Jim Brady, the bullet he took in the head exploded in his brain before it could be removed.

When we got back to the waiting area outside Dad's room, we were told that the President was awake and ready to receive visitors, provided that we went in one at a time and stayed for only a couple of minutes. For some reason I expected to find him lying semiconscious underneath a maze of tubing, but when I walked through his door he was smiling and alert and propped up in a sitting position. There were the standard intravenous tubes in place, but nothing too awful.

"Dad," I said, "how are you?" (I know, I know, it was a stupid thing to say, but it was the first thing that came out of my mouth.)

"I'm OK, Mermie," he said, "except that I was wearing a new suit when I was shot. It was the first time I ever wore it. I understand this guy Hinckley's father is a rich oilman. Do you think he'd buy me a new suit?"

Leave it to Dad to joke at a time like this. He seemed in good shape and good cheer, even if he was almost too exuberant. Obviously he was trying to put on a good show to keep up the family spirits. Obviously, too, the full impact of his injuries hadn't yet hit him.

One of the ongoing dialogues that day was between Dad and his ever-present doctors, concerning the President's scheduled commitment to throw out the first baseball of the major-league season in Cincinnati the following Wednesday. Dad's always been a big baseball fan, and he said he had waited all his life to be invited to throw out the first ball on opening day; this was his first opening day as President, and he didn't want to miss it.

His doctors told him he might have to take a rain check.

When our few minutes were up, I leaned down and kissed the President on the cheek. "I love you, Dad," I said.

He held my eyes for a long minute before answering back, "I love you, too, Mermie."

We flew back to California later that day thinking the worst was behind us.

When I returned a week later, though, Dad's condition had taken a turn for the worse. His lungs had become congested with fluids, and the doctors and nurses had to turn him onto his side every two hours to keep them clear. I waited in the next room with Nancy, and we could hear them pounding Dad on the back. It was the strangest sound; when I've tried to describe it to people, I've said it sounds like somebody slapping a side of beef. I don't know if that helps, but that's what comes to mind.

Nancy listened to the sound and turned to me and said, "That's your father they're doing that to."

There was nothing else to say.

When we were finally allowed into his room, I was shocked at his appearance. He was still sharp and alert, but he had lost a tremendous amount of weight; he looked pale and thin and drawn, and his eyes were half closed. I'll be honest with you here; he was as close to death's door as I'd ever care to see him. I don't think the White House press people who were filling in for Jim Brady ever let on how serious the President's condition was; one look at him a week after the shooting and you'd know that this was no routine recuperation.

Dad had no trouble speaking, but his lips were dry and he spoke very slowly, very deliberately. He asked me why I was in town. I told him I had been in Harrisburg, Pennsylvania, the night before and was on my way to Philadelphia, and I did my best to convince him that the most direct route between those two cities was through our nation's capital.

Again, Nancy and I didn't know what to say to each other as we walked down the corridor away from his room. Words just don't cut it at a time like that, but we were both there to support each other. We didn't need to say anything. I really felt for her, for what she was going through; it's hard enough to have your husband suffer through a difficult period without having the world watch over your shoulder. I left her with a hug in the waiting room where she maintained her round-the-clock vigil, and then I headed for the elevator.

I couldn't face the press just yet, so I had the Secret Service agent find me a quiet place to sit down and collect my thoughts. I knew there'd be microphones shoved in my face as I left the hospital. And I knew how important it was that I play up the President's fighting spirit.

"The President is still full of quips and questions, and he's resting comfortably," I said in answer to the first of many questions. I told the reporters that we'd had a nice long visit, that his recovery was coming along nicely, and that he'd be home soon. I believe I even said, "He's terrific" — but he wasn't terrific. Terrific was still a long ways away.

I don't mean to sound melodramatic here, but I think it's important that people know how close we all came to losing Ronald Reagan that spring. It's all been kind of glossed over over the years, and there's this heroic image now of the President as a man who beat back an assassin's bullet, but the truth of it is that the assassin's bullet almost beat him. Almost, but not quite. Thank God for that.

The President hung on, and once he rounded the corner his recovery was as rapid as his decline had been. Within another week I could have proclaimed his condition terrific and fallen within the reasonable limits of exaggeration. His rugged constitution, combined with massive doses of antibiotics, helped to pull him through the effects of the shooting in less than a month.

Dennis and I had talked about rescheduling our wedding date — it was less than a month after the shooting! — to allow Dad time to get well enough to make the trip. But the President insisted that we go ahead with our plans. I didn't know this, but in many cultures it's considered bad luck to cancel wedding plans for any reason, and so, with heavy hearts, we went ahead.

I'm glad we did. Oh, I would have loved it if Dad and Nancy could have joined us. But they were there in fighting spirit. I spoke with Dad on the morning of the wedding. I was staying at the Beverly Wilshire Hotel (we were doing this in high style!), and Dad was recuperating at Camp David.

Barnstorming, baby kissing, and, here, ribbon cutting in New Jersey . . . ah, the life of a campaign surrogate in 1980! *(Courtesy Maureen Reagan)*

Michael and Colleen, *left,* joined Dennis and me on the "balmy" January day of Ronald Reagan's first inauguration. Note the unused blankets on the chairs. *(Courtesy Maureen Reagan)*

The first First Family portrait, taken in the Red Room on January 20, 1981. *Left to right:* Geoffrey and Anne Davis (Nancy's nephew and niece); Dennis and me; Michael, Colleen, and Cameron; the President and First Lady; Bess and Neill Reagan (Dad's brother and sister-in-law); Patricia and Richard Davis (Nancy's brother and sister-in-law); Patti; Ron and Doria. *(Bill Fitz-Patrick, The White House)*

For some reason, this is the only picture I kept from my 1982 Senate try. That's our friend Jim Nabors, who was kind enough to put on a show to benefit the campaign. *(Courtesy Maureen Reagan)*

Tripping the light fantastic with the President in the East Room during his birthday celebration, February 6, 1981. *(Michael Evans, The White House)*

What roams Dad's ranch one year inhabits our freezer the next. This 1982 note announced the folks' traditional Christmas present — half a steer. The best part of the gift, though, is always Dad's handwritten (and hand-doodled) proclamation.

My first flight on Air Force One — to San Diego on Women's Equality Day, August 26, 1983. (*Mary Anne Fackelman-Miner, The White House*)

A special hello before the Republican Women's salute to the First Lady — Dallas Convention, 1984. (*Mary Anne Fackelman-Miner, The White House*)

The second First Family portrait, taken in the State Dining Room, January 21, 1985. New to the clan this time around: Michael and Colleen's daughter, Ashley Marie Reagan. (*© by The White House Historical Association. Photograph by The National Geographic Society*)

With the daughter of President Siad Barrah, Fatima, at a Save the Children refugee project in Somalia, July 1985. *(Courtesy of Save the Children)*

Conferring with Margaret Kenyatta of Kenya, Chair of the U.N. Conference on the Decade of Women, July 1985. *(Heinz Pfeifer, Photostudio)*

Reporting to the boss in the Oval Office on the success of the United Nations Conference in Nairobi, July 1985. "Dear Mermie," he signed the picture, "How about this? I'm to the left of you. O.K., but I'm always behind you. Love, Dad." *(Terry Arthur, The White House)*

At our annual summer get-together, which belatedly celebrated Nancy's birthday, Rancho Del Cielo, 1985. (*Michael Evans, The White House*)

What a surprise! The folks turn out for a reception in my honor at the State Department. (*Mary Anne Fackelman-Miner, The White House*)

Celebrating the President's seventy-fourth birthday with his political appointees in Constitution Hall, February 6, 1986. Joining Dad on stage are, *left to right*, Ed Meese, Jim Baker, George Bush, Nancy, George Shultz, Cap Weinberger, and me. (*Terry Arthur, The White House*)

This is one of my favorite pictures, with Dennis at the White House for the President's birthday, 1986. I am wearing a Nolan Miller creation, reincarnated from another Nolan Miller creation that I wore to the first inauguration. *(Bill Fitz-Patrick, The White House)*

Sharing a special cup of Chinese tea with Vice President Bush in his office, February 1986. *(Dave Valdez, The White House)*

Joining Hands Across America with the White House family at the North Portico. With us are Press Secretary James Brady, doorman Roland Harley (a thirty-five-year White House veteran), and children of assorted residence staff members. *(Pete Souza, The White House)*

With Boxcar Willie in the Oval Office, to thank the President for his nomination of me as Co-Chair of the Republican National Committee. Just before this picture was snapped, I whispered to Willie, "Say hello to Grandpa," which explains Dad's "Give me a break" expression. *(Bill Fitz-Patrick, The White House)*

What is Super Bowl Sunday without homemade chili? Always a traditionalist, I stormed the White House kitchen and cooked up the requisite feast in January 1987. *(Courtesy Maureen Reagan)*

A warm hello for my friend President Omar Bongo of Gabon, on a working visit to the White House in August 1987. *(Bill Fitz-Patrick, The White House)*

Greeting Soviet General Secretary Mikhail
Gorbachev (through his translator) at the state
dinner during the historic Washington summit
meeting, December 8, 1987. (You'll notice I'm getting a lot of use out of this Nolan Miller gown.)
(Bill Fitz-Patrick, The White House)

Renewing my acquaintance with
Susan Mubarak, First Lady of
Egypt UAR, during a state visit
she paid to the U.S. with her hus-
band, President Hosni Mubarak,
January 28, 1988. Mrs. Mubarak
chaired the Egyptian delegation
to the Nairobi conference.
*(Mary Anne Fackelman-Miner,
The White House)*

One more gathering of the clan, to share the President's "moment" at the Republican
National Convention in New Orleans, August 1988. *(David Johnson, The White House)*

"I'm sorry we can't be there for the wedding, Mermie," he said, "I really am, but we're thinking about you."

"I know that, Dad," I said, "and we're all thinking about you. It'll be hard for me to have a good time if you're not here."

"Listen, we all have every reason to celebrate," he said. "So just pretend we're right there with you, having a grand old time."

He was right. We did have everything to celebrate. We had survived the most harrowing, horrifying episode in our lives, and Dad's prognosis was excellent. The prognosis for Dennis and me was also excellent. I decided to cast off my heavy heart and kick up my heels. This was going to be the happiest day of my life.

And it was!

What a zoo we'd created at the Beverly Wilshire. The Secret Service had been camped out there all week, doing background checks on all the hotel employees involved in the wedding arrangements. (No matter what the occasion, security seemed extra tight in the months following the assassination attempt.) On the day of the wedding they were posted at every entrance and stair landing, and there were some other agents milling inconspicuously about the crowd. And — get this — all of our wedding presents had to be sniffed by bomb-detecting dogs before we could open them! Can you imagine?

But we chose to look past all that.

In Dad's absence, my uncle Neill did the honors and escorted me down the aisle.

"I turned my hearing aid all the way up so I wouldn't miss my cue," he joked as I took his arm.

I was wearing a Renaissance-style ivory taffeta gown, with a chiffon blouse and a brocaded vest embroidered with seed pearls. (Quite a far cry from my ten-dollar wedding dress with the stain on it, wouldn't you say?) I was also wearing a coral and white rose garland in my hair. Everything was designed for me by our friend Nolan Miller (you've seen his stunning creations on the television show "Dynasty" and elsewhere), who also pulled double duty as Dennis's best man.

Dennis looked terribly handsome in his smart blue suit, but he also looked terribly nervous.

At the ceremony we were surrounded by about seventy of our dearest friends and family members. We exchanged our own vows by flickering candlelight, in a little room with mirrored pillars. It really was quite lovely the way the whole thing was framed, over and over again, in the candles' reflection.

A champagne and buffet reception followed, with about four hundred guests — it was one of those things were everybody who had said they couldn't show up somehow managed to make it — and from there the happy bride and groom climbed into the Secret Service sedan for the ride to the Los Angeles International Airport. We were off to England, Switzerland, and Germany for ten days on a working honeymoon to scout sites for future Sell Overseas America trade shows and exhibits.

There must have been two or three hundred press people out in front of the hotel when it came time for us to leave. We knew there'd be press, but we had no idea it would be like this. They were all over the place. They had part of Wilshire Boulevard blocked off, which did not endear us to local motorists. It was a madhouse. We wanted to keep the ceremony and reception as private as possible, so we told the media types early in the day that if they cooperated and left us alone, we would stop for a photo opportunity out in front of the hotel on our way to the airport. It turned out it was a good deal for all concerned: 99 percent of the newsies kept their distance, as promised, and we fulfilled our end of the bargain with a good long photo session.

On the way to the airport, feeling safe in the comfort of my new husband (and, I should add, in the security provided by our Secret Service escort), I reflected on the past month. Remember how I said the presidency kind of sneaks up on you? Well, John W. Hinckley, Jr., changed all of that for us. I think he changed all of that for the entire country. An assassin's bullet can jolt you into a new reality, and that's just what happened. And when you survive an ordeal like that, you come out on the other side with a changed outlook, a fresh perspective. Things fall into place.

Ronald Reagan's "honeymoon" was over, and we now knew full well what it meant for him to be President of the United States.

When I visited him at the hospital, Dad told me that he had come away from the shooting knowing that his life was in the hands of a higher being, and that he would devote the rest of his time on this earth to whatever it was God intended for him to do. There were certain things, he said, that were beyond his control, and he would give himself over to those things in order to do the best job he possibly could in steering this country into a bold new era.

And now, together, the new team of Reagan and Revell was ready for whatever lay ahead.

16

A Race of My Own

For as long as I could remember I had been having a running debate with myself about standing for election. Goodness knows, I'd been asked more times than I cared to count when I would run for office — any office — but I'd always said I preferred to work behind the scenes to help elect a variety of candidates.

You have to understand, I've never been too enamored of the lifelong political types, the ones who seek election to one office simply for its value as a stepping stone to a higher office. I've supported some of them, that's true, but I've never fully bought into that way of thinking. You see people like this in every community, at every level, and always they seem to be biding their time until their two or four years are up and they can move on to the next rung of the political ladder.

To my mind that's not what politics are all about. Public service is a civic duty, not a career. For my tastes, a politician should work to enhance and enrich his community — whether that community is local, state, or federal — and then when his term in office passes and his work is done, he should step aside.

To contribute what you can and then come back and live and work in the world you've created — with your changes (even with your mistakes), not removed from them — that's public service.

And yet with Dennis's encouragement, I began to focus more and more on the notion of someday seeking office myself, particularly after the assassination attempt. John W. Hinckley, Jr., reminded me of something I should have already known — that our time here on this earth is precious, and short, and we should make the most of it while we have the chance. At the rate I was going, I could talk about it and talk about it and still never get around to running for office.

There's no time like the present, right?

For many years I'd been feeling that California was divided up into political fiefdoms by office holders who wanted to have control over a portion of the electorate but were unable to see the big picture. California was not fully utilizing its power as the nation's largest state. I had spoken a great deal about how the people — average Joes and Josephines — were so removed from the political process that they didn't know where to go to get a particular problem solved or to voice a concern. You'd be surprised how many people don't even know what the various government offices in their jurisdictions are, let alone who holds them. It doesn't have to be that way, and it shouldn't be that way. I'd always believed that we could build a bridge between our federal and local governments, and that the United States Senate was the place to start.

United States senators are unique in that they are the only two people from each state with federal responsibilities who also deal with all the levels of state and local government; it seemed to me that if we could get our senators to set up constituency committees — town hall–type clearinghouses — in all of the counties of a state the size of California, then we would really be bringing government down to a manageable size for the average citizen. We desperately needed, I said, a place where people could come and be heard on the issues of toxic waste and garbage disposal, streetlights and off-shore drilling, welfare and tax reform, a place where there were no such things as small voices or small issues.

Our United States senators, I maintained, were the only elected officials in a position to make such a program work.

On top of all this I also felt very strongly that the party

needed more women candidates, to deliver a clear message that the Republican party offered opportunities for women to exercise leadership. Even if I didn't win, a high-profile campaign for a position of national significance would send the right signals to women all over the country.

And so I set my sights on California's U.S. Senate election in 1982.

I put a call in to the White House to inform the President of my decision. He sounded pleased, I think, but also tentative. Mind you, I was not seeking his help, nor his endorsement; I just wanted to keep him up to date on a very important decision in my life. Since his first run for governor in 1966 Dad has judiciously avoided giving primary endorsements, choosing instead to help unify the party for the general elections that follow. Over the years I'd supported a number of primary candidates while he remained neutral until the party made its nomination, so I was well aware of his position. And any support he might give to his daughter's candidacy would be a slap in the face to all of the others who had hoped for his support in the past.

But before I could win the party's nomination (and my father's endorsement), I had to get past a heated primary battle. There were eight of us seeking the spot on the ticket, including Barry Goldwater, Jr. (a congressman from the San Fernando Valley), Robert Dornan (a Los Angeles congressman whose district had been decimated in reapportionment), Pete McCloskey (a congressman from San Mateo who had gained notoriety in 1972 by opposing Richard Nixon in the New Hampshire primary), Ted Bruinsma (a law professor from Loyola Marymount University), John Schmitz (a state senator from Orange County and a former member of Congress, John had been the American Independent party candidate for President in 1972), Pete Wilson (the mayor of San Diego and a former legislator and unsuccessful gubernatorial primary aspirant in 1978, Pete originally ran for governor in 1982 but was convinced to switch to the Senate race by finance people who hoped his exit would aid their candidate, Mike Curb; it didn't, and George Deukmejian became governor), and Sam Hayakawa (a first-term senator and former president of San Francisco State University).

Speculation about my candidacy created considerable interest in the primary race on the national level, so much so that the President began fielding questions about my intentions even before they were formally made known.

One afternoon, with the splendor of the Santa Ynez Mountains as a backdrop, the President stepped from the front door of his ranch house to sign the historic 1981 tax bill. The usual White House press corps was on hand, and when my father finished signing the legislation, the reporters began barking out questions on a variety of topics, as is the custom. One question went something like this: "Is Maureen going to run for the Senate?"

"I hope not," the President replied with a smile.

By the time he stepped back into the house he realized what he'd just said, and he commented to an aide, "Well, I think I just blew it."

He had indeed.

Dad got me on the phone right away. "Mermie," he said, "I think we have a problem." He paused to collect his thoughts, and from the way he sounded, it appeared he'd rehearsed what he was going to say. He told me what had happened and how sorry he was, and he tried to prepare me for what might happen next. He said he was sure his comment would be misinterpreted. "What I meant to say," he explained, "was that having campaigned myself, it's not something I would wish on anyone. I was trying to be facetious, but I don't think it came out that way. I certainly didn't mean to imply that you shouldn't be running, but I know that's the way it will appear on the evening news. I just want you to know I'm sorry."

"It's OK, Dad," I said, knowing his intentions were good. "It sounds a lot like some of the things I used to say back in 'seventy-five when they would ask me if you were going to run for President."

"I remember," he said. "Well, I guess we're even."

But the fact that I'd let him off the hook didn't erase what he'd said. His remarks would be misinterpreted, and it would come off looking like we were at odds over my entry into the race. That was not the case at all. In fact, a story appeared in the next edition of *Newsweek* suggesting that my father was supporting Senator Hayakawa's candidacy and that my plans to run had caused a rift in the family. I'm all but certain that that story was planted by my old friend Mike Deaver. It was well known in the administration that *Newsweek* reporters had what amounted to an open-door policy with Mike Deaver in the White House. Whenever something showed up out of nowhere in *Newsweek*, you could bet money that Mike Deaver was behind it. I'd bet anything that was the case here.

So this supposed family feud emerged out of a simple misunderstanding, and the President and I had to go through a very public clearing-of-air before I could get on with my campaign. I'm absolutely certain my candidacy suffered for it. Making light of the problem would not undo the political damage, and it would not make all the talk and speculation disappear, so Dad decided to set the record straight in a letter to Dr. Tirso del Junco, chairman of the California Republican party. He explained that he had made the remark in jest, and that there was no truth to the rumors that he opposed my candidacy.

"Maureen and I have discussed the possibility of her seeking office," he wrote. "She understands that I must and will be absolutely neutral, which I believe my position requires. The decision is hers to make."

Of the eight Republican candidates in the U.S. Senate race, I was the only woman. Invariably we earned ourselves the nickname Snow White and the Seven Dwarfs. Yours truly was Snow White, while Senator Hayakawa, who was frequently caught napping on the Senate floor, was tagged with the sobriquet Sleepy. San Diego Mayor Pete Wilson, who did not have the sunniest of dispositions, was nicknamed Grumpy, and Barry M. Goldwater, Jr., whose ability to govern was often in dispute, had to shoulder the burden of Dopey.

It was going to be a below-the-belt campaign, and it wasn't long before I received my first hit. One of the candidates said in an interview that he had heard I was pregnant and would be dropping out of the primaries. It was mentioned as an aside, but it was an obvious ploy to dismiss my candidacy, to diminish me, and to remind voters that as a woman, I might have other priorities than the office I was seeking.

The press called me on it immediately. "This puts me in a tough position," I said. "Pregnancy is not an illness, so it should not interfere with a campaign, but I am not pregnant, so it's not an issue."

Being Ronald Reagan's daughter was a mixed blessing for my own political ambitions, I quickly discovered. Yes, my father's name brought me instant publicity and voter recognition and, to a degree, credibility, but I also had to work against the assumption that I had no ideas of my own. Almost everywhere I went, people expected a mere recap of my father's policies. Others felt that I should drop out of the race because I disagreed with the President on the ERA. I was accused of not being a dyed-in-the-wool Reaganite and of being too liberal, even though ideologically I've always considered myself right smack in the middle of the Republican party and right smack in the middle of the President's way of thinking.

Some voters were convinced that my only accomplishment was in being the President's daughter. Even my uncle Neill, who should have known better, publicly accused me of riding on my father's "coattails" (his term). "Just because her father is the President of the United States," he told a reporter, "is no reason for her to get very busy and ambitious."

Neill Reagan had some problems getting used to the fact that his younger brother was the President of the United States. Oh, he wasn't jealous of Dad — on the contrary, he was quite proud — but my father's latest career move had put kind of a crimp in Uncle Neill's retirement plans. People he hadn't seen in thirty years crawled out of the woodwork. There were all kinds of demands on his time. People would ask him to arrange personal tours of the White House, or make other ridiculously impossible requests. Like the rest of us, Neill didn't have a staff to help him cope with the volume of mail that came pouring in. I think he saw my candidacy as just more of the same thing; maybe he couldn't face the idea of having to deal with any more than he already had to deal with.

I like to think that was the case, but most likely I'm being generous here. In the plainest of terms, things got pretty ugly with my uncle during the campaign, and the years since then have done little to heal the wounds. He behaved very badly in the several months leading up to the primaries in June 1982. It all came about when he served as one of four cochairmen of Pete Wilson's campaign. Of course, that alone would have been fine; I certainly respected his right to work for whatever candidate he believed in. His support was not owed to me by blood. But he actually went out and made a radio spot in which he said, "We Reagans urge you to support Pete Wilson."

Now, Neill and I had always been friends — hell, he gave me away at my wedding, only a few months before this campaign! — but this was something I could not look past. I was bewildered and hurt and, yes, angered by his behavior.

Pete Wilson, meanwhile, was busy telling campaign audiences about his proximity to the President. He made himself sound like a second cousin who came around for Christmas dinner. Yeah, right. This was the same Pete Wilson who had opposed my father when he chaired Gerald Ford's 1976 campaign in California and when he campaigned in New Hampshire bemoaning the faults and excesses of Ronald Reagan's governorship.

Even my opponents thought my uncle — and Pete Wilson — had gone too far on this one. His radio campaign carried with it an implicit endorsement from the President. We demanded that the commercial be pulled. Dennis was acting as my campaign manager, and he called my father and played him a tape of the commercial over the phone. The President agreed that Pete Wilson's campaign advertising was misleading and unethical, and he sent a telegram to Dr. del Junco reaffirming his longstanding position of neutrality in primaries.

Neill countered that the commercial was not misleading; it merely stated that he and his wife, Bess, were endorsing Pete Wilson. Not misleading? Give me a break! Wilson's campaign manager refused to scrap the ad and continued to run with it as scheduled.

I don't know what has transpired between the President and his brother since that time, but I do know that my relationship with my uncle has never been the same, and it most likely never will be.

There were other obstacles to my senatorial campaign, some of them not familial. As the only woman in the field, I had a tough time being taken seriously by the press, and I had a tough time raising serious money. It became an unbreakable circle: you are not taken seriously, so you can't raise serious money, and you can't be taken seriously because you haven't raised serious money.

And despite the President's neutrality, Washington continued to get in my way. Influential Republicans, including some of my father's most trusted aides and financial supporters, tried to push me out of the GOP primary. They were aided and abetted in this effort by none other than Mike Deaver. I always believed that he was burning up the phone lines to California during the campaign, sending out the message that the President and the First Lady would not take kindly to anyone who contributed to my effort. Every time I thought I'd seen the worst of Mike Deaver, he'd outdo himself.

One morning I received a phone call from Henry Salvatori, a Reagan supporter since Dad's first run for governor in 1966, who suggested that I run instead for California secretary of state, because "there's already a woman in the office, so it will be easy." He told me that I'd never run for office before and was therefore unqualified, but I pointed out that Senator Hayakawa — his candidate — had never held office until he was elected to the Senate. I added that his U.S. Senate seat was the only office George Murphy ever held, and that Barry Goldwater, Jr., one of my opponents, had been elected to the House of Representatives with no political experience. Salvatori also told me that I had no track record, so I reminded him of a campaign we had worked together on in 1969, when he had thought my advice was worth taking.

The last straw came when I picked up a copy of the *Sacramento Bee* and saw a quote from Ed Rollins, who was then working in the White House political office. "She has the highest negative of any candidate I've ever seen," he said.

The "negatives" he referred to came from polls conducted by the independent pollster Mervin Field; in his surveys Field would list all of the male candidates' occupations, and then he would list me as "Daughter of the President." Not only was that an incredibly sexist thing to do, it was also incredibly partisan. He set things up so it looked like my lineage was all I had going for me. (I thought I was back in that Las Vegas revue!) His techniques made me furious, and I was delighted when his professional skills came into question in the next several months.

(Later that year, on election night, Mervin Field appeared on the CBS television station in Los Angeles, where he was under contract as a political pollster and commentator. During the station's election coverage, he projected without equivocation that Democrats Jerry Brown, who was running for the United States Senate, and Tom Bradley, who was running for governor of California, would win their respective races, based on his exit polling. Well, Field failed to account for the fact that the Republican party had just completed the largest absentee-ballot campaign in our history, and that those votes would provide the margin of victory for our candidates — Pete Wilson and George Deukmejian. Every other reporter and so-called political expert in California had the story straight, while Mervin Field had enough egg on his face to make an omelet. Justice, and breakfast, were served.)

When my campaign workers called at seven o'clock on a Saturday morning to read me the *Bee* article, I called the President immediately.

"Dad," I said angrily, "this has gone too far. I'm out here fighting to keep your neutrality in this primary, while every other candidate is insisting he's your choice for the nomination."

"You're right, Mermie," he agreed. "I understand your problem, but what would you like me to do about it?"

"Just keep your Washington people from butting in," I insisted. "I can handle the rest of it."

"I'll take care of it," he said.

And he did.

Meanwhile, we continued to fight the good fight. We had only meager funds and virtually nonexistent media support (excepting, of course, all of this negative media support), but we succeeded in building a new grassroots organization, with hundreds of volunteers statewide. We ran an honest, ethical campaign and didn't spend our time cutting up the other candidates. (Oh, how I would have loved to cut up some of the other candidates.)

I traveled over sixty thousand miles in seven months, just in California alone. I saw the north coast, with its depressed timber industry, where loggers were waiting for construction starts to pick up in the more populous south so they could sell their trees. I talked to farmers in the Sacramento Delta, where too much water was breaking through the levees, and to farmers in the San Joaquin Valley, for whom there would not be enough water without state and federal water projects.

The term I used to define what I saw as the main issues in that election was "people concerns." "You will notice," I would say in my speeches, "that other candidates regale you on why they should be in the Senate to dabble in international relations. I dabble in international trade every day in my office here. I don't need to go to Washington for that. But you need someone in Washington who cares about what's going on here, someone who will come home to California every week to stay in touch."

I advocated welfare reform through an education and jobs system in which our expenditures would be investments in the future and not a maintenance of the status quo. I suggested increased use of community "food banks" to augment food-stamp programs and to give people a better chance to help themselves and their neighbors. I outlined my idea of constituency committees to make all levels of government more accessible to all people. I also put forth the idea of a tax deduction for community volunteers; giving tax credits for volunteer hours has since become a hot issue, and as far as I know, it started with my platform in that campaign. Our country will not function without the selfless and tireless work of the community volunteer, and a tax credit of, say, one dollar per volunteer hour would go a long way toward boosting volunteerism.

We were pressed for cash, and we needed to get our message out, so Dennis discovered the extreme cost-effectiveness of the new cable-television industry; the local access channels were perfect for our campaign.

He's a brilliant event man, my husband, and he organized some wonderful fund-raisers for our cause. As the campaign wore on he got so completely involved in keeping me busy that he lost track of his calendar. As the night of our first wedding anniversary approached in April, just six weeks before the date of the primary, Dennis sat me down to go over my schedule. He said he wanted me in this place and that place and the other place on this date and that date and the other date. I was wall-to-walled with events. One fund-raiser, I noticed, was scheduled for the night of our anniversary.

"Excuse me, Dennis," I said, "but I don't think I can make it to this one."

"Oh," he said. "Why not? Is there something else we've got scheduled?"

"Well, kind of."

"What? Do you have to be in Washington?"

"No, it's not that."

"What is it, then?"

"Well, it's our wedding anniversary, and I have other plans."

"Aha," Dennis said, turning red. "I see. Should I plan on being there?"

I looked at him and laughed. "I don't know whether you just screwed up as my campaign manager or as my husband," I teased, "but you certainly screwed up."

Later that spring Dennis suggested that we commit ten thousand dollars — a sizable chunk of our campaign budget — toward a televised candidates' debate. I thought it would be a wonderful way to get my ideas out there alongside my male opponents', but I was more than a little concerned about the expense. Dennis had lined up twenty-six local cable stations throughout the state that would carry the debate live via satellite or play it back later on tape delay. The exposure would be terrific, I admitted, so we decided to explore the idea further.

We contacted the other candidates, and as they all agreed to participate, the idea gathered enough steam to attract two public television stations, in San Diego and San Francisco, that wanted to air the debate live and offered to absorb the cost.

Well — wouldn't you know it? — each candidate tied himself to Ronald Reagan like a Siamese twin. But each one broke with the President on key economic and budgetary issues, and as they all spoke, it became more and more clear to me that these people did not fully endorse my father's programs, though each expected to receive an endorsement from him.

"I can't believe what I'm hearing tonight," I said when my turn came around. "You've all missed the point completely. Ronald Reagan is doing exactly what we elected him to do. The Republican party, for as long as I can remember, has begged our office holders to hold the line on spending and to reduce the tax burden on the middle class. As we've said for many years, you cannot build welfare program on top of welfare program and still expect to afford the overhead. You cannot use our national defense budget as a petty-cash fund to finance other social programs.

"Ronald Reagan is keeping his promise with us, as we all knew he would. Now it is time for us to keep faith with him. If he fails, we get some of the blame; if he succeeds, we get some of the credit.

"And I'll take my share of the credit, because I've been a Republican longer than Ronald Reagan."

I'd gotten a few things off my mind, but it was not enough to get me elected. By that point the fallout from the President's unwitting swipe and the sabotaging damage done by my Washington foes and by my uncle Neill were irrevocable. My opponents' message — that the absence of the President's support (to which they had all laid claim) amounted to silent disapproval of my candidacy — had hit home for too many voters. Nothing either of us could say would sway public opinion.

But get this, people. The President may not be allowed to endorse a candidate in a primary election, but he still retains his rights as a United States citizen, and he is allowed to vote in a primary election. The Economic Summit was to be under way in Europe on primary day, so it was still several weeks before the first Tuesday after the first Monday in June 1982 when the President of the United States, my father, cast his vote in California's Republican Senate primary for Maureen Elizabeth Reagan.

I may have come in a disappointing fifth, with only 5 percent of the vote, but I came away from it all thinking I had won something very big indeed.

17

Mending Fences

Politics is an expensive business.

In the past, whenever I'd helped out on a campaign, my job was always over on Election Day. Of course, there were always loose ends, but win or lose, my duties for the most part ended when the polls closed.

Oh, I always knew there was more to it than that. I just never knew how much more. In the months immediately following my failed Senate bid, Dennis and I were faced with the task of erasing my substantial campaign deficit. I know a lot of candidates walk away from their debts, but that never even occurred to me. I was not about to leave vendors hanging; there were dozens of hardworking people who had offered honest goods and services on our behalf, and they needed to be paid for their time, for their materials, and for their expenses.

We needed to raise somewhere between sixty and seventy thousand dollars; actually we needed to raise somewhat more than that because we had to factor in the cost of our fundraising efforts — mailings, phone bills, dinners, entertainment, and so on. So we devoted most of our time over the following six months to paying off our debts, with dinners, banquets, speeches, auctions . . . you name it. As I said,

Dennis has a terrific flair for organizing events, and he kept us pretty busy. It seemed that hardly a day went by when we didn't make at least one appearance to raise money. When we looked up at the other end, we'd paid off every last bill, and I don't think that's a claim that more than two or three of my former opponents could make.

I should add here that women candidates in particular have a tough time rebounding from a losing campaign. Have you ever noticed that when a man runs for office and loses, he'll turn up over and over to try his hand again as a candidate? With women, though, the tendency is for an unsuccessful candidate to disappear from politics, at least for the near future. When I lost in the 1982 California Senate primary, for example, I wasn't even invited to contribute to a political fundraiser, let alone asked to speak, for a full year following the election. I don't know why this is, but if you ask any woman politician, she'll probably tell you the same thing: if you run for office and win, terrific, but if you lose, it's unlikely that you'll ever seek the same office again.

Soon, though, I was back to devoting my full attention to the promotion of United States exports overseas. When I found time (and I always found time!), I'd do what I could to promote whatever else I believed in — women's issues, party concerns, and local campaigns. I was keeping my distance from Washington, though — partly because there was no clear role for me in my father's new world, but mostly because I was made uncomfortable by some of the people he surrounded himself with. I'd visit with the folks at the White House when I was invited or when I had business in town (why pay for a hotel when you had accommodations like that, right?), but other than that I'd steer clear.

Of course the folks always made me feel welcome when I was in town. They'd just about roll out the red carpet for me. In fact, the more I saw of Dad and Nancy as his first term in office wore on, the more I felt at home in the White House. Dinners around the table in the President's second-floor dining room were a regular family affair. There's a wonderful eighteenth-century chandelier overhead and spectacular wallpaper about the room depicting our battle for independence more than two hundred years previous, but the historic and

formal setting could never take anything away from the relaxed atmosphere. We were the First Family, that's true, but
around the family dinner table we'd try to be just plain folks.

On Memorial Day weekend in 1983, Dennis and I were vacationing in Bermuda when we were awakened by a middle-
of-the-night call from Nancy. Since Dad had become President, Nancy had begun to rely on the family more and more
for support and friendship and honest advice uncluttered by
outside influences. It was not at all unusual for Dennis or me
to answer the phone and find Nancy at the other end, just
wanting to talk.

Tonight she wanted to talk about a brewing family crisis.
An article had appeared that day in the new issue of *Redbook*
magazine, in which Michael and Colleen had criticized the First
Lady for spending too much time with the foster grandparent
program she was sponsoring and not enough time with Michael's children. I'm sure they didn't mean the quote to sound
quite as vicious as it came across — the way the magazine
played it up, it was a real blast at Nancy — but I'm sure also
they were feeling somewhat slighted by Dad and Nancy's new
responsibilities. Given some perspective, it was an easy-to-
understand misunderstanding, as it turned out, but at the time
Nancy was very stung by the article, and she very much needed
to talk to someone about it.

About ten minutes into our conversation she pulled back
and said, "You sound tired, Maureen. Did I wake you up?"

"Don't worry about it," I said, borrowing an old line from
a vaudeville routine Dad once taught me. "I had to get up
anyway to answer the phone."

"Seriously, why were you asleep so early? It's still early out
there. Are you all right?"

"Oh, we're all right, but we're not in California. We're in
Bermuda. It's one hour ahead of you here, not three hours
behind."

Before I continue here, let me just quickly explain how it
was that the First Lady didn't know where she was calling.
You see, every time she and Dad made a call it was placed
through the White House switchboard. The operators there
are like a professional team of sleuths; they can find anybody,
anyplace, anytime. Just give them the name, and they'll make

the call. Wherever you are, they'll find you. So as often as not
Dad or Nancy would call and would have no idea where we
were. It was the strangest thing. One time the switchboard
connected the President to a very sleepy member of Congress,
and Dad asked, "Where are you? What time is it there?" When
the Congressman informed the President that he was in Aus-
tralia, where it was three o'clock in the morning, Dad said,
"Oh, it's not me, it's an imposter. I'm sure the real President
will call you back at a decent hour."

Anyway, Nancy sounded really down about this *Redbook*
magazine article, and Dennis and I were due to leave Bermuda the day after next, so I suggested that we stop off in
Washington on our way back to California to try and help
smooth things over.

All of this explains how I happened to be sitting across from
the President in the family dining room of the White House
when Dad asked casually, "Mermie, do you still make
speeches?"

"Occasionally," I replied. "Why?"

"Well," he said, "I'm very concerned about our image with
women. I've appointed three women to my Cabinet, and there
are many other women in key policy positions. I just don't
think we deserve the criticism we're getting from some wom-
en's organizations."

"And what is it that you think I can do about it?"

"I'm wondering if you might mention some of these things
in your talks," he said, only sort of asking.

I knew full well about the criticism the President was referring to. By the spring of 1983 I had received dozens of letters
from Republican women office holders who felt completely
isolated from the administration and the party. The advice and
opinions of their male colleagues were sought on key issues,
but the women were never consulted. I also heard echoes of
the same from feminists and active party loyalists. I was getting the sense that these women were no longer willing to
give blind support to a political structure that completely ignored them.

Dad was getting the same sense, which meant he was facing a very difficult problem indeed. I thought for a good long
while before I answered him. Did he really want to hear what

I thought needed to be done? Or was his asking me like this, over a casual family dinner, just the kind of lip service or going-through-the-motions that these women so objected to? Well, I reasoned, he wouldn't have asked if he wasn't concerned, right? I looked across the table and saw that he was anxiously await-ing my response, which I took finally as my cue.

"OK, Dad," I said, "listen. I could give a speech every day of the week talking up what your administration is doing for women. If that's what you want, I'll be glad to do it, all you have to do is ask, but let me tell you, I don't think it will do any good."

"Why not?" he asked.

"Because it isn't enough. You have to do more. You have to speak out more. You have to reach out more. Frankly, Dad, you're not talking to the right people. The people you've got dealing with this issue publicly are all white males between the ages of forty and sixty. Nobody's listening to them."

The President has never been one to shy away from a prob-lem, and after I'd made it abundantly clear to him that he was approaching this dilemma from the wrong angle, he was all ears. We moved from the dining room into Dad's study, which is decorated with all sorts of family photographs and personal furnishings Nancy had shipped from California; here, only a room away from the museumlike confines of the President's dining room, we were on Dad's own turf, and we spent the rest of that evening banging out a strategy, talking all about form and substance, about perceptions and deeds.

What you have to understand about this room is that the way it's decorated — in a homey red floral print (the curtains match the upholstery on two overstuffed chairs) with a bright red carpet — makes it one of the few places in the White House residence where the folks have put their own touches to work. I remember I was leaning up against a needlepoint pillow em-broidered with Dad's initials — a gift from an old family friend — and Dad was relaxing in a sweater and slippers. We went over the whole issue, and every related issue, from top to bottom. I really wanted to be of some help to the President on this and at the same time help the women of the party. Of course, at one point in our discussion Dad let on that Mike Deaver was in charge of the "gender gap" issue, which made the whole business seem to me like an uphill battle, and I figured this was as good a time to deal with him as any.

"I'm not sure Mike Deaver knows what the gender gap is," I started in. "The gender gap he should be worried about is the differential between men and women voters. When you ran for governor, Dad, in nineteen sixty-six, fifty-one percent of the electorate was female, and no one cared. When you ran for President in nineteen eighty, fifty-three percent of the electorate was female, and still no one cared. The only reason your people are suddenly interested in all this today is that they've finally realized that by nineteen eighty-four there will be six million more women voters than men."

He seemed interested, and so I went on.

"There are issues of unique concern to women, but these issues don't end with women," I outlined. "The problems of child care for working parents, equal pay for equal work, equal pension benefits, availability of credit, and enforcement of civil-rights statutes all uniquely affect women, that's true, but when a woman is discriminated against, her children are discriminated against, her husband is discriminated against, her community is discriminated against. All office holders have to address these women's concerns, because they are also family concerns and community concerns."

"But what about the appointments we've made?" my father interrupted. "Don't they count for something?"

"They count for something, but they're not nearly enough. Do you remember when you were selecting your Cabinet in nineteen eighty, and the reporters came back to you and told you that I'd said Jeane Kirkpatrick's appointment was not enough?"

"I remember."

"And you laughed and they quoted you as saying, 'Maureen won't be happy until they are all women.' Well, since then you've put three women in the Cabinet and a woman on the Supreme Court. I'll admit to a degree of female chauvinism here, but you'll have to admit that if the appointment of one woman is good, then the appointment of more women is better."

As long as I had the floor, and a rapt audience, I decided I'd toss out some ideas I'd been hatching for quite some time.

It was then that I suggested we celebrate the birthday of the suffragette Susan B. Anthony the following February, an idea that would take hold in a much bigger way than anyone had expected.

Dad was eager to try anything. The polls were showing that 57 percent of all men endorsed the President's job performance, but only 39 percent of all women were supportive. "Since he took office, President Reagan has been plagued by the 'gender gap,' " a March 1983 Gallup poll reported, adding, "This sex differential cuts across all social and economic boundaries and is found in every region of the nation." Dr. Richard Wirthlin, the President's pollster, reported similar numbers.

At the President's request I met the following day with Mike Deaver, who, as I'd expected, was not the least bit interested in what I had to say. He couldn't wait for our meeting to be over. He assured me that the administration was doing "many good things that will be very good for women," though he was unable to be any more specific than that. He told me he didn't need any help from me on this matter.

Fine, I thought. Mike Deaver might not need my help, but the President certainly did. So I continued forward. The best way to reach out to women voters, I proposed, was to use our women office holders as the first line of defense. The women who spoke before their constituents on a daily basis were best equipped to transmit to us the thoughts and concerns of women in every part of the country, and to transmit the President's thoughts and concerns back to them.

Finally, with the help of Dr. Wirthlin's number crunching, I presented my plan to Frank Fahrenkopf, chairman of the Republican National Committee, making the case that this kind of two-way communication on the local levels was the best way to turn our situation around.

He agreed, and I began acting as consultant to the party chairman on what was supposed to be a part-time basis. But I knew from the start that the only way to achieve our goal was through a round-the-clock commitment, so for the price of a part-time consultant, the chairman got himself a full-time operative.

It was a good deal for all concerned.

I began shuttling back and forth from Los Angeles to my temporary quarters in the Lincoln Bedroom of the White House. Now, finally, more than two years after the inauguration, I was working for the President in an official capacity — a part of his world — and I was glad all over about it. I quickly discovered that Washington is a very difficult town, particularly for someone named Maureen Reagan during the Reagan administration. As in any field, there was a lot of backbiting and turf wars and petty bickering, even though you'd think officers of the federal government would be above all that. Ambassador Vernon Walters, a retired Army general and longtime deputy director of the CIA who served the President for several years as an ambassador-at-large, once explained to me his theory of presidential access as a three-step transmogrification:

Step 1: "I will decide when you may see the President."

Step 2: "I will decide if you may see the President."

Step 3: "I will give the President your message."

His theory was that White House insiders begin by showing you that they have all this power, even if it takes a while before they start demonstrating and exercising that power. The theory fit several members of Dad's administration, Mike Deaver among them.

Washington is the kind of place where every political newcomer is evaluated first as a threat and only later as a colleague or possible ally. I soon found myself the object of a great deal of scrutiny, and I hadn't been in town long before I heard that "the boys" were calling me "the six-hundred-pound gorilla." (The reference, incidentally, comes from an old joke, as in, "Where does a six-hundred-pound gorilla sleep?" The answer: "Anywhere he wants.") Well, I've been called many things in my life, and very few of them were less flattering, but I quickly found out who had started the practice and let it be known that I'd identified the wit behind the nickname. (I'll let him remain anonymous here, though I will say that we've since become friends.) The behind-the-back talk died down. My having accurate sources seemed to impress the insiders, and it erased their claims that I was uneducated in the ways of the political world. I had been pushed aside for too many years not to have learned how to push back.

It was true that as the President's daughter I had a certain amount of clout — to borrow Michael's term from the convention — but I was determined to use my muscle judiciously and toward positive goals. I wasn't out to advance my own political career, because after my run for the Senate I didn't think I *had* a political career. There was important work to be done if the President was to mend his political fences with women, and I didn't have time for distractions.

With my small staff at the Republican National Committee, and with the folks at the Campaign Fund for Republican Women, I began to plan for our Susan B. Anthony celebration in February, which would double as a fund-raiser to benefit the party's women candidates. The President had agreed to speak. In addition, we collected the names and addresses of all the Republican women elected to state and federal offices so we could publish a directory. Working from these lists, we secured dates on the President's calendar beginning in early 1984, and invited these elected women to the White House for a series of briefings; they would meet with members of Congress, the Vice President, and some key women in the administration, and then they would have lunch in the State Dining Room with the President and the First Lady. It was an ambitious undertaking, but it seemed to all of us that we were headed in the right direction.

Through it all, though, we continued to take a beating in the press from analysts insisting that women would defeat the President in his reelection bid. I knew if we could just hang on until the new year, many of our programs would mature and we would lift ourselves onto a more level playing field. The President believed in my plan, and because of his support the White House skeptics kept quiet, even though they were convinced my efforts would get us nowhere.

The first White House briefing went very smoothly, even with a minor snafu at the luncheon. The schedule called for the President to make some prepared remarks and then, at his insistence, to open the floor to questions from our invited guests. In the interest of time, it was agreed that he would take three random questions.

By the time he got around to the first question, though, we were already running several minutes behind schedule. He took a second question, and a third, and then he kept right on going. He loves this kind of thing, my father, and he was having too much fun to stop.

Nevertheless, he had a busy calendar that day, and before long one of his aides had worked his way through the tables and was tugging on my skirt and whispering, "Get him out of here, the secretary of state is waiting."

I waited for my father to finish his answer, and then I raised my hand. The President looked right past me, as though he hadn't seen me, which I knew he had. He called on someone else. I waited again, and this time I shot up my hand and shouted out, "Excuse me, Mr. President, but are you deliberately avoiding my question?"

The room turned so silent you could hear a press pass drop. The reporters present craned their necks to locate the rude questioner, and those listening in over the intercom in the press room thought they'd have themselves a headline for their afternoon editions.

Dad and I fixed our eyes on each other, and as I stood to reveal myself to the group he said, "Yes, I was avoiding your question, because I knew you'd tell me it was time to get off."

A titter of relief spread throughout the dining room, and I offered up my version of the President's standard sign-off line: "I was going to say — 'Thank you, Mr. President.' "

Dad mumbled something about "how sharper than a serpent's tooth . . . ," a Shakespearean reference to an ungrateful child, and then he stepped off to greet his guests personally.

The briefings had the desired effect. We heard from many women office holders afterward who reported that for the first time they had been able to reveal in their respective caucuses some inside information from the highest levels of government; for the first time, they said, the men had listened.

Now, I don't mean to give short shrift to the other domestic and international issues of that campaign, but I believed then and I believe now that the major issue facing our party that year was women. At least that was the focus for me. Remember, the Democrats had built their whole campaign around the theme that women were going to return them to the White House, so that was what we were up against.

The main event, then, was still to come.

The Susan B. Anthony birthday celebration on February 15, 1984, was quite a big deal, despite the nay-sayers in the White House who thought the whole thing was just a big waste of the President's time. It was held in the Hall of Flags, at the U.S. Chamber of Commerce Building in Washington, D.C., with all proceeds going to benefit the Campaign Fund for Republican Women.

We had the whole thing set up with a kind of carnival theme. We served these wonderfully elaborate desserts. The tickets were a hundred dollars apiece, and we also had a small photo-opportunity session with the President and the First Lady for some of our major contributors. In all we raised over a hundred thousand dollars that night, which went a long way toward shoring up the campaign efforts of a great many Republican women.

In addition, we were hooked up via satellite to local events nationwide, which meant that women candidates around the country could hold their own fund-raisers if they had access to a Holiday Inn or some other hotel with a down-link capability so they could pick up our program and be a part of our festivities. So a substantial sum of money was raised by individual candidates in connection with our event as well.

The highlight of the program was to be an address from the President. I had personally made the scheduling request with his office and with the First Lady's staff and said we needed the President to speak for fifteen to twenty minutes. A speech of this length is considered a "major" address by the White House, and it requires complicated preparation by the President's advance office.

Well, two days before Susan B. Anthony's birthday I received the draft of the President's remarks, and they seemed awfully light. Remembering Lyn Nofziger's concern back at Dad's first Inaugural in 1966, I walked down the hall and asked the President how long he thought the speech would run. He took the speech and looked it over. "Five minutes," he said, and then, weighing the papers playfully in his hand, added, "maybe six with applause."

"Dad," I protested, "the schedule says this is supposed to be a major address."

He looked at the draft again and shook his head. "This isn't a major address," he said, and then he handed it back to me.

What's a six-hundred-pound gorilla to do? Well, this ape sat herself down and started working the phones. I called the speechwriter assigned to prepare the remarks, and then I called the head of speechwriting. Six hundred pounds is a lot of weight to throw around, and it turned out to be more than I needed, because by the next night we were back on track. The next draft of Dad's address would have about ten minutes' more worth of substance.

I got roped into turning thespian for the evening. We decided that the best way to tell the story of Susan B. Anthony was to have someone dress up as Elizabeth Cady Stanton and tell it. Stanton, by the by, was Anthony's best friend, and she wrote extensively about our "birthday girl" in her autobiography, *Eighty Years and More*.

Of course the job fell to me, and to tell you the truth I wasn't all that upset about it. We made a tape, which we ran at the very top of our program, and I laid out the story of how Susan B. Anthony, who devoted her life to the struggle for women's equality, fighting for the right to an education and for the right to own property and, most of all, for the right to vote, had come to represent such an important moment in our quest for equality. I talked about how she traveled the land, organizing women's groups, writing pamphlets, and speaking at conventions. And I talked about how in 1872 she registered and voted to dramatize her cause, and how for that simple nonviolent act she was arrested and tried and fined. (Incidentally, I pointed out, Susan B. Anthony voted Republican.)

I was out working the room when the tape was running, but the President and the First Lady were backstage, getting ready to go on. I'm told that when they saw me on the monitors, dressed in nineteenth-century garb as Elizabeth Cady Stanton, the President said, "Good heavenly days! It's Mermie!"

Indeed it was.

We had other taped messages, from the Vice President and from people like Elizabeth Dole and Margaret Heckler, who were out of town and unable to attend. And a whole host of notable speakers, including the chairman and cochairman of the Republican party, Frank Fahrenkopf and Betty Heitman, the president of the NFRW, Betty Rendel, U.S. trade representative William Brock, and former Secretary of Housing and Urban Development Carla Hills, who acted as emcee.

Finally Nancy came on to introduce the President with the line "Behind every successful woman is an understanding man." Dad got a wonderful kick out of that.

Dad read his address off the TelePrompTers, which confirmed that I'd won the battle of the major speech. (Simple remarks from the President are generally read from the podium, but a full-blown speech is almost always delivered with a TelePrompTer assist.) My stock around town rose dramatically as soon as it became known that we'd gone from five minutes of fluff to a large-scale TelePrompTer address. This apparently is what it takes to impress every advancer in Washington. I may have been imagining things, but I swear people were looking at me with a new respect.

"All of us share a dream of America as a great force for peace and good will among nations," the President concluded. "And all of us share Susan B. Anthony's dream of America as a land where every citizen is judged not according to color or sex, but on the sole basis of individual merit, a land where every woman and man is free to become all they can be. I believe that, under God, we're making that great dream come true."

Gray Terry, the White House advance man assigned to the event, was even moved to consult with me on a logistical problem. "Maureen," he said, taking me aside, "if the President stays until the end of your event, the press is going to get caught in the crush of people getting out of here, and we're never going to get him home." (The President, as you probably already know, travels with a large motorcade and press pool and security types, so moving him from one place to another is never easy.)

Nancy had just returned from one of her antidrug campaign trips and was very tired, and I'd told the folks that it was up to them whether or not they stayed through the whole event. "But," I pleaded, "it would be fantastic if you could stay as late as possible." You have to understand that no matter what the event — a major dinner or a small gathering — whenever the President and the First Lady decide to leave, everybody else leaves with them. Nobody likes to be seen at an event after the President leaves.

So Gray Terry and I struck a deal. "Listen," I told him, "if they stay until the end, you have my word he'll be out of here a full five minutes before everyone else."

"I can live with that," he said.

Later we were sitting on the stage, and the President finished up his now-major address and then sat back down. Half the people in the audience were up out of their seats, putting on their coats, thinking that the President would leave at that point, but he wasn't going anywhere.

I spotted Gray Terry toward the back of the room, and he flashed me a wink.

Dad and Nancy were staying put. They were having such a wonderful time, and they knew that their staying on meant a lot to me and to our effort. They sat through our entire program.

When we were about five minutes short of closing, I stood up and announced, "Ladies and gentlemen, we want to thank our honored guests very much for being with us tonight. Why don't we all give them a big hand and let them go home."

As the audience stood to applaud, Dad and Nancy looked over, and they both said, "Do you want us to go?"

"Yes," I told them. "It's OK, you can go home now."

Dad and Nancy got a laugh track and a standing ovation as they were leaving.

Gray Terry got his five minutes to get his people out of there.

And I got my feet wet.

18

The Second Time Around

RONALD REAGAN kept America guessing in early 1984.

Everywhere you turned, it seemed, there was some speculation or rumor about his intentions of seeking a second term in office. But Dad was playing it close with everyone.

For about a year I'd been urging him to run again, for the simple reason that the American people needed and deserved a full two-term President. Remember, it'd been nearly twenty-five years since Dwight Eisenhower completed his second term, and there were many young Americans who had never known the reassuring stability of an eight-year administration.

If it ain't broke, don't fix it, right?

But the President was cagey, even with us. One night in early January I sat with Dad and Nancy before a crackling fire in his White House study. There was a cold rain slapping against the window outside. I tried to push him on the subject. "Listen, Dad," I said, "I've traveled more than fifty thousand miles in the past six months, trying to bring women into the mainstream of the party, and I'm prepared to double that in the next six months. I'm willing to visit every corner of every state to help us keep the presidency. But you have to answer me one question: am I doing all of this for you, or am I doing all of this for the party?"

Dad looked over to Nancy for a good long time, and in the way he crinkled up his eyes I knew I'd pushed him as far as he needed to go. "Well, Mermie," he said finally, "can you keep a secret?"

He didn't have to say any more. I let out a bottled-up shriek of happiness and leapt up to give him a big hug. "Thank God," I cried. "It's a lot easier to keep up this schedule for love!"

When the President managed to pry me loose, he explained that he felt there was still a lot of work left to do, that he had been tentative about his plans because he was tentative about prolonging the strain the office had put on his family, that he was anxious for a new round of international trade negotiations, and that he was simply not ready to vacate the premises.

"I haven't talked to anyone but Nancy about this," he reminded me, "so for heaven's sake, keep it quiet."

It was tough, but I kept my word. I didn't even tell Dennis. Well, I gave him about a five-minute head start on the rest of the world, but that doesn't count. We were all walking along the colonnade between the White House residence and the Oval Office for the televised announcement of Dad's candidacy. Only then did I confide to Dennis what all Americans would soon know. "He told me," I whispered, biting back a big grin. "He's running."

Dennis and I joined a small handful of well-wishers in the Oval Office and looked on at this momentous occasion, but as the President started to speak I began to worry if I'd gotten my information straight. He had been playing up the suspense of his decision for so long that it had worked its way into his remarks. "It's been nearly three years since I first spoke to you from this room," he started out. "Tonight I'm here for a different reason. I've come to a difficult personal decision as to whether or not I should seek reelection."

For an instant I wondered if he'd had a change of heart. His expression was solemn, his delivery was thick with drama, and I felt certain that when he was through he'd have pulled his hat all the way out of the ring. He went on to talk about the accomplishments of his first term, sounding themes from his Inaugural address, and still he hadn't revealed his intentions. The suspense was woven throughout his speech, and even with my inside information I was on the edge of my seat.

I had no idea which way he was going.

Finally he got to the point. "We have made a new beginning," he announced. "Vice President Bush and I would like to have your continued support and cooperation in completing what we began three years ago. I am therefore announcing that I am a candidate and will seek reelection to the office I presently hold."

There were only a few of us in the Oval Office — Nancy, Dennis, Chief of Staff Jim Baker, and longtime California politico and speechwriter Ken Kachigian — but we sure made a lot of noise. We really whooped it up, clapping each other on the back and the whole business. It was an announcement we'd all expected — one we'd certainly hoped for — and yet because of the way Dad strung it out like that, he still managed to take us all completely by surprise.

Afterward I went up to the President and said, "You made me a little nervous, Dad. I thought maybe something happened to change your mind."

"That's one of the dangers of having inside information," he said with a wink.

I was absolutely delighted by his decision. For one thing, I hadn't been able to think of a better man to hold the office four years earlier, and I certainly couldn't think of a better one now. On a personal level, though, I had finally been privileged to make a contribution to the Reagan White House, and now that I was "inside," so to speak, I didn't want to be asked to leave. For Dad and Nancy this was wonderful news, for the country this was wonderful news, and for me this was wonderful news. Dad would have a chance to finish what he'd started four years before, and I'd have a chance to finish what I'd started just over these past several months.

The reelection campaign for the incumbent President was unlike any other campaign I've ever been involved in. National and international crises are not suspended because the President is involved in winning an election; campaign stops have to be squeezed into an already overburdened schedule.

Plus, there's the Secret Service to contend with, for the entire First Family, and there's the ever-present press pool; the logistics of an incumbent campaign can get pretty staggering.

I took Dad's televised announcement as my marching orders. I would have thought I couldn't campaign any harder than I'd been campaigning, but the thought of another four years in the Reagan White House made me kick up the pace a few notches. By the time we were through I had made my way to all fifty states, sixteen of them once and others as many as eight times. We logged more than 250,000 miles in the twelve months leading up to the election.

It was a lonely, hectic life on the road, but I kept at it. We would all build in little touches of home whenever we could. Dennis stayed behind in California, where he was launching his own public-relations firm, and we would speak on the phone whenever I had a few minutes to spare (and sometimes, to the dismay of the campaign staff, when I didn't). Once in a while he'd surprise me with a visit on the campaign trail, and when he did, we'd sneak in a picnic or a movie or a quiet dinner. One time we even went snowmobiling in Alaska — what fun! — and for a few moments there the campaign was the furthest thing from my mind.

We also stole a peaceful weekend with the folks at Camp David. Let me tell you about this place: in the dictionary, under "retreat," there should be a picture of Camp David. It's in the mountains of Maryland, up by the Pennsylvania border; the compound is set off in the woods, and there are about seven or eight small, rustic cabins, a larger lodge where everyone takes their meals, and a couple of clay tennis courts. The folks would go nearly every weekend, and I understood why on my one and only visit. The place is blissfully quiet. When you live in a house where tourists come through every day and where the press camps outside your front door, you need to get away every once in a while, and when you have a place like Camp David to run away to, every once in a while can't come soon enough. Oh, how Dad would relish his peace and privacy there!

As I said, I was only there once, during the campaign, and it was a visit I'll never forget. I had a lovely moment there with my father, which I will always cherish as one of my fondest presidential memories. We were out horseback riding, and Dad started talking about how important it is for a person to always be learning something new.

"You must be kidding, Dad," I said when we'd slowed to a leisurely gait. "You're the President of the United States. You deal with more new information every day than any other person in this country."

"I suppose that's true, Mermie, but that's not what I'm talking about."

"OK, so what are you talking about?" I wanted to know.

"Well, I've begun memorizing the Robert Service poem 'The Cremation of Sam McGee.' I've learned eight stanzas so far, and it's very relaxing to lie in bed at night and put everything else out of my mind and run through the poem."

The image of our President lying awake at night in his White House quarters, kept from sleep not by domestic and world affairs but by the rhythms and cadence of an old poem, flashed happily through my mind.

"Have you had an audience for it yet?" I asked.

"Not yet," he said. "Would you like to hear it?"

"Love to," I said.

So there we were, father and daughter, riding through the majestic Catoctin National Forest on a pair of beautiful horses, with the lilting words of Robert Service echoing through the trees:

> *There are strange things done in the midnight sun*
> *By the men who toil for gold;*
> *The Arctic trails have their secret tales*
> *That would make your blood run cold;*
>
> *The Northern Lights have seen queer sights,*
> *But the queerest they ever did see*
> *Was that night on the marge of Lake Lebarge*
> *I cremated Sam McGee.*

We have pictures of absolutely everything from Dad's time in office — every conceivable pose, on every conceivable occasion, in every conceivable setting. The images of his entire presidency are recorded in glossy prints and sealed in scrapbooks and behind picture frames. But this was one moment I did not need a picture of. This was a moment — sandwiched in the back-and-forth frenzy of a presidential campaign — I would never forget, a treasured moment that will remain forever in my heart. For a moment such as this, you don't need a camera.

But as always, we were back at it soon enough.

The big issue of the campaign, as it evolved, was the Democrats' nomination of Geraldine Ferraro as Walter Mondale's running mate. I had mixed emotions over the announcement. As a woman I was privately thrilled that one of us had finally made it to a national ticket. It was about time. But the political advancement of women could no longer be a bipartisan issue, at least not on this level, and as a Republican and an emerging player in the President's reelection campaign, I felt that Geraldine Ferraro presented us with some very sticky problems.

While her nomination was making big news in San Francisco, our offices were being staked out by the national media for a reaction. I remember having a conversation with Ed Rollins, who was now working as our campaign manager, about how to play the whole thing. Despite our encounter in 1982, Ed Rollins has become a good friend, and he continues to be one of the keenest strategists in the business.

"The best response to the Ferraro nomination," I reasoned, "is, 'Good, now we know what we're running against.' Under no circumstances should anyone question her qualifications. We shouldn't even use the word *qualified*."

Ed Rollins agreed, and after some deliberation he asked me to appear on all three network morning shows the next day with the Republican response to the Ferraro nomination. After he talked me into it, I gave him a little bit of a hard time. "It's not nice to send a woman through a minefield first," I chided him. "Isn't that why your friends are opposed to the ERA, to keep us out of battle?"

I had dinner with the President and the First Lady the night before my early round of network appearances. Dad asked me what I thought of the Ferraro move.

"I'm not sure I understand it," I said.

"How is that?" he said.

"Well, she's a woman, and she's a terrific campaigner, that's true, but she comes from the same liberal wing as Mondale, and she comes from the Northeast. I don't think she brings anything to the ticket that wasn't already there, other than her gender."

"My feelings exactly," the President responded. "If they wanted to go with a woman, there were other ways to go."

It was well known in political circles that the leaders of the National Women's Political Caucus and the National Organization of Women, and other women leaders, had threatened to join a floor fight on rules led by Jesse Jackson if the party did not select a woman for the number-two spot. The Mondale campaign apparently chose not to do battle on two such volatile fronts and agreed to the women's demands. According to my sources, the call went out to Speaker of the House Tip O'Neill for a recommendation, and he was one of the first to urge that Ferraro be nominated.

As we discussed the events leading to Ferraro's nomination, our conversation naturally turned to the list of women qualified for a spot on a presidential ticket. We talked about Democratic women like Mayor Dianne Feinstein of San Francisco or Louisiana Congresswoman Lindy Boggs as candidates who would have broadened Mondale's appeal.

"You know, it's amazing," my father said, "but when you look at any list of potential women for a ticket, the vast majority are Republican."

Indeed, that was the case, and it remains so today. Number one on my list would have to be Senator Nancy Landon Kassebaum of Kansas. She has built for herself an enviable national and international reputation, though she has never gone out and sought recognition. Senator Kassebaum has simply done her job, become well versed, spoken her piece, and stood up for the rights of human beings throughout the world. No list would be complete without Elizabeth Dole, who has held many government positions but has never run for any office. I don't know that the vice presidency is the place for her to start, but she should be on anyone's list of people who know how to govern. Both women, as we saw in 1988, received serious consideration for the number-two spot by the Bush campaign.

The problem we have, as the President and I discussed that

night, is that there aren't enough women to choose from, Republicans or Democrats. Forgive me my little feminist burst here, but I'm almost done. There are thousands of men who hold public office in the United States, out of whom you can count on one hand the men you would like to see as President or Vice President of this country. By comparison, women hold only hundreds of jobs, and the fact that we can think of another handful of women we would like to see elevated to that position speaks very well for the women we're discussing; it proves they are head and shoulders above their male counterparts.

Anyway, I did my bit on the three morning shows the next day, muscling my way through rush-hour traffic on the tightest of schedules. When you do three shows like that back to back, answering the same questions, it is sometimes difficult to remember what you've already said on each particular program. You start to think about making such and such a point, and then it occurs to you that you may have already made such and such a point. It can all get terribly unnerving, but I think I managed to pull it off. I tried to avoid any discussion of Ferraro's qualifications, as Ed Rollins and I had agreed, and focused instead on the issues of the campaign. Concerning the headline-making nomination of a woman to the ticket, I said that I hoped the Democrats had nominated a vice-presidential candidate who happened to be a woman, and not a woman who happened to be of vice-presidential timber.

When I got back to the White House, there was a call for me from the Vice President.

"You did a great job this morning," he said, "and I want to thank you."

A light went on in my head. George Bush! As far as I knew, he hadn't been consulted on yesterday's developments! I was panicked. "George," I said, "has anyone discussed any of this with you?"

"Not yet."

Not yet? Talk about your sins of omission! I couldn't believe all of us supposed geniuses had been sitting around talking about this and talking about this, and no one had thought to bring George Bush in on the dialogue. The Vice President.

The one person who was going to face Ferraro head-on in the campaign. Can you imagine? He should have been the one to make the network rounds that morning, not me.

"George, I'm so sorry," I said, and then I all but pleaded with him to attend a briefing for some women office holders and candidates in the Old Executive Office Building later that morning. I knew his schedule was tight, but I thought even five minutes of his time would make a world of difference.

An hour later I introduced him to the women at the briefing as our "now and future Vice President." When he stepped in to a boisterous standing ovation, the Vice President knew for the first time that the Reagan-Bush ticket would not be deserted by the women of our party.

I was the only one of the "Reagan children" (oooh, I hate that phrase!) on the campaign trail. Patti was busy with her own life — she had been married to yoga instructor Paul Grilley in a beautiful ceremony at the Bel Air Hotel; almost the entire family was there, and I remember the President danced with almost everybody at the reception. Michael was busy racing boats to raise money for charity and couldn't attend.

Ron had donned a journalist's hat, and he would be covering the convention for the *Dallas Morning News*. He even interviewed me on our attempts to open the door further on women's equality issues. One of his pieces ran in *Playboy* magazine, and when it came out I called him and said, "Ron, do you know how humiliating it was for me to stand on the sidewalk in New York City and buy this crappy magazine so I could read your article?"

"Not as embarrassing as the pictures of you buying that magazine that are going to be in the next issue," he joked back.

The 1984 convention was held in Dallas, and even with an incumbent ticket, we managed to pack in our share of drama. The President's acceptance speech was one of the most stirring and moving he's ever made. He was interrupted more than eighty times for applause and cheering; I know because that's when I lost count. He talked about his achievements of the past four years and the promises he'd kept. And he talked about a little girl in Chambersburg, Pennsylvania, who was asked by her teacher to describe the President's duties: "The

President goes to meetings," she wrote. "He helps animals. The President gets frustrated. He talks to other presidents."

"How does wisdom begin at such an early age?" he said, after quoting from her letter.

He closed his address with the line, "In this springtime of hope, some lights seem eternal. America's is. Thank you. God bless you and God bless America." And then he stepped back from the podium to bask in the warmth and enthusiasm of the delegates.

As everyone had anticipated, my father's age was a major issue in the campaign. The Democrats charged that he was too old to do his job effectively. Mike Deaver poured gasoline on the already hot issue when he revealed to the press that he'd seen the President dozing in Cabinet meetings. I had been with my father after several Cabinet meetings, and he was much too energized and excited by the proceedings not to have participated with full attention.

(I will admit, though, that Dad did nod off during a meeting with Pope John Paul II. In the President's defense, he was suffering from jet lag and extreme fatigue, and unfortunately His Holiness's gracious but exceedingly long welcome had a soporific effect. I was watching it all live on television; it was early in the morning for me back in California, and I wasn't suffering from jet lag, but even I managed to fall asleep twice during the Pope's remarks.)

When he could, Dad would turn the age issue back on Mondale and the Democrats. At the end of one of his speeches he borrowed from those Smith Barney ads with John House-man that were popular at the time and said, "Our opponents treat each new idea the old-fashioned way — they spurn it."

The question of the President's stamina, though, was raised again and again, particularly after the first Reagan-Mondale debate, in Louisville, Kentucky, on domestic policy. I watched the debate on television in Charlotte, North Carolina, where Dad was scheduled to speak the following day. As the debate went on I kept sinking lower and lower in my chair; it was clear to me that the people who had briefed him were ob-sessed with numbers, and the President was getting bogged down with statistics.

The next morning in Charlotte his speech was lackluster and

labored. Missing was the trademark ease and affability we'd come to expect from Ronald Reagan, and in its place was a man just going through the motions. The President seemed not at all at ease with his material.

After the speech I walked over to Lee Atwater, one of the President's aides, and asked, "What have you done to my candidate?"

"Nothing," Lee replied. "We didn't do anything."

"Well somebody must have done something," I said. "Last night was bad, and today was even worse. Something is wrong."

That afternoon Dad and I flew back to Washington on Air Force One. Now, Air Force One is set up in a real compartmentalized way; the President has his quarters and the First Lady has her quarters and the President's staff and the White House press corps have their quarters. There's a galley toward the back of the plane, though I've never been back there. Everything is somewhat tight and cramped — it's an old 707 aircraft, which gives you an idea of its size — but they've got it all so cleverly configured that you don't realize right away how pressed for space you are. In Dad's quarters there's a good-size desk, room enough for four or six people to sit down and meet, and a couch where he can relax. My favorite personal touch on board: on every seat there's a tiny jar of jelly beans. (During President Carter's term there were jars of peanuts — no kidding.)

Anyway, I sat down across the desk from Dad in his quarters, and I took full advantage of our few minutes alone as we finished up our lunch and asked him how he felt about the debate the night before.

"Frankly," he said, "I don't feel very good about it at all."

"Well," I admitted, "I don't feel good about it, either, but I don't think it was quite as bad as you think." Truthfully, it was as bad as he thought, perhaps worse, but I was trying to cheer him up. "I'm pretty sure that the majority of Americans didn't notice anything," I continued. "There are millions of people out there who loved Ronald Reagan before last night, and I'm sure there are those same millions who love Ronald Reagan today."

"I still don't feel too good about it," he said.

He didn't, that was plain to see. What people don't know about my father is that he is a fierce competitor. He comes across as low-key and matter-of-fact, but he's a sportsman at heart. He hated the fact that he hadn't won against Mondale, hadn't even come close, and he didn't know how to get over his disappointment. I looked on to try and gauge his mood for the rest of the flight, and I swear he was wearing the longest face I'd ever seen him wear.

As soon as Air Force One touched down at Andrews Air Force Base, a helicopter picked us up and flew us to Baltimore for a Columbus Day celebration. It seemed as if the entire Italian population of Baltimore was out to greet their President. It really was quite a reception, and as we were driving through the streets of the city I thought that this was just what my father needed to boost his spirits.

But it wasn't enough. Nancy was waiting to greet us when our helicopter landed at the White House, and she sensed something right away. As soon as we stepped inside Dad excused himself and said he had some work to do, and Nancy leaned over to me and asked, "What's wrong with him? Did something happen?"

"He's lower than a snake's belly," I said. (Sorry, but when you grow up on the sets of so many Hollywood westerns, you tend to talk this way sometimes.)

That night at dinner Dad was unusually quiet, and Nancy and I kept flashing each other these "Do something!" looks as we tried to keep up a happy conversation for the President's benefit. He wasn't sulking so much as he just wasn't his bright and cheery self; I don't think anyone but Nancy and I would have noticed the difference, but to us it was a very big difference indeed.

Finally I slammed my hand down on the table and looked at him accusingly.

"Dad, how dare you?" I started in. "Thirty thousand people came out today in Charlotte, and thousands more came out in Baltimore. They came out to see you because you make them feel good, and you didn't let them make *you* feel good."

He looked startled at first — after all, I did have the volume on a little high — but then he started laughing. "Nancy put you up to this, right?" he said.

"Not really," I said, quieting down, "but we are both worried about you."

"Well, you're both right," he said. "I'm going to stop brooding about what happened last night and start preparing for the next debate."

"Just do it your way this time," I coached, "and give Mondale hell."

Dad went to bed that night in high spirits, but in the next few days I noticed that his briefing books were getting thicker and thicker. As he was preparing for his second debate — this one on foreign policy — I worried that he was digging himself into the same hole all over again. A briefing book with too many pages tends to overload the brain cells. Now, despite what his critics say, Ronald Reagan has the closest thing to a photographic memory that I've ever seen. He is probably the best in the business in the way he can sort through masses of information and consolidate and process it all in such a way that he understands it and the people he explains it to will understand it. He can look at a program and tell you where we are in the scheme of things, and where we're going, and in two months' time you can ask him again and he'll have total recall.

But when the briefing books get too thick, you just glaze over. Anybody would. I glaze over when they do that to me. They'll send in this three-hundred-page-long thing for a Republican National Committee meeting, and I'll just laugh (usually because it arrives the night before the meeting). It's just ridiculous. How about a few salient points, folks? We don't need a blow-by-blow on every little thing. There's just too much to remember.

I took all of this as a sign that the second debate would be a repeat of the first, so I took it upon myself to call Bud McFarlane, Dad's national security adviser. After I made my case, he agreed that the debate process was indeed getting bogged down because so many people were getting involved.

Great, I thought, so now let's do something about it.

A few days later, as I was getting ready to leave the office, I was visited by Phil Kawior, the Republican National Committee's research guru. "A group of our opposition-research people came up with some good stuff for the debate," he said, plopping himself down in my chair. "We've put down every one-liner Mondale might use and several possible responses for the President. We've even come up with some one-liners for the President."

He left me to look over his notes. I liked what I saw. There was a lot of substantive material, but the most important passages, to my mind, were the lighter parts. I called Bud McFarlane. "I'm sending you some really good material that will help with this debate," I said. "It's funny, and even if we don't use any of it, it'll help to lighten up the process."

After dinner, over coffee in the living room, I curled up on the sofa and told the President that his opposition-research staff had come up with some pretty funny stuff I thought he might like to see. As I handed him the few pages I'd brought home, I said, "Why should some researchers have all the fun, and not the candidate?"

He went off to read over the material as Nancy and I stayed and lingered over our coffee. We flipped through some magazines and talked about this and that, and every few minutes we'd hear a chuckle from his corner of the room, and I knew we were back on the right track with this thing. It's a shame, but most of the material never worked its way into the debate and has disappeared over the years, but it did serve a tremendous purpose. It put some fun into the tedious business of preparing for a presidential debate.

A spoonful of sugar helps the medicine go down, right?

The last two days of the campaign were nearly marred by a mild concussion — Nancy's. The folks were in Sacramento for a rally, and they were staying at an inn with beds on raised platforms. When Nancy got up in the middle of the night, she forgot to step down and fell and cracked her head against a chair. Dad stayed up with her all night, applying ice packs to her head and trying to talk her into going to the hospital. Trooper (and stubborn mule) that she was, she refused. She did go to see the White House doctor, who confirmed that she had suffered a mild concussion, but Nancy kept playing the whole thing down. She kept telling everybody she was fine. She just did not want to do anything to take attention away from the campaign.

I saw her two days after the accident, on Election Day. She

was sitting in a friend's office, eating a banana. To this day she does not remember seeing me or eating that banana, so clearly she must have been in pretty bad shape. But as she told me later, "Those were the final two days of your father's last campaign, and I was determined not to miss them."

I knew exactly what she meant. My final campaign appearance was on the Monday before the election, in Ohio, and I looked out at the faces of our tireless volunteers and was overcome by the thought that this was the last campaign speech I would ever make for Ronald Reagan. I was let into the game late — I completely missed the chance to campaign openly for him for governor — and now it all seemed to be over just when it was getting started.

The inauguration this time was only a little less hectic. For one thing, we had a nicer place to stay. There was a huge family reunion at the White House. There were Reagans (and Davises) everywhere, filling up all fourteen bedrooms. Dennis and I were assigned our usual quarters in the Lincoln Bedroom. (Dennis, at six foot seven, is so tall that President Lincoln's eight-foot Victorian bed is the only one in the White House that can comfortably accommodate him.) Michael and Colleen were there with their son, Cameron, and their twenty-month-old daughter, Ashley, as were Ron and Doria and Patti (whose new husband wasn't able to make it), Neill and Bess, and Nancy's brother, Richard, and his wife, Patricia, with their kids, Geoffrey and Anne. . . . We really were one big happy family during the week of those festivities. It was a joyous time for all of us. The President even built a snowman in the Rose Garden with his grandchildren. (Now that's one I'd like to have a picture of!) And in honor of the occasion, I made a pass at reconciliation with my uncle Neill over his treatment of my Senate campaign.

We all had dinner together on the Sunday night before the inauguration in the downstairs family dining room. Many years ago the President and his family took all their meals downstairs, until Jacqueline Kennedy put a kitchen and a dining room up on the second floor, which made things a little less formal. But on this occasion a little formality was more than appropriate. Besides, there were too many of us to all fit around the table upstairs.

At his first inauguration Dad had earned a special piece of history, as the oath of office was administered for the first time on the west face of the Capitol. This time the brutally cold Washington weather (there were frostbite warnings in effect!) forced us into another historic location — the Rotunda of the Capitol. Only about ninety members of Congress, the Cabinet, and the Reagan family and friends were able to squeeze into the makeshift "hall" to hear the President's live address. The other thousands who had come to Washington to witness the event had to watch it on television along with everybody else.

"My fellow citizens,'" he said. "Our nation is poised for greatness. We must do what we know is right, and do it with all our might. Let history say of us, 'These were golden years, when the American Revolution was reborn, when freedom gained new life, and America reached for her best.' "

As I listened, a chill still ripping through my bones even though we were now inside, I let my mind tally up the achievements of Dad's first term. His popularity was at an all-time high — goodness, he carried forty-nine of our fifty states in the November elections! — and he had managed to restore to the American people a sense of patriotism and pride. The economic recovery he had promised was a reality. Inflation had dropped, and millions of new jobs had been created. On the international front, our show of force in Grenada in the months just past was a great achievement, and it marked the first time in years that the United States had sent a clear signal to the Soviets and the Cubans to back off.

And as of late, he was setting a shining light for women and women's-rights issues, which was something even his supporters had questioned his ability to do. And — the best part — there were even better days ahead.

I couldn't wait for the next four years to start.

19

White House Musings

WHEN I BECAME MORE DEEPLY INVOLVED in the work of Dad's administration, I began to spend more and more time with the folks in their "government housing." After I signed on as a special consultant on women's issues, I did everything short of moving in. Before long my time was being evenly split between Washington and California.

Nancy assigned me to the Lincoln Bedroom; that was where I hung my hat whenever I was in town. I wound up spending so much time there that I had the press office add the following line to my published biography: "In Washington, she stays at her parents' lodgings." That always got us a laugh when we used it in formal introductions.

My parents' lodgings were quite something. Really. In eight years I never lost the feeling of wonder and majesty and history I had the first time I drove through the gates leading up to the White House. The place just takes my breath away. I know it's a corny cliché, but that's the only way I can think to describe how I felt whenever I came into town for a visit. If you've ever taken the White House tour and just been overwhelmed by the beauty and splendor of the place, well, just multiply that out by about a thousand and you'll get a good idea of what it's like to arrive there with a proprietary interest.

Indulge me on this one story: on one of my very first visits there, I ran around with Dennis looking to snatch up some appropriate souvenirs to send back to our friends in California. Anyway, the second and third floors of the White House, the residence floors, are referred to as the President's House. The matchbooks the White House staff leaves lying around don't say "The White House," as you might think; they say "The President's House." I always thought that was kind of neat. The first time I saw one of those matchbooks, I picked it up and showed Dennis and told him this was exactly what I was looking for. He wanted no part of my little caper, but I rounded up as many matchbooks as I could reasonably get my hands on; every time I passed a table, I'd pinch a matchbook. Every so often I'd leave one behind, just for appearances. I needed about twenty of them to send back home, and I figured I'd have no trouble meeting my quota.

Dennis couldn't believe what I was doing, but I was having great fun. (Remember, I was the one who made Dennis snap my picture that first time we saw the Oval Office; always the tourist, right?) So I kept at it until I had more matchbooks than I knew what to do with. Finally I looked around the West Hall, where we were staying, and the tables really looked bare. There'd be a matchbook left on one table and then there wouldn't be any others, and so I said to Dennis, "Well, maybe if I just take them all, they'll think they just didn't put any out."

"I can't believe you," Dennis said. "You really don't think anyone will notice?"

"Well," I said, "it's worth a try."

So I went around and picked up the few I had left behind. By the time we left, the place was absolutely clean of matchbooks. Everybody back home got one (or two, depending), and for good measure I sat down and wrote everyone a nice note on some lovely White House stationery. I stayed up all night and sent out my little care packages to everybody in my phone book.

Dennis, I'm sure, was right; somebody must have noticed. But the terrific thing, which I hadn't figured on that first time, was that even if somebody noticed, nobody would have said anything!

The White House is really quite a place to stay. I love the Lincoln Bedroom and its sitting room, with its oversized and ornately carved rosewood bed. There's some wonderful Lincoln memorabilia, like a signed holograph of the Gettysburg Address and a dance card from his Inaugural ball. It has a kind of museum feel to it, the way everything is set out just so. All of the pieces are authentic, from Lincoln's period, but not all of them were actually used by the President. The room used to be the Cabinet Room, where President Lincoln signed the Emancipation Proclamation on January 1, 1865. He had just stood on a public receiving line where more than a thousand Washington citizens came by to wish him a Happy New Year. As he sat down to sign this historic document, he paused and took a deep breath. His Cabinet members wondered aloud if the President was having second thoughts, but Lincoln put them all at ease when he said, "My arm is sore from shaking all those hands. I want to be sure my signature doesn't waver or history will record I was unsure of this decision."

The room positively pulses with history. It's impossible to spend any time there without feeling Lincoln's stately presence. In fact, Dennis and I could swear the room is haunted. I know, I know, it sounds hard to believe and weird as all get-out, but we've each seen a ghost during our stays there. I can just imagine the *National Enquirer* headlines now: "President's Daughter Sees Ghost, Claims Lincoln Haunts Her Bedroom!"

Laugh if you will, but it's true. Dennis was the first to see a shadowy figure by the fireplace late one night. I thought he was crazy when he woke me up and told me about it, but it wasn't long before I had a vision of my own. One night I woke up and saw, in the half-light, what appeared to be a man wearing a red coat. My first thought was that my intruder was my father — he sometimes wears a red bathrobe — and I remember wondering what the President was doing in my room. But then as I looked closer I realized that what I was seeing had no substance whatsoever. He was transparent. I could see right through him to the windowsill and the magnolia tree outside. A chill crept through me. The "man" just stood there, staring pensively out the window at the tree. I couldn't make out any distinguishing features, but it was very definitely a human form. Then he slowly turned around and stared at me before vanishing into thin air.

Now, it could have been a dream, I'll grant you that, but I don't think it was. I called Dennis out in California to describe to him what I'd seen, and my account fit exactly with his. The similarities were indisputable. Whether we were seeing the image of Abraham Lincoln or possibly of Andrew Jackson (who planted one of the three magnolia trees on the White House grounds in memory of his wife, Rachel, who died shortly after he was elected to office) or just of some abstract presidential figure, we were certainly seeing something. We knew we had seen the spirit that has been a part of White House lore for many, many years.

Dad thought we were loony-tunes. We tried to tell him about our middle-of-the-night visitor, and he just laughed and laughed. "If you see him again," he said, "send him down the hall. I have some questions."

But even our skeptical President had a run-in of his own before long. One night when the Lincoln Bedroom was empty, the folks' dog Rex began inexplicably and slowly stalking that end of the hall. There was no one there, but Rex kept up his chatter and Dad followed him. Rex kept barking and headed directly for the Lincoln Bedroom. Dad opened the door and Rex hugged the floor and growled, his eyes fixed on something. The President went into the room to see what was causing Rex's commotion. He couldn't find a thing. The room was as empty as a deserted Hollywood set. (He's a regular ghostbuster, my father.) Rex calmed down but wouldn't go inside the room, so the President began to think that maybe we were onto something with our "visions." It's funny that he wouldn't take his own daughter at her word, or his son-in-law, but he'd begin to believe a barking dog. Or maybe he thinks we're all a bit bonkers.

Dad loved everything about the White House, not just his after-hours prowls with Rex. He loved the mansion's charming, unpretentious architectural style, its warm and elegant staff, its spacious rooms and historical furnishings. He even loved the squirrels. There were a few oak trees on the White House grounds, but no acorns, which of course were in great supply at the President's Camp David retreat. So each fall when the folks returned from spending the weekend at Camp David, the President would bring back a large plastic sack full of acorns he had gathered. As the week wore on, he would scatter the acorns outside the door of the Oval Office each morning, and throughout the day he would look up from his desk and see the squirrels scurrying off with their treats from the country.

He used to say that by Friday the squirrels would practically nose up to the windows and give him a sad, pleading look, reminding him to bring back some more goodies after the weekend.

In the period just before the 1984 election and during my father's second term in office, I spent a lot of time in Washington. If I had to put a number on it, I'd say I spent about a week or two each month in the White House, which gave me a nice ringside seat for the presidency. The thing that struck me most of all was that the President never had a day off. Never. Not even on his so-called vacations. No matter where he is, there are always some briefing booklets for him to study, documents for him to read, speeches to write, and decisions to make. It's unending. There is not a single day — not Saturdays, Sundays, or holidays — when the folders of work do not constantly appear for his attention.

The President's routine when he was in Washington was, well, routine. I never paid any attention to what the press said about his nap-shortened workdays. From where I sat, the country got its money's worth out of Ronald Reagan, believe me. He'd put in a long, tiring day, usually with dozens of ceremonial functions, staff meetings, and briefings with other elected officials. And he'd have an endless stream of paperwork to deal with. When there was no evening function he needed to attend, he would come upstairs at about five o'clock and exercise with weights for about an hour. After a shower he'd watch the early network news feeds, and then he'd enjoy a nice leisurely dinner. After dinner he would usually retire to his study for another two or three hours of work, though on occasion the folks would treat themselves to a night off and screen movies or watch a special television program or read.

When he wasn't in the Oval Office, Dad could usually be found in his study. He felt at home there. Most of the furniture in the President's House was standard White House issue — priceless antiques, yes, but also standard White House issue — but here and there were Nancy's unmistakable touches, like Dad's study, done up in bright red (the family color) for the carpet, the upholstery, and the draperies. Lovely green plants would dot the room, with red-flowering buds. Even the different woods on his desk and tables and credenzas were so deep and rich they positively oozed mahogany. The room was filled with mementos, including a desk lamp made from a fire chief's silver horn and dozens of family photos — every flat surface (Dad's desk, the console television set) was covered with silver picture frames!

Informal family meals at the White House were for the most part simple, healthy fare. Nancy tended to watch over the folks in the kitchen, to make sure we were all getting our three squares.

As often as not the menu would lean toward the presidential favorites — macaroni and cheese and meat loaf. Now, Dad has been known to favor all varieties of the former, from the canned and boxed and frozen styles sold in the local supermarket to the homemade-from-scratch kind he'd be treated to from the White House kitchen. I take special pride in knowing that my recipe for macaroni and cheese ranks among his favorites. (Here's a hint: I take canned milk and whip it up with an egg until it's almost souffléed.)

It seems to me I'm always on a diet, so I would rarely get the chance to roll up my sleeves and dig in along with Dad, but I'll admit to a weakness for the stuff myself. I guess it runs in the family. My favorite, though, is liver, which Nancy also loves. Dad can't stand it, but every once in a while we'll prevail upon the kitchen staff to prepare some, and when we do, Dad just sours up his face in the same "Yech! Liver!" pout you'll find on little boys across the country.

Most times, though, Dad would get his way in the family dining room. Nancy softened her health kick somewhat on behalf of the presidential sweet tooth. Every night the kitchen staff would wheel out some wonderfully decadent pastries or soufflés or some exotic new flavor of sorbet. Nancy, with her perfect size-two figure, would look on and just smile as the rest of us dove in.

Nancy's figure, as long as we're on the subject, has long been the object of many a family ribbing. (Where Nancy's concerned, I use a word like *ribbing* with some hesitation.) Although we know she has the requisite number of vital organs, none of us can figure out where they hide in her pencil-thin frame. If we pressed her to eat more, she would mutter something about having just eaten lunch, which would prompt one of us to remark, "I know, I just saw it move!"

One of the great fringe benefits of my spending so much time in the White House was the chance it allowed for Nancy and me to become really well acquainted. Not since I was a little girl, on our long car rides out to the ranch or up to Chadwick, had we spent so much time together. We'd always marvel at the way the press kept insisting we didn't like each other, but the truth of it is that we spent more time together during the last five years of my father's administration than we ever had before, and we came away from the experience liking each other a whole lot more than we ever had before.

We're great friends now, actually. She's even taken to mothering me in my old age. I'll never forget one time, just before Dad's second inauguration, when I was terribly sick with the flu. Nancy must have called the doctor three times a day to make sure I would recover in time for the festivities. Of course, I was ready to get back on my feet long before Nancy thought I was, so I accepted an invitation to a party on a Sunday evening early in January.

Well, when the folks returned from Camp David that Sunday afternoon, Nancy put her foot down over my plans. "Maureen, you can't possibly go to that party," she insisted. "You're sick."

"No, I'm much better," I tried. "I really am."

But Nancy, the quintessential doctor's daughter, wouldn't budge, and before long we'd erased the past thirty or so years and I had my hands on my hips and was saying things like "Aw, gee, everyone will be there. I have to go."

Of course, we all laughed at the scene, but I failed to realize how serious Nancy was about the whole thing. I ignored her pleas and went to the party as planned, but when I got there I discovered that the First Lady had already called the hostess with orders that I was only to stay at the party for one hour.

Sure enough, I arrived back at the White House exactly one hour, plus driving time, after I'd left. "What are you, a Jewish mother?" I asked playfully on my way back to the Lincoln Bedroom.

"Yes," Nancy said, "that's exactly what I am." Then she called the kitchen and ordered me some soup. "Did you take your medicine?" she wanted to know.

"Yes."

"Did you eat?"

"No."

"You know you're not supposed to take your medication on an empty stomach."

"Well," I said, "I planned on eating something at the party, but I wasn't allowed to stay long enough for the food to be served."

That's Nancy.

Of course, no discussion of life in the White House would be complete without mention of the Secret Service. They're everywhere. The first thing they do is give you a code name so they can keep track of you in their own shorthand. Once a code name is established for the President, the names for the rest of the family must all begin with the same initial. Mine was "Radiant." I don't remember everyone's (there are a lot of us when you count grandchildren), but Michael's was "Riddler." I'd love to tell you what the President and the First Lady go by, but they're still under Secret Service protection, and I don't want to jeopardize their safety in any way. (I'll give you a hint, though, in case you haven't figured it out: they start with the letter *r*.)

They also ask you to come up with a travel name so travel agents and airline reservation people won't be tipped off to your plans. I was sitting on a commuter plane about to take off from D.C. to Harrisburg, Pennsylvania, when the Secret Service detail leader told me that for security reasons, I should travel under an assumed name. "We don't like for your real name to appear on an airline's computer," he said.

"Fine," I said. "Anything you come up with will be fine with me."

"Well," he said, "we were kind of hoping you could come up with one yourself. We're not clever in that way."

He's right. They're not clever in that way. After eight years you tend to notice things like that.

So there I was, staring out the window onto the runway and trying to come up with a clever and exotic name for myself. Nothing came to me until we started down the runway; as we were taxiing, approaching takeoff, we suddenly came to a screeching halt. A jet took off diagonally across our path. Everyone on the plane gasped, and I could hear a man up front shout out to the pilot, "Does this happen often?" It really gave us all quite a scare.

Just then it hit me: "Mandrake." As in Mandrake the Magician. As in "Now you see us, now you don't." I thought it fit in quite nicely with the precariousness of my new life-style. Now you see me, now you don't. OK, I thought, what goes with "Mandrake"? For some reason "Ramona" came quickly to mind, and so I nudged the agent sitting next to me.

"From now on, when we're on the road, you may think of me as Ramona Mandrake," I said.

"You're kidding?" the agent said hopefully.

"No, I most certainly am not."

They hated the name at first, my Secret Service friends, but as time wore on they grew to like it. In fact, the ones who were too shy to call me Maureen and too professional to use "Radiant" and too close to my own age to call me Ms. Reagan took to calling me Ramona. Eventually so many of them got a kick out of my alias that they dubbed my detail Ramona's Raiders.

For eight years the only time any of us were alone — Dad, Nancy, and all four of Dad's children — was when we were inside the walls of our own houses. In the White House that meant the Secret Service agents were in all the hallways on the residence floors but not in the actual President's House. At home, in California, it meant they were always parked outside in front of my house. The rest of the time Ramona's Raiders were with us. For eight years we had to notify someone before going to the market for a quart of milk or walking the dog. For eight years Dennis and I had company on our romantic dinners and on our walks on the beach.

It's hard not to resent the presence of the Secret Service, but you try. They are of course there for our protection, even if they get in the way sometimes, which can sometimes be as funny as it is aggravating. When we were first married Dennis was still living in Orange County, California. We spent a lot of time at his apartment, and whenever I traveled, the Secret Service had to establish some sort of temporary headquarters wherever I was staying. They also had to do this as inconspicuously as possible. After some discussion it was agreed that the agents would install a phone jack on the outside wall of Dennis's apartment building and wire it to their post in the car. After they had plugged in their phone to the jack, they would string a very long cord across the sidewalk to their car. Not exactly inconspicuous, but I suppose it just had to do in a pinch.

One afternoon as they were sitting in the car with the phone beside them on the sidewalk, a man came walking down the street. Seeing the phone, the man bent down and picked up the receiver and listened for a moment. To his amazement, there was a dial tone, and so he followed the cord until he reached the jack in the wall of the apartment building. Then he unplugged the phone and started off down the street. I guess the guy just thought the phone would look better in his living room than it did on the sidewalk.

Well, I don't know how they managed it without revealing their identities, but the Secret Service agents managed to persuade the man that the phone was theirs and that they always kept an extension out on the sidewalk like that, and they asked him to please return it at once.

On our honeymoon/business trip to Europe, Dennis and I decided to have dinner one night at a restaurant called Tiddy Dol's, in London's Shepherd Market. As was becoming our custom, my agents accompanied us and dined at a nearby table. (They lived pretty well during that trip, come to think of it.) They had visited the restaurant earlier in the day, identifying themselves only to the manager, who promised not to reveal their identities to anyone.

But even if their cover was safe, they did make an odd picture. At one point a waitress went up to the manager and asked why the six men in dark suits at the far table all had these wires and plugs coming out of their ears.

Thinking quickly, the manager said, "Those poor chaps are

all hard of hearing. One of them told me they all recently graduated from a school for the deaf, and they're here to celebrate."

Well, the waitress went back to her "hard-of-hearing" customers and proceeded to shout at them for the rest of the evening. At the top of her lungs. Every head in the place turned every time she went over to their table. In the entire eight years that we were together, I have never seen the men on my detail look so flustered.

One of the agents on the "Radiant" detail had earlier spent some time on the President's detail, and he once told me a story about a desperate-looking character leaping on the hood of the presidential candidate's limousine when the motorcade was passing through New York City. Instinctively the agents had reached for their guns, and then they stared on in amazement as three policemen, one after the other, bounded across the top of the car in pursuit of this strange man, who by this time was sprinting down the street. The agent said that when he turned around to see the President's reaction to all the excitement, my father was grinning broadly and giving him the thumbs-up sign.

Dad's always been a fan of the Secret Service, from the very beginning. He got his first dose of protection in June 1968, when he was considered a candidate for President. In those days Dad liked to practice shooting at tin cans. He said it reminded him of his days making westerns, when of course all he'd had in his gun were blanks. One time, accompanied by his Secret Service agents, he went outdoors to do some can shooting, and on his way out to set up he told one of the agents about an article he'd read in a shooting magazine that recommended that you crouch when you shoot, for a quick, accurate draw.

"Governor," the agent replied, "we don't crouch when we shoot."

Nothing the agent would say could convince my father that this crouching business wasn't a better way to shoot. Dad even got down and demonstrated. He missed. Then the agent took his turn, and standing perfectly straight, he demonstrated his method. He hit the can.

"But the article says you'd be even better if you crouched," Dad insisted.

"Governor," the agent explained, "when I'm shooting at something, I'm standing between it and the target. I'm not allowed to crouch."

Dad said that from that moment on, he was filled with respect for the Secret Service.

The only problem he ever had with his agents was their strict rule not allowing him to open any windows. The President is a fresh-air freak, and this was a tough rule for him to obey; he was forever opening up windows behind his agents' backs, just to sneak himself a quick breath of the outdoors.

Besides Secret Service agents, our other constant companions were our four-footed friends. Dad regarded his pets as members of the family, and they pretty much had the run of the place, even at the White House. For as long as I can remember, Dad has seldom been without a dog, or two or three or four. The apple didn't fall far from the tree in that respect. After Barnae, Dennis and I eventually acquired two other dogs, a small gray mutt named Fang and a miniature apricot poodle named Boxcar Willie. (My sweet Barnae is buried at the ranch, in our family pet cemetery, which we've named Mount Rhino after an early pet; as he does for all the departed Reagan animals, Dad carved Barnae's name on a headstone for the ceremony.)

As she got on in years, Fang couldn't see very well, and when she was about fourteen she fell off the balcony of our Sacramento apartment and broke her back. The poor thing! The accident left her paralyzed, and the vet was recommending that we put her to sleep, but Dennis wouldn't hear of it. He loved that dog. She had an incredible will to live, and before long she'd taught herself to walk on two legs. We also jury-rigged this harness with small wheels for her hind legs. She was incontinent, but fortunately newborn-size Huggies work as well for aging dogs as they do for babies.

Fang really made quite a sad little picture in her harness and diapers and whatnot, but when we brought her to the White House for the first time she wanted to look as dignified as possible. When we introduced her to her presidential host —

Nancy's King Charles spaniel, Rex, the one who'd seen our Lincoln ghost — Rex just gave her the oddest, longest stare. He didn't find Fang at all dignified in her getup. He just found her weird.

Thanks to Dennis's loving care and devotion, Fang was with us for a year and a half after her accident. When she left us, it was because she was ready to go, and not because some vet wanted to put her down. Fang's heir apparent came into our life in 1986, when Dennis was dining in a Sacramento restaurant. Dennis was about to get into his car, where Fang was waiting, when he noticed what looked to be a small group of homeless people picking through a garbage can. Perched on top of their shopping cart was a tiny orange dog. The street people wandered over to Dennis's car, and when they saw Fang on the front seat, they began flashing these wide toothless grins. They'd never seen such a ridiculous sight as a dog in diapers!

So Dennis struck up a conversation with them, and when he asked how they'd happened to acquire the apricot puppy, they explained that they had done some yardwork for some people who refused to pay them at the last minute and offered them the poodle instead.

"But it's not easy with a dog," one of the men told Dennis. "He whimpers all the time, and we can't always find food for him." Dennis offered to give them some money to buy some food for themselves and the puppy, but another one of them said, "Look, we live on the street, and the street is no place for a dog."

A light bulb went off over Dennis's head, which I'm sure is just what these men were hoping for. Dennis emptied his wallet — I think he had about forty dollars and change — and he gave the money to them in exchange for the puppy.

No sooner did we bring Boxcar Willie home than the vet informed us that the dog had a serious heart defect and needed open-heart surgery. (Don't they ever give you good news, these veterinarians?) Open-heart surgery for a dog costs practically as much as it does for a human-type person, and doggie medical insurance isn't exactly Blue Cross/Blue Shield. But Dennis and I dug deep into our bank accounts without a second thought.

He was up and about in a few days, chewing on the leg of our sofa. Before long we decided it was time to take Boxcar Willie east to meet the rest of his First Family. Willie's got some wonderful friends at the White House, most notably a kindly staff butler named Alfredo. Alfredo simply adores Willie — most everybody does! — and he'll usually get down on all fours and play with him whenever he turns up at the door.

There are people on the White House staff who assist the President and the First Lady with walking their dogs (yes, we follow pooper-scooper laws on the White House grounds), but when Dennis and I are there with Willie we do most of our own walking. Except one time when, after a state dinner, I woke up with a horrendous headache and called down and asked Alfredo if he wouldn't mind taking Willie out for me. "If you're really Willie's friend," I asked, "would you mind taking him downstairs for me, since the sunlight would just be murder on my eyes?"

Alfredo thought that was the funniest thing he'd ever heard, being asked to walk the dog like that. I guess if you're in the White House long enough, you see everything.

Willie could turn anyone into a friend (and I do mean anyone). On Willie's first visit to the White House, Dennis took him over to the West Wing to introduce him around. As they were walking down the hall, Tom Dawson (assistant to the President's chief of staff, Donald Regan) came out of his office, took one look at Willie, and said, "Oh, the Chief has to see this."

So Tom Dawson led Dennis and Willie to Regan's office; they opened the door and Willie bounded in, jumped up on the desk where the chief of staff was working, and proceeded to lick him all over the face. Now, Don Regan is usually a man with no time to spare for anybody, but Dennis told me he permitted this overwhelming display of affection to go on for a good twenty minutes.

And they say dogs are such terrific judges of people.

20

Nairobi

IN JULY 1985 I had one of the most frustrating, agonizing, exhausting, and (ultimately) satisfying experiences in my political career; at the same time, in a completely unrelated forum and half a world away, those very same emotions were put into play for me on a personal level.

Late in 1984, after the election, I was invited to lunch by my old friend Nancy Clark Reynolds. Nancy had left a career in broadcasting to join the Reagan administration in Sacramento back in 1967, and she remained with the governor, both in and out of office, for the next ten years. She beat him to Washington, though, by a couple of years, and when she left she joked that she was headed east as the first member of the Reagan transition team for 1981. (It turned out she was right.) Anyway, in 1984 Nancy was working as the president of Wexler, Reynolds, Harrison and Schule, a well-known public-affairs firm, and serving part-time as a United States representative to the United Nations' Commission on the Status of Women.

When we sat down to lunch, she got right to the point. "Jeane Kirkpatrick and I think you should chair the U.S. delegation to Nairobi," she announced. Nairobi, Kenya, was to be the site of the third of three United Nations world conferences the following summer — the first two had been held in Mexico City (1975) and Copenhagen (1980) — marking the end of the U.N.'s Decade of Women. The goal of the Nairobi conference, I was to learn, was to achieve consensus among member delegations on a document with the rather unwieldly title "Forward Looking Strategies to the Year 2000," which had the entirely wieldly and noble purpose of addressing the growing needs of women in developing countries.

"I'd be honored," I said, "but I didn't think we were participating in any more of these conferences." The United States delegation and the Reagan administration, I knew, viewed the first two conferences as social successes but substantive failures. In fact, at Copenhagen the U.S. had led the vote against signing the document that was to have emerged from that conference because of objectionable language that equated Zionism with racism; without consensus documentation, the conference was unfairly reported in the world press as little more than large-scale spinning-of-wheels.

"No," Nancy said. "There's some debate about that, but we'd like to go ahead. If you agree with us on this, then together we can wage the battles necessary to ensure U.S. participation."

Nancy had always been an enthusiastic supporter of my efforts, and a good friend, and there was no way I could say no; besides, I thought it would be a real chance to bring hope and light to women on an international level, against considerable odds — a combination I could not easily turn down.

So, under the protective wings of Nancy Clark Reynolds and Jeane Kirkpatrick, I began my tutelage in the ways and wonders of the United Nations. I spent the next several months immersed in the history of these conferences and in policy and procedure. We put together a thirty-six-member U.S. delegation that included Kansas Senator Nancy Kassebaum, Congresswomen Marjorie Holt of Maryland and Lindy Boggs of Louisiana, and Assistant Secretary of Health and Human Services Stephanie Lee Miller. (Margaret Heckler, secretary of Health and Human Services, had attended the Mexico conference as a member of Congress but was forced to drop out of the Nairobi delegation for health reasons.)

By the time of our final preparatory meeting — which was

held at the U.N. facility in Vienna in February 1985 — we had already announced the members of the U.S. delegation, putting an end to Soviet-backed disinformation that we would not attend. The Soviets and their radical allies had hoped that without U.S. participation, the longstanding attempt to delegitimize Israel by equating Zionism and racism would continue unabated. Additionally, nonparticipation by the U.S. would guarantee that other contentious issues would be accepted without a major battle, including such thorny subjects as mandatory sanctions against South Africa; a Palestinian homeland; and forgiveness of international debts for developing nations.

Among the major players on the Commission for the Status of Women (CSW) was Tatiana Nikoleava, who had represented the Soviet Union for over thirty years. A stickler for parliamentary procedure, Tatiana was well known for her ability to filibuster any subject over which she wanted to build disagreement; she was a formidable adversary, and nothing Nancy Reynolds could have told me about her would have prepared me for our first encounter.

We met in Vienna. After exchanging a cursory hug with Nancy, Tatiana turned to me and said, "Why do you want to destroy my country?"

"I don't," I said evenly. "Why do you want to destroy mine?"

She paused a minute and then started in again. "The success of Nairobi depends on Geneva," she said, referring to the site of the then-stalled arms negotiations.

"The success of Nairobi depends on Vienna," I said.

She stared at me for another minute and then walked away. I thought I'd handled her pretty well, for a rookie.

Sure enough, Tatiana Nikoleava lived up to her reputation. She filled the first two days of the preparatory meetings with extraneous debates and other parliamentary stalling tactics. We were getting nowhere, and if things kept up this way the CSW would not be able to take action on the agenda, rules, or documentation for the upcoming conference; Vienna was looking like a bust.

During one of our breaks Nancy and I huddled into a phone booth in our hotel lobby and tried to put a call through to Ambassador Kirkpatrick, who was in Rabat. "Jeane," I hollered into the phone, "something strange is going on here. Tatiana has filibustered the entire meeting. At this rate we won't have time to get anything done."

Our connection was lousy, but I heard a chuckle at the other end. "Welcome to the U.N.," Jeane laughed. "I'll bet you've never seen anything like it."

"To tell you the truth, it's a lot like a Young Republicans convention," I said.

"I can imagine."

"Look," I continued, "we're wondering if you have any information on why the Soviets are acting this way."

What we pieced together later, after the passing of Soviet General Secretary Chernenko, was that Madame Nikoleava had had instructions to ensure that no action was taken by the CSW before the new government of Mikhail Gorbachev could establish its power. She followed orders very well; when we left Vienna, it looked as though Nairobi was doomed to fail.

Back home, I vented some of my frustrations over dinner with Dad and Dennis.

"My gosh, Mermie," the President said at one point, "why in heaven should the U.S. go any further with this conference?"

Good question. Fortunately I had some answers. I told him how essential it was to talk with the African women on a "woman-to-woman" basis, and not a "government-to-government" one, because that way we would no doubt gain a new perspective on their problems. I told him about the women of Burkina Faso, who leave home in the evening, walk ten to fifteen miles, rest beside the mud wallows, gather water, and then return home before the heat of the day. I told him about a woman in rural India who remarked to a visiting Member of Parliament at a seminar on water resources: "You talk about water resources, but you do not really understand the situation. In my village water is so rare that a woman gets a bath three times in her life. When she is born, when she marries, and when she dies." I reminded him that 78 percent of the world's agricultural workers were women, and that women owned less than 1 percent of the land. And I made the case that Kenya was not a drought-stricken country like some of her neighbors; there were a number of educational, health-related, and income-generating projects already under way there that were worthy of world attention.

"If we're there, we can find like-minded advocates on important world issues," I said. "We can get a dialogue going on literacy and domestic violence and development — on any number of issues. If we stay home, we'll miss that opportunity."

"What about the document?" Dennis asked.

"Well," I admitted, "it's going to be real tough to get a consensus, and without it the U.N. will continue to talk about these problems but won't take any positive action."

"Sounds to me like it's worth a try," the President said with only a hint of skepticism. "Why don't you talk to Bud McFarlane and George Shultz and see what they say?"

A few days later I had breakfast with Bud McFarlane, who agreed that we should attend. He said that we had left the playing field in these world conferences to our adversaries for too long, and he felt very strongly that we should assert ourselves in this area.

Great, I thought. One down, one to go.

Later that day I met with George Shultz. "Mr. Secretary," I pitched, "we can probably resolve ninety-nine percent of the issues in the documentation, but there is the issue of Zionism and racism, and the three normal political issues that always cause us problems."

"What do you mean by 'normal political issues that always cause us problems'?" he asked back.

From the look on his face it seemed he clearly knew the answer; I got the feeling he was testing me on this one. "Those issues we always face," I said, "which there is no consensus language for — the Palestinians, apartheid, and the international debt crisis."

The secretary of state smiled. If it was a test, I had passed. "Well," he said, "Bud and I will talk, but it is my opinion that you must beat back the Zionism and racism language. If you can do that and limit the number of paragraphs on which we must vote no, then it seems to me we might join consensus on the document."

I came out of that meeting feeling better than I had in weeks.

We made our plans for Nairobi.

When I told the President we were definitely going to the conference, he said, "Gee, Africa in July? Have we done you a favor?"

"It won't be too bad," I said. "It's south of the equator, so it will be winter there."

Of course, Nairobi is just about nine miles south of the equator — as the President was kind enough to point out — so I use the term "winter" very loosely here. But the city is forty-three hundred feet above sea level, so the weather was quite pleasant during our stay.

Unfortunately the dates of the conference overlapped with the President's planned colonoscopic examination, which had been scheduled for some time at Bethesda Naval Hospital. I had wanted to be in Washington during the procedure, but I was assured that it was a routine matter and that my presence, though welcomed, was not needed.

Two days before we were due to leave, the President received a memo from his doctor outlining the diet he was to follow in the forty-eight hours prior to his surgery. "I'm going to starve," Dad gasped when he saw his menu. He looked to me for sympathy. "Mermie," he said, "while you're winging your way to Africa, think about your poor father stuck here eating plain macaroni."

"Oh, you poor thing!" I teased.

On Thursday, July 11, the day before our departure and two days before Dad's surgery, the President and the First Lady hosted a gala send-off luncheon for the Nairobi delegation in the State Dining Room. "Maureen tells me you will come home victorious," the President told the group, to great cheers.

We certainly hoped so.

As it turned out, many of our so-called heavyweight players were not actually in Nairobi for the conference — Congress was in session, for one thing, and Ambassador Kirkpatrick was with us "on call" and only able to join us in an emergency — but they were all active participants in our preparations.

Despite press accounts to the contrary, this was the best-prepared and most highly motivated U.S. delegation to a U.N. conference ever. We had spent an entire weekend together in

May, going over United Nations procedures and all of the major issues and major players. By the time we touched down in Nairobi after a twenty-one-hour flight with refueling stops in Shannon, Ireland, and Cairo, Egypt, our team was ready to do battle.

We worked all that Friday evening, leading up to the first day of preconference consultations on Saturday. That morning I was interrupted in the committee room with the news that the press wanted to see me; it seemed there was something wrong with the President. Aha! I thought, the colonoscopy. They want a comment. Nothing to worry about. The press can wait; our preconference committee meeting can't. So I returned my attention to the business at hand.

A few minutes later, though, a little voice told me there might be something going on I'd want to know about. It turned out there was a lot going on. Dad's doctors had found something during the colonoscopy. I put a call in to the President's doctor, Dr. John Hutton, at about noon Nairobi time, which made it about five in the morning Washington time. When I roused the poor doctor out of bed, I learned that he had indeed discovered a growth, possibly a tumor, in Dad's colon. The President would be undergoing colon surgery in a few hours.

Cancer! Oh, my God. I didn't know what to do or how to react. I flashed back to March 1981, when Dennis had called with the news of the assassination attempt. Why is it that I'm always thousands of miles away whenever something happens in my family? My first thought was to leave Nairobi right away, but then I realized that even if I left at that very moment, it would take at least a day to get home. The logical thing to do was to stay put and see what Dr. Hutton had to say in twenty-four hours. I was needed here; there was nothing I could do for my father or Nancy from an airplane. Besides, I thought, we've always been a "show-must-go-on" kind of family, right?

I returned to the committee room and sank knee-deep into the back-and-forthing of the preconference consultations. It was as good a place to wait through the ordeal of the President's surgery as any.

It was Sunday afternoon before I got a call. By that time I

was frantic, but I told myself to be patient, that if there was any news — good or bad — somebody would have called. It was Nancy, and she said everything was fine. They had removed the tumor, and the President was resting comfortably. She sounded awful, and I knew that she was going through what she'd been through in 1981 all over again, and that it was overwhelming her. I tried to talk to her about it, but there was very little I could do to comfort her from such a long distance. Again I thought about returning home to be there for Dad and Nancy, but again I realized that it would be more than a day before I'd arrive, and by then the worst might be over. Again I was staying put.

I didn't get very far reassuring Nancy that everything would be all right, and we hung up promising to call each other as soon as we heard anything or even if we just wanted to talk. As soon as I got off the phone, I called Dr. Hutton, who filled me in on the details. The surgery had gone well, he said, but it would be a day or two before they knew the results of the pathology report on the tumor. The media, he told me, were having an absolute field day; every station had some so-called medical expert who claimed to know better than the President's doctors did what Dad's condition was. One of these quacks apparently even went on the air and predicted a postoperative longevity of under five years. Can you imagine? Didn't they think the President might be watching the news? Or didn't they care?

"What did the President say when he heard this?" I asked Dr. Hutton.

"He looked at me and very quietly said, 'They don't sound as optimistic as you.' "

"Well," I agreed, "they don't."

"Listen," Dr. Hutton assured, "I'll tell you exactly what I told the President. These medical experts were not there in the operating room, they have not participated in the President's case, and they know nothing firsthand about the general health of the patient." He told me that the President had seemed satisfied with that, and he hoped I would be, too. He also said that the constant media harangue was taking its toll on the First Lady. That much I already knew.

OK, I told myself. I'm here, Dad will be fine, so let's get

down to business. The conference was to begin the next morning.

It took one more phone call before I knew that the President would be his old self again. Dr. Hutton called to let me know the results of the pathology report. As he explained it, the malignancy was contained within the mass and the intestine wall, which had all been removed. They were very sure they had gotten it all. He admitted that he would have been happier if the malignancy had been confined just to the mass itself, but he said his prognosis was excellent just the same. "Your father is a very healthy man," he said, "and he is going to be fine, so don't listen to what the newsies are saying."

Then the doctor went on to tell me a story that went a long way toward lifting my spirits. Apparently he had been with the President and the First Lady the night before. Dad had been reading a Louis L'Amour novel, which he had by his bedside. When it came time for the First Lady and Dr. Hutton to leave for the evening, Nancy insisted that Dad turn out the light and get some sleep. He did, and they all said their goodnights. But as the doctor closed the door behind them, he noticed from the crack under the door that the President had turned his light back on. He wanted to read a while longer.

That was all I needed to hear. Not even a little thing like colon surgery could keep Dad from one of his westerns. I knew he'd be fine.

By the first day of the conference my full attention was back in Nairobi. I made the opening remarks for our delegation. I spoke about the toil of the African women, and I spoke about the wholesale loss of basic human freedoms. "I realize that this conference offers to many women a platform from which to speak that may be denied to them elsewhere," I said in closing. "I am blessed to be a citizen of a nation where women are free to speak out for their ideas to prevail. That is what I have done for my entire adult life. I would never deny to any woman an opportunity such as that presented here to use this platform, no matter how much I disagree with her position. We are willing to discuss political issues but not subvert the conference to political whim."

We were under way.

Meanwhile, across town, at a university campus, a forum

for nongovernment organizations was monopolizing much of the world press attention focused on Nairobi. The same thing had happened in Mexico City and Copenhagen, which effectively stole some of the CSW's thunder. I can certainly understand why the media would look elsewhere for a story during the early days of a U.N. conference; the proceedings tend to be dry, drawn-out affairs, and the big news and resolutions do not come about until the last day.

At the university, Bella Abzug was holding a forum (believe it or not, entitled "When Women Rule the World") under a tree, and Angela Davis was running around telling the press that she was going to head a sit-in at the entrance to the Hilton Hotel, where the U.S. delegation was housed. The press was eating it up.

After our first encounter during her book tour ten years earlier, I had very little patience for Angela Davis. So when a reporter asked for a comment on her threats of a protest, I said, "I have enough Communists to worry about with the Soviets, Cubans, Nicaraguans, Afghans, the ANC, and the rest of that crew without worrying about some homegrown variety. Tell her I said to come on and do her worst. I can't think of anyone I'd rather step over."

I won't weigh you down with the details of the conference, because it can all get pretty confusing. What you need to know is that the conference was divided into three areas: the Plenary, where general statements were delivered and where final decisions would be made, and two committees to discuss the 350 draft paragraphs and any draft resolutions. Committee I would deal with the contentious political paragraphs, and Committee II would debate the real meat of the documents, the unique concerns of women.

What you also need to know is that our most heated debates, as expected, centered on the Zionism and racism language.

Meanwhile, I got another call from Nancy. The President was doing well, she said, except he had a tube down his throat, which made it very difficult for him to talk. "His staff keeps trying to set up meetings for him," Nancy said, "but he needs to rest for a few more days."

Nancy, I'm told, could have used some rest herself. Dr.

Hutton reported that she hadn't been eating well, and so I asked her about her appetite.

"You know me," she said. "I'm not hungry when I'm upset."

"How about a banana?" I urged. "Can you choke one of those down?" (Yes, I can mother with the best of them.)

She promised she would try, and I made another call to Washington to make sure there were plenty of bananas nearby, at the hospital and at home; I knew Nancy would never go out and seek something to eat at a time like this, but if something was handy, then she might nibble.

Later that week I spoke to the President on his return home from the hospital. The first thing out of his mouth when I called was "I'm glad you didn't do something foolish like come home."

"I thought about it," I told him.

"I know you did," he said, "but you made the right decision. I know you wanted to be here, but we needed you there. By the way, how are you enjoying your Nairobi winter?" (Great, I thought, he's still got his sense of humor; that's a good sign, right?)

"I've hardly been outside since we got here," I said.

"Well, we're keeping up on what you're doing there, and I think you can still win this battle."

I was glad for his encouragement, but mostly I was glad that he was home and OK, and that that particular crisis had passed.

But now I had a whole bunch of crises of my own to deal with in Nairobi. As the conference wore on, I received a cable from Secretary of State George Shultz, concerning the paragraph with the objectionable Zionism and racism language: "If paragraph 95 is presented as drafted, the U.S. delegation will speak against it," the cable instructed. "If necessary, U.S. delegation will ask for a vote and will vote no. If paragraph 95 is adopted in its present form, no U.S. delegation member is allowed to remain in the room."

This was turning into quite a fight.

I informed the other members of the delegation of the administration's position. I urged them all to be in the room at the time and to expect fireworks. I was torn, I really was, as I spoke to this wonderful group of highly motivated and passionate and intelligent women. They had given so much of themselves over the past few months — during the past two weeks particularly — and now they had to be told to be prepared to walk away from it.

As I sat down behind the United States of America placard, I surveyed the scene. I knew only that Canada and the Netherlands would vote no on the document if paragraph 95 was included; most of the other Western countries would abstain. I started to scratch out some notes on a yellow legal pad to explain away our almost certain departure: "Five months ago I came to the U.N. system full of hopes and dreams and thrilled at what this conference would tell us about ourselves, about the Decade of Women, and about the future," I wrote. "I came with the passion necessary to take on the political system of the U.N. and with the experience to remain upright as the tidal waves of divisiveness battered us and our work."

As I was writing, it occurred to me that I had spent my entire adult life in communications and politics, and that if I miscalculated on this one, I'd have to find a new line of work.

We didn't come to paragraph 95 until five o'clock in the afternoon. It had already been a long day, but my spirits were brightened somewhat when the delegation from Côte d'Ivoire surprised us all and announced that they didn't like paragraph 95. Then the delegation from Mexico, as leader of the Latin American group, released its colleague nations from any group commitment. Suddenly, all around the room, placards were in the air to indicate various delegations' disagreement over paragraph 95, including the delegation to our immediate right, Uruguay.

Maybe we wouldn't have to walk after all.

At that moment the chair called a ten-minute recess, which lasted for the next two and a half hours. During this time the Soviet negotiator kept hard to his position and insisted that the language not be changed; throughout the room intense negotiations were under way, with the Palestinian representatives flitting from one delegation to another. A dinner break was finally called.

The session started again at ten o'clock that evening — a full five hours after our "ten-minute recess." The U.S. delegation took this as a bad sign. We fully expected that with five hours to work their negotiating black magic, the Soviet delegation would have solidified support for their original wording, and that we should therefore be prepared to walk. I told the other members of our delegation to expect an ugly scene. We figured the likely scenario would have Israel speaking first and then walking out of the conference amid jeers and catcalls. And then it would be our turn.

But things happened a little bit differently. Just when we thought all was lost, the host delegation, from Kenya, took the floor to offer a proposal — that we strike the word *Zionism* from the disputed paragraph and insert the phrase "and other forms of racial discrimination" in its place.

Yes, I thought immediately, that would do it.

Egypt, India, Algeria, and Mexico all took the floor to support the new language. Even the Soviet Union agreed to accept the amendment, and a PLO representative made a ten-minute speech on how it all meant the same thing.

Paragraph 95 was adopted by consensus, as amended. The United States delegation stayed put.

Of course it was eleven o'clock at night, and we still had nearly 250 paragraphs to plow through, including those on the Palestinians, apartheid, and the international debt crisis. (Maybe we should have walked out, I thought to myself in a fit of extreme fatigue; at least then we would have gotten some sleep!) Our delegation had been on the phone with the State Department all night long, and as our problem areas passed we were given the green light to join the consensus. At five o'clock in the morning, when the chair asked if there was consensus, our silence was the signal that there would be a "Forward Looking Strategies to the Year 2000" document. In all we had reserved on three paragraphs, voted no on three, and abstained on one.

I looked back at the notes I'd made to myself on my yellow legal pad: "There is such pain in my soul that those, and you know who you are, who disrupt this conference will stay and we who came with such hope and love must leave. But I feel so strongly and my government feels so strongly that this scandalous abuse of women's hopes and dreams cannot be allowed to continue. My delegation is willing to take the ultimate step. Mexico, Copenhagen, and now Nairobi. It must stop and it must stop now. Women of the world, sisters all, we came to build the future, we leave to ensure the future. We will meet again, and our issues will prevail."

Thank goodness I never had to say those words.

Even though it was our Kenyan host delegation that came up with the new, acceptable language for paragraph 95, I firmly believe that the conference would not have produced a consensus document if the United States had not sent a delegation to Nairobi in the first place, and if the highest levels of our government had not voiced such strong opposition to the contentious paragraphs. Finally, after eleven years and three tries, we could demand the United Nations' programmatic attention to issues that had for too long been overlooked. Millions of women who didn't even know that our conference was taking place would be touched by the political and social successes of Nairobi.

21

Roving Ambassador

FINALLY, a Russian leader stayed alive long enough to answer one of Ronald Reagan's letters. The President met with Soviet General Secretary Mikhail Gorbachev that fall in Geneva. It was to be the first time, after several attempts, that Ronald Reagan met officially with a Russian leader.

This was to be just a formal get-together on neutral ground. There were no major negotiations on the agenda and no great expectations on either side, except of course the President's long-held wish for a kind of friendship with the Russian people.

The world press descended upon Geneva like a swarm, but the only news to come out of the meetings was the hope that there would someday be other meetings. There was some historic footage of the world leaders departing the Geneva summit, with the two men shaking hands and leaning into each other for a last, private exchange.

Over dinner one night at the White House after his return, I asked the President what it was they had said to each other.

"I said, 'I would like you to come and see my country.' "

"And he said?"

"He said, 'I will do it, and you must come see mine.' Then

I said, 'I want you to come next year,' and he said, 'I will do it.' "

I would go on from our triumph in Nairobi to succeed Nancy Clark Reynolds as the U.S. representative to the United Nations Commission on the Status of Women in October 1985.

What a warm welcome I received! Secretary of State George Shultz and Assistant Secretary Alan Keyes hosted a reception at the State Department in my honor, with two very special surprise guests. I couldn't believe the folks had kept their invitation a secret from me; the schedule for the President and the First Lady is very much a matter of open record within the White House, and I hadn't even had a clue that they were penciled in for my reception.

The President had some wonderful things to say about me that day, and because it'd be bad form for me to say wonderful things about myself in my own book, I think I'll let him have the floor for a while. "Some of you may think it's a little unfair to catch Maureen off guard like this," Dad began his remarks after stepping into the reception room, "but I can assure you I'm only returning a favor she's been doing for me all my life. The truth is, Maureen's been surprising me and making me very proud for a very long time.

"If you'll just let me tell this one little story. I think all of you know that when a candidate for President gets the required number of votes at a political convention, it's traditional for the press and cameras to come bursting into his hotel room for pictures of the family celebrating. Well, back in nineteen eighty, when we were in that gigantic Renaissance Center in Detroit, I noticed just before the magic moment that everybody in the Reagan clan was there except Maureen. And naturally, with only a few minutes to go, I started asking everyone, I'd say, 'Where's Maureen? Where's Maureen?'

"Then, sure enough, it hit me and everyone else in the room. And only a few seconds later there was confirmation right there on the television set in front of us. Maureen wasn't in the room with us because she had duties to perform as an alternate delegate and leader of the California delegation. And one of those duties, come to think of it, was voting for me.

"Now, I hadn't been in politics as long as some people, but I did know that that was the wrong moment to start taking anything for granted. So as I listened to Maureen on television, just this once, I was glad she was on the floor and not with us.

"And there's a little sequel to this. Last year, I kept seeing in the press all those reports about the U.N. conference wrapping up the Decade of Women. I think some of you remember that there was a good deal of speculation that the whole conference was going to become politicized, a propaganda exercise on extraneous matters rather than a serious exchange on issues that uniquely affect women. And there was some talk, too, about how the American delegation which Maureen was heading was going to be outsmarted, outmaneuvered, and probably embarrassed by all of this. And, you know, every time I read one of these reports, I got this big Cheshire cat–like grin, because I was thinking to myself, Somebody out there sure doesn't know my daughter.

"Well, those of us here today do know Maureen. At State, you know her by the wonderful job she did in Nairobi. You know how effectively she worked to get agreement on the consensus documents that would make the conference the success that it was, and bring the American delegation the credit it deserved. And you know, too, that she'll do a fine job as our representative to the U.N. Commission on the Status of Women.

"And, of course, for Nancy and me, Maureen is someone we love dearly, and yet someone whom we also recognize as the extraordinary individual that she is. And that isn't all that easy. As I said, it's always a little bit of a surprise for a father, just as it was that night in Detroit, to realize that that's your daughter up there on the TV screen, not only a grown woman, but a leader, a mover, someone who is making the world a whole lot better place to live.

"So, I want to thank Maureen today, as her father, for making me so proud of her on this occasion and so many others, but also as her President, on behalf of the American people, for distinguished service to her country and the cause of human freedom and dignity."

Thanks, Dad. I couldn't have said it better myself. I wouldn't have wanted to try. Seriously, though, I hadn't been on the "inside" long enough to be used to Dad's praise; these were his own words, from the heart, and after I'd spent so many years in the wilderness of his political life, they were like music to me. It was amazing to me that he remembered all the things I hadn't thought he knew about in the first place. As I sat and listened to him that day, I realized for the first time that my father was also my friend.

It was a nice realization.

After Nairobi I had assumed the mantle of "unofficial ambassador-at-large to anyplace in Africa"; whenever there was an event that required U.S. participation, I would invariably get the call. I didn't mind at all. Actually I started to tabulate how soon it would be before I made state visits to all of the African nations (there are more than fifty!).

One of my most memorable trips was keyed to the coronation of the new king of Swaziland, a small tribal kingdom surrounded on two sides by South Africa and on one side by Mozambique. It was such a beautiful little country; in parts it even reminded me of the topography in California. While I was there, a round of bilateral meetings with various African heads of state were scheduled back-to-back-to-back in the city of Mbabane.

On my first stop (the reason for the trip) I delivered a letter from the President to the new leader, King Mswati, an eighteen-year-old youth who until his coronation had been attending school in England. Royal protocol required that we converse through a minister who sat between us, and when our audience ended and I handed him the letter, he reacted like a typical teenager. He looked right past the President's message to the signature and marveled, "Ronald Reagan . . . gosh!"

I was tickled.

From there I met with P. W. Botha, the president of South Africa. From my briefings I was expecting to look into the eyes of this soul-weary man and see some light for a better tomorrow for his people. Instead I saw steel. He had put up a wall, and I couldn't see through it.

My marching orders had been to engage the president on any level on the possibility of further reform in apartheid, so I elected to attack the problem from a political perspective. "Mr. President," I started in, "although I am not an official of my government, I still must tell you that in my political judgment we will be faced with veto-proof legislation on sanctions against South Africa by the end of this year."

Since at that point — April 1986 — there was no legislation on South Africa pending in our Congress, Mr. Botha naturally thought I was lying. He looked at me with disdain, but I continued and pointed out that President Reagan had expended a tremendous amount of political capital to fight off sanctions and buy South Africa time to conduct their own reform, but I added that time was running out. "It is our hope that you can offer the President more ammunition for this battle," I said, "because if we cannot demonstrate that there is an end in sight to apartheid, then I'm afraid sanctions are inevitable."

"That's your problem," Botha said, "not mine." He waved his hand as if to dismiss me, which in effect he did.

It was clear to me that Botha wanted to see the U.S. impose sanctions on his country because then he would be politically free to break from our influence. I was terribly unsettled by his attitude — even frightened — not only for the people of South Africa but for their neighbors in Swaziland, Botswana, and Mozambique.

As I gazed into Botha's cold, expressionless eyes, I became aware of a nagging ache in my hands. It was the strangest sensation. I glanced down and realized that I was becoming so enraged by what he was saying that I was digging my fingernails into my palms.

I couldn't get out of that room fast enough. I was seething. I thought immediately of my father, still supportive of Botha, who would have been utterly disappointed to learn that the energy he'd spent on behalf of the South African government was being met with such ingratitude.

Next up was an audience with President Samora Machel of Mozambique, whose warm and engaging personality made my encounter with President Botha seem like a bad dream. Unlike the South African president, Machel was absolutely charming, with a quick and wonderful sense of humor; he was also anxious for our friendship, which in his presence couldn't help but be forthcoming.

A former guerrilla leader and now the president of this one-time Portugese colony, Machel wanted America to understand that Mozambique's independence had been facilitated by aid from Moscow; but he stressed that he knew the future of his country lay with Western development, and he sought a place among the nonaligned nations.

On Machel's first visit to the United States, he and the President had taken quite a liking to each other, so I knew he would appreciate my first question: "Mr. President," I said, "my President would not ask you this, but I will. How was your last trip to Moscow?"

"You're right," he answered, with only a mildly disbelieving glance from the corner of his eye. "Your President would not ask me that."

And he tactfully would not answer, though we did move on to a discussion about the Reagan-Gorbachev summit in Geneva the previous fall. Machel's message, which he wanted me to convey to the President, was that the United States was breaking the spirit of Geneva by engaging in a new round of weapons testing that the Soviet Union would be compelled to answer. I explained that the U.S. had suspended testing in hopes of a new agreement, while the Soviets had continued their testing program unabated.

"Mr. President," I concluded, "if anyone is breaking the spirit of Geneva, it is Mikhail Gorbachev. He promised my President in Geneva that he would visit the United States this year, and now he won't set a date for a meeting."

Machel wondered if that meant there would be no summit in 1986. I told him I didn't know, but I assured him there could be a summit if Gorbachev would keep his word and visit our country.

With this President Samora Machel's eyes narrowed, and he looked at me for a long, almost awkward moment. "Are you telling me this," he finally said, "because you think I am a friend of theirs?"

"No," I said. "I'm telling you this because I think you're a friend of ours."

Machel burst out laughing and told everyone in the room that this was the best meeting he'd had on this trip to Swaziland.

I must have made some impression on him, because the next day, when we were seated among fifty thousand people in the city's soccer stadium to watch the coronation festivities for King Mswati, Machel gave me a most sensational greeting. There, after receiving a huge ovation from the crowd, he stepped up on stage and, after greeting each of his peers, stepped over to where I was sitting. With a politician's wink, he embraced me in a huge bear hug, and then he turned and waved to the crowd to let them know we were friends.

I made a second trip to southern Africa in 1986 to help Botswana celebrate its twenty-five years of independence, and while I was in the neighborhood I made plans to tour Mozambique. President Machel put together an extensive program for my visit. We had in-depth discussions with women leaders, toured the national dance school, engaged in a meaningful dialogue with the minister of education (who happened to be Machel's wife, Graca), and spent the better part of a day at one of the many cooperative farms on the outskirts of Maputo. The farm was run by women, which is not all that unusual in Africa, where 90 percent of farm labor is female. The women on this farm worked from dawn to dusk and earned only the equivalent of about eighty-five dollars a year, which was not even enough money to buy shoes for their children.

But despite their extreme poverty, the women were warmhearted and generous. Before I left they gave me a present — three stalks of bananas, two crates of vegetables, and two live ducks. They could live for many days on the food they were offering! I told myself I had to find a way to leave some of it behind without insulting them. I accepted the fruit and vegetables (which we later distributed to the people in Maputo), but I seized on the ducks as my answer. I told the women I did not eat meat and asked if I could leave them behind and if they might be allowed to live another day in my name. I thought I'd gotten myself out of a sticky situation with some diplomacy, but as soon as my wishes were translated for these women, they started giggling like teenagers. They thought my request was the funniest thing in the world — they'd never heard of someone refusing meat!

Later, at a dinner hosted by President Machel and his family, I heard our host grumble that he was unable to obtain any California wine in his country. He had grown very fond of the stuff on his trip to the United States. Well, by a lucky coincidence, we happened to have some on board our plane. A member of our group, Jonathan Miller, a former U.S. Peace Corps director in Botswana, had seen to it that we were traveling with a wine cellar stocked with several cases from his family's California winery.

"Mr. President," I offered, "we have a negotiation we'd like to carry out with you. We have some bottles of California wine on board our aircraft, which we hope to be able to exchange for some of your country's wonderful cashews."

Machel got a big kick out of my offer, but he took it seriously enough to send a nod to his chief of protocol, after which I was sure the deal had been struck.

Before I left, after we'd completed our sensitive wine-cashew negotiations, he took me aside for a private conversation. "Tell your father he is a man of tremendous courage," he said, taking hold of my hand. "I know what a chance he is taking by going to Reykjavik" — the Iceland summit was to begin in a few days — "and please tell him I wish him to be strong but also to be wary. He is my friend, as we are friends, and that is of great value."

A few weeks after I returned home, the radio alarm went off in my Los Angeles apartment at five-thirty one Monday morning, and I awoke to the sad news that President Machel and at least thirty-four members of his government had been killed in an air crash in South Africa. I was crushed. Almost everybody who had attended that lovely dinner at his home was on board, with the exception of his immediate family. I really felt a friendship with this warm and caring man, and I'd been so looking forward to maintaining and nurturing that friendship with him and his countrymen for many years to come. He had so much good, proud work still left to accomplish. In the past few weeks I had been talking him up as a man who would rival Rajiv Gandhi for leadership of the nonaligned movement, and now he was gone.

I was asked to be the United States representative to his funeral. I was going anyway, with or without portfolio. Nothing could have kept me away. I don't think I'll ever forget the ashen look of grief and shock on the faces of the president's wife, Graca, and his eight children, or the devastated faces of the people of the city of Maputo, who lined the streets to watch his coffin pass.

The entire trip took less than sixty hours. We were back before the newspapers said we'd gone.

In addition to my new role with the U.N., I had stayed on as a consultant for women's campaign activities at the Republican National Committee. It was election time again in America in 1986, which meant that when I wasn't spanning the globe I was traveling our own back roads and getting out the word for our female Republican candidates. That year saw a record number of highly qualified women seeking office, and we were all hopeful that those candidacies would translate into a record number of new women in key offices that fall.

We still had to put these women in office, but the very fact that they were running, with our party's endorsement, suggested that we were on the right track.

But even before the November elections, my role at the RNC would undergo a dramatic change. Frank Fahrenkopf informed me that he would be seeking reelection in January as party chairman, and then he dropped the bomb that the President had selected me to succeed Betty Heitman as cochairman of the party.

I took Boxcar Willie with me to the Oval Office to tell Dad how much I appreciated the vote of confidence. "Thank you very much," I said, and then I added, "I think."

"You're very welcome," Dad said back, "I think."

As anticipated, my appointment created a minor flap within the party. There were some people who maintained that my father had given me the job simply because I was his daughter; now, I was his daughter, there was no disputing that, but what my nay-sayers failed to acknowledge was that a sitting President always chooses the chairman and cochairman of his party, and that I had been active in party politics for many years. I wanted to do things that would help strengthen the party by bringing new ideas and people into our ranks and giving women more encouragement and more opportunities to serve, and I knew that was the legacy Ronald Reagan wanted to leave.

Personally I thought he'd made a fine choice, and I was determined to prove it.

After all of this the election itself was a letdown. Like me, Dad had crisscrossed the nation, pushing hard for our Republican candidates, but despite the President's all-out effort, the Democrats gained control of the Senate by a 55 to 45 margin over the Republicans. As much as I was disappointed by the results, I wasn't surprised. Since there were twice as many Republican incumbent senators as Democrats up for reelection in 1986, the odds were against our holding control of the Senate. The press played the loss of control up as a personal defeat for the President, but I didn't see it that way. Rather, I thought our showing pointed out some holes in the party organization, holes I would seek to fill in my new position as RNC cochair. Our losing campaigns for the most part had dismissed the all-important grassroots organizing efforts in favor of high-priced media. That was a mistake.

As for women, our showing was also discouraging. Despite the record number of candidates, there were only twenty-three women in the House of Representatives when the elections were over, and only two in the U.S. Senate. Those numbers were far below my expectations. The biggest disappointments, though, came in the governorship races. There were eight women running for governor in 1986, five of them Republicans; I had been hopeful that we'd wind up with at least three women governors, but as it played out, we ended up with only one.

And as far as our one victory was concerned, well, we women knew going in that we had that one sewn up. Kay Orr, who became the first Republican woman to be elected governor of Nebraska, defeated Democrat Helen Boosalis in a historic election marking the first time two women from major party tickets competed against each other in a gubernatorial election.

Behind every cloud there's a silver lining, right?

22

Iran-*Contra*

A DAY BEFORE THE 1986 ELECTIONS, a story appeared in *Al Shiraa*, a Lebanese weekly magazine, reporting that the United States had sent military spare parts to Iran after a secret visit to Teheran by former national security adviser Bud McFarlane. According to their account, Bud had made the secret trip in an effort to gain the release of American hostages held there.

It was quite a piece of news.

In the next several days the story grew even hotter, as it was revealed that the United States had not only sold arms to Iran but had used the profits from those sales to benefit the *contra* rebels seeking to topple Nicaragua's Marxist government. This was the most explosive story of Dad's administration, and the revelations kept coming. Initial reports pointed to Lieutenant Colonel Oliver North, Vice Admiral John Poindexter, who had succeeded Bud McFarlane as national security adviser, and McFarlane himself as the masterminds behind the operation.

Now, there's one thing you have to understand about Washington, D.C.: it sometimes seems as though it's a city of just about one hundred people. What I mean is that the number of key players on our national political scene can be counted on the fingers of about twenty hands. That includes the President and his advisers, certain members of the press, and influential movers and shakers in the House, the Senate, and the private sector. When something like the Iran-*contra* scandal breaks, there is an immediate and urgent and pervasive bunker mentality that takes hold. Everyone feels like they're in the middle of everything, and events tend to get inflated beyond perspective.

If you ask me, that's what happened here.

Almost immediately Washington was rife with rumors and speculations. You couldn't turn on the news or open a newspaper without finding some new wrinkle to the Iran-*contra* developments. There was even a story making the rounds that CIA director William Casey, who was in a semi-coma following surgery for a brain tumor, had known about the diversion of millions of dollars to the Nicaraguan rebels a month before it was disclosed to the public.

Of course the President's role in the negotiations was immediately called into question, and it was variously reported that he knew full well about the diversion of funds, that he knew nothing at all about them, and that he knew and then conveniently forgot. I'd like to go on record here in my father's defense. He was devastated by the revelations of the scandal, largely because of the holes they pointed out in his administration, that's true, but mostly because he felt the American public no longer believed in him. Oh, was that hard for him to swallow! My father has always been a man of integrity, and he couldn't stomach the notion that people thought he was lying about his involvement in the Iran-*contra* affair. In the days before he formed the Tower Commission to investigate the scandal, he kept insisting that he should go on television just one more time, and then just one more time again, to try to convince the country of his honesty.

In typical Ronald Reagan fashion he tried to keep up a good fighting front, even though inside he was hurting something fierce. During the weeks of the Tower Commission investigation, he was determined that all would be business as usual in the White House. He tried not to let it get to him, but it got to him.

It got to all of us.

I remember that at the height of all the speculation there was a meeting in town of the party's major donors. I kept hearing all this talk about what trying times these were for Ronald Reagan and his administration, and all this nonsense about how the President still had something to hide in the matter. The group was concerned that the scandal would make it difficult to sell tickets to their fund-raisers.

"Horseshit," I exclaimed, getting up to say my piece. I couldn't stand to listen to any of it anymore, particularly not from these good people who counted themselves among Dad's earliest and most enthusiastic supporters. I wanted to grab their attention and shake them back to something resembling reality. With an opening line like that the floor was all mine, so I continued: "These are not trying times. The President of the United States did not do anything wrong. I can understand all this talk from the press, and I can understand a certain amount of skepticism among the American people. But you? You know him. If there's one thing everyone in this room knows about Ronald Reagan, it's that Ronald Reagan doesn't lie to us."

I was angry, and I was taking it out on Dad's supporters, who I'm sure were justified in their concerns.

Of course word got back to the President of my ringing defense on his behalf, particularly the part about the emphatically colorful language I'd used to open my remarks. This he needed to verify.

"You didn't?" he said one night at dinner, only sort of asking.

"I did," I said.

In the first weeks after the story broke, the betting line was that Secretary of State George Shultz, Chief of Staff Donald Regan, and Admiral Poindexter would soon resign or be dismissed from office.

Now, I will leave to others the task of re-creating a blow-by-blow account of the entire Iran-*contra* mess. Entire books have been written and will continue to be written on that one subject alone. I am not a journalist or historian. Rather, I am a politician and a member of the First Family and, as such, a passionate and privileged observer of one of the most dramatic episodes in Ronald Reagan's administration; I didn't have a front-row seat to this particular piece of history, but I was sitting in the orchestra.

First, let me point the finger — at Donald Regan. Whether the President's chief of staff was directly responsible for the Iran-*contra* negotiations, I can't say, but I am certain that he was aware of them and that he allowed them to continue.

You have to understand, the President of the United States is the ultimate arbiter of policy debate. He is responsible for the execution of thousands of ideas by literally hundreds of thousands of employees. There is a large White House staff, and there are Cabinet departments and sub-Cabinet-level agencies, administrations, boards, and commissions. The organization of all these under-levels of our government is left to the White House chief of staff and all of the division heads. It is not the President's job to peek behind every office door and micromanage the people working there. It is the chief of staff's job to have people in place who look and listen and report back, and to keep the machinery functioning.

When Donald Regan signed on for his post, he immediately filled the White House with his choices. He wanted to recast the highest levels of our government in his own image. No longer was the chief of staff managing "the President's staff"; he had transformed the operation into "the Chief's staff."

Yes, I'll admit that the ultimate responsibility for the conduct of his own government does indeed rest with the President. Ronald Reagan will admit to you the same thing. But I am utterly convinced that the only failing in this particular President, throughout this particular scandal, was in his placing so much trust and authority on a man like Donald Regan.

Let me tell you a little bit more about this guy. When he first came on the scene, during Dad's second term, there were nervous rumblings about his management style almost immediately. I went to check him out for myself, and to tell you the truth he seemed pleasant enough; I wasn't particularly uncomfortable with him. I did, however, remark to Nancy that I hoped he was as good as he sounded.

By our second meeting I had deduced that Donald Regan didn't think much of politicians or politics, and that he didn't think much of me. He seemed to suffer from that rare snobbery of the greedy rich, the attitude that suggests, *If you're so smart, how come you ain't rich like me?* In politics wealth of knowledge is the currency, but he didn't consider politics to be all that important. This troubled me, believe me, but I figured the President wouldn't be facing another election and so I was not overly dismayed by Regan's way of thinking.

In the months after that he began to drive away from the White House dozens of people who had served the President well. He carried the self-styled nickname the Chief and the press-styled nickname the Prime Minister, and he did his best to live up to both of them. Bud McFarlane may never admit it, but I'm sure he left his post over a rift with Regan. Ed Rollins, too, fell in the chief of staff's wake.

And women, despite our gains in recent years, no longer had a place in Donald Regan's White House.

It wasn't long before he started to annoy the hell out of me. He had his offices remodeled to include an outdoor patio similar to the President's. He also took it upon himself to refer to my father as Cousin in public, a habit he quickly abandoned after the President pointed out that "the Chief" might be accused of benefiting from nepotism. (Good going, Dad!)

During a network television profile on the new chief of staff, Regan was shown seated at his desk, picking up the phone and barking curtly into the receiver, "Get me the President!" Can you imagine? First of all, as anyone who's ever been the subject of a television news profile can tell you, the footage was clearly staged; network cameras would never have been in the room if Regan actually had some business to conduct with the President. But the fact that he chose that kind of image of himself to present — as someone who could command the President's attention at his whim — was unforgivable. I burned when that profile aired, because of what it showed about the man and because it followed on the heels of Regan's informing senior White House staff that he would examine all material requiring a presidential decision and would decide in advance which options for action would reach the President's desk. He was actually limiting the President's access to ideas, thereby inhibiting the President's ability to make decisions and giving the unfortunate impression of a President who was out of touch with the process.

The man was out of control.

The first major congressional vote during Regan's tenure was on the MX missile. The White House staff members responsible for lobbying the Hill worked day and night, and the President personally phoned and visited with undecided members of Congress in an effort to pass the legislation. After the successful completion of the effort Regan sent everyone involved a paperweight with a paper insert inscribed "You made my day" and signed Donald T. Regan. The chief of staff had apparently decided he would be chairman of the board and would allow the President to retain his title.

The folks, though, were blind to the real Donald Regan. Every time I tried to demonstrate to them what this man was doing to his office and to the office of the President, they would come up with some logical explanation in his defense. In hindsight I should have pushed them harder, but at the time I figured that the man was just a nuisance, nothing more, and that if the President was happy with his performance, then it wasn't my place to make a stink.

Pity the poor person who made Donald Regan angry. His "explosions" quickly became the stuff of White House legend, though I was not on the receiving end of one of his tirades until the close and controversial *contra* vote. One night Nancy put me on the phone with him — as in, "Hold on, Don, Maureen wants to talk to you" — and I offered my opinion on what I thought was a poorly planned "pep rally" to drum up enthusiasm for the administration's support of the freedom fighters.

Before I could get another word out, he erupted. "Goddamn it!" he began. "Who the hell do you think you are? You have been trying to run the West Wing for too long, and I'm going to stop you!"

Wait, it gets better. "You are a pain in the ass," he continued after I told him I was well aware that the RNC and other organizations in Washington had been asked to supply bodies for what promised to be a thinly attended press event. "And if I find out who is talking to you, then you won't have any more sources."

That was really the last interaction I had with the "Prime Minister," but it wasn't the last time we would lock horns. I learned how to go around him, since I had no intention of ever giving him an opportunity to cough up such venom again — at least not at my expense.

Our last clash would be over the "Hands Across America" event on Memorial Day weekend in 1986. It was to be one of the most exciting people movements in our history, with Americans linked from coast to coast in a chain of human spirit and charity, all to help our nation's homeless. I thought the President should be involved; Donald Regan thought otherwise.

On the Thursday evening before Memorial Day, Dennis and I sat watching the evening news with the folks. We were in Dad's study. On NBC that night Chris Wallace reported that the White House had announced that the President would not participate in the event for security reasons. Dad seemed quite surprised to hear that piece of news from Chris Wallace, and he indicated that he would have liked to have been a part of all the excitement.

I wanted to say something, to try and talk him into putting his foot down on this, but I held back.

Next up was Sam Donaldson at ABC, who told us the story for the second time. This time Dad mentioned that he'd been reading about "Hands Across America" for months, but he hadn't realized that it would come through Washington.

Still I held back. (I had to bite my tongue, but I didn't say anything.)

On CBS we heard the same story yet again, and this time I could not contain myself. Dennis, too, had a thing or two he wanted to say.

But the President beat us both to the punch. "Gee," he said, "I would have liked to have been a part of that."

"What do you mean, 'would have'?" I said back. "It hasn't happened yet. It's not too late to get involved."

"But Don Regan says security is a consideration," he reasoned.

"Dad," I said, "we'll worry about security later. Look, this is your kind of event. You've always talked about solving our problems through community commitment. You're a community-activist person. This is the ultimate example of that. You have to be there."

"Well," my father said, thinking out loud, "that's true. It *is* a perfect fit. But how do we even know it'll come by the White House?"

"Mr. President," Dennis chimed in, "if you want it to come by the White House, then it will come by the White House."

"Yes," I said, getting caught up in the exciting prospect, "we could create our own link right up the drive and out the other side, and that should take care of the security problem."

The President seemed intrigued but not entirely convinced. But Dennis and I had been in the political-organization business for our entire adult lives, and we knew that if we wanted to do it, it could be done. I told Dad to think about it, and Dennis and I left to refine our plan. Back in the Lincoln Bedroom later that night, I wrote Dad a note outlining a basic plan for his participation.

The next morning Dennis was feeling guilty that Dad's senior staff was going to be surprised by the President's change of heart, so he put in an early call to the chief of staff's office to tell him there was a very good chance the President would want to participate in "Hands Across America."

What happened, as Dad told us later that night, was that Dad walked into his office, apologized for the fact that he was about to disrupt everybody's holiday weekend, and let it be known that he really wanted to be a part of the event. Regan, after Dennis's warning, was steeled in his opposition, and he told the President that he had reviewed the matter just that morning and that the senior staff was sticking with its earlier decision that the President should not get involved.

With that my father smiled, whipped out the note I'd written to him the night before, and said, "Here, Don, this is how it can be done, and we will do it."

Bravo, Dad.

We wanted at least five hundred people at the White House that day, but Regan insisted on only 250, so the line between the two north gates in front of the White House was rather thin. Those who did participate were White House "family" — the kitchen staff, groundskeepers, electricians, and so on, with their families. Even the on-duty chef turned up, complete with his white hat, and when the President saw him he joked, "We won't worry if dinner's a little late."

Dad was joined by his press secretary Jim Brady, who was still recuperating from the near-fatal bullet of five years earlier; his road to recovery had been slow and trying, and it was uplifting to see him at the President's side for an occasion such as this.

Also sharing center stage was Mr. Harley, a White House doorman who has faithfully served our Presidents for over thirty-five years.

It was a beautiful moment — in spite of Donald Regan — but the press covering the White House angle of this national event failed to capture the real story. They missed the honor and pride on the faces of the White House employees and their kids as they shared something personal and meaningful with their President. They missed the sense of family we all shared on that day. They missed the little boy who was holding the President's hand, and who whispered to his friend after the event, "I'll never wash this hand again!"

They also missed the sight of Donald Regan and Larry Speakes, who refused to participate in the warmth and glory of the day and instead chose to stand off to the side as all of this was going on, making fun of the proceedings.

I was not at all surprised, then, to learn that the President had not been kept fully informed about the Iran-*contra* negotiations. I was furious, but not surprised. When the story broke, Dad was put on the point to make a speech, which proved to be factually inaccurate, and he subsequently had to call a press conference to explain the inaccuracies.

Nancy was out of town the night before the press conference, and so the President and I dined alone in the study, on tray tables in front of the television. The folks very often take dinner in Dad's study. We're not talking TV dinners here, mind you, but the regular sumptuous White House fare. On this night Dad was sitting on his chair in open collar and slippers, and I was in Nancy's chair, to his left. We were watching the news, which of course featured the latest developments in the Iran-*contra* scandal at the top.

"Dad," I said, "do you think you are totally up to speed on this thing?"

Filled with pictures of his family, this was my father's safe haven during the Iran-*contra* crisis, the one place I could put such a question to him with no fear of encroaching on his office in any way. He paused for a moment and looked up from the television and then down at the briefing books in front of him. "Yes," he said slowly. "I think so."

I hoped so.

As it turned out, the second set of briefings prepared for the President by Admiral Poindexter was as inaccurate as the first set; the press conference was a disaster, and it marked the second time in the early days of the Iran-*contra* scandal that the President was sent out in public without sufficient or sufficiently accurate information.

All through November and December, members of Congress began to call for Regan's resignation, party leaders started insisting he was a liability to the political process, and editorial writers laid wagers on how long he could last.

Meanwhile, as I mentioned earlier, the President had formed the Tower Commission to investigate the National Security Council staff, and he announced that he would not comment further on the scandal until he read the commission's report. The timing worked out well for the President, in that the investigation coincided in part with his recovery from prostate surgery; it was the perfect opportunity for him to regain his strength while national press attention was focused on the investigation.

Donald Regan, though, didn't see it that way, and he insisted that the President resume a harrowing travel and appointment schedule the week following his operation. Nancy was in a snit. The "Prime Minister" had already made headlines when he hung up on the First Lady — not once but twice — and now he was getting in the way of her husband's health. That was just too much! As soon as word got out that the First Lady was on Regan's case, she began getting calls from nearly everyone in Dad's administration, all offering up enough ammunition to urge his early departure.

On the Monday of Presidents' Day weekend, when they returned from Camp David, Nancy called me down the hall for a talk. It seems Ron had filled the folks in on my most heated altercation with the "Prime Minister," which I had related to him just a month before. They wanted to hear it from me. I re-created the story for them as best I could — complete with Regan's street-level language — and they listened in shock.

"If Don feels so powerful that he can speak that way to me," I reasoned, "then just think of the tyranny he is imposing on the people downstairs who can't fight back."

Dad was horrified. All week long he had been hearing horror story after horror story about his chief of staff, and this one seemed to ice it all for him. The look on his face, with his squinting eyes and pursed lips, and the indignation in his voice reminded me of that night in New Hampshire nearly seven years earlier — "I paid for this microphone!" — and he said he realized that something had to be done, and he would take care of it.

At last!

Within a few days the White House rumor mill was on overdrive with the word that the President wanted Regan to resign. Ninety-nine percent of the "one hundred" residents of Washington, D.C., got the message — all, of course, except Donald Regan. Now, my father is not one of those "fire them now" administrators; most people aren't. The hint should have been enough, and Regan should have taken the opportunity to resign with dignity, without causing the President, or the White House, or himself, any further embarrassment. But the "Prime Minister" wouldn't budge. At week's end the President gave Regan another chance for a graceful exit when the press stopped him on the south portico and asked whether the chief of staff would be leaving: "I don't know, you'll have to ask him," the President said. When they did, Regan's reply came back, "I don't know, you'll have to ask him," indicating the President.

No matter what we've learned about his role in the mess since and no matter what we will learn about it in the future, I will always be convinced that it was Donald Regan — with his smug insistence that he knew better than the President what was best for the President — who allowed it all to happen. Donald Regan had taken Ambassador Vernon Walter's three-step transmogrification to another level, and Colonel North was allowed to roam around the deck of the ship of state like the proverbial loose cannon.

One of the things the Tower Commission discovered was that Oliver North had been carrying too much authority. Under the system, he should have been reporting to at least three people — one for Central America, one for the hostages, and one for drug interdiction. Because he had given himself all this portfolio, everyone thought he was reporting to someone else.

The national press began to report that Oliver North claimed that he had had private meetings with the President, dinners in the private residence, and weekends at Camp David, none of which ever took place.

The fallout from Iran-*contra* was widespread and swift. The most troubling piece of news came that February, when we learned of Bud McFarlane's near-fatal overdose of Valium — an apparent suicide attempt.

I was having dinner alone with the President — Nancy was in California — when we heard the news on television. Again we were behind tray tables and in front of the television. CBS was the only network to run with the story as an attempted suicide. Dad and I talked long into the night about what it would take — assuming that the CBS report was accurate — to drive a man to such a desperate act. For some reason we commented on the fact that Bud McFarlane and I were about the same age.

The President had always liked and respected McFarlane and valued his advice a great deal. "I feel just terrible about this," he said to me that night. "Bud is one of my favorite people."

"I always think of Bud as a fatherly type," I let on. "You know — someone who will make things all right."

"And now this," Dad said.

"And now this," I concurred.

There was nothing else to say.

Later that evening, after the President went to bed, the White House switchboard operator called to say that Mike Deaver was on the phone and wanted to talk to me. How strange, I thought, since we rarely communicated, but I took the call. (In fact, this was to be the last conversation I ever had with the man.)

"Maureen," he began in his normally abrupt way, "the switchboard says the President has retired for the evening. I don't believe that, but they wouldn't put me through, so I thought I'd try you. Did you hear the news tonight about Bud?"

"Yes, we did," I said, happy to learn that Deaver now knew what it felt like to be shut off from the President. "In fact, we talked about it."

"Well," he continued, "I want you to go down the hall tomorrow morning and tell the President that he must call Jonnie McFarlane" — Bud's wife — "first thing."

Now, to put this in context for you, Mike Deaver was no longer working in the White House at the time of this call, but the folks for some reason still valued his opinion, even if I didn't.

"I don't think that's the best idea," I said.

"It's not important what you think," he snapped. "This is a friend in trouble, and you are to tell the President to make the call."

"The friend in trouble at the moment is the President," I shot back, "and I don't want to see the television news speculating on whether the President is trying to cover something up by calling at precisely this moment."

"No one asked your opinion," he yammered. "Just do it."

On that night I decided that Michael Deaver gave chutzpah a bad name.

I called Dennis to sound him out on this. I was upset at being put into a position of giving orders to the President — my father — by a man who no longer served him. I knew, however, that if I failed to deliver Deaver's message, the little creep would find out about it and would manage to get it through to the folks that somehow I had failed them. Dennis and I talked through a couple of scenarios, and we agreed that I'd sleep on it before taking action in the morning.

The next day I staked out the White House elevator so I could join Dad on the brief ride to the ground floor. "Mike Deaver called last night," I said, almost in passing. My father flashed me a look that suggested that perhaps he was getting tired of Deaver's unsolicited advice. I continued: "He said that if you were contemplating a call to Jonnie McFarlane this morning, he wanted to vote yes."

I thought I finessed that pretty well.

The President said he indeed intended to call Jonnie Mc-

Farlane and wanted to be of whatever help he could to Bud and his family during this crisis. If that's the way he wants to handle it, I thought, that's fine; I wasn't about to try to talk him out of it, as long as it was his own idea and not Mike Deaver's.

But maybe I should have said something. In the weeks ahead I watched a very bitter Jonnie McFarlane, in a televised interview, brush aside the President's call as though it was a Band-Aid on a severed artery.

Perhaps it seemed that way to her.

Meanwhile the question of Nancy's role in the Don Regan ouster was still dominating the headlines. Dad sought to take the pulse of the situation and invited the party chairman, Frank Fahrenkopf, the cochairman, yours truly, and various Republican leaders to lunch at the White House to discuss the Iran-contra affair and its effect on the party. The President seemed reassured by our assessment that the fallout would be short-term and that if all went well, the party should remain strong and healthy.

After lunch a briefing was scheduled in the White House press room, where Frank Fahrenkopf had selected certain participants to tell reporters how the President planned to put the scandal behind him. I had not been invited to the press conference — I didn't even know about it until it was announced at lunch — so I headed back up to the residence to go over some paperwork.

Along the way I ran into Sam Donaldson, Helen Thomas, and Chris Wallace outside the press room.

"Oh, Maureen," Helen Thomas said, "are you coming to see us?"

"No, sorry," I said. "I'm not one of the participants."

"Afraid of us wolves?" Sam Donaldson kidded.

"Of course not," I insisted.

Then, just as I was getting ready to continue down the hall, Deputy Press Secretary Marlin Fitzwater walked up and asked me to join the press conference.

Inside, Frank Fahrenkopf hadn't given the newsies much to chew on, and for some reason they set their sights on me.

"Is the Republican party mortally wounded by the Iran-contra affair?" someone barked in my direction.

"Wounded?" I responded. "Do I look wounded?"

The questions started coming all at once:

"How does your father feel about all the criticism of his administration?"

"Why has the President not met with the press?"

"What's your father's reaction to all this?"

"Look," I said, trying to tackle all of the questions at the same time. "It was a very difficult waiting period for the President, and for all of us, until the Tower Commission completed its report. It has been very frustrating not to be able to respond. I think the President was very angry when he learned of some of the things that had been done without his knowledge. In fact, 'royally p.o.'d' might be a very good term for it. I cleaned that up just for you guys."

"Is it true, Maureen," the next question came, "that at a Republican rally in North Dakota a week or so ago, you said that Poindexter and North should be court-martialed?"

"Yes," I admitted. "I said that a member of the United States military who lies to his commander-in-chief is guilty of treason and should be court-martialed."

"How do you know they lied?"

"Because by omission or commission, they did not tell the President what they were doing. And that's a lie."

When the stories about the press conference ran on television that evening and in the newspapers the next day, they touched off all manner of speculation on what I'd meant by "p.o.'d." Johnny Carson cracked me up that night when he figured on the "Tonight Show" that it must have meant "presidentially offended."

At the height of the Iran-*contra* affair and during its immediate aftermath, there were many stories in the press about the gloomy atmosphere at the White House and about how grim and despondent my father had become. They were only partly true. The assumption was that the First Family did nothing else all day but sit around and talk about the crisis; that might make for good copy, but it wasn't the case. When we gathered for dinner we talked about many things — family matters, our day-to-day activities, other national and international developments — and tried to keep the controversy in perspective. Now, we acted this way not because we were trying to pretend the Iran-*contra* situation didn't exist, but because we were confident that everything possible was being done to get the facts out into the open. All the way into the open.

It was true that it was a bad time, but our family had been through bad times before, and it never occurred to any of us that we wouldn't get through this one. I think the hardest thing of all for the President was having to deal with the fact that Americans thought he wasn't telling the truth. It pained him to have to study all the polls that showed that the people still liked him — they just didn't believe him. That ate him up inside. But he did his best to keep that from us.

In late March 1987 we all attended the annual Gridiron Club dinner. Some past Presidents had been "presidentially offended" at the irreverent snipes by Washington journalists at their administrations, and had refused to return to subsequent banquets, but not Ronald Reagan. He looked forward to this night all year, every year.

As I was walking into the huge reception that preceded the dinner and revue portion of the evening, Helen Thomas came running over to me and said, "Maureen, I'm so angry — I'm playing you and they won't let me dress sexy. They're making me do it in a pinafore and Mary Janes, and I'm really furious!"

I wondered what was in store for me, but I didn't have to wonder long.

Helen Thomas came out done up in a frilly short dress and Mary Janes, and she gazed adoringly across the room at the President and sang the following lyrics (to the tune of "My Heart Belongs to Daddy"):

> *I've led some fights for women's rights,*
> *   But not as a liberal baddie;*
> *The GOP is my cup of tea,*
> *   'Cause my heart belongs to Daddy;*
> *Each day I scoff at Fahrenkopf,*
> *   And his '88 handicapping;*
> *My Dad will choose the one who can't lose,*
> *   Just as soon as he's done napping.*

I got such a big kick out of Helen's impression — the folks did, too — that I couldn't resist sending her flowers the next day. "You were terrific," I signed the note, "but sexy would have been better." (The note I got back from Helen Thomas — informing me that she had watched my activities since the Schlafly meeting in the basement of the Sheraton Hotel in 1967 — closed a twenty-year political cycle and proved to me once again what a small world it is.)

That night at the Gridiron, however, it was the President who stole the show, with his jokes about himself and the First Lady and even the Iran-*contra* affair.

He threw out one-liner after one-liner:

"Oh, by the way, Nancy," he said, "I got a call on the hot line the other day — and it was for you."

"They said a while back that I read important papers during the commercials on television at night. That's not true. I watch the commercials. I read my papers while the news is on. This is part of my new strategy. I'm going to try to establish relations with the moderates in the press."

"Nancy and Don tried to patch things up the other day. They met privately over lunch — just the two of them and their food tasters."

As he worked the room the way only an actor-turned-President could, it became clear to everyone in the audience that night that Ronald Reagan was in top form, back in control of the agenda.

(As long as I'm on the subject, let me slip in a quick memory of the Gridiron dinners: over the years the President would often try out his material on me, and often he'd wind up running through his lines while I was under the hair dryer. In the White House, you see, there is a tiny room that was made into a tiny beauty parlor by Pat Nixon. Well, one year we were all getting ready for the dinner; Nancy was under the dryer and I was in the chair as the President leaned against the wall and rehearsed his material. Just at that moment a young woman who had worked at the White House for only a few days came through the door with a delivery. Her mouth fell open and she hollered out, "Oh, my God!" as though she'd just seen the most startling thing in the world. I can just imagine how it all looked from where she stood, with the President dressed casually and telling jokes and the First Lady under a hair dryer, and all of us in these cramped quarters. I don't mean this as a slur on any of Dad's jokes, but the look on this poor young woman's face was the best gag of all!)

Congressional hearings began on the Iran-*contra* affair in July. Because of his busy schedule Dad could only watch them intermittently, but I saw most of them. I'll admit it, the hearings were compelling theater. Naturally I was curious about what Colonel North and Admiral Poindexter were going to reveal about their clandestine operations. I hoped their testimony would put an end to the wild rumors of a "smoking gun" that had haunted us for months.

North and Poindexter made it clear that they had conducted their secret operations without the President's knowledge, but I must admit there were aspects of their testimony that I found puzzling. I wondered why there was so little interest, for example, in North's testimony that he had shredded documents in front of Justice Department lawyers — even though the lawyers later proved he was not even in the building at the time. I was also curious about why no one pressed North on why he'd tried to gain access to the White House on Thanksgiving Day, after his pass had been revoked.

Was there something in particular he'd wanted?

Many of us — myself included — passionately support freedom fighters around the world, and the *contras* in particular. But unlike North, we do not exercise that support at the expense of the American presidency.

At the time of the hearings, while Ollie North was putting on his dazzling performance as a brave Marine with a chestful of medals and a disarming grin, I told Dennis that I thought he would be indicted. As it turned out, I was right. In March 1988 Colonel North, Admiral Poindexter, the international arms merchant Albert Hakim, and retired Air Force Major General Richard Secord were charged by a federal grand jury with conspiracy to defraud the government and theft of government property, among other things, in connection with their roles in the Iran-*contra* operation. As of this writing, they have asked a federal judge to dismiss the charges against them, maintaining that their case has been "tainted" by the widespread testimony they gave in the summer of 1987 under grants of limited immunity from prosecution.

I don't know that we'll ever get all the way to the bottom

of the Iran-*contra* scandal. I think we'd be there by now if the military had handled the investigation of its own personnel, as they should have in the first place.

But I hope we get there soon. For my father's sake and my family's sake and for the sake of the country, let's remove this blemish from Ronald Reagan's presidency and place the full blame where it belongs. If there's one thing I know as sure as sunshine, it's that Ronald Reagan was not trading American arms for American hostages in Iran; he was not doing business with the Ayatollah.

There's a part of me that won't rest easy until everyone else knows that, too.

23

Summit

FOR ALL THE DRAMA of the Iran-*contra* hearings, the following several months packed their own brand of wallop for the Reagan administration and for the Reagan family.

Almost as soon as the hearings were completed, the administration was plunged into an entirely new controversy, this one over Judge Robert Bork's nomination to the Supreme Court of the United States. Bork pushed Iran-*contra* right off the front page, where it was now his turn to hold forth for the next several weeks.

I had absolutely no doubt that the Democrats were playing games with the President's nominee, trying to keep the seat tied up until 1989, when they hoped one of their own could fill the position with another one of their own. I'm sure they resented the fact that the appointment came up during Dad's term. Remember, during the 1984 presidential campaign Walter Mondale and Geraldine Ferraro tried to win over voters with the argument that Ronald Reagan would continue to appoint reactionary conservatives to the federal bench and to the United States Supreme Court; what they forgot to tell us was that their party would do everything in its power to keep the President from making any appointments whatsoever.

I knew Judge Bork to be an intelligent, well-grounded man of the law; his credentials were impeccable. The objections, I think, went no further than the fact that Ronald Reagan had selected him. I actually thought it was kind of funny, in a depressing sort of way, to see three of the least reputable senators the Democrats could find being trotted out to question the judge's integrity. Imagine: a presidential candidate who plagiarized another politician's speeches, a man who resigned from the Senate Intelligence Committee after leaking materials to the press, and a political veteran whose flagrant violations of decorum and decency had been well documented — all gathered together to scrutinize the integrity of another man. Joseph Biden, Patrick Leahy, and Ted Kennedy were hardly the trio I would have rounded up to question somebody's character. The whole thing struck me as one big procedural oxymoron.

But despite the reputations of the Democrats' three blind mice, the Bork nomination was rejected.

Enter Judge Douglas Ginsburg, Dad's second nominee to the high court. As it happened, Ginsburg played right into the hands of the Democrats who were hoping to spin our wheels until 1989. On his own the judge admitted that he had in the past used marijuana, a disclosure that set off a storm of protest and effectively disqualified Ginsburg from consideration.

As I listened to the way the media jumped on the bandwagon to rail against Ginsburg's one-time marijuana use, I wondered if we were entering a new age of press scrutiny that might successfully eliminate an entire generation of Americans from holding public office. Would our baby-boom politicians be voted out of office if it was learned that they'd experimented with drugs or protested against the 1960s establishment?

Curiously, in the next two weeks we listened as every candidate with his hat currently in the ring called a news conference to confess any past indiscretions and explain away his behavior; then each went out and hit the trail running. The thinking must have been that it was better to come clean with any skeletons in your closet — however small the bones — before the press beat you to the front page.

After a while all of these confessions became so boring that the subject died, but so did Ginsburg's appointment.

Before long I got a call from White House political director Frank Donatelli, who was seeking my support for Dad's third nominee, Judge Anthony Kennedy of California. This was a problem for me, and I said so. I'd supported Bork and I'd supported Ginsburg, but I could not put myself behind Kennedy in any way. Of course, for the good of the party I would do nothing to oppose the nomination, but I wasn't about to support it.

Here's why: Judge Kennedy's decision in a 1984 case in the state of Washington — in which he refused to rule on whether the state should revamp its pay scales to reflect the fact that positions held predominantly by women were in lower-paying categories, stating that the legislature should make laws, not the courts — put him on the wrong side of the comparable-worth issue in my book.

I gave it to Frank Donatelli as straight as I could. "My best judgment," I told him when he asked me about Kennedy's chances, "is that the Democrats have pulled out every stop on Bork, and they've utilized every chit they have with civil-rights groups. My information is that the people who will be opposing Kennedy will be Democrat feminist organizations. You have to know something about feminist politics: the Dems will never go to the wall for their women. They never have and they never will. If Kennedy is opposed only by feminists, you've got an appointment to the Supreme Court."

And that's exactly how it happened. The only organizations opposing Kennedy were women's political groups, and the Democrats paid no attention to their objections.

In September the President had lent me a book called *Against All Hope*, written by the Cuban poet Armando Valladares; the book, which was given to the President by the author after he testified for the United States at a U.N. Human Rights Commission meeting in Geneva that spring, is Valladares's shocking and vivid account of life as a political prisoner in Cuba. Armando Valladares spent nearly half his life in Cuban prisons for his refusal to put up a Communist poster in his office.

Through years of work by various international organizations, and after the intercession of President Mitterrand of France, Valladares is a free man today; he is now an American citizen and divides his time between the United States and Spain, writing and managing a human-rights organization.

I was so moved by Armando Valladares's story that I began to cast about for new ways to boost our campaign against Cuban atrocities.

One night at dinner I tried out one of my ideas on the President. "What would you think of Armando Valladares as our ambassador to Human Rights in nineteen eighty-eight?" I asked. "It's our last chance to win an investigation of Cuba, and he's perfect for the job."

The President said he would think about it, and apparently he was true to his word, because a short time later Armando Valladares was appointed as the United States representative to the U.N. Human Rights Commission, with ambassadorial status.

(Incidentally, before the commission adjourned in 1987, it was decided to send a delegation to examine human-rights violations in Cuba; for the first time in over thirty years, an international agency would have complete access to Cuban prisons. What this meant was that for a period of one year — during the six months it took for the delegation's investigation and the following six months until they issued their report — Cuban prisoners were properly fed and clothed. No matter what the long-term impact of the delegation's findings, Armando Valladares and others on the commission succeeded in bringing at least temporary relief to a situation that cries out for world attention.)

Dennis and I built in a break from the tumultuous events back home. In October we spent two weeks as guests of the People's Republic of China, visiting the capital city of Beijing, the terra-cotta soldiers in Xi'an, the thriving metropolis of Shanghai, the Silk Embroidery Institute in the garden city of Suzhou, and the southern city of Guangzhou (known to most of us as Canton).

We were in sightseers' Heaven!

While we were there I met with some of my friends from the All China Women's Federation, and I had a chance to renew an acquaintance with Li Peng, the soon-to-be premier of

China, whom I had met on a trip to Botswana the year before; Minister Li and I continued our meaningful dialogue on development in southern Africa and continuing educational opportunities for Chinese students in the United States.

We returned home invigorated by our visit, but we were met with more bad news. While we were away, Nancy's regular mammogram had revealed a tiny but malignant tumor in her left breast, which required surgery. She had been waiting for two weeks for a break in her schedule to have what would unhappily turn out to be a mastectomy.

In order to avoid having her situation torn apart on network television — we'd all learned our lesson following Dad's colon and prostate surgeries — the White House did not announce the news of the malignancy and the upcoming surgery until the First Lady was on a plane returning from an antidrug event in New Hampshire on the very day she would enter the hospital.

They really kept this one under wraps — or at least they tried to. The folks even had to postpone any conversation on the subject between themselves when Nancy's condition was first diagnosed; the Crown Prince and Princess of Japan were their guests for a formal dinner that evening. "I knew," Nancy told me later, "that if I started to cry, I would never get through that dinner."

We were right about the First Lady's condition being picked apart on the nightly news, but there was nothing we could do about it. It's amazing to me the lengths to which some of these newsies will go to run a story.

"If you hated the graphic displays on colon cancer or prostate surgery, " I warned the President on the night before Nancy went into the hospital, "then wait until you see what they do with breast surgery."

Dad and I talked, and he seemed to me to be OK about the whole procedure. I mean, this was a very personal ordeal for my father and his wife, and I didn't want to invade their privacy in any way. I tried to look on from the sidelines, wondering, Are they talking to each other? Are the lines of communication open? They were, on both counts, so I sounded my warning about the press and backed off.

Nancy was to check into the hospital on a Friday evening

and would be operated on the following morning. Sure enough, that first night we found a male medical expert on one of the networks, standing in front of a blackboard with a drawing of two breasts; to demonstrate the procedure, he erased one of them. And the folks had to sit through this stuff! Everywhere you looked in the few days following Nancy's hospitalization, you'd find all these interviews with women and doctors second-guessing the First Lady's decision to have a mastectomy. She should have had a lumpectomy, they cried, or radiation. They made it sound like she was letting down all of womankind!

The surgery went well, and her prognosis for a full recovery was excellent. Her cancer was a common form and was confined to a duct. It had not spread to other areas of the breast, but her doctors did remove some lymph nodes as a precaution.

I flew in on the red-eye the morning after her return from the hospital. I called the switchboard as soon as I got to the White House to see if she was awake. She was having breakfast, I was told.

Wonderful. So I called her up and asked if she wanted any visitors.

"Where are you?" she exclaimed.

"Down the hall."

"Well, come on," she said. "I've been waiting for you." Within three minutes we were plopped down together on her recovery bed, and we spent the next hour or so trying to figure out what it was about the news media that turned our lives into such a feeding frenzy.

"I don't understand why people want to be so mean," Nancy said.

"We're good copy," I said. "They think they're just doing their jobs."

Throughout her recovery it seemed to me that Nancy was having the hardest time dealing with the controversy in the press generated by her decision to have a mastectomy. She handled the loss of the breast itself quite well, considering; it was the constant media harangue that got to her.

"I couldn't possibly lead the kind of life I lead and keep the schedule I keep if I had to have radiation or chemotherapy, " she explained to me one day. If she had opted for a lumpectomy, as some cancer groups had advised her, she would have had to undergo such treatment.

Again I checked in on Dad to see how he was holding up. I poked my head into his office that afternoon, and he seemed just fine about the whole thing.

When I left the folks to return to California, Nancy seemed in good spirits. She had already begun doing the exercises the doctors had prescribed to strengthen the muscles under her arm. She was getting her energy back, and she was doing what she could to put the incident behind her.

But by the time I arrived home we'd all received another blow. And Nancy, at the worst possible time, was hardest hit. Her mother, Deedee Davis, had died of a stroke in her Phoenix, Arizona, apartment. I was overcome by the news, but my first thoughts were for Nancy; she had only been out of the hospital for four days, and I wondered how she was going to deal with her mother's death, and all of the small traumas that went along with it, so soon after her own ordeal.

The folks flew immediately to Arizona. Ron and Doria arrived the next day to help Nancy sort through her mother's things. (The President could not stay on and had to return to Washington.) Dennis and I arrived later in the week to do what we could.

My heart was breaking for Nancy, but when I stopped to catch my breath I realized it was breaking some for me, too. Deedee Davis was one of the truly memorable people who touched this earth, truly a rare and special bird. We were not related, not technically, but I'd known her nearly all my life and had always thought of her as my grandmother. Whatever our relationship, she was warmhearted, funny, and feisty, and she and I were good friends.

Her passing touched off so many memories for me. One of the reasons Deedee and I got on so well, I suppose, was because of our well-known use of expletives; we were like a couple of truck drivers, the two of us. Deedee's dirty jokes were legendary. I remember a story Senator Barry Goldwater related to me about his attending a wedding in Phoenix some twenty years earlier and feeling a tap on his shoulder. There, kneeling in the pew behind him, was Deedee, and she wanted to share with him a bawdy new joke she knew he'd enjoy.

That was Deedee.

Goldwater, incidentally, was one of Deedee's biggest fans. How he loved listening to her stories! But when the senator endorsed Gerald Ford in 1976 over Ronald Reagan, he did so at great cost. He had to go cold turkey. Deedee called Goldwater's brother on the phone and told him to tell that #!$&!#! brother of his that he had heard his last dirty joke from her; as far as any of us know, she kept to her word.

Once, in the 1970s, I found myself in Phoenix as a luncheon speaker for a very conservative Republican party organization. Deedee was there. I became embroiled in a philosophical dispute on the Equal Rights Amendment, and according to the group I was taking a very "radical" position. Well, after the luncheon a woman came up to Deedee and asked quite suspiciously if she agreed with my position. Deedee's hearing was not the best at this point, and she had not heard all of my speech, but she did not approve of this woman calling into question the good judgment of her "granddaughter," so she shook her finger in the woman's face and said, "If my granddaughter says that's what we ought to do, it's what we ought to do."

Too bad familial support isn't always that easy to come by.

I thought of some other favorite stories that day. Like the time during one of our many White House crises, when the President and I looked on in disbelief as Nancy let fly with a mild burst of profanity. It was so unlike her. We just stared at her, and when she finally recovered she pointed at me and said, "I learned it from her."

"Oh, no you didn't," I responded, "you learned it from your mother." We all broke up at this, with Dad laughing loudest of all.

One Christmas, when the entire family was gathered for dinner, Dad decided to tell a joke that he'd originally learned from Deedee. I've forgotten the joke over the years, but the punch line had something to do with stuffing a turkey with gunshot and "blowing its ass off!" Dad, however, decided to tone things down a bit and substituted the more genteel kicker "blowing its keister off." After the laughter subsided Deedee turned to her son-in-law and said, "Ronnie, darling, I love you and I told you that story. I remember distinctly using the word *ass*. Now, if you are not going to repeat my jokes accurately, I'm not going to tell you any more stories."

We all knew enough from her handling of her old friend Barry Goldwater to take such a threat very seriously indeed.

For her memorial service, at a beautiful Phoenix church, the altar was decorated with bouquets of all white lilies, carnations, and gladiola, with sprigs of greenery. Dad returned from Washington to deliver the eulogy. Paraphrasing Winston Churchill, he said, "Meeting her was like opening a bottle of champagne."

We all still miss her terribly.

While we were in Arizona, though, we received some sensational news. (It was about time!) The President announced that he was going to meet in December with Mikhail Gorbachev to sign an arms accord banning medium- and shorter-range warheads. Wonderful. We were all standing outside the church waiting to go in for the service when he delivered the news. For our family the timing was perfect; it lifted all our spirits, even Nancy's. For the first time in our history the language of arms control would be replaced by arms reduction, in this case the complete elimination of an entire class of U.S. and Soviet nuclear warheads.

The General Secretary of the Soviet Union's Communist party was coming to the United States to sign Ronald Reagan's treaty, the same treaty the Soviets had walked away from three times. Ever since Dad took office in 1981 his so-called zero-option proposal had been criticized by his opponents as impossibly visionary and unrealistic. The Soviets would never agree to something against their empirical designs, his critics said. The quest for arms control was one thing, but asking the Soviets to destroy the weapons they'd already built, well, that was another thing entirely. Speculation held that the President was holding fast to a proposal he knew the Soviets could not accept just so he could go down in history as a "peacemaker."

I never bought any of that talk, and neither — thank God — did Ronald Reagan. Ever patient, the President outlasted the Soviets in Reykjavik, and now, in Washington, D.C., we were all about to take a major step in the direction of world peace, thanks to his persistence. After Reykjavik Michael and I both asked the President for his assessment of the meetings. "I think things are going to get better between our two countries," he said with a knowing smile.

"Dad," I wanted to know, "those pictures we saw of you and Gorbachev getting into your cars when it was all over — what did he say?"

"He said, 'It's not too late?' " (Meaning, of course, that they could still come to a disarmament agreement if the President would relinquish S.D.I.)

"And you said?"

"And I said, 'It is for me.' "

That was their last meeting before the upcoming summit.

Of course, not everybody saw things in the same positive light that my father did. Several well-known conservatives (and I use that term loosely here) designed a new fund-raising gimmick for themselves around the summit meeting by calling the President "a useful idiot of Soviet propaganda." It seems to me the only useful idiots in this picture were Dad's conservative foes; they failed to recognize what was going on behind the scenes. You have to understand that it is well known in diplomatic circles that the Soviets have an entirely different negotiating style than we do here in the United States; their goal is to win at all costs, and even if they are being defeated on some negotiations, it becomes imperative to them that they appear to be defeating their opposition. In the United States we generally negotiate with the idea that we will get more if there is no apparent winner or loser — you have to give something to get something, right? — so the administration did not respond with hostility when the Soviets began telling the Europeans that "zero option" had really been their idea all along. Fine, the President thought; the objective is to reach an agreement, not to debate where the idea originated.

So it was Dad's conservative opponents — the useful idiots — who were playing right into the hands of Soviet propaganda by perpetrating the myth that the whole treaty was a Soviet gambit and not a U.S. triumph.

Of course, the Gorbachev visit did not come off without its share of snafus. When the date was set for the summit meeting, the First Lady wrote a letter to her Soviet counterpart, Raisa Gorbachev, inviting her for tea on Wednesday afternoon, the second day of their visit to Washington. Weeks went by, and Nancy never heard a word. Privately the folks stewed over Raisa's oversight; publicly they sought to be accommodating. Meanwhile Raisa had accepted an invitation arranged by Anatoly Dobrynin, our old friend with Barnae's "First Dog Inaugural Flight" button, to a luncheon that Thursday, hosted by a well-known Democrat fund-raiser, Pamela Harriman. But still Nancy's invitation went unanswered.

As time went on the American officials arranging the visit came right out and asked the Soviets if Raisa was going to accept the First Lady's invitation. Yes, they were informed, she did plan to come, only not at three o'clock, as invited. The Soviets said that Raisa would be available for coffee at eleven-thirty on Wednesday morning; though the mornings were most difficult for the First Lady, who was still recovering from her surgery, she agreed to the new time.

The day of Gorbachev's arrival was cool and damp, but nothing could dampen the spirits of that great day, not even Raisa. The trumpets sounded, the drums rolled, and the clatter of rifles cut through the still winter air as our soldiers went through their military exercises dressed in Revolutionary uniforms with fife and drum. It was quite a salute. The U.S. Marine Corps Band played the "Star-Spangled Banner" and the Soviet national anthem.

In his welcoming remarks the President spoke of democracy and *glasnost* and of the futures of our two great nations. "Mr. Gorbachev," he said, "I hope that during your short time here you will see that we Americans are a dynamic and energetic lot, people of enterprise and an abiding love of freedom. We believe in God and care about others who are in need. We are proud and independent. Like the people of your country, we believe our country should be strong, but we desire peace. Have no doubt about that. The longing for peace runs deep here, second only to our fervency for the preservation of our liberty. Americans believe people should be able to disagree and still respect one another, still live in peace with one another. That is the spirit, the democratic spirit, that I will bring to our meetings."

But apparently Raisa Gorbachev still had a thing or two to learn about our democratic spirit, and a whole bunch of things about diplomacy. A few hours after the coffee, as Dennis and I came downstairs to join 250 invited guests to witness the historic signing ceremony in the East Room of the White House, we were stopped by Barbara Bush. "Has Nancy told you what happened this morning?" she inquired.

Dennis and I both shook our heads no.

"Well," she continued with some exasperation, "as you know, the First Lady invited some of us for coffee with Raisa. Let me tell you, all that woman wanted to do was lecture all of us on the glories of the U.S.S.R. and the shortcomings of the American political system. She wouldn't let anyone else get a word in. She'd just cut you off and keep talking. I've never seen anything so rude. I don't know how Nancy kept her cool."

Later, when I asked Nancy about Barbara Bush's story, she just sighed. "That is what always happens with Raisa," she finally said. "Now maybe someone will realize what a chore it is to spend any time with her."

At two o'clock that afternoon the President and the General Secretary signed a treaty banning medium- and shorter-range nuclear warheads. How proud I was of Dad on that day! Dennis and I looked on at our two most influential world leaders, sitting side by side at the Treaty Table, which had been brought down from its permanent place on the second floor. This table, incidentally, has been used many times over the years for historic treaty ceremonies such as this one, and in the last century it was often used as a Cabinet table. I wondered what stories future generations would tell about this table after today's meeting.

"We can only hope that this history-making agreement will not be an end in itself," the President said before he signed the treaty, "but the beginning of a working relationship that will enable us to tackle the other issues, urgent issues, before us."

Mr. Gorbachev, before giving his signature, reiterated some of the President's thoughts through his interpreter. "It is our duty to take full advantage of this chance and move together toward a nuclear-free world," he said, "which holds out for

our children and grandchildren, and for their children and
grandchildren, the promise of a fulfilling and happy life, without fear and without a senseless waste of resources on weapons of destruction."

The real pomp and ceremony of the occasion was to come
later that night at a state dinner honoring the Soviet leader
and his wife. Now, state dinners are the closest thing we have
to the royal command performance; it usually works the same
way each time out. The guests — about a hundred to a hundred
and twenty-five people — all gather in the East Room for the
reception portion of the evening at about seven o'clock. Cock-
tails are served. At exactly seven-thirty the President and the
First Lady and their guests of honor come down the grand
staircase, and then the drinks are collected and there's a receiving line as the guests make their way out to the Green
Room and down the Grand Hall to the State Dining Room.

The State Dining Room is a grand old room, dominated on
one side by a portrait of Abraham Lincoln, which is framed
presidentially atop the room's fireplace. The President sits at
a round table with about eight of his guests, just in front of
the fireplace. There are another eight to ten tables flecked about
the room. Underneath the tables is the largest Persian rug I've
ever seen — when the room is clear of furniture, the rug looks
about the size of a football field! Fresh flowers of the season
decorate the tables. There is a stunning chandelier overhead,
but most of the light comes from the candles at each table. It's
all very elegant.

With the President at his table you'll usually find the wife
of whichever head of state is being honored on that particular
night; the visiting head of state will typically sit at the First
Lady's table. In the tradition of formal dining, seating is arranged in "boy-girl" fashion, drawing from a guest list that
normally includes a mix of foreign diplomats, businessmen,
First Family members like myself, entertainers, members of
Congress, and so on.

During Dad's administration Nancy instituted a wonderful
innovation in the routine with the strolling string music of
U.S. Army musicians; the guests are serenaded as fantastically
decadent desserts (courtesy of pastry chef Roland Mesnier) are
served. The newsies are then let in for the President's toast;

they line up along the side of the room, and everyone tries to go along with the proceedings as though they aren't there. I'd always get a lot of mileage, though, out of pointing out to the other guests at my table the way the White House press staff has got one of the room's stately pillars rigged to accommodate the harsh klieg lighting for the news cameras.

"You'll love this," I always tell my dinner partners just as the pillars open up to reveal the bright lights. They always do.

After dinner the guests retire to the Blue Room, where coffee is passed around and after-dinner drinks are served. From there it's back to the East Room, where the evening started. While the guests have been at dinner, the White House gremlins have been afoot setting up chairs and getting things ready for the evening's entertainment. The performers usually have some tie to the guest of honor. When Italian President Sandro Pertini and his wife were honored one evening, for example, Italian-American singers Frank Sinatra and Perry Como did the crooning; for King Hussein and Queen Noor of Jordan, Benny Goodman was on hand to entertain the visiting jazz buffs.

The entertainment usually lasts about twenty minutes, and then the evening turns to champagne and dancing to the music of the United States Marine Corps Band. The President and the First Lady share a dance or two and then retire at about eleven-thirty; most of the guests leave shortly thereafter, though on occasion the joint is really jumping and the dancing goes on until the early part of the wee hours.

During Ronald Reagan's two terms in office, state dinners were held about six or eight times each year. I would attend whenever I was in Washington, which as our White House years wore on amounted to more often than not. One time, though, I had to miss out because I'd had my wisdom teeth pulled earlier in the day. I was in no condition to help the folks entertain anybody, let alone the dignitaries they'd assembled downstairs, and I sat up in the Lincoln Bedroom all night, listening to the music first of the strolling strings, then of the evening's entertainer, and then of the Marine Corps Band as it came wafting up through the floorboards. I felt like I was a kid again, being sequestered upstairs during one of my parents' parties. Alfredo, Boxcar Willie's friend from the White House staff, was kind enough to bring me up a plate of the wonderful dinner I was missing out on downstairs.

Some enchanted evening.

Anyway, let me get back to this particular state dinner. The guest list for the Gorbachev dinner included Soviet and U.S. government dignitaries and many prominent people from our business, sports, and artistic communities. Among those on hand that night were the industrialist Dr. Armand Hammer, Olympic gymnast Mary Lou Retton, actress Claudette Colbert, author Saul Bellow, and baseball immortal Joe DiMaggio.

Now, state dinners usually last for about four hours, sometimes longer, but the Soviets had requested that we keep this one down to about two hours; the reciprocal dinner they had planned to honor the President and the First Lady would last two hours, and they didn't want to be upstaged. Fine. To accommodate them, the private reception before the dinner was canceled, as was the "coffee break" between the dinner and entertainment portions of the evening. Oh, and of course the Soviets also requested that the evening not be "black tie," as is the custom, because they saw such dress as a display of bourgeois capitalism; the White House held firm on the formal dress but stressed to the Soviets that many visiting dignitaries had attended these functions in the past *sans* black tie, and that anything Mr. Gorbachev chose to wear would be appropriate.

It seemed to me there were as many negotiations over the peculiar social dance between our two nations as there were over our arms-reduction accord. But with all the back-and-forthing finally over, the majesty of the evening took hold. As expected, Gorbachev wore a business suit and Raisa wore a black brocade gown. Dad was in black tie, and Nancy looked exquisite in a black beaded Galanos gown with floral-pattern sleeves. Both couples proceeded to the East Room to receive their guests, to the strains of "Ruffles and Flourishes" and, of course, "Hail to the Chief."

The receiving line was the slowest one I've ever been in! I usually bring up the rear at these things, so the folks know that when they see me, the receiving line is over; it usually gets me a big smile, but on this night all it got me was a pair of aching feet and a rather unusual exchange with Raisa Gorbachev.

Nancy introduced us, saying to Raisa, "This is our daughter Maureen."

Raisa grabbed my hand in a death grip and said through her interpreter, "Ah, children grow up so fast."

"Especially in California," I replied, in an innocuous attempt to cut short our conversation; I tried to withdraw my hand, but she simply would not let go.

"Do you have children?" Raisa wanted to know.

"No."

"Well, that's why you don't agree with me," she insisted.

I hadn't realized I'd disagreed with her. I wanted my hand back. I later learned that every person on the line had been engaged in a "meaningful" conversation with our distaff guest, which explains why it all took so long.

Finally we were seated for the dinner. The circular tables had been set with vermeil flatware and the red Lenox china that became known during Dad's administration as "the Reagan china." The White House florists outdid themselves on this one; the room looked (and smelled) spectacular. The kitchen, too, worked overtime. We dined on a first course of Columbia River salmon with lobster medallions; as an entree we enjoyed a beautifully presented loin of veal with wild mushrooms and zucchini boats filled with fresh vegetables. A tea sorbet inside honey ice cream with petit fours was our light dessert. California wines, of course, accompanied the meal.

A wonderful story took root at our table. Joe DiMaggio was seated to my right, and at one point in the evening he floated his desire to get the signatures of the President and the General Secretary on the same baseball. What a marvelous idea, I thought, but I knew the odds of pulling off something like this would be very long indeed.

Nevertheless, I agreed to help. My first concern was where to get a brand-new baseball, one clean enough for such notable autographs, at this hour of the evening.

"I just happen to have one downstairs in my coat pocket," Joe assured me.

I still can't get over the fact that Joe DiMaggio arrived at a

White House state dinner, in black tie, with a baseball in his pocket! Does he travel with one everywhere, I wondered, or did he bring it along especially for this occasion?

"OK," I suggested, "I'm not making any promises, but if you leave the baseball with the ushers when you leave, they'll get it to me and I'll see what I can do."

Soon we were well into the entertainment portion of the evening, featuring the piano virtuosity of my old friend Van Cliburn. (The connection here is that Van Cliburn had been the first American to win the coveted Tchaikovsky Piano Competition in Moscow; he came out of retirement to perform for this historic occasion.) As I listened to the music I gave long and serious thought to Joe DiMaggio and his baseball. I knew the President was a big baseball fan — and a big fan of DiMaggio in particular — so I figured I'd just put it to him straight out and see what he thought about the whole idea.

It couldn't hurt to ask, right?

So the next morning I staked out my usual territory and waited to ride down in the elevator with the President on his way to the office; over the years I'd learned that this was the best time of day to approach him on matters such as this, before his busy calendar got the better of him. On the short way down to the first floor, I started in innocently enough with, "How do you think it's going?"

"Well, Mermie," the President said, "we've got a lot of work to do, but I really get the feeling the General Secretary is here to do business."

"Speaking of business, Dad," I said, "I have a strange question. Joe DiMaggio asked me if it might be possible to get your signature on the same baseball with Gorbachev's." I handed him the ball and continued: "I thought maybe you might need something to lighten the mood over the next few days, and this might be a good way to do it."

Smooth, huh?

The President looked at the ball, and then back at me, and then back at the ball; then he tossed the baseball up into the air and put it in his pocket. "Mermie," he said, "you're right, that's one of the strangest things you've ever asked, but I'll see what I can do."

Sure enough, several hours later the baseball was back in

my hot little hands — signed by Ronald Reagan and Mikhail Gorbachev — and I sent it off to Joe DiMaggio and figured the story would end right there.

It wasn't until about a month or so later that I found out how the President had pulled it off. Dennis and I were sharing a pizza with Ken Duberstein, who was then the deputy chief of staff, and his wife, Sydney. Ken was holding forth with some wonderful stories on the Gorbachev visit when suddenly he started in on a tale that sounded utterly familiar. "You'd never believe this," he said, "but the morning after the dinner, the President came walking into his office tossing a baseball in the air and wondering aloud how to entice the General Secretary into joining him in signing the ball for Joe DiMaggio."

Why wouldn't we believe that? I thought to myself, but I didn't want to let on until Ken finished the story.

He continued: "So I suggested to the President that he hold the request in reserve for one of their private sessions, to make the point of 'playing ball' on reaching an agreement. I thought it might be a light way to get them off dead center on a troublesome issue."

When he finished his tale it was clear that Ken Duberstein was very proud of his contribution to world peace and to Joe DiMaggio's autographed baseball collection, but as he looked across the table at Dennis and me, all he got were smiles and a few muffled giggles.

"All right," he finally said. "What's so funny?"

We'd strung him along long enough. "Where do you think he got the baseball?" I said finally, and then I filled him in on the rest of the story.

Not bad teamwork, if I do say so myself — every bit as good as a double play.

In a very real sense, the summit had put a cap on Ronald Reagan's presidency; it marked one of his most significant achievements in office and was sure to leave a lasting mark on the course of world history. But to me it also signaled an end. After Gorbachev's visit I couldn't shake the thought that we were all coming down the home stretch.

As we headed full steam ahead into 1988, I noticed caps to Dad's term in office everywhere I turned. Everything this year was a last — as in last State of the Union address or last visit to Camp David or last trip aboard Air Force One.

The last Gridiron dinner, which the folks had attended faithfully over the years, made perhaps the most fitting cap of all. New York Governor Mario Cuomo was one of the major speakers at this year's event, and he brought down the house with the line "I dreamed the devil came to see me and told me I could be President, but he said I'd have to sell my soul. 'Yeah?' I said, 'What's the catch?' "

(Every time I repeat that line, I wish that a Republican had come up with it!)

Nancy took the stage for a rendition of "Thanks for the Memories," with apologies to their old friend Bob Hope. And then it was Dad's turn. By tradition the President is the final speaker at these affairs, and by the time he got up to speak we'd been there for over five hours. "You invited us for dinner," the President quipped, "but you didn't say it was to spend the night."

As much as the Gorbachev visit had signaled an end to my father's presidency, so too did this last laugh with the Gridiron Club tell us that a very special time in our history had come and gone. It reminded me of how well my father had gotten on with the press and with the American public. And it reminded me that despite everything that's happened to him over the years, Ronald Reagan has never lost his sense of humor.

I'm sure he never will.

When I left the White House for the airport following that final Gridiron dinner, I took time to breathe in these last months of my father's presidency. Every time I drive through the gates of the White house, I get a thrill. Still. And on these last times the thrill began to resonate more and more. As we wound our car around the south grounds, I would take these mental snapshots of the lawns, the trees, the flowers. On my last nights in the Lincoln Bedroom I would stay awake and stare at the silhouette of the giant magnolia tree outside my window; sometimes I'd even lie in wait for a visit from my ghostly roommate. I wanted desperately to remember everything about this place. I didn't want to forget any of it. I knew the day would come, soon, when these memories would fade.

I never liked "Hail to the Chief" — it always seemed pompous to me, and overblown — and yet I'd grown quickly fond of it the very first time I heard it played for my father. But soon Ronald Reagan will hear "Hail to the Chief" played in his honor for the last time. He and Nancy will board Air Force One and head back to California, and for the first time in eight years he won't see the squirrels scurrying for their "imported" acorns outside his office door; he won't have the national and international press poised to record his every move; he won't have to dress impeccably, every day, for formal luncheons and dinner parties; he won't be pulled from some of the things he loves best — horseback riding, mending fences, clearing brush — by some pressing world crisis.

Ronald Reagan's time will once again be his own. And his family's.

EPILOGUE

New Orleans, 1988

IT AIN'T OVER till it's over, but we're getting awfully close.

The 1988 Republican National Convention in New Orleans, for me, was charged with emotion and purpose. On a personal level, it marked the end of a compelling chapter in our family history. From where I sit, as the cochair of the party, it marked the so-called passing of the mantle to Vice President George Bush, who would lead the party into the 1988 elections as its nominee for President. And for me as an American citizen, it marked the close to eight years of strong leadership and stability and a return to pride of country, community, and family.

And on all levels, it marked the first ceremonious ending to Ronald Reagan's presidency.

It was quite a scene.

I sat there on the first night of the convention in the presidential box with the rest of the family, looking on at a film the Republican National Committee had prepared to help introduce my father. As I watched along with thousands of delegates in the hall and millions of Americans at home, it stirred up a whole range of memories.

I thought about the time my father dropped me off at

boarding school when I was a little girl, and I stood, alone, and watched the turquoise of his convertible disappear over the horizon.

I thought about the time I was stuffing envelopes in Washington for Nixon's presidential campaign in 1960, when I found out to my horror that my father was a registered Democrat.

I thought about our after-hours swearing-in at Sacramento in 1967, and the way we all celebrated, in the middle of the night, the new turns our lives were taking.

I thought about my last-minute trip to Miami in 1968 for what was to be my father's first political defeat, and about my clandestine meeting with the governor in the Florida Keys.

I thought about Kansas City in 1976, when none of us knew if there would ever be another chance at the presidency; we had come so close, and we worried that we'd never be this close again.

I thought about Detroit in 1980, when in the middle of our crowning glory, Michael's young son, Cameron, was running around the platform like it was Recess; we all took turns chasing after him during the benediction.

I thought back to that cold day in March 1981, and John W. Hinckley, Jr.

I thought back to our second Inaugural, when Dad romped in the snow outside the White House with his grandchildren.

Prompted by the film on the convention-hall monitors, I thought about the overwhelming tragedy of the space shuttle *Challenger* in January 1986, and the way our President sought to comfort a wounded nation. The *Challenger* crew, he told us, had "slipped the surly bonds of earth to touch the face of God." I remembered the memorial service for the crew at the Johnson Space Center in Houston, when I saw the look on the face of a little girl who'd lost her father in the explosion. I wanted to reach out to her and say, "Take my father, please, and let him make you feel better." I was his daughter, but in our grief we were all his children. I would share him then, just as I would share him throughout all his days in public life.

And I thought about his last State of the Union address, only a few months earlier, when the President stood before a national television audience and made a dramatic plea against congressional excesses and mismanagement. He dropped a three-thousand-page appropriation-package document on a conference table with a thud that resounded in every corner of this land, and he warned the members of Congress to never again present a document to their President that nobody could have the time or the stamina or the wherewithal to digest, no matter who their President might be in the future.

It all seemed like yesterday. And at the same time it seemed like several lifetimes ago.

So much has happened to me over the years that it's hard not to be changed by it all, transformed. I am a different person now than I was more than forty years ago, going through the pain and anxiety of my parents' divorce; I am a different person now than I was nearly thirty years ago, when I struggled through an abusive marriage; I am a different person now than I was twenty years ago, when I was told I would have no part in my father's campaign for governor; and I am a different person now than I was just eight short years ago, when Ronald Reagan took office and I worried how and where I would fit into his new world.

And we are a different family to each other.

But as much as some things have changed, there are tremendous constants in our lives. My relationship with my father hasn't changed with the years. I still feel for him the same love and respect and admiration I've always felt; if anything, those feelings have deepened with time. He will always be a big, warm, cuddly teddy bear of a father to me, and I will always be his wise-eyed, precocious little girl. The man who taught me the poetry of Robert Service on our drives out to the ranch when I was young is the same man who, as President, recited the words of the same poet to his same little girl.

He is a unique human being, my father; the White House hasn't taken that away from him. He's always had the ability to make you want to be what you instinctively know you're capable of becoming, and what you know instinctively he knows you're capable of becoming. You just know when he talks to you what he expects of you. He's been that way with his children, with his friends, and with the people who've worked with him and for him in government.

He has always been the most forgiving person in the entire

world. It's enough to drive you nuts. I have seen him look me in the eye and swear that someone who is his mortal political enemy couldn't possibly have done anything wrong, so therefore I must be mistaken. He sees the absolute best in people, all people, and then he's sometimes quite surprised when they don't live up to it, because he knows that if he can see it, then it must be there.

And he's always been shy. That may surprise a lot of people — after all, the man served for eight years as the President of the United States! — but he's a private man, my father, and he plays things very close. He doesn't like to open himself up, even with us.

I'll tell you what I mean. About a year before he left office, my father asked me to look over some books he wanted to give me. They were thick and hardcover and pretty cumbersome. Anyway, once he saw that I liked the books, he disappeared into his study and came back with a worn, weathered, and very well-used brown leather briefcase.

"Here," he said, opening up the briefcase, "you can use this to take them home."

A leather briefcase? To cart home a couple of books?

I sensed something was up. "There's more to this briefcase, right, Dad?" I said.

"Well, no," he said. "I mean, I do have a new briefcase, so I don't need this one anymore."

"Uh-huh," I said, waiting for the explanation I knew was going to come.

"Well," he continued, "this is the briefcase I used for the whole time I was governor and through my whole first term as President." He started to sound like a salesman, convincing me to take it: "You'll notice that the lock on it says 'one-three-three,' for the thirty-third governor of California, and that there's this little tag on it that says 'Ronald Reagan, Governor of California.' "

"Uh-huh," I said. "What else?"

"Nothing else. I just thought you might be able to carry those books home in it."

"And then you want the briefcase back, right?"

"Well, no," he stammered. "It would be all right if you kept it for a while."

I thought it was the sweetest gesture. My father wanted me to have the briefcase that he'd used as governor of California and during his first term as President of the United States, and he was treating it like a satchel. Can you imagine? It meant a lot to him for me to have it, I knew that, but he was tentative about giving it to me and so he cooked up this ridiculous scheme with the books just so he could kind of slip it to me without having to attach any significance to it. Either he was worried that I wouldn't want it or he didn't want to make a big deal out of it, or both.

Of course Dennis and I have put the briefcase to use in the same spirit in which it was given, a use that only a man like my father would appreciate. It sits in our closet and holds all of Boxcar Willie's gear. That's where we keep his snowsuit and his Frisbee and his bathing suit.

In our house that's a very special place indeed. Dad knows that.

I've never met anybody like my father, and I don't think this country will see another man like him anytime soon. He's the warmest person I've ever come across, and it's a warmth that runs so deep inside him it just kind of pulls you along like a magnet. People respond to that in him — perfect strangers, even — and if he can get that kind of response out of just plain folks on the street, just imagine what he does for the people who know him.

The picture I have of my father, and the one I wanted to bring across in this account of our lives together, came into focus for me in the vast hall of the New Orleans Superdome on that first night of the convention. There on the platform, the President was swatting playfully at red, white, and blue balloons, with Nancy at his side. He'd just finished a rousing speech to kick off the 1988 Republican National Convention — he'd whipped the delegates into a frenzy of party loyalty and affection and enthusiasm — and as the balloons tumbled from the ceiling, he couldn't keep from batting a few of them around. I loved it! He walked to one end of the stage and Nancy stepped to the other, and they were both reaching up for the balloons and sending them back out across the floor to the delegates.

I never wanted this moment to end.

Later, when I looked at tapes of the network coverage from

that night, I got to see up close the look of sheer joy and wonder and triumph on my father's face. It was a look I knew I'd find. His eyes sparkled the way we'd all seen them sparkle so many times before, and the lines on his face were crinkled up in a smile.

Those lines also wrote his legacy in office; they told the story of the way his administration was able to diffuse the enormous power of the central government in Washington; they told the story of his glorious successes at the negotiating table with Mikhail Gorbachev; they told the story of his attempts to make the world a safer place for democracy to flourish. Most of all, they told the story of Ronald Reagan's dream for a simpler, richer, and more prosperous America, and how that dream was coming true for so many people.

As the curtain was coming down on his presidency and the nation's eyes were focused on New Orleans, the leader of our grand old party was having himself a grand old time.

This is the Ronald Reagan America will remember, I told myself then — serious and persuasive one moment, playful and energetic the next, proud enough of himself and his country that he can stand before a national political convention and play with balloons.

That's my father.

Index